Moonshine

CHRISTINA JONES

D0334283

piatkus

PIATKUS

First published in Great Britain in 2009 by Piatkus
This paperback edition published in 2010 by Piatkus

5 7 9 10 8 6 4

FT
Pbk

A CIP catalogue record for this book
is available from the British Library.

ISBN 978-0-7499-0945-1

Typeset in Bembo by M Rules
Printed in Great Britain by Clays Ltd, St Ives plc

Papers used by Piatkus are from well-managed forests
and other responsible sources.

MIX
Paper from
responsible sources
FSC
www.fsc.org   FSC® C104740

Piatkus
An imprint of
Little, Brown Book Group
Carmelite House
50 Victoria Embankment
London EC4Y 0DZ

An Hachette UK Company
www.hachette.co.uk

www.piatkus.co.uk

Praise for Christina Jones:

'Read it on a wet and windy winter's day with a
mug of hot chocolate in front of a roaring fire,
and you'll soon be warm inside and out'
News of the World

'As feel-good and cosy as a goosedown duvet,
and bursting with sparkle and joy'
Jill Mansell

'H. E. Bates for the twenty-first century'
Katie Fforde

'Bubbles with more joy than a magnum of champagne'
Peterborough Evening Telegraph

'A fabulous story of friendship and
eccentric local traditions'
The Times

'Bloody good read . . . Funny, romantic book . . .
a lively romp through rural England'
New Woman

'Sexy . . . unputdownable . . . a heart-thumping read'
Company

'A working class Jilly Cooper'
The Mirror

Christina Jones has been writing all her life. As well as writing novels, Christina contributes short stories and articles to many national magazines and newspapers. Her first novel was chosen for WH Smith's Fresh Talent promotion, and *Nothing to Lose,* was short-listed for the Thumping Good Read Award, with film and television rights sold.

After years of travelling, Christina now lives in Oxfordshire with her husband Rob and a houseful of rescued cats.

Find out more about Christina Jones and her books by visiting her website: www.christinajones.co.uk

Also by Christina Jones

Hubble Bubble

Seeing Stars

Love Potions

Heaven Sent

Happy Birthday

The Way to a Woman's Heart

Never Can Say Goodbye

An Enormously English Monsoon Wedding

That Red Hot Rock 'n' Roll Summer

For the most beautiful boy in the world

Acknowledgments

With many thanks to Emma and Donna, my superb editors at Piatkus, who were wonderful in their professionalism when mine deserted me, and for their unstinting help, support and friendship.

Many thanks also to Broo Doherty for simply being Broo and being brilliant.

And to Mags Wheeler – my lovely friend and *Moonshine*-deadline buddy – who never stopped being there when I needed her despite being deep in a deadline hell of her very own.

Chapter One

'. . . and . . . Oh, look, I'm terribly sorry, but before we go any further, I'm really going to have to ask. Were your parents Egyptologists?'

'Jazz fans,' Cleo explained for the zillionth time in her thirty-five years. 'You know? Cleo Laine . . .?'

'Ah, yes. Really? How very, um, original.' Mimi Pashley-Royle didn't quite manage to disguise her amusement. 'Still, look on the bright side. If you'd been a boy they'd have named you Acker.'

Cleo sighed.

Mimi Pashley-Royle, her slender shoulders still twitching, composed herself by twiddling an as yet unused gold fountain pen between expertly manicured fingernails and peering down at a piece of paper resting on the vellum-bound desk diary in front of her.

Cleo noticed for the first time that the diary pages were blank. All Cleo's details were scribbled on the single sheet of paper. Like the fountain pen, Cleo assumed the diary was probably just a prop for this strangest of job interviews.

As soon as her shoulders had subsided, Mimi took a deep breath and looked up from the diary. 'Sorry, Cleo, I'm forgetting my manners. That was extremely impolite of me. Mortimer, my husband, is always telling me there's a very fine line between my being curious and appearing downright rude, and is constantly chiding me to *think* before I speak.'

Cleo, suddenly warming towards the unknown Mortimer Pashley-Royle, simply smiled and reminded herself of just how desperately she needed this job. 'It's OK. I'm not offended. I'm used to people finding my name unusual.'

'That's very gracious of you, dear. You're certainly far better mannered than I am. But, yes, it is an unusual name –' Mimi Pashley-Royle peered down again at the piece of paper in front of her '– Cleo, um, Moon?'

'Moon is my maiden name,' Cleo said. 'I've reverted to it since my divorce.'

'Really? Cleo Moon . . .' Mimi Pashley-Royle imbued the words with plum-rich vowels. 'It sounds like a new breed of clematis . . . Cleo Moon . . . You must have gone through hell at school. In my experience, children can be so cruel. There must have been endless jokes about mooning and moon-face and being a Moonie and . . .'

'Yes, all of those,' Cleo admitted. 'And plenty more. But I'm still more than happy to be a new Moon again.'

Mimi chuckled softly, then leaned forwards like an inquisitive bird, clearly forgetting Mortimer's dire warnings. 'What was your married surname then? Surely it must have been an improvement on Moon?'

'Sneezum.'

'Nooo!' Mimi Pashley-Royle screamed with laughter. 'Oh, no . . . Sorry . . . but no, surely not?'

'Yes, sadly. Dave's – my ex's – family originally came from Norfolk. It's quite a common name there.'

'Goodness me.' Mimi attempted to regain some self-control. 'How appalling for you. I mean, er, I can quite see why you chose to become a Moon again. Lord above . . . Oh, dear . . . Sorry. Sorry, we seem to have digressed. Where were we?'

Cleo, pretty sure this was a hypothetical question, said nothing. She was just glad they'd left the name stuff behind. If this hadn't been a job interview, and if she hadn't been absolutely desperate for employment, and if she hadn't been properly brought up, she may well have joined in the merriment by pointing out that "Mimi" wasn't exactly run-of-the-mill. Well, not in rural Berkshire. Not unless you were a poodle.

She shifted a little in her sumptuously upholstered brocade chair and, as she had ever since the interview started, tried to avoid looking at her reflection in the huge ornate gilt mirror on the far wall in case the desperation showed.

She had to remember to relax; to look calm and nonchalant. She was sure that if the autocratic and imperious Mimi got wind of just how important this PA appointment was to her, she'd make her life hell.

Damn! Now she'd looked in the mirror.

It was slightly disconcerting to see her own curvy self,

with her big brown eyes, billowing mass of dark hair and chain-store clothes, and the at-least-a-decade older, slim, blonde, elegantly designer-dressed Mimi, reflected together in the looking glass, with this gorgeous drawing room spilling out around them.

Chalk and cheese, Cleo thought. Straight from central casting. Just as it should be in this situation. The lady of the manor bestowing largesse on a peasant.

'Where had we got to?' Mimi Pashley-Royle pursed her very full lips and beamed again. 'Before I was swept away at a tangent by your delicious name? Ah, yes, the end-tying. So, is there anything you'd like to ask me?'

Cleo shook her head and smiled her best interviewee smile at her achingly glamorous interrogator. 'No, I don't think so. I think you've covered absolutely everything I could possibly want to know about the position, thank you.'

Nicely done, Cleo thought. Polite, slightly distant, not over keen. Nothing was more off-putting than someone absolutely panting to be thrown a lifeline. Not to mention clearly asking to be a doormat.

'Good.' Mimi Pashley-Royle heaved a sigh of relief. 'I do so hate interviewing for staff. So, despite my obvious lack of manners, do you think you could bear to work for me? Will you take the job?'

'What?' Cleo blinked, just managing not to grin madly and leap up and kiss the regal Mimi on her surgically enhanced cheek. 'You're offering it to me? Now? Just like that?'

'Well, yes.' Mimi raised her eyebrows as far as the Botox would allow. 'Why wouldn't I be? I need a PA, like, yesterday, as the children say. You were the only applicant, you're local, you haven't got any family dependants to cause a hindrance, you're newly single, you're unemployed, and I sense you're desperate.'

Cleo flinched. Chaff it! She hadn't managed to disguise the neediness. And the litany of awfulness was all true, but maybe it could have been dressed up just a little to soften the blow. Not, she reckoned, that Mimi was the sort of woman to soften blows. And, she thought ruefully, PA was so far off the mark that Mimi Pashley-Royle should be sued under the Trades Descriptions Act.

Personal assistant? With the list of tasks Mimi had already listed, drudge and dogsbody would better fit the bill. But what choice did she have?

Play it cool, she told herself. Be sweetly grateful but not too ecstatic. Keep the upper hand.

'Well, yes, thank you. It sounds, um, fascinating, and I'm very interested, of course, but it's not the only job I've applied for, and I do have other offers to consider.'

'Really?' Mimi suddenly looked very put out. 'Well, of course I'm aware that it might be considered a step down from your previous positions, but if you feel unable to accept straight away, then I'd better look elsewhere.'

Nooo! Cleo squeaked inside. There was playing it cool and there was behaving like a prat. 'Well, of course, what I meant was that I've had other interviews, but I haven't heard the outcome of those yet.'

She dared to glance across the room at her reflection. She was sure her nose would now be Pinocchio length.

Mimi shrugged. 'Well, there I feel I have the advantage over the others. I'm offering you this job now. However, if you want to wait and risk seeing if you can find something you'd prefer more, then we'd better say goodbye and –'

'No – sorry, I mean, yes, thank you, then. I'd love to accept the post.' Cleo did some inward deep-breathing exercises to stop the excitement showing, outwardly smiling across the expanse of polished mahogany desk. 'But as I'm new to this sort of work, maybe we could arrange some sort of trial period?'

'I'm not entirely sure that you're the one who should be dictating terms,' Mimi said frostily. 'Goodness me, there are dozens of people without work through no fault of their own, who'd be ecstatic to be offered this opportunity.'

Sensing the job offer slipping away again, Cleo gritted her teeth and decided that being a doormat was infinitely preferable to being unemployed. 'Sorry, yes, of course. I'll, er, let the other places know that I'm no longer seeking work. But what about my references? And police checks? After all, I could be *anybody*.'

Mimi Pashley-Royle flapped her long and expensively bejewelled fingers. 'Oh, yes, well, of course, there will be the usual boring personnel business minutiae to attend to, but Mortimer, my husband, always says I'm a good judge of character. You look decent enough to me – and anyway, if you don't suit I can always sack you, can't I?'

Thanks a bunch, Cleo thought. Thirty seconds into being employed again and there was already talk of dismissal. She squeezed out another smile. Honestly, much more of this inane beaming and her face would set in a permanent gurn.

Mimi closed the untouched diary and laid aside the unused fountain pen. 'So, now we're both happy, can you start tomorrow? And yes, on a temporary basis if you prefer, to see if you're happy with such a menial post and until such time as I've delved into your murky past.'

'Sorry?'

'Merely a figure of speech, dear.' Mimi Pashley-Royle stood up, clearly indicating that the interview was at an end, and stalked on slender heels across the acres of Aubusson towards the door. Then she paused and looked quizzically back to Cleo. 'Or have you actually got one?'

Cleo, scrambling to her feet, shook her head. 'Not really. Not at all, in fact. My entire life has been boringly virtuous to be honest. Even the divorce wasn't my fault.'

'Well, you would say that, wouldn't you?' Mimi beamed across the panelled room. 'But in my experience it takes two to –'

'Tango?'

'Good Lord no. I despise clichés. Sod up a marriage, I was going to say.' Mimi shrugged her catwalk-thin shoulders. 'And I should know. Right then, Cleo. Let's see how it goes. You toddle off back to your encampment now, I'll go and disembowel the florist for sending bloody crysanths instead of the Autumnal Tumble I'd ordered, and we'll meet here again at nine tomorrow morning.'

Cleo nodded, assuming that from nine tomorrow morning, as Mimi's PA, disembowelling florists would be just one of her many new and exciting tasks.

After another brief beaming session, and an even briefer handshake, Cleo and her new employer parted company in a class collision of man-made fibres and cashmere.

Outside Lovelady Hall, Cleo exhaled in the mild golden September afternoon. Well, that was that then. It had gone quite well considering, and at least she'd managed to convince Mimi that this job wasn't the be-all and end-all. Despite it coming very close to disaster, that was another hurdle, er, hurdled.

Since Dave had announced that he wanted a quickie divorce, she'd hurdled quite a few obstacles this year: leaving her ten-year marriage and becoming rapidly single again; leaving her smart – if boringly cloned – development semi in Winterbrook; leaving her last job – well, as Dave's secretary it would have been impossible to stay happily typing up his software orders in the spare bedroom while snarling, 'Drop dead, you two-timing, double-crossing bastard'; leaving behind everything and everyone that she knew, and at the tender age of thirty-five, moving a few miles across Berkshire to start a new life.

In a new home.

In the hamlet of Lovers Knot.

And now – Cleo looked back cheerfully at the glorious mellow manor house with its swathe of vivid Virginia creeper, sitting in the obligatory sea of manicured lawns, spotless gravel drives, and the just-turning autumnal ochre and russet shrubbery – she'd got a new job too.

Mimi Pashley-Royle was no doubt going to be a vixen to

work for. But surely, after the upheavals of the past few months, Cleo could cope with that, couldn't she? And at least she'd be earning her own money again. Which meant that the dwindling amount in her bank account might start to move in a more positive direction.

Feeling that life might just be on the up, Cleo clenched her fists in delight and did a little exultant dance of jubilation on the immaculate gravel.

'Yessssss!'

Just a fraction too late, she noticed Mimi Pashley-Royle watching her and laughing from one of Lovelady Hall's tall leaded windows.

Chapter Two

Feeling absolutely mortified at having been spotted mania-
cally capering and celebrating getting a job she'd more or less
said she didn't want, Cleo drove her ancient but much-loved
hatchback through Lovelady Hall's towering filigreed gates as
quickly as possible, and headed the two miles home along a
high-banked single-track road.

Home . . .

Actually, Cleo thought, as she paused briefly at the overgrown crossroads with the skew-whiff signpost indicating
that anyone misguided enough to want to could find
Fiddlesticks, Bagley-cum-Russet and Hazy Hassocks
within a few miles radius, Lovers Knot *was* slowly becoming home.

Home – the word that for ten years had always conjured
up Dave and the Winterbrook semi – was strangely becoming synonymous with one of Berkshire's smallest hamlets.

A crow-flying mile from Fiddlesticks, Lovers Knot had a
single-track through road, bordered on either side by a

straggle of higgledy-piggledy slate-and-shuttered council houses; a huddle of cottages round a lush village green where people gossiped, children played and cricket matches drew picnicking crowds in the summer; a collection of large red-bricked villas hidden along twisty lanes; and a small general store.

Sheltered by the Downs on three sides and the dense tangle of Lovers Spinney on the other, Lovers Knot was either one of England's hidden rural gems or the last place on earth any sane person would want to live, depending on your point of view.

Cleo, who was gradually coming round to the former, smiled to herself as she drove towards Lovers Knot Caravan Park.

'Trailer trash?' Cleo's mother had shrieked when the move to Lovers Knot had been announced. 'You're going to become *trailer trash*?'

And Cleo had laughed and protested that as the entire Moon family had been raised in a two-up two-down council house on the Bath Road Estate in Hazy Hassocks, she didn't see that her mother had any room at all to be snobby about mobile homes.

'But your father and I have *bought* our house now.' Mrs Moon had puffed herself up. 'Surely you could have done the same? You had a lovely little place in Winterbrook. You need bricks and mortar, Cleo, not a tin box in a field with, well, what must be the dregs of society.'

And Cleo, who had never really seen eye to eye with her mother's social climbing or the capitalist attitudes of her

11

terrifyingly upwardly mobile brothers, had merely shrugged and said nothing. And since she'd moved on to the caravan park, she hadn't seen anything at all of her family.

And now, she thought, as she carefully negotiated the deep wheel ruts and narrow gateway of the mobile home site, Lovers Knot *was* home, and, if she was to survive, any lingering pangs about Dave and the Winterbrook semi and her family in Hazy Hassocks and her previous life, had to stay firmly in the past.

The grandly named Lovers Knot Caravan Park, which, for Cleo, had originally conjured up a vision of sprawling sylvan farmland, dew-damp fields, rippling crystal streams and lashings of Enid Blyton picnics, was actually a small and rather bleak concreted area on the edge of the hamlet.

It housed two dozen mobile homes, a mixture of single and double static caravans, dotted in four rows of six; each one surrounded by a small fenced garden, with a car-parking space and a shed for the gas bottles.

The gas bottles had been the most frightening thing about Cleo's new venture. The prospect of hauling huge LPG canisters around and connecting up mysterious pipework and Einstein-fuddling gauges to fuel her central heating and cooking had filled her with trepidation.

But she needn't have worried.

Delighted to have an excuse to visit their new neighbour and delve into all the most intimate details of her personal life, the caravan site's residents had rallied round and given her a crash course, not only in the gas bottles, but in all the finer points of being a mobile-home dweller.

And how, Cleo thought with a grin as she parked the hatchback, her mother and her brothers and her even more snobby sisters-in-law would loathe her new neighbours . . .

The Reynolds, who had a double unit on one side of her – a down-to-earth working class couple with three children – were what her mother would have disparagingly called salt of the earth. Which meant, Cleo reckoned, that their left-wing views, lack of qualifications, sportswear outfits that never saw the inside of a gym, total belief in the tabloids and addiction to trash telly, meant, as far as her mother was concerned, that they were also into drug-dealing and benefit fraud and murder and all manner of even more heinous crimes.

In fact, Ron and Amy Reynolds were friendly, helpful and hard-working. And their noisy, exuberant and brightly inquisitive children, particularly Elvi their sixteen-year-old daughter, were a delight.

Living in a single unit on the other side of Cleo's caravan were the middle-aged spinster Phlopp sisters – christened Beryl and Phyllis – but known to everyone in Lovers Knot, naturally, as Belly and Flip.

Phlopp . . . Cleo chuckled to herself. Now there was a name for Mimi to conjure with. It made Sneezum sound positively classy.

Belly and Flip worked together behind the scenes in some government department in Reading – jobs they'd had since they left school. They set off to catch Lovers Knot's one and only bus 'up town' early each morning and returned again in the early evening. They remained loudly cheerful, incurably

13

nosy, and with their lifestyle still rooted somewhere in the mid-1950s.

Then also on the site, there was Rodders – an elderly man who wore dirty overalls and heavy-duty gloves and was obsessed with making sure the caravan site's drains ran freely. Rodders patrolled daily with his bag of extendable poles and constantly grubby hands, hauling up gratings and rooting around in the resulting gunge as blissfully happy as a pig snuffling for truffles. And there was Wilf and Maudie, a very ancient married couple, who lived quietly with their grown-up son Jerome. Jerome had his very own social worker and an eye-wateringly large collection of Davy Crockett caps and an imaginary horse and galloped round the caravans insisting he was Hopalong Cassidy.

Cleo giggled to herself. Oh, yes – her mother would love all of them.

But probably not as much as Salome – a much-painted, over-hennaed, stick-thin woman of indeterminate age – who wore more make-up than the entire Debenhams cosmetics department and teetered round Lovers Knot on stilt-high sandals wearing a smelly and moth-eaten fur coat and jauntily swinging her patent-plastic handbag. Or Raymond and George, who kept themselves to themselves and who were brilliant at knitting Fair Isle tank tops which they wore with gay pride.

And then there was Mrs Hancock . . . Mrs Hancock had cats. Lots and lots of cats. Her own and other people's. If any cats went missing in Lovers Knot, then Mrs Hancock's caravan was the first port of call for the distraught owners. And they'd find them, curled on a satin cushion, in front of the fire, being hand-fed chicken breast and evaporated milk, having been rechristened Belinda or Nigel. And Mrs Hancock would weep copious tears when they were reclaimed by their rightful owners.

Ah yes, Cleo thought, her mother would have a field day in Lovers Knot.

Like any small community, they were a hotchpotch of ages and characters, and the only thing they had in common being their reason for living in a caravan in Lovers Knot: Hobson's choice.

However lovely they were, Cleo hoped, as she climbed the three rickety steps and unlocked her front door, that none of the neighbours had noticed her arrival. She hadn't told anyone, except her best friend, Doll, and Elvi Reynolds, about the interview at Lovelady Hall – just in case she didn't get the job. Her recently discovered sense of self-preservation was working overtime. If the other caravan site residents spotted that she was 'all dressed up', they'd feel it was their God-given right to know every last detail of where she'd been and why.

Managing to close the door behind her without being spotted, and shedding her one good jacket and kicking off her one remaining pair of heels, Cleo breathed a sigh of relief. Right now she just needed some time to have a cup of coffee and sort through her sparse wardrobe for suitable PA outfits without interruptions and a lot of cross-questioning.

Her neighbours, once they got the bit between their collective teeth, would put Torquemada to shame.

Moving with swift economy round the tiny rooms, Cleo changed into her jeans and sweater in the pretty pale-green and white bedroom that always made her think of spring mornings at one end of the caravan; checked the telephone's answering machine – no messages – in the scaled-down but perfectly furnished neutral living room at the other; and made her coffee in the kitchen-in-the-middle, which was probably no bigger than a ship's galley.

And that, with the addition of the smallest bathroom known to man, was the sum total of her living accommodation.

One thing about living in a mobile home, she thought, leaning against the draining board and relaxing after her first much-needed mouthful of caffeine, it had cured her of her natural untidiness. There was simply no room for clutter. And as an inveterate hoarder, Cleo had had to make some huge lifestyle changes. The caravan had a place for every-thing and, as long as she remembered to keep everything in its place, then it was wonderfully snug and cosy.

As she'd bought the mobile home fully furnished, Cleo had left most of her past behind in the Winterbrook semi with Dave and her replacement; pared down her wardrobe into just the basics; culled her belongings into two crates of things-she'd-die-if-she-was-parted-from; and was gradually getting used to the fact that she could walk from one end of her new home to the other in a matter of seconds.

'Cleo? Are you in?'

Cleo groaned, then, recognising the tall slim outline of Elvi Reynolds from next door through the frosted glass, smiled. 'Yep. Come in . . . the kettle's just boiled.' She unpeeled herself from the draining board and reached for another mug. 'Just don't let anyone else see you – I'm not in the mood for the mass third degree just yet.'

Elvi closed the door behind her, beaming broadly. 'So – did you get it?'

'I did.'

'Knew you would. Congratulations. Mimi's a putrid cow, of course, but you'll be able to handle her. Oh, thanks – coffee. Just what I need after treble French and a sneaky test on Chaucer.' Elvi grinned, shedding folders, bags and a backpack on her way through to the living room. 'And is there any of your fantastic cake going?'

'In the tin,' Cleo said, looking fondly at the almost six-foot Elvi, with her bone-straight chestnut bob, and her hoiked-up grammar school uniform and her endless legs in opaque black tights. 'Though God knows how you manage to stay looking like a supermodel. I've never known anyone eat as much as you.'

'Adrenaline, genes and metabolism.' Elvi sprawled on the sofa with the cake tin. 'And you make the best cakes in the world – so it's your fault if I lose my youthful good looks and stunning figure any time soon. So, when do you start at Lovelady?'

'Tomorrow morning.' Cleo curled in a fireside chair. 'I was the only applicant.'

Elvi spluttered crumbs of coffee and walnut cake. 'Not surprising. Mimi must have exhausted all the locals by now. No one stays at Lovelady Hall for more than a few months at most. Money OK?'

'Good enough. It'll do until something else comes along anyway. The job market's horrifically depressed at the moment, so anything's better than starving – and what's left of my share of the house money after buying this place has all but disappeared.'

'Don't know why you didn't get a massive divorce settlement out of Dave the Rave so you could live in luxury.' Elvi helped herself to more cake. 'I would have done.'

Cleo sighed. Elvi, young and idealistic, had so much to learn.

'Well, I didn't. Wouldn't. Once I knew he wanted to end the marriage I just wanted to get out as quickly and cleanly as possible. After the remortgage, he paid me my share of the house plus a bit for the goods and chattels – as the solicitor so sweetly called my furniture – and that was it. No maintenance, no nothing. I'm completely free of Dave as he is of me.'

Elvi blinked huge green eyes beneath a lash-long fringe and wiped her fingers on her blazer. 'Do you miss him?'

'No.' Cleo shook her head. 'Not any more. Honestly. The marriage was well into injury time. We were bored with each other and our life together. We'd grown up and grown apart, although finding out he'd been having a six-year affair with Wobbly Wanda from the post office was a bit of blow to my pride, of course. Being replaced by an older model doesn't do much for an already battered ego.'

Elvi sniggered. 'Oh yes, Wanda – the putrid other woman. I'm not surprised you were gutted. If she'd been some young blonde bimbo –'

'It might have been easier to under̲ ̲ ̲
Wobbly Wanda's fat and fifty-something.' ̲ ̲ ̲ ̲
fully. 'Grey hair, mumsy clothes, a penchant for ̲ ̲ ̲
quiz shows and bingo.'

'And he honestly preferred her to you?'

'Seems like it. He's very happy now, so I've been told.'

'Christ!' Elvi shook her head. 'He must be barking. She sounds like my nan.'

'Wanda's one of those as well. Three children, six grand-children – maybe that was the attraction . . .'

Cleo stared down into her coffee. Maybe if she and Dave had been able to have a family things would have been different. If the IVF attempts hadn't failed, if maybe they'd persevered . . . She sighed again. She'd been down that sad route too many times. It just hadn't been meant to happen. And just as well, really. At least there were no children to be hurt by this particular divorce.

Elvi leaned forwards. 'Oh, Cleo, sorry. Me and my big mouth. I forgot . . . Mrs Baxter, our form tutor, always says my mouth is in top gear while my brain's still in neutral.'

'Please don't worry about it. The divorce wounds are well healed by now.' Cleo smiled, finding that the words were almost true. 'Now, if you've gorged yourself to bursting on cake and before you rush off to immerse yourself in your homework, I need to pick your brains a bit – so shift them out of neutral, OK?'

'My brains have atrophied.' Elvi sighed dramatically. 'And it's only just the start of autumn term and I'm only in my third week in the lower sixth. God knows what it'll be like per next year. It's right rotten wicked and cruel – as my nan would say – the way they force us children to learn stuff.'

Cleo laughed. Elvi was academically brilliant. She'd gained a scholarship to Winterbrook's indie grammar school and soaked up facts like a sponge. Elvi would sail through her sixth-form years and on to a good university with no problems whatsoever.

'You poor little soul – you should have tried battling your way through the 1980s educational hell that was Winterbrook Comp like I did. Now that really *was* cruelty to children. Anyway, this shouldn't tax you too much – now I know I've got the job, I just want a bit of background info on Mimi, on the Pashley-Royles, and on the set-up at Lovelady Hall before I start working there. I'd hate to make a huge gaffe on my first day . . . I mean, I suppose Mimi married Mortimer Pashley-Royle for his millions and –'

'Wrong straight away.' Elvi reached for more cake. 'Mimi's old money. Lovelady Hall is hers – passed down through the generations. She was putridly wealthy in her own right before she hooked up with Sir Mortimer.'

'Sir?' Cleo raised her eyebrows. 'Blimey – I had no idea he was a *Sir* . . . Which means Mimi is Lady Pashley-Royle, I suppose.'

'Yup. But she was a ladyship long before she married him. She inherited her lady-dom because her father was a minor duke of some sort, I think. Mort got knighted quite recently in one of those New Labour honours lists, which was probably a huge relief to him.'

'So it was a match made between the balance sheets, was it?'

'Rumour has it that they actually *fell in love.*' Elvi wrinkled her nose. 'Gross! I mean they must have been so *old* and they'd both been married before so you'd think they'd have known better, wouldn't you?'

'Maybe they did fall in love,' Cleo said, grinning. '*Old* people do, you know. So, is Mortimer a gold-digger or are they evenly matched on the Rich List?'

'Well, he's a *noveau riche* gutter slob really. She's blue blood and breeding, he's self-made and snobby with a class chip. But, yeah, they're probably about equal in the money stakes. He made his millions in the media – iffy indie radio stations, sleazy-ish lads' mags, dodgy tabloids, that sort of thing. Sold out the entire Pashley-Royle empire before the shares collapsed and now runs his new business from Lovelady Hall.'

'Does he? I didn't see him – or any sign of a flourishing semi-porn industry.'

'Oh, he's given up on the tarts 'n' tits,' Elvi said cheerfully, finishing her cake. 'He runs his new company from what was the old stables at Lovelady.'

'And the new company is what then? I suppose I should know this stuff – just in case.'

'In case you ever need a Maserati or three?' Elvi giggled. 'Mortimer indulges himself sourcing and supplying luxury cars for the even more disgustingly rich. Even if Mimi's family money hadn't quite kept up with deflation, Pashley's Passion Wagons would have continued to keep Mimi in the fabulous style that she believes she deserves. As it is, even in

21

the latest recession, they're both wallowing in loadsa money – while the rest of us grub around for what we can get.'

Cleo nodded to herself. It was nice to know that in these straitened financial times there were still pockets of unbelievably wealthy people to make sure she felt even more impoverished.

It was as it had always been.

'If that's all you want to know, I suppose I should go and face Mum and Dad and the brats – and make a start on my *hours* of homework.' Elvi stood up. 'Thanks for the cake. Forget about being Mimi's next slob-outer – you should make cakes for a living. You're brill at it. Oh, but don't let Mimi know – she'll have you up to your armpits in sponge mix in the kitchen before you know it.'

'I think "a little light cooking" was actually on my list of PA duties.'

'I bet it was,' Elvi snorted, collecting up her bags and folders. 'Olive used to do all the cooking at Lovelady before they carried her off screaming. They've never replaced her on a permanent basis. Mimi wouldn't know what to do with a kitchen, so she's always using outside caterers or on the lookout for someone local to produce Nigella-style dinner parties. If you want to stay sane up at Lovelady, my advice is you'd best keep quiet about knowing one end of a pickled caper from the other.'

Oh, Lordy, Cleo thought, what exactly have I let myself in for?

Chapter Three

After Elvi had gone, Cleo busied herself laying out her clothes for the morning, making a cake to replace the one that Elvi had demolished and preparing her evening meal. It was, she'd found since living alone for the first time in her life, important to keep occupied. There had been many fleeting moments of painful loneliness since she'd moved to Lovers Knot. But tonight, with the television burbling chattily in the tiny living room, the radiators humming against the autumnal chill as dusk fell, and the lights in the caravan dimmed to a faint glow, she felt, well, if not ecstatically happy, then at least contented.

And that, she thought, attempting to empty eggshells into the bin, was pretty good going, considering.

'Oh, sod it.' Cleo glared at the bulging swingbin as the lid refused to shut. 'Now I'll have to trek outside in the pitch darkness and empty this in the dustbin – and it's probably raining and I knew I ought to have found an electrician to fit an outside light before the nights drew in and –' She stopped and laughed. That was something else she'd really have to sort out: talking to herself. It had become a rather worrying habit. Maybe she should get a cat to discuss things with, then the one-sided conversations would seem a little more, well, normal. Maybe she should have a word with Mrs Hancock. Mrs Hancock's cats were always having kittens as Mrs Hancock felt neutering 'went against the laws of nature, duck'.

She'd always wanted to have cats – and dogs – but Dave hadn't liked animals. Cleo knew now that should have rung early-warning bells. And then her mother had said that having cats would turn her into some sad mad childless old woman who was using them as a baby substitute.

Nice woman, her mother.

Not, Cleo thought, as she heaved the bin liner out and carefully knotted the top, that the talking-to-herself really mattered. There was no one here to notice that she now talked not only to herself, but also in a Shirley Valentine way, to all her kitchen utensils and some of the furniture as well.

Unlocking the door, Cleo put one foot on the top step in the darkness, trod on something large, soft and squashy, and screamed.

'Jesus,' a deep, upper-class voice groaned. 'Careful, Olive.'

'I'm not Olive.' Cleo, her heart pounding, hissed at the man sprawled on her top step in the shadows. 'And this isn't a dosshouse. Just clear off before I call the police.'

'Please don't shout, and why –' the figure uncurled himself and peered up at her '– would you want to call the police? Oh – you're really not Olive, are you?'

24

'No.' Cleo gripped the rubbish bag more firmly. As a weapon it wouldn't have been her first choice, but it'd have to do if he turned nasty. 'I've no idea who Olive is and why you're here, but just clear off.'

The man stood up unsteadily, rocked a bit, then stepped back onto the ground and fumbled in his pocket.

A knife? Cleo thought wildly. Or a gun . . .?

The situation, at first annoying and a little worrying, had suddenly upped into something altogether more threatening. Her mouth was dry with terror. Surely this couldn't be happening to her? Not in quiet, sleepy, miles-from-anywhere-urban Lovers Knot?

Instinctively, she swung the bulging rubbish bag with as much force as she could muster and whacked the intruder neatly across the side of the head.

He went down like a stone.

Oh God, oh God, oh God – Cleo peered at the body – I've bloody killed him.

Would it be manslaughter? Could she plead diminished responsibility? Surely it had to be self-defence at least?

'Bugger,' the man groaned. 'I'm covered in egg and shit.'

Hallelujah! At least she wouldn't be spending the next ten years in Holloway.

Cleo reached behind her and, with trembling fingers, flicked on the full beam of the overhead kitchen light.

In the pool of light illuminating the caravan steps, she could see – with some relief – that the intruder was sitting up now, still breathing, dripping egg shells and the residue of her lasagne supper.

And, despite the detritus, he was without doubt the most beautiful boy she'd ever seen.

Black silky hair, high cheekbones, big bruised eyes – really bruised, she realised, blinking at two of the biggest gradually emerging shiners seen outside a boxing ring – and a sexy-sulky mouth that was oozing a trickle of blood.

Oh, Lordy, had she done that? Would that count as grievous bodily harm?

Holloway loomed once more.

Cleo took a deep breath and tried to stop shaking as she stared at him. As malefactors went, his clothes certainly matched his well-bred accent. Not your usual hoodie-and-baseball-cap uniform here. Oh no. He was wearing extremely expensive evening clothes. Bits of cake mixture dribbled down his tuxedo and onto the front of his white shirt. His bow tie, hanging undone, was decorated with globules of butter.

'Why the hell did you do that?' he mumbled, wincing as he carefully removed a tea bag from its resting place above one rapidly closing eye.

'Because I thought you were going to pull a knife or something on me.' Cleo's voice trembled.

'The only thing I was going to pull –' he gripped the bottom step, attempted to heave himself to his feet and failed '– was my cigarette lighter. I thought we ought to be able to see one another. It's pretty dark out here. I keep telling Olive to get a security light fitted. Oooh, I don't feel very well at all.' He stopped and squinted at her. 'You're seriously not Olive, are you?'

26

'For the third time, no. And I've no idea why you're here or what you want but if you haven't gone in thirty seconds then I honestly will call the police. You're drunk. You've obviously been fighting – those black eyes aren't self-inflicted and they can't be my fault, neither can your split lip.' Cleo stopped and glared at him. It didn't matter how gloriously gorgeous or upper class he was, he was still an intruder who, she thought, had been going to attack her, and she read the red tops. She knew all about rife knife crime. She had *rights*.

'I'm not drunk. A little tipsy, maybe, but mostly dazed and confused.' He looked at her sorrowfully. 'And let me remind you, it was y*ou* who attacked *me*.'

'It was self-defence – and you can't say it wasn't. Just be grateful I'd put all the glass and tins in the recycling bin.'

'Oh, right – so you being green and ecologically minded is supposed to appease me, is it? That bag was still hefty enough to catch me unawares and knock me off balance, and that's outside the Marquess of Queensberry's Rules.' He gave a deep groan and hauled himself to his feet. 'Sorry, but before we go any further, would you mind standing aside? I need to use your bathroom. I think I might be about to vomit . . .'

Of course she was completely insane, Cleo thought as she paced the tiny kitchen waiting for the man to emerge from her bathroom. She should never – *never* – have allowed him inside the caravan. But then neither did she want him throwing up all over the steps . . . And he was exceptionally well

27

spoken, very well dressed and polite and didn't seem at all aggressive . . .

Still, best to be on the safe side, Cleo thought, rattling through the cutlery drawer for a large kitchen knife. There. Now, with her mobile phone in the other hand, she'd be well protected if he turned nasty when he emerged from the bathroom.

But who the hell was he? What did he want? And who on earth was Olive?

Olive? She'd heard the name mentioned somewhere recently surely? Oh, yes, Elvi had said something about an Olive having been the cook at Lovelady Hall, hadn't she? And that she'd been carried away screaming . . .

Great.

The splashing from the bathroom suddenly ceased. Cleo gripped the knife more tightly as the door opened.

'Christ.' The man, carrying his tuxedo, the white shirt now clinging damply, and rubbing his wet hair with one of Cleo's bath towels, looked at the knife and pulled a face. 'Please put that down. I knew I was taking a risk coming in here, given your violent tendencies, but I didn't think you were a knife-wielding psychopath.'

'*Me*? I'm the one taking a risk, allowing you into my home. After all, you're the one who was about to break into my caravan.'

'No, I wasn't. I was merely seeking sanctuary and you attacked me with a bag of rubbish – most of which, you'll be pleased to know, I've managed to remove from all those awkward little places.' He grinned at her. 'You're much prettier than Olive, but I'd really be a lot happier if you put the knife down.'

'Only if you promise me you'll go. Now.'

'OK. Thanks for the use of the bathroom – I don't think I've messed it up too much. I just stuck my head under the cold shower which was great, thanks. I feel so much better. Completely sober. Oh, and I wasn't sick, which is always a bonus. I don't suppose you've got any steak?'

'Steak?' Cleo squeaked, deciding the danger of attack had passed, put down the knife and the phone, making sure they were still within reach should she need them. 'You want me to cook for you?'

'No . . . Well, I am a bit peckish now you come to mention it. But actually I meant for my eyes. Isn't that what you're supposed to use on black eyes to reduce the swelling? Fresh beef steak?'

'I have no idea. My close relations with brawlers are non-existent I'm delighted to say.'

He stopped rubbing his hair. It fell silkily towards his bruised eyes. Cleo looked away quickly.

'You know –' he smiled again '– you look just like Sophia Loren.'

'She's seventy-three.'

'I meant when she was young.'

'And as you're probably no more than thirty, you're far too young to have fancied Sophia Loren.'

'Right on the age. Wrong on the fancying. Kylie and co. did nothing for me. You've no idea how much I lusted after Sophia in my youth.' He sighed dramatically. 'And Claudia

29

Cardinale . . . and Gina Lollobrigida . . . Real curvaceous, vivacious, glamorous, sparky women. Voluptuous. Like you.'

Cleo shook her head. This was too surreal. 'Fascinating, but if you've finished trying to soft soap me, let me tell you that I'm immune to all that claptrap.'

'Soft soap? Claptrap?' He sighed. 'Damn. They were some of my best lines – and – actually true in your case.'

'Really? Shame – they're wasted on me. So, if you've finished cleaning up, and if you'd like to put my towel down, perhaps you could just clear off.'

'OK, er, Olive's replacement.'

'I am *not* Olive's replacement!'

'Well, what else can I call you? I don't know your name, do I?'

'I don't think there's any point in introductions as we'll never meet each other again.'

He grinned at her as much as the split lip would allow. 'And that's a pity.'

'No, it isn't.'

He leaned against the kitchen table. 'I'll tell you mine if you tell me yours.'

'No.' Cleo tried very hard not to laugh. The playground words were so at odds with this totally beautiful, exquisitely dressed, achingly upper-class stranger.

He seemed unfazed by the refusal. 'You're no fun. Anyway, I'm Dylan Maguire. If you tell me your name I can remember my manners and write you a nice thank-you letter when I get home, can't I? And you know who I am, so you've got to share yours. That's only fair.'

'Fair doesn't seem to come into any of this, but, OK – and simply because I don't want to be known as Olive's replacement – it's Cleo.'

'*Really*? How fantastic is that? It really suits you. Dark, glamorous, voluptuous –'

'And, as I've said, all that's wasted on me,' Cleo interrupted him. 'So shut up and chaff off.'

'You're a cruel woman, Cleo. And just in case you were wondering about my relationship with Olive – she wasn't my older lover or anything remotely News of the World. We used to work together.'

Cleo peered suspiciously at him. 'Work? So, is that the same Olive who worked at Lovelady Hall?'

'Yeah – ouch – my eyes hurt . . . Do you know Lovelady then? Did you know Olive?'

'I think you probably deserve your eyes hurting. Yes, I know a little about Lovelady Hall. No, I know absolutely nothing about Olive.'

Dylan shrugged. 'When she worked at Lovelady Hall, Olive used to live here. In this caravan. She was my substitute mum. I always came to her in times of dire need and disaster. I'd temporarily forgotten, in my tired, emotional and distressed state this evening, that she'd moved. Olive –' he looked at Cleo dolefully '– wouldn't have hit me with a rubbish bag.'

'Pity.'

'God, you're so hard. Olive always understood and dished out tea and sympathy.'

'More fool Olive.'

He laughed. Cleo glared at him. Being amusing, and drop-dead gorgeous to boot, *did not* excuse him being here, unannounced, in a state of drunkenness and disarray.

'She retired and went to live with her sister in Eastbourne. I thought my heart would break. And I know you've been really good about the bathroom and not stabbing me and everything, but before you turf me out into the dark, cold night, I don't suppose you could spare a cup of back coffee, could you? I really, really need to sober up properly before I get back to Lovelady and tell Mort what I've done with his top-of-the-range Bentley Continental.'

Cleo perked up a bit. Dylan Maguire was clearly a huge liability but probably not a crazed killer. And he was going to be one of her work colleagues, wasn't he? Not that she had any intention of telling him that. Yet.

But just what had he done with Mortimer Pashley-Royle's top-of-the-range Bentley?

After the last few humdrum months, it was all much too enticing to ignore . . .

Chapter Four

'OK . . . One cup of coffee. Black. To sober you up. Then you go. Understand?'

Dylan beamed happily. 'Yeah, promise. I'll go and sit quietly in the living room . . .' He drifted elegantly from the kitchen, then whooped. 'Wow! This is cosy. Been done up a bit since Olive's day too. She had it filled with crying puppy pictures, sad squat kiddie ornaments and photos of dead people.'

'Sounds, er, lovely.' Cleo, making the coffee, stifled a giggle. 'It must have been refurbished before I bought it. I didn't see it before I moved in. I just added the fripperies.'

When she carried the coffee through to the living room, Dylan was stretched out on the sofa, watching *Coronation Street* on the television, perfectly at home. Looking disconcertingly like something drop-dead sexy from a glossy ad for designer aftershave or eye-wateringly expensive watches.

She averted her eyes. 'Coffee. Strong. Black.'

'Thanks.' He sat up lazily. 'You're a star. And I like the fripperies. Nice word. Does it mean cushions?'

Cleo sat as far away from him as possible. 'Yes, and plants and flowers and candles – you know, all the girlie stuff that men hate.'

'Some men. Not me. I can appreciate pretty things. I don't think that makes me latently gay, do you?'

Absolutely no way on earth, Cleo thought, but she said nothing.

Dylan sipped his coffee and winced.

'Did that –' Cleo indicated the split lip and bruised eyes '– happen at the same time as whatever happened to the Bentley?'

'A nasty car crash? I wish. At least I might have got a bit of sympathy. Nah. This was the result of an enjoyable dalliance with a lady called Nesta.'

'Blimey, it's not been your night, has it? Nesta turning into Ricky Hatton and then me weighing in with the rubbish bag.'

'Nesta didn't hit me. Nesta loves me – and my body. Nesta's husband doesn't.'

Cleo closed her eyes. She should have known. Dylan Maguire was exactly the type to play fast and loose with married women. Just like Dave . . .

Well, no, actually not at all like Dave. Dave hadn't been young, tall, lean, fit and toe-curlingly sexy, had he? Cleo stopped, shocked at the thought.

'Serves you right for messing about then,' she said quickly. 'So, Nesta's husband did the thumping, and then what happened to the Bentley?'

'Same as me, really.' Dylan shrugged. 'Bollixed beyond

redemption. I was showing it off to Nesta, taking her for a little spin. We were planning a nice little dinner *à-deux* before christening the Bentley's rather sumptuous back seat . . . Nesta's husband – miserable sod – followed us, cut us up, dragged me out of the car and thumped me.' He beamed lopsidedly at Cleo. 'Can't blame him really, can you? Then Nesta scampered off with him and I crawled back into the car. I was supposed to be delivering it for Mort, you see.'

'You're Mortimer Pashley-Royle's *chauffeur*?'

'Yes, well, and the delivery driver for all his limousines and flash pash supercars. The Bentley was going to a recently knighted telly presenter. It never made it.'

Cleo leaned forwards, fascinated now, hooked on the story. It was way, way better than *Coronation Street*. 'Go on . . . Will Nesta be OK?'

'Oh, yes. Her husband only hits blokes. They're probably making it up in the age-old fashion right at this minute . . . I'll see her again when the fuss has died down. She's not the only lady in my life, but she's a bit of a fox and I'll miss her.'

Cleo decided she didn't want to know the more intimate details about the flighty Nesta – or any of the other notches on Dylan's bedpost. 'And the car?'

'Is several miles off the A34. Hugging a tree.'

'So what are you going to tell Mort, er, Mortimer?'

'God knows . . . not the truth. Definitely not the truth. Not that I was driving like a demon to get away from some woman's husband and mistimed a bend on the Hassocks road. Mort's a bit po-faced about that sort of thing.'

'And can you blame him?'

Dylan smiled endearingly again. 'No, not really. But for someone who worked in the sleaze industry for years, Mort can be a sanctimonious prig. And, before you say it, no I didn't crash because I'd had too much to drink. I wasn't drunk. I don't drink and drive. I had the drinks after I'd trashed the car. I was a bit shaken up, so I walked to Fiddlesticks and drowned my sorrows in the Weasel and Bucket.'

Cleo frowned. It was at least four miles from the Hassocks road to the village of Fiddlesticks, which in turn was about a mile from Lovers Knot. Dylan had had quite a trek. He must be very fit.

She swallowed quickly. 'But why come here?'

'Because I needed a sympathetic ear and a friendly cuddle and some good advice – and I knew that Olive was the only one to deliver. In my confusion, I'd forgotten that she wasn't here any more. And then you hit me and you weren't Olive.'

'Tough,' Cleo sighed. 'Earlier, I was going to apologise for assaulting you with the rubbish. Now I'm not. You deserved it. Not only for seeing a married woman, but for crashing a car that doesn't even belong to you, and running away from the scene of the accident – isn't that a hanging offence, anyway?'

'I didn't run away.' Dylan looked affronted. 'I limped. And I rang the police and told them what had happened and where the car was and that there was no one else involved. And I rang the car-breakdown-rescue people to remove it as well. I'm not totally irresponsible.'

But he was, Cleo thought. Wildly irresponsible. And very, very attractive.

'Well, now you'd better limp back to Lovelady Hall and make your excuses to Mortimer Pashley-Royle, hadn't you? He'll probably sack you on the spot.'

'I bloody hope not. I live in the flat over the stables – which is where he keeps his cars. I'm his security guard as well, you see. I'd be jobless and homeless in one fell swoop.'

'You should have thought of that, shouldn't you?'

'Harsh. You wait till it happens to you.'

It already had, Cleo thought. Which was why she was in this bizarre situation. It was all Dave's fault . . .

Bloody men.

Dylan stood up. 'Thanks again for the coffee and the hospitality, and I'm very sorry for intruding, and scaring you. I can assure you I don't usually behave like a yob. I think it was post-traumatic shock. And I'll know where to come next time I need tea and sympathy, won't I?'

'No way.' Cleo shook her head. 'I might have inherited Olive's home, but I am definitely not taking on her waifs and strays as well.'

Dylan shrugged into his tuxedo. 'Such a pity, but then, I can't say I blame you. If you ever change your mind, you know where to find me, don't you?'

'Believe me, I don't want to find you.'

'But if you did . . .'

'You won't be there because Mortimer will have sacked you.'

'He won't. The car's insured. I work for peanuts and I'm usually good.' He grinned down at her. 'I'm actually very, very good . . .'

'Out!' Cleo stood up. 'Now!'

Laughing, Dylan blew her a kiss and within half a dozen strides had gone, closing the caravan door behind him.

The living room seemed strangely quiet and empty without him. He certainly had a presence. And, Cleo wondered with a pang of guilt, should she have offered him a lift home?

No way!

Giving herself a severe mental shake, Cleo picked up the coffee mugs and carried them into the kitchen.

Dylan Maguire, she thought, running hot water into the sink, was a charming, cheating, amusing man. Just the sort of man she'd keep well away from. But, she had to admit, the gorgeous Dylan Maguire might make working at Lovelady Hall very interesting indeed . . .

Chapter Five

'. . . and then,' Mimi Pashley-Royle said, consulting a mile-long list, 'once you've emptied the washing-up machine and put everything away as per the kitchen diagram I showed you earlier, if you'd do the ironing in the basket in the boot room. Don't touch the ironing basket in the utility room – you can do that tomorrow. I need the boot room stuff cleared first – it's only some guest-room linen and towels and things like that but it's been lurking for ages. It shouldn't take you long. OK so far?'

Cleo, who had never ironed bedding or towels in her life, nodded. Only half an hour into her new job and Mimi had already outlined enough duties to keep her busy until Christmas.

'Good.' Mimi beamed. 'And when they're done, if you could just fold them and put them into the hot cupboard on the second landing? You do remember where that is?'

Cleo nodded again. She'd been amazed by the hot cupboards, as Mimi called her airing cupboards. They were vast, and it seemed there was one for almost every en-suite bedroom. And the shelves were all labelled and colour coded.

It was a total revelation to someone who now shoved her one set of spare linen into a tiny space over the top of the cooker in the caravan.

'And then, could you start on these invitations for me, please? The names and addresses are all on the computer in the downstairs office – the one just off the small drawing room. Still with me?'

Cleo nodded yet again. The whistle-stop tour of Lovelady Hall's myriad glorious panelled rooms, gleaming carved staircases and expensive rug-strewn corridors had left her head reeling.

'Lovely.' Mimi peered at the list again. 'I'm impressed, Cleo. You're a quick learner. I've had people here who've still been hopelessly lost after an entire week. Actually, I think I'll come and join you for this one. There's a particular issue with these invitations that I really must explain. What say we have coffee at the same time? Then you won't need to break off for elevenses, will you?'

Clever tactic, Cleo thought, as she headed for the dishwasher prior to attacking the boot room's ironing basket. Very clever. And no doubt there'd be a working lunch too. Having Mimi Pashley-Royle as an employer was going to be akin to slaving on a chain gang.

Having established during the grand tour that about the only thing that didn't fall within her PA remit was gardening and heavy-duty cleaning, Cleo now heaved a sigh of relief as she tramped backwards and forwards across the ballroom-sized bespoke oak and maple kitchen, unloading the dishwasher and locating the correct homes for the crockery and cutlery.

Cleaning Lovelady Hall would be like painting the Forth Bridge: never-ending.

'The grounds are Mortimer's province really, and he employs a super man – literally – from Hazy Hassocks: Rocky Lancaster. He and his lads have worked miracles on the gardens – but cleaners! That's another thing altogether!' Mimi had thrown her hands in the air in mock despair when Cleo had finally been brave enough to ask who kept Lovelady gleaming inside and out. 'Cleaners are the bane of my life! The locals seem to think a quick squirt of Mr Sheen and a wave of a dirty duster is all that's needed. No, I employ a firm of contract cleaners who specialise in caring for stately homes and National Trust properties, and they come in on a monthly basis for a top-to-bottom scrub, and then Zola and Zlinki do a couple of hours three times a week to keep the cobwebs down and the patina up.'

'Zola and Zlinki?'

'Sweet girls,' Mimi had drawled. 'Polish or Latvian or something similar. Students. I thought they were possibly studying English, but no. They speak English far better than most of the locals. They're going to be barristers.'

So, Cleo thought, as she trudged across the miles of tiles with some exquisitely patterned soup bowls, she now knew that she wasn't the sole Lovelady employee. There was also Rocky Lancaster, and Zola and Zlinki – and, of course, Dylan . . .

As she managed to stack the soup bowls without dropping any, she wondered – not for the first time – how Dylan had fared in his confessional with Mortimer over the fate of the Bentley. And, yes, OK, if he'd survived, whether she'd see Dylan in the course of her new job. Not that she wanted to see him in any sort of *fancying* way, of course, but he had been gorgeous and amusing and, yes, a welcome diversion from the dull routine of her evening – and it would be really funny to see how he reacted when he realised that she was Olive's replacement in more ways than one.

Maybe, she thought, blinking slightly at the fact that one huge cupboard had several shelves of dinner services, all labelled EVERYDAY, FAMILY, BUSINESS GUESTS, COUNTY, and ASK FIRST BEFORE USING, Dylan had been sacked on the spot and was at that very minute trying to woo his way back into Nesta's good books and she'd never see him again...

Would that bother her? Nah. She shook her head. Well, yes, OK, maybe just a little bit . . .

Anyway, she was curious about Dylan. Why would someone of his class be working as a chauffeur-cum-delivery driver? Well, of course, a lot of graduates and public schoolboys found it difficult to find slots in their normal city bolt holes in these days of severe economic cutbacks, but even so . . .

She could always ask Elvi about Dylan, of course. Elvi seemed to know everything about everybody. But Cleo wasn't sure that she wanted to hear a catalogue of Dylan's misdemeanours from Elvi – and she certainly didn't want a lecture on why Dylan Maguire was the pits and under no circumstances should she allow him near the caravan again. Which was why she wouldn't be telling her best friend Doll about Dylan either.

No, Cleo decided, she'd keep Dylan's nocturnal visit a secret between her and whichever piece of kitchen equipment was her current confidante of choice.

She straightened up from the last cupboard. All this bending and stretching would at least keep her fit. It was a universal unfairness, she thought, that some people, like Elvi, had genes that handed you slender elegance at birth, and others – like hers – tended towards curves and wobbly bits.

She squeezed the little roll of wobble above the waistband of her black polyester trousers and laughed. Voluptuous, Dylan had said . . . Which was a far lovelier way of describing her curves than Dave-the-ex had used. Oh yes, Dylan certainly had a silver tongue – and he clearly knew how to use it.

Cleo suddenly felt very hot.

Maybe, she told herself severely, if she really wanted to hang on to this job, she should just forget all about Dylan Maguire and get on with the ironing.

An hour and a half later, sitting in the downstairs office with Mimi, the computer and a jug of very good coffee, Cleo knew she'd been right about Mimi. Mimi *was* a slave driver, but to give her her due, she was appreciative and had thanked Cleo profusely for the ironing and all the jobs that had preceded it.

'So many people just skimp things.' Mimi sipped black coffee. 'You've done everything as I would do it myself if I had the time or the inclination for menial tasks. Most impressive. Right, now the invitations. You're all right with finding your way round this computer? Good – now, you'll find all the names and addresses on this list, and the invitation template is stored under "social". Just change the occasion to Harvest Home, the date to 19 September and the times to from eight until late. All the invitations will have to be printed off and sent snail mail as a lot of the villagers aren't online – I'm sure they think the internet is the work of the devil in Lovers Knot.'

Cleo somehow doubted this as Mimi drew breath but felt it probably wasn't the best time to say so.

'Harvest Home?' Cleo frowned. 'As in "gathering in all the sheaves of corn"?'

'Exactly that. Lovelady has been holding Harvest Home supper for hundreds of years. It matters not that we no longer have a working farm attached to the manor – this is a tradition. We don't need literal sheaves of corn to celebrate. We're very big on tradition. Centuries ago the Lovelady Harvest Home indicated survival for everyone for another year. It was well worth celebrating – and the villagers do so enjoy having a bit of a shindig.'

'And you have it here? And invite everyone from Lovers Knot?'

'Everyone.' Mimi straightened her silk cashmere sweater and pulled a face. 'Not, of course, that we allow the hoi polloi to run amok through the house of course. No, we stick with tradition and do it as they did in the old days and have the whole thing al fresco in the courtyard.'

'And if it rains? Do you have an "in the village hall if wet" contingency?'

Just too late, Cleo remembered Mimi's tendency to take everything literally.

Mimi looked puzzled. 'Lovers Knot doesn't have a village hall. You should know that – you live there. The nearest village hall is in Hazy Hassocks and that's too far away . . . No, no, if it rains we have it in one of the barns. It's not a problem. I always feel the majority of the guests feel quite at home in the barns.'

Cleo bit her lip and clicked on the computer's 'social' link.

Mimi peered over her shoulder. 'Lovely . . . I can see you're as computer literate as you claimed in your interview. Sadly, it's not one of my skills. I've never had the time to learn. So, can I just say that the really important thing to remember with the invitations is that, to avoid any problems, we cross-reference with the provisions list and clearly state who brings what.'

Cleo, who had just managed to find the template and was poised to start typing in names, frowned. 'Sorry?'

'Food. For the Harvest Home,' Mimi laughed. 'Goodness me, you don't think I provide it all, do you? Lord, I'm not that publicly spirited. And this is *tradition* after all. In the good old days, the Big House provided the meats and game mainstays of the feast, and the villagers all brought something home-made or home-grown from their own harvested store to bulk it out and share amongst the others.'

'Very democratic.' Cleo smiled. 'So, when I send the invitations, I have to put "Fred Knobble: vegetable marrow", do I?'

'Well, yes –' Mimi looked doubtful '– except of course there's no one called Fred Knobble on the list, and we don't actually want anyone to bring a vegetable marrow. It would take too much cooking and no one would eat it. That sort of thing is fine for the harvest festival church service in Hazy Hassocks – where I actually believe they now roll up with tins of baked beans and packets of desiccated noodles – but it's not what we want here. Heaven forbid.'

Cleo stared hard at her screen and tried not to laugh.

'No,' Mimi continued, 'Mortimer and I will provide the pig roast and the more robust carnivorous things – they all seem to love something on a spit – but we have to stick with the traditions, so they still bring something of their own making. And to make sure we don't get eighteen plates of flaccid sausage rolls, I like to stipulate – see, there, against Mary Benwell I've got cheese. Mary keeps goats. She makes some superb cheese. And Geoff Glass has a small orchard and turns out a simple super shortcrust pastry – and who am I to mention his sexual orientation? – so he's down for apple pies. Simple.'

Still trying not to giggle, Cleo nodded.

'Right.' Mimi poured more coffee into both cups. 'So we're clear on the invitations? Good. Oh, and you'll be free for the nineteenth will you?'

'Yes,' Cleo said without thinking.

There was no need to check. She had no other social events looming.

Apart from Doll Blessing, her best friend through school and beyond, most of the friends of her marriage had drifted away. Some had taken Dave's side in the break-up and now accepted Wobbly Wanda into their circle, others had just found it too awkward including the newly single Cleo into things that used to involve Cleo-and-Dave: the Couple.

Doll and, oddly, Elvi were probably now her closest friends, and evenings out were something of a rarity.

It would be fun to be a guest at something which should, if her memory served her well, be reminiscent of a painting by Bruegel, with villagers sitting at trestle tables and on hay bales and quaffing huge quantities of ale and munching on great legs of some poor roasted animal, and being generally – well – Bruegel-ish.

It would be wonderful to join with the Phlopps, and Elvi and her family, and Rodders and Salome and Mrs Hancock and the others from the caravan park at such a bucolic party. Oh, and especially Jerome. She wondered if Jerome would be allowed to bring his imaginary horse . . .

'Super.' Mimi smiled. 'And what's your speciality? What can you bring to the table?'

Remembering Elvi's warning about not letting Mimi get wind of any sort of latent Nigella-skills, Cleo didn't answer straight away.

'Um,well, I do love making cakes, so –'

'Oh no, not cakes. Definitely not cakes. Belly and Flip make cakes. They've always made cakes for Harvest Home. We mustn't tread on their toes. No, sorry, Cleo, cakes are out.'

Bugger the Phlopps. Cleo sighed. Cakes were easy – now she'd have to think of something else.

'I had no idea that Belly and Flip were cake-makers.'

'Oh, yes excellent. Such large-handed clumsy women, but a wonderfully light touch with a sponge. Do you know the Phlopps then? Oh, of course I suppose you would. They live on your caravan encampment, don't they? Such odd women I always think. Something not quite right there: middle-aged sisters, dressing identically, working all their life in the same civil service office . . . but they make melt-in-the-mouth fancies, so I shouldn't be unkind.'

No you shouldn't, Cleo thought irritably, concentrating on the computer screen again and glancing first at the list of names and then at the list of produce, and wondering what she could possibly make for Harvest Home that some Lovers Knot resident hadn't already laid claim to for the last nine hundred years.

'We'll have to put our heads together and see what we can come up with for you to concoct.' Mimi pursed her glossy lips. 'But if you're a dab hand with cake-making, does that mean you could rustle up other little confections? I know we agreed on a little light cooking – which I was thinking would be rustling up a hot snackette for brunch – but . . .'

'Welsh rarebit I think was mentioned at the interview,' Cleo said quickly. 'Light lunches in an emergency.'

'Yes, well any fool can use a toaster or the George Formby – what I'm looking for is another local person to cook at my supper parties. Caterers are all very well, but one has to book them in advance, and sometimes it's useful to have someone on hand who can whisk up something at a moment's notice. And puddings are always such a tricky area – sadly the Phlopps and Geoff Glass have always turned me down.'

'Oh no, sorry,' Cleo said even more quickly. 'I'm pretty useless at everything apart from cakes.'

'Oh, what a pity.' Mimi gave a little snort of disappointment. 'Ah well, can't be helped. Right, now can I leave you with the invitations? You clearly know how to cross-reference the names with the allotted provender, the address labels are in the right-hand drawer, envelopes in the left. Stamps are there in the tray. Pop them in the postbox on your way home tonight, please. All OK?'

'Perfectly, thanks. I can't see any problems at all. Oh, and thank you for inviting me to Harvest Home. I really appreciate it.'

'Inviting? Good Lord, Cleo, you're not a *guest*. You'll be working. Waiting on tables and what have you. As we all will. Tradition, you know.'

Bugger again. Cleo continued to peck away at the keyboard. She should have realised that anything to do with Mimi would involve working. Still, maybe she'd get overtime. And then again maybe she wouldn't . . .

'Heavens, where has this morning gone? I must go and get ready for lunch. Charity you know? I'm chairing the committee.' Mimi stood up in a waft of something exclusive. 'Committees and lunches and fund-raising take up most of my time and – Oh, hello, darling.'

Mimi's tone had changed so dramatically that Cleo looked up in surprise as the office door opened.

'*Darling*' was a short, rotund, balding man wearing country-gent ginger cords and a Tattersall checked shirt, and who simply *had* to be Sir Mortimer Pashley-Royle.

Cleo blinked. From Elvi and Dylan's descriptions, she'd imagined him to be some oleaginous, perma-tanned, multi-blinged porn baron, so this benevolently smiling roly-poly ball, who was possibly a foot shorter than Mimi, came as a complete shock.

'Mortimer, meet Cleo. She's an angel. An absolute whiz at everything,' Mimi gushed happily. 'Cleo, let me introduce my darling husband, Mortimer.'

Mortimer's eyes twinkled in their rolls of fat and his handshake was firm. 'Lovely to meet you, Cleo, my dear. Mimi was so pleased you'd taken the job. Welcome to Lovelady Hall. I hope you'll be very happy here.'

'Er, yes, I'm sure I will be, um, thank you . . .'

Now Mimi and Mortimer were holding hands, Cleo noticed, and smiling into one another's eyes. How weird was that? Elvi had said it was a love match, and it certainly appeared to be. It just went to show . . .

What it went to show, Cleo wasn't entirely sure, but the cliché seemed appropriate.

'We'll leave you now,' Mimi said, still beaming at Mortimer. 'So much to do. If you have any probs at all you have my mobile number – and I'll see you again tomorrow morning, at the same time? Good. Now I really must dash.'

And, still holding hands and giggling together like

teenagers, the Pashley-Royles closed the office door behind them.

Well! Cleo shook her head. That was a turn up . . . And while Mortimer didn't look at all like a stereotypical sleaze merchant – not that she'd ever met one, but she was pretty sure they all followed a definite physical pattern – neither did he appear angry or like someone who had just sacked a vital member of staff. And Mimi had seemed calm and unruffled, which surely she wouldn't if her beloved Mortimer had been unhappy, so maybe Dylan had survived even if the Bentley Continental hadn't?

And as she wasn't going to think about Dylan Maguire, Cleo told herself sternly, she really ought to crack on with the invitations.

With a sigh, she consulted her list again.

That evening, having showered, thrown on her cuddly bunny pyjamas and a fluffy dressing gown, eaten a hastily concocted Spanish omelette and a chocolate mousse in front of the television, Cleo sorted out a fresh shirt to go with her polyester work trousers and yawned.

She was totally exhausted. Mimi's duty list for the day had been completed by just before six, and a similar hefty catalogue of duties loomed for the morning.

'Sad,' she said cheerfully out loud. 'Thirty-five years old and ready for bed at 8.30. Life is truly over . . . Oooh, damn, the rubbish bin has to go out tonight. Can't risk leaving it until the morning, they always collect them so early. I'll just do that then it's bed and a good book for me. And I really am going to have to see Mrs Hancock about getting a cat to have these conversations with.'

She hadn't even had Elvi to talk to tonight. Elvi, Cleo knew, was reluctantly at one of what the local authority called Social Integration evenings, apparently devised to introduce the pupils from single-sex schools to the delights of getting to know the opposite gender in a responsible manner, without having to resort to gallons of alcopops and falling out of nightclubs in the early hours, or fighting like badgers at the Hazy Hassocks kebab van.

Cleo hauled herself from the sofa, wrapped her dressing gown more tightly round her and unlocked the door.

Stupid, she thought, as she felt a pang of disappointment at finding the doorstep empty. Had she really expected Dylan to be there? No, of course not. Did she want him to be? Definitely not! No way. Not at all. Well, yes, OK, just a little bit . . .

She hurried across to the tiny lean-to shed in the blustery darkness, then switched on the dim overhead light and bent down to drag out the dustbin.

'Come along,' Cleo encouraged the bin, 'there's no point in hiding, you've got to go out. And I really must stop this talking-out-loud thing. Ooof!'

She tugged the bin from its cubbyhole between several large packing cases of empty bottles and large oddly shaped glass jars, beneath one of the lopsided shelves.

'Oh, sod it!'

A pile of bags, boxes, books and old newspapers cascaded to the floor. Like the bottles and jars, they'd been in the shed when Cleo had moved in and, like the bottles and jars, had been on her to-sort-out list ever since, but as they were out of sight they were also very much out of mind.

Scrambling the papers up into her arms, she shoved them back on the shelf to be dealt with at a later date. They must have belonged to Olive, she thought, thrusting some 1979 *Woman's Weekly*s into an untidy heap, and been abandoned in the move to Eastbourne. Ah well, one day she'd get around to sorting through them.

Just the collection of exercise books to go. Olive seemed to have amassed an awful lot of folders and binders and old books – ooh, that was pretty, though . . . She squinted at some vividly coloured illustrations that had flapped from one of the buff-covered books.

Aw, sweet – Olive must have cut things out of magazines and collected them into some sort of scrapbook. Or maybe they were knitting patterns? Or handy hints? Idly, Cleo flipped through the vibrant pages. How odd . . . All the gummed-in illustrations were of drinks. No, not just any drinks – these were all pictures of wine – wine in rich, deeply hued glasses and bottles.

There were dozens of wine glasses on the pages, lustrous with ruby and crimson and purple liquid. Brimming bottles, glowing with all the colours of autumn.

Was Olive a secret lush then? Cleo grinned to herself. That would explain the myriad empty bottles, and might also explain why Dylan had visited her so regularly.

Fascinated, she flipped through the book's yellowing sheets a bit more – now there were pages of – what –

recipes? Yes. Detailed, handwritten recipes, but not for food. These recipes were for wine. Home-made wine. Wine made from wild berries and hedgerow fruits.

Cleo laughed out loud, the tiredness gone, the dustbin forgotten. Hallelujah! This was what she could make and take to Lovelady's Harvest Home. No doubt this is what Olive had made for years – and she knew from the invitation list that no one else was bringing wine.

Fantastic!

She'd follow in Olive's footsteps and make home-made wine for the party – oh yes, and even better, she'd keep it a secret from Mimi, and then it would come as a really big surprise.

Chapter Six

'Putrid,' Elvi groaned, stretching out her long legs in front of her. 'These things are a truly putrid waste of time.'

Her best friends, Sophie and Kate, sitting on either side of her on the window ledge of Winterbrook Girls' Grammar School's assembly hall, nodded in agreement.

'It isn't even,' Elvi continued, 'as if *they* want to integrate with *us*.'

'*They*' were the sixth-form boys of Gorse Glade College, a public school from the other side of Berkshire, which promised a second-to-none traditional education for the sons of anyone wealthy enough to afford the eye-watering fees. There was always a smattering of minor royalty and embryo cabinet ministers included in the Gorse Glade ranks.

The boys looked about as enthralled with Social Interaction as the girls. Harsh overhead lighting did no one any favours, and a soundtrack of appalling 80s electro pop, clearly the staff's era and therefore party music of choice, filled the hall. Everyone clutched a beaker of tepid fruit punch.

'Well, I'm not panting to integrate with them anyway.' Kate hitched up her skirt a bit more, undid several buttons on her blouse, and pouted. 'There you go – they're all completely gay. Not one of them took any notice. There's not one decent fit lad amongst them as far as I can see.'

'We haven't seen them all,' Elvi pointed out. 'The ones over by the stage have kept pretty well hidden.'

Sophie shook her head. 'Doesn't matter – they'll be dorks, too. Nerds. Geeks. Rich-kid saddos.'

'You'd think,' Elvi said, watching a clutch of boys in their individual lounge suit uniforms all huddled together in the middle of the hall as some of the more desperate Winterbrook girls fawned and gushed and were more-or-less ignored, 'that as they're all boarders, they'd be rampant with hormones and mad to get at girls – any girls.'

'We're not posh enough, *dahling*,' Kate giggled.

'Nah.' Sophie shook her head. 'I reckon we're *too* posh. At least educationally. Who they want to socially interact with are the girls from Winterbrook comp. Not only do they not have to wear a bloody silly uniform, they'd be fun and refreshing and uncomplicated. They wouldn't have guilt complexes about not having done their English essays or revised for the next French test. The Gorse Glade boys must have education thrust down their throats from morning to night – they wouldn't want it in their social life.'

Elvi pulled a face. 'And you're clearly doing way too much putrid A-level psychology. God, what's the time? How much more of this do we have to put up with?'

'Half-eight,' Sophie said. 'Only another half-hour to

go, and my dad's picking us up so we can make a quick get-away.'

'I won't need a lift,' Kate said. 'I'm, um, I'm . . .'

Elvi and Sophie raised their eyebrows.

'You're not?'

Kate nodded. 'But don't you dare tell my mum. I've told her this ends at eleven.'

Elvi exhaled. Everyone in the lower sixth knew that Kate was having sex. Proper sex. In a proper relationship. With Mason. Mason was eighteen, on Job Seeker's Allowance, wore a hoodie, was ace at hip-hop, and hung around with his gang in Winterbrook precinct looking vaguely menacing.

Kate was besotted.

Elvi was half shocked and half jealous. Not that she'd want a boyfriend like Mason because he was – well, to be honest, he was a bit scary. And despite being Berkshire born and bred on the Hazy Hassocks Bath Road Estate, he spoke like a gangsta rapper and sometimes she couldn't understand him. But he did seem very fond of Kate in a kind of rough and gruff way, and Kate wore his knuckle-duster sovereign ring on a chain under her school uniform and said they'd get married as soon as she'd done her A levels or got pregnant – whichever came first.

No, Elvi thought, she definitely wouldn't want a boyfriend like Mason, but a boyfriend of some sort would be lovely. Someone to share things with, someone who would make her giggle like Kate, and give her something else to think about other than tricky long-winded Chaucer, and horrid Shakespeare with his screamingly obvious plot devices, and sodding dreary squeaky prissy mimsy Jane Austen.

If it wasn't for Tennyson and Larkin and Dickens and Stella Gibbons and the wondrous Harper Lee, Elvi was pretty sure she'd have ditched A-level English by now.

She sighed. Her entire life revolved around school and studying, and because her parents were so proud that she had a brain and used it, she knew that she'd have to go to uni and couldn't let them down. So it looked like at least another two years of enforced celibacy loomed.

Then again, look at Cleo. Cleo was so cool. Cleo had had the together-forever and lost it, and seemed really happy without it. Maybe relationships weren't the be-all and end-all – but it would be nice to *know*.

'Girls!' Miss Chamberlain the chemistry mistress bore down on them. 'Come along! This is all about socialising and integrating. I haven't seen any of you doing either of those things all evening. Now, split up, and go and mingle. Introduce yourselves. This is a lesson, you know. Teaching you to become young ladies. Teaching you how to behave appropriately in social situations with members of the opposite sex.'

Kate sniggered loudly.

'And split up!' Miss Chamberlain said sharply. 'Kate, you go over there. Sophie, over to the group by the doors, and, Elvi, you can join the boys by the stage. Quickly!'

Reluctantly peeling themselves from the window ledge, Elvi, Sophie and Kate did as they were told because any sort of disobedience was simply not tolerated at Winterbrook.

The group of boys by the stage had their backs to her. Shellie and Bex, both lower-sixth social climbers, were hovering on the periphery, giggling.

Elvi, trying to ignore the overhead blast of the Human League, took a deep breath.

'Hi, I'm Elvi Reynolds.'

The nearest back – clad in a loud houndstooth check – turned and stared at her. He was all pink and white and baby-looking, with a fluffy incipient moustache and acne.

Elvi, determined not to judge a book by its cover, smiled. 'This is pretty boring isn't it? We've got to do it several times this term and I bet they'll all be putrid. What about you?'

Ignoring the question, the houndstooth check wrinkled his nose. 'Is Elvi truncated? Or is it a proper name?'

'It's Welsh. My dad's family originally came from Wales.'

'*Dad*,' houndstooth drawled. 'And no doubt you say "lounge" and "settee" and "toilet", don't you?'

'Nah.' Elvi shook her head. 'As I live in a caravan we don't have room for a lounge, and we sit on boxes and use the outside bog.'

Houndstooth roared with laughter. 'Touché! That's me put in my place. I'm Henry Bancroft. It's a pleasure to meet you, Elvi. And yes, these things are frankly, pretty unbearable. However, as we're incarcerated in our ivory-towered seat of educational excellence for thirty weeks of the year, any escape is more than welcome. What are you studying?'

'English, French and history. You?'

'Classics.'

'Putrid.'

'Very much so.' Henry laughed again. 'And are you up for Oxbridge?'

'God, no. I'm only in the lower sixth, but it'll be Durham I hope, and if not, Exeter.'

'I have to get into Christ Church. The Bancrofts have been educated at Christ Church for generations. Ah, here comes the booze.'

The Human League turned into Ultravox. Elvi really hoped Henry wouldn't keep laughing. It was more of a high-pitched hiccupping haw-haw and people were looking at them. Henry Bancroft, pleasant as he undoubtedly was, certainly wasn't going to be The One.

'Booze? You mean you've got proper alcohol? Here?'

'My enterprising chum smuggled in some vodka. We've been lacing this God-awful fruit pee all night. He's just returning with refills.' Henry waved a loudly chequered arm above his head. 'Over here!'

Elvi turned to see which other chinless wonder was clever enough to be spiking the drinks and stopped.

Ohmigod!

The pale boy in the baggy, dark-grey suit, was very tall and bone thin. His hair, which hung in a long silky fringe over his large eyes, was black, dead straight and spiky.

'Bugger.' He grinned at her as he reached them, his brown eyes on a level with hers. 'If I'd known we had company I'd have brought another beaker. Here – you can share mine.'

'Thanks.' Elvi took a sip. It was very strong.

'She's Elvi,' Henry brayed, glugging at his vodka punch. 'She's not only beautiful but she lives in a caravan and she's smart.'

The tall, thin boy grinned again. 'Hello, Elvi. I'm –'

'Zeb Pashley-Royle. I know.'

'Bloody hell! Are you psychic?'

Elvi handed him the beaker. 'I live in Lovers Knot. My mum used to clean for your mum at Lovelady Hall before she got the job at Big Sava.'

'What?' Henry looked amazed. 'Is your mother working in a supermarket, Zeb? How very democratic.'

'*My* mother,' Elvi giggled, 'not Lady Pashley-Royle.'

'You really live in Lovers Knot?' Zeb seemed stunned. 'But how come I've never seen you?'

'Because,' Elvi said sweetly, 'I doubt if you've ever strayed into the village – or on to the caravan site where I live. And years ago, before you went to Gorse Glade, when you *were* around at Lovelady Hall, I was always there as the cleaner's brat, or later waitressing when your mother hosted a charity lunch, which would make me invisible. And because since then you were always at school or away skiing or out doing putrid posh things . . .'

'Sod it – I always knew an expensive education would have massive drawbacks. So, did you know I'd be here tonight?'

'Nope. I honestly didn't know you were at Gorse Glade. I just knew you boarded at some Rich-List kids school. Eton, Harrow, Radley . . .'

'Bugger,' Zeb sighed, passing the beaker to her again. 'I'd

have asked to be home-educated had I known you were on my doorstep.'

They smiled at one another.

Elvi looked away first and gulped at the drink, savouring the moment, knowing she'd remember for the rest of her life the very second when she fell in love with a smile to an Ultravox backing track.

First love: wondrous, intense, heady, intoxicating, never to be forgotten . . .

Henry guffawed some more, the other boys pushed and shoved round them and Shellie and Bex were giggling shrilly at something someone had said.

Elvi wasn't aware of any of it.

She was only aware of the tall, skinny, spiky-haired, achingly cool and deliciously gorgeous Zeb Pashley-Royle.

And, amazingly, it seemed, he was only aware of her.

Ultravox had been replaced by Marc Almond. Elvi hoped 'Tainted Love' wasn't an omen. She somehow felt it wasn't. Although, of course, fancying Zeb Pashley-Royle was all a bit upstairs downstairs – or did she mean Montague and Capulet? Oooh no, not that. That was a teenage love affair that was very tainted indeed.

Zeb sighed. 'So we've wasted simply years of knowing one another.'

'Not really.' Elvi passed the beaker back. 'We were only children before. I was aware of you being around but you were just a skinny kid. As I was.'

'And now?'

'And now –' Elvi smiled, refusing the beaker because her head was spinning slightly '– you're still a skinny kid while I'm an elegant young lady of sixteen. Girls mature so much faster than boys.'

'A fallacy,' Zeb said, his eyes wide through the long strands of his coal-black fringe. 'And I'm an extremely adult seventeen, so that gives me the edge, I reckon.'

'OK, it might just do, although I'm not saying you're right, of course. And, on the plus side, the year difference means if you're in the upper sixth and doing the same boring A levels as me, I can pick your brains.'

'Chemistry, physics and maths?'

'Sod it,' Elvi said, still feeling ecstatically giddily happy and knowing now it wasn't anything to do with the vodka. 'English, French and history . . . And I was going to suggest we used study notes as an excuse to meet up next time you're home.'

'We won't need an excuse.'

'Oh,' Elvi mocked happily, 'you say the nicest things.'

Zeb laughed. It was a nice laugh. Deep and throaty – not loud and braying like Henry's – and it crinkled his eyes. He had extremely long eyelashes.

'Seriously, I'll be back at Lovelady for Harvest Home. Just a couple of weeks away. We can meet then, can't we?'

Elvi stared at him. 'Meet? As in casually pass in the rutted furrows of my putrid hamlet? Or meet as in on a date?'

'The latter. Definitely.' Zeb suddenly stopped smiling. 'I mean, if that's what you'd like, er, I mean . . .'

'I'd love it!' Elvi forgot to be cool and play for time and all the things the magazines said you should do to keep a boy interested and not appear over keen.

With some relief she realised it didn't seem to have put Zeb off.

'Fantastic.' He grinned. 'We can fix it up when you're at Lovelady for Harvest Home, can't we?'

'Well, yes – but don't forget I'll only be there as a token yokel guest. While you'll be the young lord and master.'

'Who'll be waiting on the so-called yokels, as per Lovelady tradition.'

'Oh, yes, of course, the egalitarian evening!' Elvi beamed. 'Oh, that'll be really cool. You dancing to my every whim. I like it.'

'Good.' Zeb drained the beaker. 'I'm glad we've set the ground rules – I shall spend the rest of my life dancing to your whims. And don't forget that this Social Integration crap also means that we get to host a return match at Gorse Glade. These sessions are always home and away, aren't they?'

'God, yes. I'd forgotten that. You get to see our putrid 1960s concrete breeze-block-and-plate-glass monstrosity, and we get to see your mellow, crumbling, totally gorgeous sixteenth-century abbey.'

'And my study. And my dorm.'

'Dorm?' Elvi chuckled with delight. 'You sleep in dorms? Like in Harry Potter?'

'Absolutely nothing like Harry Potter. Well, yes, the younger boys do, but when we get into the upper, we're treated as young gentlemen. We get single rooms.'

'For entertaining young ladies?'

'God no. We'd get hung, drawn and quartered and then sent down. That's strictly against the rules. But being a Pashley-Royle has taught me one thing – rules are always more fun when they're broken.'

They laughed together. Elvi supposed that somewhere close Henry was still braying, the electro-pop was still booming and the rest of Winterbrook Girls' Grammar School were yawning their way through Social Integration, but she could see none of it, hear none of it.

This was *it*, she thought dreamily. This was what Kate felt about Mason. Now she could understand why Kate would risk everything simply to be with her man – well, boy – and knew she'd do the same . . .

Then the music died.

'Right, ladies and gentlemen!' Miss Chamberlain clapped her hands. 'That's the end of our Social Integration for tonight. I'm sure you'll agree it's been a super evening. So let's say thank you to the Gorse Glade pupils and staff.'

There was a round of ragged applause. The Winterbrook mistresses and the Gorse Glade masters uniformly heaved a sigh of relief. The boys all rushed for the hall doors, the girls almost beating them to it.

Nooo! Elvi thought. It can't be over already! It simply can't.

Miss Chamberlain and her cohorts were collecting beakers, straightening chairs, returning the hall to normal, ready for the next morning's assembly.

'Here.' Zeb pushed a piece of paper into Elvi's hand. 'My mobile number. What's yours?'

She told him, watching carefully as he copied it into his iPhone.

'I'll text you tonight. As soon as we get back.' He stared at her. 'Oh, shit, now I really wish I went to Winterbrook comp and we could see each other every day.'

'Me too,' Elvi said softly. 'And thank the Lord for social integration – that's in lower case, by the way.'

Zeb laughed, then Henry beamed at Elvi and, with a mock bow, grabbed his arm and tugged him in the direction of the rest of the disappearing Gorse Glade boys.

As the lights dimmed and the hall emptied, Elvi stood and watched him go. Then, alone, she turned away. She felt blissfully happy and desperately sad and more mixed up than she'd ever felt in her life, but more than anything she wanted to run after him.

What if he didn't text her? What if she never saw him again? Oh, what if the next time she saw him was at Harvest Home and he blanked her? What if –?

'Elvi . . .'

She looked round.

Zeb grinned at her. 'I didn't say goodbye.' He pulled her against him and kissed her.

'Oh, I say!' Henry trumpeted from somewhere behind them, but Elvi didn't care.

It was her first proper kiss. Not just some fumbling youth club disco snog, but a proper, blissful, mind-blowing, grown-up kiss.

She trembled, feeling Zeb's bone-thin body shivering too, and kissed him back.

'Zeb!' Henry snorted. 'Come on!'

Elvi opened her eyes and reluctantly, Zeb moved away from her.

'See you soon,' he said softly.

And this time he was gone.

Elvi, still shaking, drifted dazedly towards the doors.

'Where did you get to?' Sophie grizzled, shoving Elvi's coat and bag towards her. 'I couldn't see you in the hall, so I thought you were already in the cloakroom but you weren't. Kate's sodded off to get her paws on Mason and my dad's waiting outside so we'd better hurry. Elvi? Elvi? Are you OK?'

'What? Oh, er, yes, fine.'

'Good.' Sophie linked her arm through Elvi's. 'Well, thank God that's over. Jeeze – those prats were the biggest bores on the planet, weren't they?'

'What? Oh, yeah.'

Sophie groaned. 'God, I bloody hate the idea of Soc Int – and that one was a real crap fest, wasn't it?'

'Mmm,' Elvi agreed dreamily as they walked outside into the windy September darkness. 'Totally putrid.'

Chapter Seven

'Tell me again exactly why we're doing this?' Doll muttered, tightly muffled against the autumnal chill. 'Why are we trudging through Lovers Spinney, in the freezing cold, foraging stuff into Big Sava carrier bags on my one child-free afternoon, when I'd been looking forward to some girlie gossip and one of your cakes in the warm?'

'Don't grizzle,' Cleo puffed, reaching upwards towards some perfect specimens on a scrubby crab apple tree. 'I need the raw materials for my home-made wine, four hands are better than two, and you're my best friend. It's what you do. Look, just grab that branch and hold your bag open – thanks.'

Doll shook her head, grabbed the branch with one hand, and obediently opened her already-bulging bag with the other as Cleo plucked the crimson and gold crab apples.

'Aren't they lovely? They look like little Fabergé Eggs, don't they? Only without the gems and the sparkle, of course.' Cleo let the branch twang back, showering them both with leaves and small twigs, disentangled her hair from the tree, and sighed happily. 'I think that's enough for now. What have we got? Damsons, crab apples, wild plums, sloes, elderberries – oh, and those blackberries that you said we shouldn't have touched.'

'Because,' Doll said cheerfully, 'you should know, being born and bred in the country, that any blackberries picked after 6 September have been peed on by the devil.'

Cleo scraped her abundant hair back into an untidy heap on top of her head. 'More likely to be peed on by the yoof of Lovers Knot. Anyway, I don't believe in all that superstitious claptrap – while you, as the daughter of a witch . . .'

'My mum is *not* a witch! She's an accomplished country caterer who, um, uses ancient rural herbal recipes to great effect in her cooking.'

'As I said, a witch. Mention Mitzi Blessing's name to anyone round here and they immediately cross their fingers, genuflect, spin round three times and say about twenty Hail Marys.'

'And she'd put a hex on you if she heard you say that.'

Giggling, Cleo linked her arm through Doll's and, with the loaded bags knocking against her jeans, happily kicked her way through the lush undergrowth of Lovers Spinney.

'And anyway,' she said as they emerged from the spinney's dark-green depths and into the daylight, 'you won't have to worry about the devil's pee on the blackberries – I'll be giving everything a good wash.'

'Thank God for that – although I still won't be touching the stuff. Home-made wine! Lord! It's always so grim.

Mum's neighbour Clyde makes home-made wine – parsnip and cowpat being his favourite. It's undrinkable, inflammable and should be condemned as hazardous waste. And please tell me when we get back to your caravan we won't have to start chopping and mashing and stuff. I'm only here for a bit of R & R away from the joys of motherhood.'

'Which you shall have in spades,' Cleo said warmly, as they slipped and slithered along the sloping, narrow paths, away from the tightly packed trees of the spinney and headed towards the caravan park. 'You deserve it after being such a star with the fruit.'

'I've quite enjoyed it, actually. Like when we used to scrump apples or collect conkers when we were kids. The Big Sava bags are a bit of let-down though.' Doll frowned. 'Surely, if you're suddenly going to become a rustic earth mother, we should be a-gathering-in nature's bounty in a wicker trug?'

'Big Sava were all out of wicker trugs and I'm all out of money. Right – now we're on the site, don't stop to speak to anyone. Especially not the Phlopps. I don't want anyone to know what I'm making. It's a secret.'

'Why?' Doll smiled as she waited for Cleo to unlock her mobile home's door. 'No, on second thoughts, don't bother. Ah, warmth and civilisation. Shall I put the kettle on? Coffee?'

'Please,' Cleo puffed as she dumped the heavy bags on and under the kitchen table and inhaled the delicious fragrance of outdoors and fresh air on ripe, rain-washed fruit. 'And I'll get the cake . . . I'll sort through the berries and stuff tonight, and decide which flavour wine I'm going to make first, and the rest can go in the freezer. This is going to be easy.'

'Is it?' Doll frowned, manoeuvring the kettle round a plethora of oddly shaped glasses, bottles and jars, washed and gleaming on the draining board and almost every other surface. 'It looks more like some sort of complex surgical procedure to me. And where's the recipe book?'

'Here.' Cleo nodded towards Olive's collection of ancient buff exercise books with the cuttings and closely written faded and fragile pages. 'I think it was meant to happen – the winemaking, I mean. I sort of inherited these from the previous occupant.'

She stopped and concentrated on wrestling the lid from the cake tin. She wasn't going to mention inheriting Dylan as well. After all, he hadn't repeated his mistaken-Olive visit in the last three days, and she hadn't seen hide or hair of him at Lovelady Hall either. In fact, Cleo was beginning to wonder if she'd actually imagined the whole bizarre encounter.

And anyway, if she mentioned Dylan's visit to Doll, Doll would immediately leap on it and assume that Dylan was going to replace Dave in Cleo's life – which was *so* not the case – and then there'd be ages spent on mulling over Cleo's singledom. Again.

No, Cleo thought, slicing hefty chunks of apple and cinnamon cake on to two plates, as Doll made coffee, she wouldn't mention Dylan to Doll, any more than she'd mentioned Dylan to Elvi – for much the same reasons.

'I'm not sure you should be doing this.' Doll pursed her

lips as she scanned the winemaking instructions. 'These are clearly decades old and are probably breaking every health and safety rule. And, seriously, it's sort of how my mum got started, and look what happened there.'

'Oh, yes,' Cleo said as, followed by Doll and the coffee, she carried the cake into the living room. 'Awful. She made a complete business success, and had a total career change, and was rejuvenated by cooking and supplying the recipes in that ancient book she found, didn't she? I'd really hate to achieve something so spectacular – not!'

'No, but really –' Doll curled into the caravan's fireside chair with her coffee and cake '– you need to be careful with these old country things, Cleo. There were all sorts of strange side-effects to mum's cooking. People still swear that she works magic – not that I believe it, of course.

'No, you wouldn't,' Cleo laughed over the rim of her coffee mug, 'it didn't work for you, did it? Oh no – let me think – what happened to you after you'd eaten Mitzi's stuff? You fell in love all over again with the only bloke you've ever had and were bored to tears with, married him after fifteen years of shilly-shallying, and produced three babies in as many years.'

'Yes, well.' Doll looked a bit abashed. 'Mum and Lulu *swear* it was magic, of course. I just think it would have happened anyway.'

'Yeah right,' Cleo snorted in disbelief. 'Anyway, how is Lu?'

'Revoltingly happy for a hippy. Still with Shay. Still madly in love. Still working for the RSPCA. Still adopting animals willy-nilly.'

'Chalk and cheese, you two. Never guess you were sisters. So all's well in the world of Blessing is it?'

'Fantastic . . . oh, this cake is sublime. Why on earth aren't you making cake for this thing at Lovelady?'

'Because Belly and Flip are. Don't ask.'

'Not going to. Wouldn't dream of it. And anyway, how come, on the first Friday afternoon of your first week in your new job, you're not actually working?'

'Because –' Cleo helped herself to more cake '– Mimi is having a charity supper party at Lovelady tomorrow night. She's been let down by whichever poor soul was going to be waiting on table and she asked if I'd do it. I said yes because Saturday nights are still the worst – all that imagining everyone else in the world out there having a great time while you're stuck in, home alone, with *Casualty* and a microwaved curry.'

Doll sighed. 'You could always come over to us. Any time. You know that. Brett loves seeing you, and the kids adore you . . . Oh, perhaps you'd rather not –'

'For the millionth time, I don't have a problem with you having babies and me not. I'd love to see your gorgeous children – and Brett – and we'll have to arrange something really soon.'

'I'll keep you to that. So, go on about this waitressing thing . . .'

'Well, Mimi could give Shylock a run for his money, so rather than pay me overtime for working on a Saturday night, she gave me this afternoon off instead. Which has tied in nicely with seeing you – and getting on with winemaking.'

Doll leaned forwards and nabbed the last slice of cake. 'Oooh, this is great. And don't tell me how many calories there are in each slice. It's why I love being a multi-mum. It means no one mentions my spreading waistline. Actually, while I'm not sure I approve of this winemaking venture, *if* – and I say *if* very cautiously – *if* it works and is in any way drinkable, I might have a little money-making proposition for you.'

'Oh, goody. I'm always up for those. Go on. Now I'm intrigued.'

'Well, Mum's having a belated birthday party next month. She usually ignores her birthdays but this one is a bit special, and Joel insisted that she celebrates it. Sooo, she's having a 60s Sixtieth in Hazy Hassocks village hall.'

'Wow! That sounds amazing. What a great idea.'

'Joel's idea actually. Her birthday was earlier in the year and he took her on that wild cruise, remember? But now he says she should have a really suitably mad Hazy Hassocks party for all her friends and family.'

'Ah, sweet – although I still can't believe Mitzi's sixty. She looks years younger than that.'

'She says that having a sexy, much-younger live-in lover keeps her youthful and trim.' Doll pulled a face. 'Far too much information there for a daughter to hear if you ask me. Anyway, yes, it's going to be a real retro party. Everyone dressed in 60s costumes, and she's having the JB Roadshow for the music – a genuine 60s soul band – and –'

'Do you want me to be a waitress for the evening?' Cleo interrupted. 'I don't mind at all. In fact I'd love it.'

'Nooo. Course not. I'm not Mimi Pashley-Royle. I don't want my pound of flesh. You'll be there at the party as a guest.'

'Oh brilliant, my social calendar has just improved one hundred per cent, but where's the earning potential then?'

'Well,' Doll said with a shrug, 'I may regret suggesting this, of course, but I thought you could supply some home-made wine for the night – only if it works and is drinkable, of course. It'll prevent Clyde offering his toxic brew and would go brilliantly with Mum's home-made rustic food and be in keeping with the retro theme. And we'll pay you per bottle, of course.'

'And knowing the quaffing abilities of the Hassocks residents, that'll be an awful lot of bottles.' Cleo beamed happily. 'See – an entrepreneurial venture on the cards already. Who knows where it may lead? Done! Thanks, Doll, that'll be brilliant.'

'Don't go getting all excited just yet. I shall want a tasting first, remember? Right, now, must tell you this before I forget. You're not going to believe the latest about Viv at the dental surgery and the bald bloke who makes the false teeth . . .'

By six o'clock that evening the caravan was redolent with the biting autumn scent of pounds of chopped damsons. Cleo, humming along to the radio, had thoroughly enjoyed her afternoon with Doll and, buoyed by the suggestion of supplying her wines for Mitzi's party, was now more determined than ever to become a sort of bucolic vintner.

If she could make a success of this wine thing, she thought, as she squinted at Olive's spidery writing on the yellowing pages, she might be able to become self-employed. Then she'd be in charge of her own destiny on all fronts – emotional and financial – wouldn't she? And how wonderful would that be?

She straightened up, pushed her long hair back into its high ponytail and rolled up the sleeves of her sweater. If she was going to rival Grants of St James's she really ought to make her first brew.

Right . . . so she'd washed and prepared the damsons, now what was next? Ah, yes, boiling the water and adding a pound of sugar. But . . . what was that? She screwed up her eyes – God, Olive's writing was awful. The word 'water' was crossed out and replaced with – what? *Lovers Cascade*?

What was Lovers Cascade, for heaven's sake? Cleo frowned. She hadn't noticed that before on the list of things she needed.

A trip into Winterbrook on the previous evening had provided her with all sorts of mysterious winemaking items listed on the flimsy pages. Things like campden tablets and citric acid and pectub-destroying enzymes and finings and yeast. But – sod it! She'd completely missed out on the Lovers Cascade, whatever it was . . .

She scanned the pages again. No, there was no explanation. Maybe Lovers Cascade was simply some rustic name for tap water? Like Adam's Ale? So, should she just use the plain old water she'd measured into a bucket and take a chance? Put her own slant on Olive's recipe?

Just as she'd decided that if she was ever going to stun

Mimi with her home-brewing abilities, not to mention making a go of being a supplier of fine wines to the local community, she really ought to get a move on with this first batch, there was a knock on the door.

Oh, good, probably Elvi, Cleo thought. She might be able to help with the translation of Lovers Cascade. Elvi had been behaving oddly for the last couple of days – all dreamy and distant – so it would be a good opportunity to chat to her, make sure she wasn't working too hard.

'Come in!' Cleo yelled above the murmur of the radio. 'The door's open!'

'Fantastic.' Dylan Maguire, wearing designer sunglasses, stepped into the kitchen. 'I've reached first base without being assaulted. Oh, and you look stunning and you're cooking. What more could a man ask for?'

Cleo stood and stared. Her mouth wouldn't work. Words seemed to have failed her.

'These are for you.' Dylan crossed the tiny kitchen in two strides and handed her a huge bunch of sweet-scented freesias. 'To say sorry for being such a pain the other night, and as a thank you for your hospitality. I could have Interflora'd them, but that seemed too impersonal after you'd been so kind – and of course, would have done away with the visit. And I know it should have been red roses, but they always seem a bit clichéd, so . . .'

'Er, thank you.' Cleo took the flowers clumsily. 'No, they're absolutely perfect. They're really beautiful. Um, how are your eyes?'

'Sore. And turning technicoloured. Hence the shades,

which I have to say, give me an added air of mystery and are therefore quite a talking point for the ladies.'

Dylan was totally incorrigible. Cleo buried her face in the freesias' fragrance to hide her confusion. The exquisite evening clothes of the previous visit had been replaced tonight by casual jeans and sweater and a scruffy leather jacket. It didn't detract one iota from his dark gorgeousness.

She looked up. 'So, er, you've still got a job? Mortimer didn't sack you for the loss of the Bentley?'

'He was a star, actually. Really sympathetic about my little mishap. Said it could have happened to anyone. Mind you, I didn't give him all the details. Anyway, the Bentley has been retrieved and is being repaired and the recipient is eagerly awaiting a slightly later delivery date at a much reduced price, which was Mort's attempt at damage limitation. So he may be slightly out of pocket, but he's kept a customer, and I've kept my job.'

'And you're not working tonight?'

'No. Just got back from a few days away on, er, business – couldn't wait to get out of the tux and into civvies. Mort always insists on me delivering the cars looking like James Bond. Still, the ladies love it, especially with the addition of the Ray-Bans.'

Cleo smiled to herself as she put the freesias in one of the scrubbed bottles on the draining board. The business had no doubt been mixed with more than a little pleasure. And the few days away would explain why she hadn't seen Dylan at Lovelady. It was nice to know she still had that little surprise to spring on him.

He removed the sunglasses, displaying a selection of multi-coloured bruises, looked quizzically at the array of jars and bottles, then sniffed appreciatively. 'So, what are you cooking? Plums? Ah, no, damsons. Are you making jam? I love damson jam. Olive made fabulous jam.'

'Um . . .' Cleo moved slightly away from him. 'It's not jam. Actually, it's wine – and you might be able to help me.'

'Wine – wow! And you want me to be a taster? Sounds right up my street – Oh, sorry, that's my phone. Excuse me.'

Cleo tried not to listen as Dylan chatted, his deep, upper-class voice low, but she couldn't miss the sprinkling of 'darlings' and 'sweethearts' and 'love you toos'.

Nesta? Or some other lady who'd occupied him during his recent absence? And did it matter? Not a bit. And was it any of her concern? Of course not.

'Sorry.' Dylan beamed, snapping his phone shut. 'I should have switched it off. Very impolite of me. That was Cassie.'

'You don't have to tell me,' Cleo said quickly. 'And you can leave your phone on. I'm not fussed about you having private conversations. Anyway, thanks again for the flowers – I love freesias – and before you go rushing off to Cassie, maybe you could just help me with this, as you spent so much time with Olive.'

'Glad to, but I wasn't intending to rush off anywhere. Cassie was last night. A sort of last-minute substitute because Nesta has finally decided to become a born-again faithful wife.' Dylan sighed. 'I hate it when they do that.'

Cleo laughed. 'Faithful obviously doesn't figure in your personal dictionary.'

79

'Don't judge me too harshly. I'm a graduate of the Neil Young school of romance. You know? "Love the One You're With" . . . It always works for me. Now, what was it you wanted to ask me?'

Cleo pointed to the spidery writing. 'Lovers Cascade. I've no idea what it means, have you? I guess it's just water. Maybe Olive –'

'Does that say Razzle Dazzle Damson? Is that what this wine's called?'

Cleo nodded. 'Cute isn't it? They've all got really sweet names. Blackberry Blush, Plum Pucker, not to mention Elderberry Ecstasy. And I'm very intrigued by Crab Apple Captivation. Your Olive must have been really poetic.'

'No, she wasn't. She was as prosaic as they come. And that's not Olive's writing.' Dylan frowned, peering at the wine recipe. 'Olive was a chapel-goer and strictly teetotal. She never touched alcohol so she certainly wouldn't have ever made her own wine. She used to give me hell when I'd drunk too much – or anything at all come to think of it. What made you think this stuff belonged to Olive?'

Cleo explained about finding the books containing the recipes, illustrations and instructions in the shed's junk.

'Ah, then my money's on it being Mad Molly's,' Dylan said. 'She lived here before Olive. I didn't know her, of course, but her reputation lives on. She used to make all sorts of things apparently. Not just wine, but herbal remedies and things like that. Lovers Knot folklore has it that people would come to Mad Molly rather than go to the doctor. Rumour also has it that she killed more than she cured – in a manner of speaking. Seriously, Olive said Mad Molly's concoctions caused mayhem.'

'Really? But why would Molly's stuff still be in the shed? Even if Molly left it here when she moved, why would Olive keep it?'

'Oh, Olive never threw anything away just in case it came in useful. Wartime mentality – make do and mend. She was a dreadful hoarder. So, you're making something of Mad Molly's are you? That's brave.'

'Brave? Or foolish?'

Dylan looked at her. 'I'd never accuse you of being foolish. If you want to try out one of Mad Molly's brews for whatever reason, then I'd say go for it, but I'd also advise you to keep quiet about it. There are enough people round here who still remember the chaos she caused. Molly probably got it all wrong – mixed up her ingredients and quantities and poisoned people as a result – so as long as you stick to the exact measurements, I'm sure you'll be fine.'

'I hope so,' Cleo said doubtfully. 'But maybe without the Lovers Cascade the wine won't work anyway. Maybe I should just forget it.'

'Why? You don't look like a quitter to me. And it could be fun. And anyway Lovers Cascade isn't a euphemism – it's the waterfall in Lovers Spinney.'

'What? I've never seen a waterfall in Lovers Spinney. And I spent most of the afternoon there. It must have dried up or something.'

Dylan shook his head. His hair fell silkily into his still-bruised eyes and he brushed it away with a slender long-fingered hand. 'No, it's still there, but you've got to know where to look. It's not in the main tanglewood part of the spinney, it's in the fairy glade.'

'The *what*?' Cleo laughed. 'Pul-ease. Aren't you getting a bit *Lord of the Rings* here? What fairy glade?'

'It's a tiny hidden clearing, all moss and briars and dog roses. Really pretty and totally secluded. Great for, um, assignations, actually. The locals think that it's where the fairies live – and who am I to disabuse them?'

Before she could voice any opinion on the sanity of Mad Molly or the gullibility of the villagers, Dylan's phone rang again. With an apologetic face, he had another whispered conversation, much along the lines of the first.

'Sorry.' He grinned, sliding the mobile into his pocket. 'Alicia. She's a sweetie. But slightly clingy. Keeps talking about commitment and what wallpaper we'll have and choosing names for our babies. Alicia's getting slightly heavy.'

'Then tell her,' Cleo said sternly. 'You shouldn't string them all along.'

'I don't. I've never promised any of them anything except a damn good time and all my attention and affection when I'm with them.' He smiled winningly. 'I can't help being irresistible, can I?'

'I'm finding you extremely easy to resist.'

'I know,' he sighed. 'As I said on our previous meeting, for all your luscious curves and voluptuous Latin looks, you're a bloody hard and cruel woman.'

'And your chat-up lines are totally wasted.'

'I know, and it kills me,' Dylan sighed. 'Anyway, where were we?'

'Before we got sidetracked by your phone calls, clichés and fascinating love life? Discussing Lovers Cascade. So, you think that according to Mad Molly's recipe, her wine only works with water from this waterfall then?'

Dylan shrugged. 'Christ knows. But I'm sure she wasn't called Mad Molly for nothing, so maybe she believed it. And maybe she wasn't so mad after all, and was right. Who knows? Maybe the wine just won't taste the same made with tap water.'

Cleo sighed. 'Damn. Having found all this stuff, I really wanted to stick to the original recipe in its entirety.'

'How much water do you need?'

Cleo peered at the scrawled notes again. 'Um, well, this recipe is for a gallon of wine which takes four litres of water, but I'm doubling up on quantities, so . . .'

'Eight litres. That'd be, oh, I'd say, one large or two small buckets. That should be easy enough to carry – assuming you've got the buckets. Ah yes, there they are alongside the other weird and wonderful paraphernalia. Oh, and those big water containers might come in handy too. Might as well get as much as we can. Right, grab your coat and wellies.'

'Why?'

'Because,' Dylan said with a grin, 'I'm going to introduce you to the delights of Lovers Cascade.'

Chapter Eight

Bizarre, Cleo thought as she followed Dylan's long denim-clad legs up one of the overgrown rutted inclines of Lovers Spinney. Totally bizarre. How mad was this? Here she was in the autumnal twilight, with a drop-dead gorgeous but completely amoral man who just happened to be practically a total stranger, heading into an isolated thicket. With buckets. To collect magical water from a cascade in a fairy glade . . .

She giggled to herself.

Dylan turned round. 'Did you sneeze? Are you OK?'

'I'm fine. It was a giggle not a death rattle,' Cleo puffed. 'How much further?'

'A couple of yards. At the top of this slope.'

'Oh, goody.'

'I'd offer to help you up the last bit, but as I'm being gentlemanly and carrying all the buckets I'm sort of otherwise occupied.'

'I'm fine.' Cleo puffed a bit more as she climbed the final

stage of the rutted path, ducking under low hanging branches in the gathering dusk, and sidestepping snaking brambles. 'Maybe a little unfit but nothing terminal. And how can a glade be at the top of a slope anyway? That defies geographical definition.'

'You'll see.'

· Cleo exhaled. Dylan had sure-footedly negotiated the steepish inclines with all the agility of a mountain goat – and he was handicapped by the buckets and water containers. Huh! Must be all that sex that kept him so fit and in such perfect physical shape . . .

She pushed the thought quickly from her head and concentrated on climbing.

'There.' Dylan put down his cargo and held out his hand. 'Come on – just one small step for womankind.'

Ignoring his hand and grabbing a branch, Cleo hauled herself to the top of the slope to where the spinney fell away sharply downwards into a tiny secluded dell of mossy green grass banked by briar bushes on three sides and Lovers Cascade on the fourth.

'Oh, wow!'

She'd intended to be scathingly disinterested in the silly-sounding waterfall and the superstitions of the Lovers Knot residents and the madness of Mad Molly, but the reality was breathtaking.

'It's . . . It's absolutely fantastic.'

Cleo stared in delight at the cascade of fast-flowing clear silver water as it raced and gurgled from between the mass of trees opposite, tumbled over rocks and plummeted forever downwards in a spume of spray, to froth and bubble into the depths of a dark pool.

The waterfall was a dull constant roar, deadened by the thickness of the spinney. No wonder she'd never seen it. It was a true hidden treasure.

Below them, the hidden glade curved round the pool, and in the strange half-light, Cleo could easily understand why the villagers might think it a magical place, a home for fairies, a haven of mystery.

'Impressive, isn't it?' Dylan raised his voice above the water's babble. 'And a well-kept secret.'

'I'm not surprised.' Cleo continued to stare. 'If this got out the place would be overrun with tourists and townies. No wonder the locals spread the rumours of it being mystic – they wouldn't want to share it with anyone.'

Dylan smiled. 'Oh, they really *believe* it's magical. Even though it's so beautiful, you won't find many Lovers Knot residents here – ever. Which has always suited me perfectly.'

She shook her head. 'Does your mind ever stray above your waist?'

'Frequently. I'm extremely well educated and have some pretty impressive academic qualifications. Actually.'

'Well, get you!' Cleo mocked, while wondering again, if that was so, why Dylan was wasting his education and brain in driving flash cars for an ex-porn baron. Not that it was any of her concern, naturally. Or of any interest to her what-soever. 'So, if we're going to collect this water, Mastermind, how do we get down there?'

'Watch and learn.'

'Don't push your luck.'

'Do you want to make this wine properly or not?'

'I do.'

'Then –' Dylan smiled '– stop being stroppy and follow me. It's easy, honestly, but I'll catch you if you fall.'

Cleo, who had absolutely no intention of falling, took a deep breath and, slithering, grabbing overhanging trees and treading very, very carefully, followed Dylan downwards towards the glade.

Again she wondered briefly about the sanity of what she was doing. Dylan, charming and amusing, just like Dr Jekyll in polite company, could well turn into a murderous Mr Hyde alter-ego as soon as they reached the foot of Lovers Cascade. But, Cleo thought, giving a little shriek as she slipped down a few feet more quickly than she'd anticipated, she had her mobile phone to call for help and a really loud voice.

'OK?' Dylan turned and looked at her. 'Did you slip?'

'A bit. Don't worry about me.'

'Oh, I don't. I already know you're a very resourceful woman. Anyway, we've nearly reached the bottom now. There . . .'

Panting slightly, and pushing her dishevelled hair away from her face, Cleo sidestepped Dylan and looked around her.

'Oh, it's so beautiful. Even in this dismal weather and the dusk, it's truly beautiful.'

And it was. The thick vivid green grass was cropped short, the moss was springy underfoot, and the glade formed a perfect horseshoe round the deep, dark bubbling pool. The briars and brambles had entwined with the trees to form a natural overhead canopy, and it was as if this place was separated from the rest of the world.

'It's so quiet – apart from the waterfall – and it's really still, and much warmer than up there in the village. How weird.'

'Magic?' Dylan raised his sunglasses and smiled at her. 'Or just natural phenomena?'

'The latter,' Cleo said firmly, 'but fabulous nonetheless. And as neither of us has a torch, I think we ought to collect the water quickly before it gets properly dark. Shall we just try to scoop it out from the pond?'

'What? Absolutely not. Well, not unless you want to give everyone who drinks the wine a nasty dose of cryptosporidium. Have you looked at that water? The pool is really deep and, without the input from Lovers Cascade, completely stagnant. Goodness knows what's in there. The pool may be pretty, but it's lethal, and totally useless for skinny-dipping –' he stared at her '– which is a pity.'

'I've never skinny-dipped in my life,' Cleo said hotly. 'And I don't intend to start now.'

'Shame. With those gorgeous curves and that tumbling hair you'd look exactly like Botticelli's Venus.'

''Armless?'

'Oh, ha-ha. And actually,' Dylan grinned, 'as someone who was force-fed history of art at school, I'll have to take issue with that joke.'

'Well, OK. I know it wasn't Peter Kay material but –'

'It was the Venus de Milo that was 'armless. Botticelli's Venus was the fabulously curvy lady rising from the sea with her hair hiding her assets and —'

'Oooh, get you! I'm dead impressed with your superior knowledge of the classical masters — not.' Cleo laughed. 'Anyway, we both know I'd look like an overweight thirty-five-year-old turning blue with all my cellulite on show, freezing to death in a Berkshire pond.'

'Allow me to be the judge of that.'

Cleo giggled. 'No. No way. Not ever. Never. So, if we can't use the water from the pool . . .?'

'Well, as the water from Lovers Cascade is straight from several Downland springs and absolutely pure, it's into the waterfall for us.'

'But we'll get wet.'

'And have fun getting dry.'

'In your dreams,' Cleo said, not meeting his eyes. 'OK, so let's do it. Er, not the having fun getting dry bit, though. Or, well maybe I should do it on my own, as it's my wine. I mean, I quite understand if you don't want to get drenched. You've been really kind so far.'

'Kind?' Dylan wrinkled his nose. 'I'm not being kind. I'm really enjoying myself. More than I have for ages. I love doing crazy spur-of-the-moment things, don't you?'

Cleo considered this. 'Not usually, no. I like to know what's happening and why and having things planned. I like order and routine and get uncomfortable with changes. This is completely out of character for me. I think . . . I think I just got caught up in the winemaking thing — maybe Mad

Molly's madness is infectious . . . but I still think I should be the one to collect the water.'

'No way. We're friends and we're in this together, and if you're going in, then so am I – Oh, shit . . . Sorry.'

Dylan's mobile trilled noisily again.

Cleo wandered away, across the soft, springy turf, closer to the pool while he talked. The tumbling roar of Lovers Cascade drowned the conversation. The spray tickled her cheeks. In the strange light, the still, warm air was scented with rich earth and sweet briars. Cleo peered into the deep brown bubbling pool, fringed by reeds and bordered by the flat pancakes of water-lily pads. It was even more spectacular close to. Sylvan. Other-worldly. Certainly a place worthy of creating mysterious dreams.

She could almost believe that on hot, drowsy summer nights the glade would be peopled by a host of flitting, glittering gauzy-winged fairies, and that bejewelled unicorns, tails swishing, would be drinking lazily from the pool.

Almost.

'Sorry,' Dylan said, catching up with her. 'I've switched it off now. That was Jessamine. Hot date for tomorrow night.'

Oooh, yes, Cleo thought, tomorrow night. What sort of hot date did she have lined up? Waiting on Mimi's supper party table. No contest.

'As I'm not the keeper of your social diary, you don't have to keep telling me about what a great catch you are. I'm not even slightly impressed, you know. Right – now what's the best way to get the water?'

Dylan shrugged. 'Actually, gathering water from Lovers

Cascade isn't something I've ever done before, so your guess is as good as mine. But we'll assume that Mad Molly actually managed it for her winemaking, so it must be doable.'

'But she was mad,' Cleo argued, 'so she probably just plunged in and got wet, which we're so not going to do.'

'Spoilsport.'

They stood side by side, staring at the non-stop sheet of water and the slippery surrounding rocks.

Eventually, Dylan nodded. 'OK then, looking at it from here, I reckon if we squeeze round the right side of the pool by walking on that rocky ledge, and hold the buckets right under the waterfall we should catch quite a lot without getting saturated.'

Cleo nodded. 'Yes, that makes sense, and honestly I think I should do it alone. No point in us both getting soaking wet and risking falling in at the same time.'

'I beg to differ. I bow to your independence, but I'm stronger than you and water is heavy as I recall from my physics lessons, so let me collect the water and I'll pass the buckets out to you. And let's not argue about it because it's getting dark and if we fall in and drown no one will ever find our bodies until it's far too late – and there'll be dozens of distraught women thinking I've simply abandoned them.'

'And we couldn't have that, could we? OK. You win. But please don't sue me when you die from pneumonia. Let's just go for it.'

They did. Slipping and sliding, they negotiated the rocky outline of the pool and eventually managed, amazingly without falling in, to reach the perpetual torrent of Lovers Cascade. It was far colder there, and much noisier, and, despite her protestations, Cleo realised they were both going to get very wet indeed.

Miserably drenched within seconds, she held on to whatever anchorage she could find as Dylan carefully stepped behind the sheet of water, then passed him the first bucket. She watched anxiously, disorientated by the movement of the water, irritated by the spume, deafened by the non-stop roar.

There was a lot of swearing, some laughter, and a considerable amount of splashing from behind Lovers Cascade but eventually Dylan thrust the first filled bucket back into her wet hands.

One further bucket and the two large water containers followed. It took far longer than she'd anticipated.

Mad Molly nothing, Cleo thought. I'm the one who's mad. Completely doolally. What on earth am I doing? And all because I want my homemade wine to be the genuine article.

'OK!' Dylan shouted. 'That's it. All full. I'll carry this one out and grab the other container. You take the buckets.'

Slowly, with a bucket in each hand, Cleo edged her way back from the waterfall, hampered by the weight of the water now, very cold, and terrified of falling on the slippery rocks.

There! With a huge sigh of relief, she took one last step away from the pool and on to dry land. Then she watched, her heart in her mouth, as Dylan slowly negotiated the same exit strategy, the water containers threatening to tip him off-balance with every step.

'Bloody hell!' He shook the water from his hair like a dog. 'Forget *Venus de Milo* – you look like a drowned rat.'

'Pot-kettle-black.' Cleo grinned delightedly. 'And thank you so much for doing this. I don't know how I'll be able to repay you.'

'Well, as it clearly isn't going to be in prolonged physical pleasure, I guess a bottle or two of your home-made plonk will have to suffice. But right at this minute I'd settle for a hot shower and a cup of coffee.'

'It's yours,' Cleo puffed as she hauled up the two buckets. 'It's the least I can do. Now let's see if we can climb back out of here without spilling anything. It'd be a right sod to have gone to all this trouble collecting the Lovers Cascade water only to lose it on the last stretch.'

The buckets were incredibly heavy, and awkward, and annoyingly knocked against her legs, and water slopped into her boots, but eventually, slowly, carefully manoeuvring the overhanging branches in the dusk, Cleo emerged victorious and relatively unscathed from the fairy glade and back into the rural normality of a deserted Lovers Knot evening.

'Brilliant,' Dylan panted, putting the two large containers down beside the buckets and stretching. 'You're ace. You managed that without losing very much at all. But I think hypothermia is about to set in, so let's get back home before anyone sees us and asks awkward questions.'

Smiling rather stupidly at Dylan's casual assumption that her caravan was now 'home', Cleo picked up her buckets and, falling into step beside him, set off on the final stage of the journey.

An hour later, having stowed several stoppered containers of precious Lovers Cascade water in the ice-cold shed, hauled the sloshing buckets into the kitchen, showered and dried, and warmed up with coffee and cake, Cleo peered at Mad Molly's Razzle Dazzle Damson wine recipe again.

The whole caravan was misty with rich damson-scented steam as the mass of fruit, citric acid and sugar bubbled in the carefully measured Lovers Cascade water. Rolling up the sleeves of her favourite oversized cosy sweater, Cleo raked through the winemaking ingredients for the strangely named pectub-destroying enzyme, found it and added it to the mixture.

Dylan looked up from the tumble-dryer, which was adding to the cosy humidity. 'My clothes are nearly dry – only a few more minutes – so is there anything else I can do to help?'

Cleo giggled. Again. Dylan was wearing her fluffy pink dressing gown, tightly belted. The fact that he was naked beneath it was something she was trying very hard not to think about.

'Make some more coffee, if you don't mind. We deserve another break after our labours. Oh, and if the cake's all gone there's another one in the blue tin.'

'Is it another apple and cinnamon? That was out of this world.'

'So you kept saying. I think –' she scanned the spidery writing again '– this is nearly done now.'

Dylan, humming to the radio, his hair drying spikily, was really quite domesticated, Cleo thought in surprise, as she watched him moving economically round the tiny kitchen, sorting out the coffee and cake. And he'd been a perfect gentleman over the undressing and showering. He'd kept out of the way until she was decent, and then used the bathroom himself with the maximum of decorum.

So far, so good, she thought – all Dr Jekyll and not a hint of Mr Hyde in a fluffy dressing gown – and wondered why she was faintly disappointed.

'Swiss roll!' Dylan exclaimed as he wrestled the top from the blue tin. 'Home-made Swiss roll! Amazingly wonderful. You really are a domestic goddess, aren't you?'

'*Venus de Milo* in a pinny?'

'Every boy's wildest fantasy come true. Your cakes are seriously good – if the wine is half as perfect it'll knock spots off Margaux 86.'

'Who's she?'

'Are you winding me up?'

'Only a bit.' Cleo stretched her aching arms, then scanned the recipe again to make sure nothing was missing. 'I might only be trailer trash with a comprehensive school education but I do know some classy stuff, you know – Oh, chaff it!'

'What?'

'This isn't going to be any good. After all the trouble we've been to – it's going to be useless. I'm such a dill-brain! Oh, sod it. I should have read the whole recipe through first. I should have *known*.'

Dylan, still munching Swiss roll, looked over her shoulder

in a cloud of fluffy dressing gown. 'What's wrong with it?'

'I've missed something vital.'

Dylan chuckled. 'Well, being Mad Molly's recipe – let me think . . . Minotaur's tongue? Manticore's toenails? Snotling's spit?'

Despite her irritation, Cleo laughed. 'You made that last one up!'

'I did not.' Dylan looked indignant. 'How sadly lacking in the innermost workings of the lives of elves and goblins was your education? Snotlings, let me tell you, are tiny, rather stupid gnomes – they're used as slaves by orcs. Their spit is prized across several continents.'

'Get away.'

'Well, OK, I made the last bit up. I know nothing of snotling spit, but the rest is true. Anyway, is that what you're missing? Because, if it is I'm buggered if I know where we'll get any at this time of night.'

Sighing, Cleo pointed to the spidery writing. 'It's nothing to do with orcs or Minotaurs or bloody snotlings. Look, it says here, after the bit about leaving the wine to stand in a warm place for two days and then straining it into the demi-johns and adding more sugar and water and yeast and nutrient, I need –'

'Yes, fine, but you've bought all the stuff you need, haven't you? So what's the problem?'

'I need,' Cleo repeated, gritting her teeth, 'to rack it every two months until clear. Every *two chaffing months*. That could take *years* – and I need it to be drinkable in less than two weeks. Oh, bugger!'

'Ah, right. Bugger indeed.' Dylan frowned. 'I'm not sure why you need it to be ready so quickly, but assuming you do, then that's a complete bastard, isn't it? I hadn't actually thought about the time it took to, well, ferment, brew, mature whatever.'

'Neither had I. And I should have done, as Molly describes Razzle Dazzle Damson as a "Full-Bodied frooty red" – I should have known that wouldn't appear overnight. Oh, sod and damn!'

They looked at each other in exasperation. Then Dylan picked up the yellowing wine recipe books and flipped through the flaky crackling pages.

'It's not good looking,' Cleo said crossly. 'We can't change anything. The one thing I haven't got is time – and no one can magic that up.'

'Maybe not,' Dylan murmured, 'but have you seen the back of this Razzle Dazzle page? There're loads of scribbly bits, some of them crossed out and written over, some sort of jottings . . .'

'Mad Molly's shopping list.' Cleo sniffed. 'No use what-soever.'

'Don't be so quick to damn poor old Molly. I think these are her vintnering *aides-memoires*. Look, there's a bit here about *not* using tap water for the wine because "it takes two durn long to come to Frootiness and Drinkiness".'

'Terrible syntax and spelling.'

'True –' Dylan unselfconsciously pushed up the sleeves of the fluffy dressing gown as he studied the mass of crossings out and rewritten notes '– but as we're not the grammar police, we'll forgive her, shall we? She also says – no, listen – "allus use the Magik Water from Lovers Cascade and the fairies will make sure yerll be able to drink yer first glass of Damson within a seven-night".'

'Really?' Cleo perked up a bit. 'And the fairies don't say anything about all you'll get is a mouthful of acid, sour fruit and a killing stomach upset?'

'Nothing of the sort is even mentioned.'

'No doubt she just put that bit about fairies and magic and quick-brewing with Lovers Cascade in to fool people, to stymie the opposition and keep her winemaking monopoly in the village,' Cleo argued. 'Knowing how damn difficult collecting water from the waterfall was – is – would put everyone off, even if the fairies didn't.'

'True –' Dylan brushed Swiss roll crumbs from the dress- ing gown '– but just suppose that on its way across the Downs, through, under and over all those primeval rocks, that Lovers Cascade collects some sort of chemical cocktail, and that chemical cocktail really does speed up the maturing process. That would be science, wouldn't it? Not magic. And even if you don't believe in Mad Molly's magic, you must believe in science?'

'Not all of it, no. But, OK, yes, if I accept, for the sake of argument, that there's some chemical mixture in the Lovers Cascade water that speeds everything up, what else does she say we should do?'

'She just says – um, let me see – ah, yes – to rack the wine after forty-eight hours, then every day after that and within a "seven-night" – that must be rustic daft old bat speak for a week? – you'll have a "Grandly drinkibble Deep ripe Red Wine".'

'Fantastic,' Cleo said half-heartedly, 'and she probably just said that because she wanted to turn her wine into a profit as quickly as possible.'

'Well, if you want to look on the glass half-empty side, that's fine. But if you – for whatever reason – want this Razzle Dazzle to be drunk in less than two weeks, then why don't you just suspend disbelief and go with it? It might just work. Where's the harm? What can possibly happen?'

Poisoning the whole of Lovers Knot at Harvest Home, Cleo thought, but she didn't say so. She shrugged. 'What choice do we have? OK, I'll go with Mad Molly and the fairies and the magical water and see what happens after a seven-night.'

'Great. Hang on – wait a second – there's some other stuff scrawled here . . . Oh, shit, it's been torn off at the bottom of the page. I think it says "Beware and Wornning" . . . and then . . .' Dylan frowned. 'No, can't decipher it – something to do with "making Sure you dunt Drink Razzle Dazzle Damson unless youn" – bugger – that's where it ends.'

'I shouldn't worry about it. She was clearly barking. It's hardly likely to be a disclaimer, is it? No doubt it was Mad Molly's way of making sure no one pinched her recipe. OK, I'm almost convinced now. Lovers Cascade is magical – well, chemically enhanced anyway – and my Razzle Dazzle Damson will be ready for drinkiness next weekend.'

'And if it is?' Dylan carefully closed the recipe books. 'What's next?'

'Oooh, Blackberry Blush or Crab Apple Captivation, I think. Might as well use up all the Lovers Cascade water while I've got it.'

'And am I invited to the tasting and making of them, too?'

Cleo pushed her rat's-tail rough-dried hair behind her ears. Should she encourage him? Was it wise? Of course it wasn't. She liked Dylan a lot. An awful lot. And Dylan liked her too — she knew that. They'd already formed a happy, joky friendship, and no doubt Dylan would be more than happy to make the very short trip from the kitchen to the bedroom, which would be impossible to resist, whatever she might say to the contrary, and fun and lovely and clearly a mind-blowing experience, but absolutely definitely not what she was looking for . . .

Ah, sod it. She'd had years of doing the right thing during her marriage and look where that had got her. She could always keep Dylan at arm's length, couldn't she?

She smiled. 'Yes, of course — unless you're otherwise engaged romping with, er, Jessamine and co. or tearing about the country delivering supercars to the rich and famous.'

'Oh, I'll keep a window as they say. I'll make sure I'm here,' Dylan said cheerfully, twirling the dressing gown's tie-belt like a stripper. 'I wouldn't miss it for the world. This is the most fun I've ever had without being horizontal. So next weekend, then? It's date?'

'Yes,' Cleo said faintly. 'It's a date.'

Chapter Nine

'Oh!' Elvi, peering round the caravan's door, groaned in disappointment. 'You're getting ready to go out.'

'Hello, stranger. Yes, sorry.' Cleo hopped out of the bedroom, trying to push her feet into her loafers and tuck in her white shirt at the same time. 'I'm working at Lovelady tonight. But come in anyway – I'm early and I've still got to put my make-up on and do my hair so we can chat at the same time.'

'Thanks. Oh, it smells lovely in here – all warm and fruity.'

Cleo thought guiltily of the Razzle Dazzle Damson wine fermenting secretly away in her collection of buckets and saucepans, hidden from view in the cupboards beside the cooker – the warmest place she could think of. There was no reason on earth why she shouldn't tell Elvi about making the wine, and she would, but not yet. Not until she knew if Mad Molly's recipe had worked.

She'd been damned with faint praise enough times during

her marriage. Dave's 'It's OK I suppose, but my mother made it far better and she used double cream *and* Belgian chocolate,' when she'd spent all day sweating over some complicated recipe to try to win his approval, still smarted.

The New Cleo – sounding, she thought amusedly, like a television car advertisement – she'd decided after the divorce, was never going to allow her feelings to be bruised again. Failures would stay strictly private. Only successes would be made public.

'Does it? That's probably because I've been baking cakes this morning, and the smell does tend to linger in these mobile homes, doesn't it? Oh, would you like some cake while we're talking? You know where it is. There's a pineapple upside down and –'

'No thanks.' Elvi shook her head. 'I'm not very hungry. I mean, I usually love your cakes but –'

'That's OK,' Cleo said, really worried now. Elvi refusing cake? Unheard of. 'Um, I haven't seen you for the last few days. Been busy? Lots of studying?'

'Mmmm.' Elvi followed Cleo back into the bedroom and slumped onto the cushiony double bed. 'This room's really lovely. All fresh and pretty. You're so lucky having all this to yourself.'

Bless her, Cleo thought. The caravan's bedroom was absolutely minute compared to the one she'd left behind in Winterbrook. 'Is yours just a single, then? That must be difficult for your school work, clothes, music, television, computer and everything else you must need.'

'It's horrid,' Elvi kicked off her ballet pumps. 'But Mum

and Dad have one double room and the boys have the other, so there's no choice. Most of my life is in storage boxes piled floor to ceiling. I can't wait to have my own space.'

Cleo applied her first coat of mascara. There was something different about Elvi. The bounce and vitality had gone, and left a sort of faint sadness. Poignant, Cleo thought. That was the word to describe Elvi tonight: poignant . . .

But why?

'Are you sure you're OK?'

'Yeah, I'm fine. Just a bit tired. What are you doing at Lovelady tonight then?'

'Waitressing. At one of Mimi's charity suppers. Hence the thick black tights, sensible shoes and indecently tight black skirt that fitted last time I wore it – or so I vaguely remembered. I certainly didn't remember all these rolls of fat. God knows what I'm supposed to wear as a waitress. I hope Mimi'll supply the natty little cap and frilly apron.'

'As long as it's not nipple tassels and a thong.'

'*What*? You are joking I hope?'

'Yeah.' Elvi smiled dreamily. 'Oh, I'm sure tonight will be decent enough, but when I was little, my mum used to tell me stories about some really wild parties they'd had at Lovelady when Mimi was much younger. My dad said it used to be a den of iniquity and that it was obscene that people like the Pashley-Royles had so much money to waste on decadence when decent hard-working people were struggling to keep a roof over their heads and food in their bellies.'

'Oh, dear. Yes, I can see it must have rankled with him.'

Cleo knew, like everyone else in Lovers Knot, that Ron Reynolds was just slightly left of Stalin in his political outlook.

'Rankled? He wanted to be up there with placards and a picket line and march "them bloody toffs" off to the guillotine.'

Cleo giggled. 'I can somehow imagine Ron getting apoplectic over what he'd see as a massive injustice to the lower orders. But presumably social events are more orderly up at Lovelady now?'

Elvi looked suddenly wistful. 'Yeah. But I used to love hearing about all that glamour and glitz. My mum said that they used to have really famous rock bands and catwalk models and proper celebs at Mimi's parties. And that there were champagne fountains and dancing girls and Chippendale lookalikes and everyone hurling themselves into the swimming pool fully dressed and then taking their clothes off and –'

'Blimey.' Cleo blinked. 'That sounds like, um, fun. But I honestly don't think it's going to be that sort of party tonight.'

Elvi shook her head. 'God, no. They've cleaned up their act since then. Now it's all putrid good works and country life. Tonight it'll either be Knobs 'n' Snobs or the do-gooding brigade – all shirtwaisters and unilateral blue rinses. Very correct and boring either way. I do wish you weren't going though.'

Cleo delved into her make-up bag and applied blusher, then reached for the mascara again. She'd need two coats tonight, definitely. For confidence. 'I only said I'd work because I thought it'd save me from a lonely Saturday night.'

'I've got one of those looming.' Elvi tucked her long skinny-jeaned legs under her and chewed the ends of her chestnut hair. 'That's why I'd hoped you'd be in.'

'What?' Cleo peered at Elvi through the mirror. 'You'd prefer spending time with an embittered old wrinkly to visiting the hot spots of Winterbrook with your girlie mates for a night of teenage debauchery?'

'Something like that. Sophie wanted to go to that new disco in Hazy Hassocks, and Kate invited me to a party she's going to in Bagley-cum-Russet, but I just didn't fancy either of them.'

Pausing in applying the second coat of mascara, Cleo frowned. 'Are you ill? You've seemed, well, a bit distant recently. And not wanting cake. And now turning down a disco and a party on a Saturday night? At sixteen? I'm getting a bit worried about you.'

'I wanted to ask you about sex.'

'Shit!' Cleo poked the mascara wand in her eye and groped blindly for a tissue. 'Sorry. Er, sex? Me? As in a sort of case study for something at school?'

'Nah.' Elvi shook her head. 'As in real life. My life. I need some advice from someone I trust and know will be honest and won't go all stupid and giggly and make putrid stuff up like Kate and Sophie, or hit the roof like my mum.'

Cleo swallowed quickly. Of course, it all made sense now.

'God, Elvi, you're pregnant, aren't you?'

Elvi laughed. 'Nooo. Course not. As if. I'm not that stupid.'

'Thank God for that.'

'But that's why I wanted to talk to you. About, well, relationships. And, well, everything, really.'

'I'm very flattered. But honestly, you probably know far more about it than me. I never had many boyfriends – met Dave early on. He was – is – the only man I've ever slept with. I'm sure you're way ahead of me.'

'No, I'm not. I'm putridly virginally innocent. Oh, of course I know the basic *details* – and I know what Kate has told me about what she and Mason get up to – which sounds pretty gross usually – and I've had a few fumbles and fancied boys a bit and been to parties and snogged and stuff, but this time –' Elvi raised huge green eyes to Cleo's through the mirror '– this time it's different. I've met someone special.'

Someone special . . . Cleo sighed at the words. Lucky, lucky Elvi. That special someone, that very special someone – someone like Dylan Maguire . . .

She blinked. Where on earth had that come from? Ridiculous!

'Cleo? Cleo? Are you all right?'

Cleo was suddenly aware of Elvi staring at her. 'What? Yes, yes. Sorry, I just, er, remembered something. So go on, tell me about this boy. Is he pressurising you to have sex? Because you don't have to if you don't want to, you know. Oh, I know according to the tabloids everyone these days is at it the minute they've finished their first SATS papers, but there's no need to feel –'

'It's nothing like that.' Elvi laughed. 'We've only met

once and he hasn't said anything, done anything. It's not him, it's me. I know I'll want to, because – well, because he makes me feel incredible. I can't eat, sleep, think about anything but him. We've texted each other about fifty million times and . . . and I . . . I love him. Really love him. It was love at first sight, and I know he feels the same. Don't laugh.'

'Wouldn't dream of it,' Cleo sighed, turning and gazing at Elvi. 'First love is a pretty intense and amazing thing. It's all-consuming – takes over your entire world, makes everything lovely, makes you laugh at silly things and read all sorts of hidden messages into things you'd never considered before and –'

Elvi stopped chewing her hair and smiled broadly. 'See! You do understand. You're so cool. That's why I needed to talk to you. I knew you'd understand. I've even found that putrid Shakespeare and Jane Austen *know* about love. Before, I thought they were just long-winded and way too silly and old-fashioned, but they *knew*, didn't they?'

'Probably,' Cleo agreed. 'No, definitely. There are very few people who love has left untouched.'

'Was that how it was with your Dave? Just like, well, all rainbows and lollipops and sunshine? Like, when he touched you, you turned to jelly, and when he smiled your heart felt like it was going to burst, and all you wanted to do was say his name all the time, and panic sets in when you think you've forgotten his face and then, when you haven't, you want to turn cartwheels and laugh out loud?'

No, Cleo thought sadly, that wasn't at all how it had been

with Dave. However, she recognised the symptoms only too well . . .

'Not exactly, no. But I know exactly what you mean . . .' She stopped, realising with a sudden shock that she really *did* understand how Elvi felt. But it had nothing at all to do with Dave.

'I knew you would.' Elvi grinned in delight. 'It's like nothing else matters in the whole world, isn't it? That every little thing in your life suddenly means something different. Words and music and just the way someone smiles – it all reminds you of him, doesn't it?'

'Whoo, you've really got it badly, haven't you? But honestly, Elvi, I don't see the problem. You're sixteen – a normal age to fall in love, have a boyfriend – and the sex thing, well, that's fine too as long as it's what you both want and you respect one another and you're sensible and make sure there's no chance of unwanted pregnancies or anything.'

'Do you think I should go on the Pill? I do and I want to, but I can't go to my GP though – she's older than Methuselah – and she's known me since I was a baby.'

Cleo suddenly felt very ancient and a little sad. If only worrying about contraception had been a problem for her. She smiled. 'In that case, what I'd advise is finding a nice friendly anonymous clinic. There's a good one in Winterbrook – I know several of my friends went there. They can advise you on all sorts of stuff like that and certainly won't judge you, and yes, the Pill is possibly the answer, but, and I know I'm going to sound really prehistoric here, I do think you should get to know each other a bit better first.'

'I know and we want to, but, being realistic, I'm not sure we'll be able to. In fact all this stuff might well be a rotten waste of time.'

'Why? If you love one another? Or is he just about to emigrate or something?'

'Nah. He's, well, he's around fairly locally. But my parents – my dad especially – will go totally ballistic. They'll never agree to let me go out with him.'

'Why not? You're certainly old enough to have a proper boyfriend, so Amy and Ron aren't going to object, surely? They're very easy-going parents, aren't they? You've got the best of both worlds with them, I think. Your dad being older and wiser so he can give you good advice, and your mum being that much younger, well, she'll understand how you feel. They love you, Elvi, and if this boy makes you happy, then I'm sure they'd be OK with it.'

'And I love them,' Elvi sighed. 'Very much. They're great. Brilliant. And I don't want to upset them. But believe me, they'll go apeshit when they find out.'

Cleo shoved things back into her make-up bag and started pulling a brush through her long hair. 'OK, yes, I can see that they'll be a bit scared because their little girl is growing up – that's only natural.'

'It's not just that.'

'No, of course it wouldn't be just that, OK, and I can also see they wouldn't want this relationship to interfere with your school work. But if this boy is as lovely as you say, then he'll understand that too. You can meet at weekends, when you've finished your studying, can't you?'

'No.' Elvi shook her head. 'And it won't be my horrid school work that Dad will worry about either. He'll just forbid me from seeing him because . . . because he's unsuitable.'

Oh God, Cleo thought as she twisted her hair into a knot on top of her head in the hope that it wouldn't trail in Mimi's soup, she's fallen in love with a Bath Road Estate chav. Hoodie, baseball cap, glottal stops, dead eyes, adenoids, drugs – oh, God, no, surely not drugs.

'Right. OK. Tell me the truth, Elvi. How unsuitable?'

'Totally. Absolutely. The worst sort of person my dad could ever imagine I'd hook up with. There's no way on earth they'll agree to let me see him.'

Cleo winced, imagining now some slack-jawed yoof peddling Ecstasy and cannabis round Winterbrook and surrounding environs. But surely not? Elvi was a sensible, intelligent girl – young woman – she surely wouldn't? But then, love played its crazy tricks on even the most sensible people, didn't it?

'And this boy, does he have a job? Or is he unemployed? I'd have thought your dad would have every sympathy with that.'

'He's still at school.'

'Oh, right.' Cleo tried to get the tendrils of her hair to stay in their anchorage and failed. 'And how old is he? I mean, is that the problem? Is he a lot younger than you or something?'

Elvi fumbled in the pocket of her jeans. 'He's seventeen. He's doing his A levels. I've got a picture of him on my mobile. He tried sending me loads that he took himself on his iPhone but they were all fuzzy, so his friend Henry took this one. See, isn't he just beautiful?'

Cleo took the mobile phone, prepared to say this spotty schoolboy oik was Brad Pitt or Johnny Depp, or whoever the corresponding current teenage must-have boys were, rolled into one to keep Elvi happy.

But she didn't need to.

The bone-thin boy with the killer cheekbones and the spiky, long-fringed black hair was certainly beautiful. And had huge friendly intelligent eyes. And was very classy look-ing. Yes, she could completely understand why Elvi found him irresistible. But that skeletal look? Was that due to heroin? And what did she know about drugs anyway? Who was she to advise Elvi on anything? Oh, this was getting very complicated.

Cleo handed the phone back. 'He's gorgeous. Very gor-geous. And I do completely understand why you've fallen in love with him. But you're going to have to be honest with me now. Why is he so unsuitable?'

'He's at Gorse Glade.'

'Christ!' Cleo blinked. This wasn't at all what she'd expected. 'Ah, yes, I can see the problem now. Your dad, being the way he is about the class system, isn't actually going to welcome someone he sees as an upper-class leech on the working man as your first boyfriend, is he?'

'First, last, one and only,' Elvi said defiantly.

Cleo nodded. Poor Elvi. It all made sense. She didn't stand a chance.

'So, does this lovely boy have a name?'

'Zeb.' Elvi purred the word, smiling from ear to ear.

'Nice. And hopefully that isn't prefixed by a title? That really would send Ron into the stratosphere.'

'Nope – his dad's got a putrid title, but it was an honour's list one so not inheritable. But he does have a double-barrelled surname.'

'Almost as bad as far as your dad's concerned.' Cleo gathered her things together and glanced at the bedside clock. She'd really have to leave now. 'Look, Elvi, I'm sorry, but I'm going to have to scoot. Maybe we can carry on tomorrow morning? Put our heads together and have a good think and maybe find some way to persuade your mum and dad that Zeb Thingummy-Upperclass –'

'It's Pashley-Royle.'

'Holy cow!' Cleo stared open-mouthed at Elvi.

'Now you see the problem?' Elvi sighed, leaning down and sliding her feet into her ballet pumps. 'No way on earth is anyone going to approve. His rotten parents will be just as horrified as mine.'

'And do they know? The Pashley-Royles?' Cleo asked faintly. 'I mean, I didn't even know Mimi and Mortimer had any children.'

Elvi stood up. 'Zeb has been away at boarding school since he was five. Shunted straight from his exclusive prep school to the even more exclusive Gorse Glade, and then will no doubt be shunted on to Oxbridge. Wheeled out on putrid family occasions only. And no, as far as I know, Zeb won't have mentioned me to them. Why would he? They'd forbid him to see me. A working-class kid from a caravan site? They'll love that, won't they? Zeb must know it won't be going anywhere.'

Cleo crossed the bedroom and hugged Elvi. 'You poor, poor things. Star-crossed lovers doesn't come close, does it? What on earth are you going to do?'

'Go on the Pill and elope.'

'Glad to see you've kept a sense of proportion about all this. Oh, love, I don't know what to say. No, that's not true. If you love one another – and you really do need to get together more often to find out – then I think you must be honest with both families. Goodness knows, aren't we supposed to live in a classless society these days?'

'You know as well as I do that that's a load of bollocks,' Elvi said, smiling sadly. 'Especially round here. And especially with my family and the Pashley-Royles. My mum was their cleaner, for God's sake, and my dad's not known as Red Ron for nothing. Oh, I don't know if I'm coming or going any more. It all goes round and round in my head and all I really want to do is to be with Zeb – and he wants the same – as often as we can.'

'Right –' Cleo reached for her jacket and car keys, and grabbed her bag '– now I'm going to say something really radical. If you and Zeb are serious about one another, then go for it. Keep it your secret for as long as is necessary. Don't upset anyone unnecessarily. I know you think it'll last for ever – and I hope it does – but if it doesn't, then no one will be any the wiser, will they? And if you're going to sleep together then get fixed up. And enjoy every bloody minute of it!'

'Oh.' Elvi threw her arms around Cleo. 'I knew you'd be the right person to talk to! Thank you! I love you. I so wish you were my mum.'

With a jolt, Cleo realised that, given the age difference, being Elvi's mum was far from being a physical impossibility. She was probably exactly the same age as Amy Reynolds. It made her feel extremely old. And sad and happy and not a little emotional.

'Sweetheart, you'd be the perfect daughter. And if you were my daughter, then I'd be the proudest mum in the world. Now, before I burst into tears and embarrass us both, you go and text Zeb and tell him you love him, and I'll go and spill stuff on the do-gooders.'

'Yeah, cool.' Elvi's eyes sparkled properly for the first time as she opened the caravan's door. 'And if you can manage to poison Mimi and Mort at the same time, that'd be extra brilliant.'

Chapter Ten

'Hello there, young Cleo!' Mortimer Pashley-Royle boomed across the gravelled drive, waving cheerily as Cleo locked her car outside Lovelady Hall. 'Bang on time! Well, a tad early actually, which is very handy, because I wondered if you could spare me a few minutes?'

'Yes, of course.'

As she scrunched her way across to him, Cleo gave a sigh of relief. Mortimer was once again clad in his country squire outfit, all cords and checks, which indicated tonight's supper party wasn't going to be formal. Her waitressing experience covered various pubs and eateries, but she'd never aimed as high as complete silver service.

Mortimer beamed. 'Mimi will be very impressed by your being early. Not that she's not impressed with you already, of course. She's singing your praises morning, noon and night. She's had such a bad time with staff, poor angel. I do hope you won't let her down, too.'

'I'll certainly try not to,' Cleo said fervently and truthfully, having a massive sense of self-preservation and no intention whatsoever of joining the swollen ranks of Mimi's ex-staff until her finances were on a far firmer footing.

'Good-oh,' Mortimer said heartily. 'I do so admire loyalty in our employees. And I like you, too. You seem like a plucky girl.'

Mmm, all a bit too jolly hockey sticks to be genuine, Cleo thought, still smiling in what she hoped was an obsequious minion manner. Mortimer had probably had to read an awful lot of etiquette books when he married into the landed gentry. And clearly most of them had been hopelessly out of date.

'You look like a proper little nippy in that get-up tonight.' Mortimer beamed, immediately confirming Cleo's earlier suspicions. 'Nice and neat. Some of the waiting staff we've had have been God-awful. Truly God-awful. You look just the ticket.'

Mortimer Pashley-Royle was a nice man, Cleo decided, even if he was still slightly out of his depth with the old money of Lovelady Hall. Underneath he might well be a raging lower-middle-class snob like her mother, but all in all he seemed OK – so far.

How OK would Mortimer be though, with his son and heir canoodling with his ex-cleaner's daughter? Not very, she thought as she scrunched her way across the gravel with him. He'd probably be even more apoplectic than Red Ron Reynolds. Poor Elvi . . .

And poor Zeb, too, if Elvi was to be believed and their feelings were mutual. How strange genetics were. She would never have believed this squat, rotund, vaguely porcine man was the father of the skinny but beautiful Zeb.

Although, yes, the eyes were the same, she thought. Nice eyes. Open and laughing. Zeb must have inherited his shivering greyhound upper-class frame from Mimi. But he had his father's eyes.

'Wondered if you'd like to take a look at my little empire before you enter the fray in the kitchen?' Mortimer beamed, bouncing imperiously, like so many small men did, on the soles of his highly polished handmade Church brogues. 'You've got a few minutes to spare. The caterers haven't arrived yet and Mimi likes to do the table settings herself when she's using the best service and the family silver.'

Thank goodness for that, Cleo thought, as her own table settings usually comprised one plate, mismatched knives, forks, spoons and the requisite number of sheets of kitchen roll. But caterers? Stupid! Of course there'd be caterers. Mimi was hardly likely to be doing the cooking herself, was she?

Mortimer rubbed his hands together. 'I'd like you to get to know the whole of the Pashley-Royle empire, so to speak. I've been meaning to give you the grand tour all week, but Mimi always has you tied up in the house during the day. You look like a girl who'd appreciate a nice motor car. That's what I do, you know. Supply nice motor cars to those who can appreciate them.'

Cleo continued to smile and nod and didn't give any indication at all that, courtesy of his delivery driver, she already knew quite a bit about his little empire. 'Oh, so does that mean that you're offering me the pick of the bunch?'

Mortimer roared with laughter. It was odd, Cleo thought, that this little ball of a man could produce such a resounding bellow. 'Clever girl! Caught me there properly. Mimi said you were as bright as a button. And who knows, one day you might be able to afford one of my little beauties. Come along, my dear, follow me.'

As Cleo reckoned it would be churlish to tell your employer's husband that you actually had very little interest in cars – except making sure that they started and stopped at the right times – and none whatsoever in chromium-plated gas-guzzlers for those who had more money than sense, obediently she did as he asked.

Mortimer trotted round the side of Lovelady Hall and Cleo followed. In the chilly September darkness, the large house was tastefully illuminated by hidden ranks of uplighters in the encircling shrubbery, which cast swathes of gold across the mellow brickwork, and turned the long leaded windows into twinkling panels of burnished copper. Where the lights fell on the Virginia creeper, the leaves glowed in a glinting, glimmering autumnal rainbow. It was exceedingly beautiful, like something stage-set by Merchant and Ivory, Cleo thought. Typical English country class.

And a million miles from the Lovers Knot Caravan Park.

Having ducked beneath the creeper-clad clock arch, they crossed the vast cobbled courtyard at the back of Lovelady Hall. Cleo hadn't been round this side of the house at all, and she looked around in pleasure as more lights sprang on as they walked, illuminating the dark sky, throwing looming shadows across the golden brickwork and casting bright pools at their feet.

This, Cleo reckoned, was where the Harvest Home supper would take place. Very suitable. Again like a stage set, nearly surrounded by the curve of Lovelady, and with a towering thatched open-fronted, empty and immaculately clean barn on one side and the refurbed stable block on the other.

Despite promising herself that she wouldn't show the slightest interest, Cleo's eyes immediately strayed upwards to the flat above the stables. There were soft lights spilling from the uncurtained windows and her heart gave a foolish lurch.

That was Dylan's home. That was where Dylan was, at that very moment, either preparing to go out to meet Jessamine, tonight's hot date, or – even worse – was already entertaining her, only a few feet away, in his own special fashion.

Cleo sighed.

Dylan had left her caravan the previous night, after dressing with decorum in the bathroom as soon as his clothes were dry, having demolished the Swiss roll and a lot more coffee and helping her in decanting the Razzle Dazzle Damson and clearing up all the winemaking paraphernalia, smiling and saying he'd had the best time ever and he'd see her next weekend, and couldn't make it before then.

'I'm going to be away all next week. And as you know, I always like to tack a bit of extra-curricular activity on to Mort's deliveries.'

He'd waved and blown her a kiss, then disappeared into

the night, and, yes, she'd known exactly what the extra-curriculars entailed. And now tonight he'd got a hot date with someone impossibly called Jessamine, and sod it, she *cared*.

Well, one thing was sure, she'd never, ever let him know.

Still staring at Dylan's home, Cleo counted the windows – six on this side, which meant it was fairly large. About three times the size of her caravan. No little poky hayloft bedsit for Dylan then. Mortimer was clearly a caring employer. And hot-date Jessamine was possibly romping naked through all that space, as she stood outside like some starving urchin, staring wistfully.

No, she shook her head. As urchins were, by law, piteously thin and waiflike, and she was anything but, Cleo immediately discounted that image. Even so, it was very galling to be so near and yet so far . . .

Hoping beyond hope that Jessamine was some hulking horse-faced woman with thick ankles and thin hair, Cleo sighed and pushed any further distasteful images from her head, trying to concentrate and look interested as Mortimer fiddled with locks and keys and pressed various security buttons.

'Open sesame!' He grinned hugely, as the massive metal doors slid open as if by magic and a zillion lights instantly flickered on inside the stables. 'Come along, my dear. Come and see my pretty boys' toys.'

Cleo, who knew she wouldn't be able to tell a Bentley from a Rolls-Royce and hoped it wouldn't matter, stepped inside.

She blinked.

The stables' interior had been completely gutted to give acres of floor space. Professional lighting and floor-to-ceiling showroom mirrors made the multicoloured paintwork of the cars dance with sparkles and spangles.

'Heavens,' she said faintly.

These cars were no ordinary exclusive expensive saloons. They were not simply limousines, but snarling, angular, scarily powerful supercars. Long and low, almost impossibly futuristic, they crouched in the stables like so many fantasy creatures, waiting to roar and spring and surge with powerful life.

'Lovely, aren't they?' Mortimer said proudly, beaming paternally as if he were displaying a particularly attractive litter of pedigree kittens to a prospective buyer. 'And not what you were expecting?'

'Not at all what I was expecting,' Cleo admitted. 'Er, they're spectacular. And I'm afraid I don't recognise any of them.'

'Not surprised, my dear. Some of these are real rarities. Of course, we do still get plenty of people seeking the classics – a Rolls Phantom Coupé or a Bentley Continental – mainly retired bankers who got out before the credit crunch with their bonuses intact. But these are the cars the youngsters want.'

Clearly delighted to have a novice as a captive audience, Mortimer ushered Cleo along the serried metallic ranks, explaining torque and power-steering ratios, and intoning with paternal pride the names of his favourites: Aston Martin

V8 Vantage Roadster, Ferrari Scuderia Spider, Lamborghini Murcielago LP640, Maserati Gran Turisimo . . .

On and on the list went, sounding, Cleo thought, something like Latin noun declensions – and just as perplexing. As Winterbrook comp had never offered Latin to its scholars, Cleo was totally bamboozled.

'But they must be worth a fortune.'

'A king's ransom,' Mortimer said smugly. 'And believe it or not there are still plenty of people out there who'll fight to buy them, even in these cold, grey days of tightened belts.'

'Really? That does surprise me. But who?'

'Oh, celebrities of all hues, my dear. Film stars, television actors, media people and sportsmen in particular – then, of course, there are the newly wealthy. The lottery winners who want to spend, spend, spend.'

Cleo gazed at the rows of cars again and knew now why Dylan had so much success with a particular type of lady on his supercar delivery travels. If you were impressed by the trappings of wealth – which, both by necessity and inclination she wasn't – how could you possibly resist one of these sexy, classic and exclusive cars driven by an even more sexy classic and exclusive chauffeur?

No wonder Dylan had eschewed any other career better suited to his obvious qualifications in favour of this one – this one that would ensure he had access to not only the sort of cars that most men would cut off their right arms for, but also a whole bevy of adoring, rich and glamorous women.

Lucky Dylan – and lucky, lucky ladies . . .

Cleo dragged herself back to the matter in hand. 'So, how

does it work? People who have far too much money and far too little time, contact you and ask you to source them a particular must-have car do they? And when you've found exactly what they're looking for, you then add on your expenses and profit percentage, and marry the two together?'

'Spot on!' Mortimer chuckled. 'Couldn't have put it better myself, my dear. You are a clever girl.'

Cleo gave what she hoped was a suitable simper and tried hard not to be affronted by the patronising tone. After all, this was Mortimer's multi-multi-multi-million pound business – and she couldn't even afford to buy a steering wheel.

'I always think of myself,' Mortimer continued, looking slightly pompous, 'as one of those people you girls can't seem to manage without.'

Doctors? Dentists? Plumbers? Electricians? No, surely not . . . Cleo gave up and looked enquiringly at Mortimer.

'A personal shopper for cars. Mimi would be lost without someone to fetch and carry when she updates her wardrobe two or three times a year – as no doubt you would too, my dear.'

Ah, right . . . Cleo said nothing. Mimi's shopping habits in Harrods and Harvey Nicks probably warranted a personal shopper. She'd never seen one offering its services in Primark.

Realising that any minute she'd say something that would show how out her depth she was, Cleo resumed her polite minion mode. 'Thank you so much for taking the time to show me round. It's been fascinating, but I really think I should be in the kitchen by now. I don't want to upset Mimi.'

'Neither do I,' Mortimer said, as they retraced their steps and he went through the security locking and bolting in reverse and the huge doors slid shut. 'I love the very bones of that woman. But I'm glad you liked the cars, my dear. And, I'm very excited because, due to the interest raised by television programmes like *Top Gear*, I've recently had enquiries for some of the newish supermodels.'

Oh great, Cleo thought, Agyness Deyn on order. Dylan would really love that . . .

'The Bugatti Veyron and the Pagani Zonda R are the hot favourites at the moment. I'm having a lot of fun trying to get hold of those. Right, well, thank you again for your delightful company – and you know your way back to the kitchen entrance, of course. I'll have to skedaddle now I'm afraid and get into my best bib and tucker.'

Chaff, Cleo thought, this time deliberately not staring up at the flat above the stables. It was going to be a formal dinner party after all. Oh, God . . .

The kitchen, filled with mouth-watering smells, was heaving with activity. Having shed her outdoor layers, Cleo watched the frantic bustle with amusement from the doorway.

An overweight man with badly bleached hair was flapping around, red-faced, looking angry and swearing violently in the manner of all the best celebrity chefs. Huge foil-covered trays were being popped into ovens, film-covered dishes were pinging in and out of the microwaves, and various tubs were being shoved into the industrial-sized fridge.

Two very pretty girls with braided hair, and wearing neat black trousers and white T-shirts were perched on the maple island, chatting casually to one another, completely ignoring the mayhem around them. Were they Zola and Zlinki? Possibly . . . And, oh my God! Working on the other side of the kitchen, Cleo noticed with some surprise, were the Phlopps.

Big women, almost identical, despite their five-year age difference, with their dough-faces and dark page-boy hair-cuts, the Phlopps, swathed in massive white aprons, were busily and messily stirring something on the top of the small-est oven.

What on earth were Belly and Flip doing at Lovelady Hall? Cooking? Surely not? But they couldn't be waiting staff too, could they? How many people had Mimi invited for Lord's sake? Was there going to be one waitress to each guest?

'Hello, Cleo, what are you doing 'ere?' Belly looked up and waved a wooden spoon. Something dropped glutinously on to the cooker top and Flip scooped it up and ate it. 'Bit late at night for PA-ing, isn't it? Or 'as 'Er Ladyship dragged you in fer a bit of overtime?'

'Er, Mimi asked me to wait on the table tonight,' Cleo shouted above the clanging, clattering noise. 'What about you? I didn't expect to see you here. I didn't think you did any, um, extras at Lovelady any more?'

'No more we don't,' Flip yelled cheerfully. ''Er Ladyship is a rotten boss – no, we're here with Giovanni. As kitchen 'ands. Catering, you knows? He does most of the prepping at 'is place and then we does the last-minute stuff on the spot.'

'Oh, right,' Cleo said, slightly at a loss.

Belly beamed. 'We 'elps out as often as is needed on his outside contracts. He comes over from Willows Lacey. Got that five-star Bisto place. Caters for all the knobs. Pays well. We saves the money for our holiday in Teneriffey.'

'Oh, right,' Cleo repeated. Presumably Giovanni was the overweight man with the colourful language.

'Um, any chance of knowing the menu?' Cleo asked. 'And are we all supposed to be serving each course, or what?'

'Best ask Giovanni,' Flip said. 'He keeps us all in order. Oh, and 'ave you met Zola and Zlinki, yet? They're waitressing too.'

The two girls sitting on the island smiled. Cleo smiled back.

Flip sucked a wooden spoon with lascivious pleasure. 'Giovanni usually 'as his own gels waiting on, but they all went on unilateral strike over this one. None of 'em wants to work for 'Er Ladyship – not after last time.'

'Last time?'

Belly shook her head. ''Orrible, it was. All them gels in tears. And all because 'Er Ladyship had a bit of a fit over the Eton mess. Well, we all said after, it's meant to be messy, innit?'

Cleo nodded. Her heart sank. This was going to be an evening she knew she'd really rather forget.

'Mind you,' Flip, added, 'it's best to keep the mess on the

plate and not all over 'Er Ladyship's lap. Language? You ain't never 'eard anything like it.'

Cleo winced. Please, please, please, she prayed silently, don't let history repeat itself tonight.

'Pet!' In an accent that owed far more to Tyneside than Turin, Giovanni beckoned across the kitchen. 'Yes, you, pet. Over here a sec.'

Cleo trotted across towards him.

'You're the third waitress then? Great. Nothing too complicated for you lasses tonight, thank God. Three courses only and she's gone for classic rather than fusion. Fusion can be a nightmare for the waiting staff, pet. Especially in a mausoleum like this.'

Tell me about it, Cleo thought.

'Right, pet. There's twelve guests including Him and Her – so that means each of you three waitresses take four meals each.'

'At the same time?' Cleo asked, wondering how she'd manage to carry more than two of anything unless they were balanced on her head.

'Naturally at the same time.' Giovanni frowned. 'Timing is of the essence. Every guest has exactly the same plate of food, at exactly the same temperature, served at exactly the same time. I thought you was a waitress, pet?'

'I've done pub grub. Two plates of something congealed and chips served to bladdered punters who are just happy to have anything to empty their ketchup bottles on.'

Giovanni shook his head sorrowfully. 'I love a lass with a touch of class. Ever been to Byker, pet? You'll just have to be a quick learner. I've given them other two the ends and near side of the table as their service area. You'll have the far side. OK?'

Cleo nodded miserably. Now she'd have further to walk and dozens of fresh opportunities to slip, fall over, throw things . . .

'Right, now,' Giovanni said briskly, 'starters is French onion soup with melting Gruyère toast. You'll have to be a bit canny with the toast, mind, pet. It's slid on top of the soup and tends to float about a bit and you don't want to end up all claggy, do you?'

Cleo didn't. There was no need for a north–south interpreter. She got the picture. Vividly. Why the hell couldn't it be a nice prawn cocktail? All contained in a tumbler? With no risks involved?

'Right. Mains is grilled sea bass. I blame the bloody telly programmes, I do – everyone wants bloody sea bass. Last year it was all monkfish; now it's bloody sea bass. Gets boring. So, sea bass, with crushed Jersey Royals and braised sea greens. Should be easy enough that one. Fish and spuds on the plate, then you hand round the veg tureens. Her Ladyship wanted table service, not dig in and help theirselves. Slower but less clarts.'

Chaff, Cleo thought. Another golden opportunity to drop fricasséed seaweed or something equally unpleasant all down the front of someone's Versace. Great.

'And afters is a white chocolate and berry pudding. Individual ramekins. Berries in the pud and in a drizzle on the side. Bit of vanilla cream too. Careful you don't let the lot slide off, pet.'

Cleo nodded, feeling very sick. So many pitfalls loomed large.

'Right, hinny –' Giovanni beamed '– I'll rely on you to let us know when they want service. You clear one course, give us a shout and I'll plate up the next. With me, pet?'

Way, way ahead of you, Cleo thought, nodding. I'm going to foul this up in a totally spectacular manner, I just know I am. She smiled. 'Yes, thanks. It all sounds straightforward to me.'

'Good lass.' Giovanni patted her in a perfunctory manner. 'You can be my right-hand woman. Them other two canny lasses over there might look bonny enough but they're as much use to me as mittens to a crocodile.'

Cleo looked at Zola and Zlinki who were chatting closely together, swinging their long slender legs, clearly far more concerned with their legal studies than worrying about Mimi's dinner party.

'I promise I'll do my best.'

'That'll do for me. Right – let's get the grit out of them greens. Oh, damn, here's Her Ladyship – best go and head her off, pet. I never like hostess interference in my kitchen.'

Belting back across the kitchen, swerving round Flip and Belly who were scraping new potatoes and lustily singing 'Blaydon Races', no doubt in a gesture of solidarity with Giovanni's roots, Cleo blinked at Mimi.

Stunning in a sheath of silver, her blonde hair gleaming, her make-up cover-girl perfect, she looked about eighteen and absolutely gorgeous.

'Cleo, lovely to see you and thank heavens you're here, I

have no faith whatsoever in Zola and Zlinki's waitressing skills. I always think their minds are on torts rather than tortes.'

Cleo, doing a lightning mental juggling act with the wordplay, laughed dutifully in the pause.

Mimi seemed pleased that she'd made the effort. 'My guests have all arrived and are just about to be seated. We're in the Duke's dining room in case you think we're eating in the Blue Room. Too small. You're au fait with the layout of the formal dining room, aren't you?'

Cleo nodded. It was a large beautiful room, oak-panelled – obviously – and decorated with portraits of ancient forebears and an obligatory stag's head which she'd always avoided looking at because it had a rather miffed expression as though it hadn't been given anything like a sporting chance.

Still, at least the Duke's dining room was a nice oblong shape, with the Queen Anne table running for miles down the centre, and two doors at either end leading back to the hall and the kitchens. Should give her plenty of room for manoeuvring.

'Super. Mortimer said you'd arrived early tonight, and I do appreciate that. I'd hoped to have a little word, but he snaffled you first to look at his cars, I understand. Never mind. Just delighted that you're here. Has, um, Giovanni filled you in on the whys and wherefores? Good – now, what I wanted to say –'

Her monologue was interrupted by a crash, a scream from one of the Phlopps and a stream of invective from Giovanni.

'Dear Lord,' Mimi sighed as peace broke out again. 'And you wonder why I was glad not to have Belly and Flip waiting on table? Sheer hell at the sharp end, isn't it? That's why I loathe these things. I could never cook for other people – such a menial and thankless task. Yes, where was I? Oh yes, I just wanted to say that my guests tonight are very influential both in the county and in supporting my charities, so please don't upset them. I know you won't of course, but this is my standard little pre-supper indemnity chat.'

'I'll try my hardest to be the perfect waitress,' Cleo said. 'Was that all you wanted me for, because I think, if your guests are sitting down, I should be sorting out the starters, don't you?'

'First course, dear. This isn't a Berni. Yes, yes – but no, what I actually wanted to say – in case I forget later – was to thank you for the way in which you've organised Harvest Home. Everything docketed and cross-referenced and checked off. People have responded straight away. I've left a list of who's bringing what on the office desk for you to deal with on Monday. It's all most impressive. So, I'm passing it all over to you from now on. Harvest Home is all yours. I'm away next week on a fund-raising mission, so I want you to concentrate on the organisation to the exclusion of everything else. That'll be all right, won't it? Good.' Beaming and without waiting for reply, Mimi spun round and in a shimmer of silver and diamonds, left the kitchen.

Reeling from the onslaught, Cleo exhaled. Great. Now she was even more terrified of spilling stuff on the great and the good – and organising the whole of Harvest Home? Eeek!

'Pet!' Giovanni waved a ladle above his head. 'I needs yer! I'm about to start dishing yer starters. Best gird yer loins.'

Chapter Eleven

Carefully balancing four beautiful soup bowls of French onion with a slice of bubbling cheesy toast floating on top like a raft adrift on a stormy ocean, Cleo, followed by Zola and Zlinki, backed into the dining room.

It was like walking into Aladdin's cave.

In the tastefully muted light, candles flickered, glassware and cutlery sparkled, and little prisms danced from every surface. The colour theme was silver and ruby. Designer arrangements of roses and embellished foliage tumbled tastefully on to the Queen Anne table, and the guests looked as though they'd been assembled by Oscar Wilde.

No one took any notice of the waitresses at all. Their entrance wasn't acknowledged. Not even by Mimi and Mortimer. They were staff. Invisible. Vital but non-existent.

Oh, poor Elvi, Cleo thought. Even if she and Zeb Pashley-Royle did make a go of their embryo relationship, how would she ever cope with this?

The roar of pre-supper conversation haw-hawed round the panelled room.

'. . . and then he had the temerity to say he might live in a council house but he had human rights too. Can you believe that?'

'. . . flew in from the States red-eye with a hot tip, made a couple of billion and was back on the Airbus before lunch. Who does that these days? I thought everyone used cyber-traders — even if there is a killing to be made anywhere, which I doubt. I said to Tommo, it had to be insider-dealing . . .'

'. . . far, far too last-season, darling, I told her. We'd be a laughing stock . . .'

Aware of a sea of expensive evening gowns, glittering jewels and neat tuxedos, Cleo took a deep breath and walked slowly to the far side of the table. Four people, two men, two women, all doing the polite dinner party thing of chatting both to left and right, continued to ignore her.

Carefully, remembering to serve from the left, she lowered the first bowl under a jowly chin. Success. And the second slid neatly under a bulging dinner jacket. So far so good. Not a drop spilt.

Now it was going to be easier. Two bowls, two hands.

Cleo attempted to manoeuvre the penultimate French onion round the slender shoulders of a gamine youthful Audrey Hepburn lookalike in a strapless dress of pale-pink sequins, who was chattering in an upper-class high-pitched little girly voice and moving her hands animatedly as she did so.

'I say.' A man with a goatee beard leaned across the vastness of table towards the Audrey clone. 'The waitress is trying to serve your soup. Sit still and give her some space, there's a poppet, Jessamine.'

Cleo froze. No way . . . No way on earth could there be *two* Jessamines in the whole of Berkshire, let alone anywhere near Lovelady Hall . . .

Her hand shaking, she lowered the bowl between the gleaming cutlery, and stared at the back of Jessamine's dark-haired tuxedo-clad neighbour.

Dylan Maguire looked round to accept his soup and stopped, staring back at her with a stunned expression.

Horribly aware of her cheap blouse, ill-fitting polyester skirt and clumpy shoes, and trying to prevent the Gruyèred toasts sailing over the edge of the bowl, she placed the soup in front of him.

'Thank you,' he said in his low, languid voice, smiling, his eyes asking a million questions. 'But what the –?'

Pole-axed with shock, but without betraying a flicker of recognition, Cleo walked stiffly away from the table, her head reeling, pushed past Zola and Zlinki, and belted back to the kitchen.

Flip and Belly were sitting at the limed oak table, alternately spooning vast quantities of French onion soup into their mouths with ladles and chewing happily on cheesy toast.

They beamed at her with twin Gruyère moustaches. 'Leftovers – cooks' perks. Mind you save us some fish and taters, Cleo, love, won't you? Not too fussed about the greens, though. We don't go too much for greens. Puddin' though – that's different. Keep us back some of the pud.'

'All OK, pet?' Giovanni asked. 'No spillage?'

'None,' Cleo muttered. 'And I'm just going to take a breather. Excuse me.'

Outside in the darkness, she sucked in the chilly early-autumn evening air. It tasted of decaying leaves and earth and mist and bonfires.

Still completely stunned at seeing Dylan when she'd least expected it, Cleo frowned, her brain racing almost as fast as her heart.

No wonder Dylan had been so keen to see Jessamine tonight. Jessamine must be a personal friend of the Pashley-Royles, mustn't she? One of Mimi's charity fund-raisers? And Dylan would have leaped at the opportunity to turn up as the escort to one of the guests at his employers' formal supper party, wouldn't he? To sit there, at that fabulous table, eating Mortimer and Mimi's extravagant spread, being treated as an equal by the people who actually paid his wages.

Oh, yes, he'd love that!

And of course Dylan wouldn't have mentioned to her that the hot date, with the willowy and exceptionally upper-class Jessamine, was taking place in the glorious Duke's dining room, because he had no idea that Cleo worked at Lovelady too, had he?

She smiled to herself. She'd be able to tease him about it when he came round to the caravan next week to test-drive the Razzle Dazzle Damson, wouldn't she? She'd rib him unmercifully, saying it was reassuring to know that his class and breeding hadn't all gone to waste – at least he'd know which fork to use.

And Dylan would have been just as surprised to see her tonight, wouldn't he? She'd kept a secret from him too. They'd no doubt pretend to be mock-shocked and joke about both being Lovelady employees, and he'd say, in that gorgeous upper-class drawl, that Cleo had found her true station in life at last in waiting on him.

Yes, that's exactly how it would be. Anyway, they were quits now, weren't they? And now she was prepared, and knew he was there, sitting beside the gamine Jessamine, looking gloriously sexy in the Duke's dining room, she'd be fine with serving the other courses, wouldn't she?

But why, oh why, wasn't Jessamine disgustingly gross instead of being a little elfin thing wearing an evening frock that clearly cost more than Cleo's caravan? And why was her stupid heart now beating fit to burst? And why was she still trembling? And why had she gone – literally – weak at the knees when Dylan smiled?

Lordy, Cleo thought, with a lightning bolt of realisation, Elvi's met someone special – and so have I.

And that wasn't supposed to happen, was it? She wasn't supposed to think of Dylan, after their pathetically brief acquaintance, as anything but a charming, amusing, rich-kid, waste-of-space, alley-catting, strange sort of friend, was she? OK, and the Most Beautiful Boy in the World. Definitely that. But when on earth did the 'special' bit creep in?

Because it had and he was.

So, how silly did that make her? Like Elvi? Like some teenager besotted with her first love? And just as futile? Probably . . . Not that she wanted to scrawl Dylan's name on her pencil case – or whatever the twenty-first century equivalent was – but yes, the mention of his name did make her smile, and the memory of their two very off-the-wall encounters made her laugh to herself, and, yes, she did want to see him again – even if it wasn't in a *going out* sort of way . . .

Oh, bloody chaff it.

'Cleo, pet!' Giovanni's voice rang out from the kitchen. 'I think you should check on thems. See if they need the soup bowls clearing. The fish is almost ready . . .'

Serving the main course was far easier than the first. Helped by Zola and Zlinki, Cleo had managed to remove the empty soup bowls without any problems at all. She hadn't even glanced at Dylan. Or Jessamine. The supper party guests still ignored her as she placed plates of sea bass and crushed Jersey Royals in front of them.

The conversation seemed to have moved on to charity fund-raising and eye-watering sums of money were being mentioned by the time Cleo returned with the tureen of wilted sea greens for her side of the table.

Crossly, she realised that her hands were shaking as she hovered over Jessamine's perfect bare shoulder, and did the two-spoons serving thing.

Concentrating hard, she gritted her teeth and managed to decant the requisite amount of shredded samphire neatly onto the plate. The urge to tip the lot down Jessamine's lovely back was very fierce. With great strength of character she managed to control herself and moved round to Dylan's left.

'Braised sea greens, sir?'

'Please.'

Oh God. The one word was imbued with an overt sexuality that made her hands shake even more. And he was smiling again. And very, very close.

Cleo's mouth was dry and her hands trembled as she dollopped greens onto Dylan's plate. Stop it, she told herself. Grow up.

'Enough?' Cleo winced. Sod it. Was she supposed to say sufficient? Or nothing at all?

'Oh, I can never have enough.' Dylan grinned. 'As I'm sure you know.'

Feeling very hot, Cleo moved the tureen away before her treacherous hands caused a disaster of epic proportions.

'Dy–lan!' Jessamine squeaked. 'You are naughty. You mustn't flirt with the staff. The poor girl will think you mean it.'

Dylan laughed. 'And you don't need to patronise this particular poor girl. Although I'd like to ask her one or two questions.'

Snap, Cleo thought, holding the semi-denuded tureen firmly and turning away just as Dylan reached out and grabbed her arm.

It was the first time he'd touched her. Her skin was on fire.

She wrenched her arm away.

Jessamine squealed as the remains of the braised sea greens flew from the dish, and settled provocatively on her shoulder for a second before slithering gloopily into her very small cleavage.

'Oh, I say!' The goatee man waved his fork. 'Clumsy!'

Cleo wanted to die on the spot.

The jowly woman and the portly gent joined in the condemnation. Fortunately neither Mimi nor Mortimer, who were engaged in conversations at either end of the table, seemed to have noticed. Yet.

'I'm so sorry . . .' Cleo started to mutter her apologies.

Dylan stopped her. 'No, please don't say sorry. There's no need. I'm the one who should apologise. It was totally my fault. I jogged your arm. Absolutely nothing to do with you. Please, carry on.' His eyes stared deeply into hers for a second. Then he looked at Jessamine. 'Oh, for God's sake shut up, Jess. It's an infinitesimal bit of samphire trying to find its way into your tits, not the massed battalions of the Grenadier Guards.'

Jessamine screamed.

'Oh, I say!' Goatee harrumphed again.

Dylan started mopping at Jessamine's chest with a bunched crested linen napkin. Cleo noticed that Goatee and Portly also had theirs scrunched at the ready. Jessamine was now purring gently under Dylan's ministrations like a well-groomed prize Siamese cat.

Humiliated beyond belief, Cleo ran from the dining room just as Mimi became aware of the hullabaloo. Oh, God, now

she'd be sacked. She'd join the swelling ranks of the unemployed – again – at the speed of light. Oooh, chaffing hell!

'What's occurring?' Giovanni raised his eyebrows as Cleo
hurtled into the kitchen and slammed the tureen on to the
nearest work surface. 'Sea bass not up to scratch?'

'I tipped greens on to a guest.'

'Bollocks!' Giovanni howled. 'They'll probably sue!'

'It wasn't my fault – honestly. One of the other guests
grabbed my arm. It was only a little bit and, um, I'm sure it'll
be OK. They've calmed down now. Just don't let anyone –
anyone at all from that dinner party – come in here looking
for me, OK? If they do, tell them I drowned in the vanilla
custard, OK?'

'Whatever.' Giovanni calmed down slightly. 'If you're sure
no one's going to get litigious. What about the puds,
though? Are you still going to be serving the puds, pet?'

'No way. I'm never going back in there again.'

'Course you are. Look, hinny, they'll have all been knocking back the fizz and raking over their friends and enemies
and talking mega-millions and won't remember a thing.
Come on, we've all done it – chucked stuff – it goes with
the territory. Can't be your first time.'

'Dumping chips into the lap of a bevvied brickie in the
Maggot and Mushroom doesn't count.'

Giovanni smiled. 'There, see, pet? You've kept yer sense of
humour. Try not to let it upset you. Take a deep breath. Go
outside and have a fag –'

'Gave up five years ago.'

'Start again, pet. No?'

Cleo sketched a smile. It would have to be Jessamine that got the spillage, though, wouldn't it? Now Dylan would think she'd done it out of spite or jealousy. Oh, damn bloody Dylan Maguire.

'Not the taters you spilled, was it, Cleo?' Flip looked up from where she was scraping residue into a swill bin. 'You didn't waste any taters?'

'Just greens. You won't starve.'

'Good,' Belly said happily 'You didn't dump them on Her Ladyship, did you?'

'No. Just down the cleavage of the prettiest girl in the room. There was a rescue attempt going on as I left.'

Zola and Zlinki, who had followed her into the kitchen, were giggling together. Cleo looked across at them and they beamed back at her in solidarity.

Maybe, she thought, it wasn't that awful after all. Maybe . . .

By the time the main course was finished and Giovanni had persuaded her she had to get back into the dining room to clear, everyone stopped briefly in the middle of their conversation to stare at her.

Dylan more than most. Cleo ignored him.

'Don't let her near me!' Jessamine squeaked. 'I don't trust her.'

'As far as I gather,' Mortimer slurred cheerfully from his end of the table, 'it wasn't our Nippy's fault at all. No recriminations needed. I'll be dealing with the true miscreant later. You carry on, Cleo, my dear.'

Knowing her face was burning scarlet, but mightily relieved that she wasn't about to be sacked on the spot, Cleo scurried round the table with Zola and Zlinki, removing the plates and cutlery. Oh God – but Mort blamed Dylan, and now he'd probably lose his job and it'd be all her fault . . .

'Cleo.' Dylan looked at her as she reached for his empty plate. 'I am sorry. But why are you –?'

'Don't talk to her, Dylan,' Jessamine huffed. 'This dress is ruined.'

'It's not even touched, but I've already said I'll pay to have it dry-cleaned if that's what you want,' Dylan said shortly. 'It was my fault. But, Cleo –'

Cleo shook her head, clattered the last of the empty dishes onto her tray and, without speaking, backed out of the room.

Mercifully, the serving of the white chocolate and berry pudding went without incident. Dylan didn't look at her again, clearly knowing that thanks to her, despite his apologies, not only would he never be allowed inside Lovelady Hall again, but he was also about to join the ranks of the unemployed. Jessamine was gulping from her crystal goblet and was already cross-eyed, everyone else was also pretty drunk, and the conversation rose and fell in a low roar punctuated by raucous laughter.

Giovanni was right, Cleo thought as she returned to the sanctuary of the kitchen, it was all a thirty-second wonder. The supper party guests were happily inebriated, had moved on and forgotten all about it. She'd have to do the same.

Belly and Flip were now joyously munching on the

remains of the sea bass and Jersey Royals, surrounded by the car-crash remnants of the supper party.

'Zola and Zlinki is doing the cheese and fruit and biscuits,' Giovanni said from the kitchen doorway where he was dragging gratefully on a cigarette. 'And they can see to the coffees and the liqueurs as well. It won't take three of you. You've done well, pet. You can get off now if you want to.'

Cleo looked round the messy kitchen. 'Are you sure? You don't want a hand with sorting out this lot?'

'Bless you hinny, no. You're a waitress, not a skivvy. Them Phlopps might chomp their way through their body weight in leftovers, but they're demons when it comes to clearing up. That's why I employ thems. Thank you, pet. And don't give another thought to the little accident. Despite that, I can see you's got potential. I'd have you working with me again like a shot.'

'Would you?' Cleo said gratefully. 'That's very kind.'

'Not kind at all.' Giovanni flicked the end of his cigarette on to the immaculate gravel. 'You're a good worker and got a bit of a brain. Any time you want a bit of extra cash, pet, you know where to come, don't you?'

'Thank you.' Cleo beamed, her spirits rising.

There, she thought as she fumbled for her coat, bag and car keys, that was all OK. Now the only thing left was to talk to Mortimer on Monday and persuade him not to sack Dylan and then –

'Cleo?' Mimi appeared unsteadily in the kitchen doorway. 'Could I have a little word before you go?'

Cleo's rising spirits sank like a stone.

144

Giovanni, the Phlopps and Zola and Zlinki all watched warily.

The words 'marching orders' hung unspoken in the air.

'Just to say thank you and that I think you did very well.' Mimi's eyes glittered. 'Oh, I know there was that little mishap – but they can happen to anyone. And Dylan says it was all his fault, which I can well believe, and Jessamine is just a silly rabbit.'

'That's, um, very magnanimous of you.' Cleo stretched her lips into a smile. 'I'm really sorry . . .'

Mimi held up a hand. 'No. No, there's no need. It will be dealt with.'

'I should apologise to Jessamine properly though. And at least offer to pay to have the dress cleaned. Dylan shouldn't have to do that. And I don't want Dylan to lose his job because of me and –'

'Jessamine is the daughter of Blondy Burgess,' Mimi said. 'Blondy Burgess owns most of Sussex. Jessamine can afford three hundred of those frocks from her monthly clothes allowance. And Dylan was itching to come out here and speak to you himself but I expressly forbade it. He has to remember his manners. Jessamine is his partner for the evening. It would be crass in the extreme for him to leave her and come and apologise –'

'There's nothing for him to apologise for. It was an accident. But please don't sack him or anything. I was clumsy – it really was just a silly accident. Please, please, don't blame him, and please don't let Sir Mortimer fire him because of it.'

The kitchen had gone very quiet.

Mimi frowned. 'Ah, you know that Dylan works for Mortimer, then, do you?'

'Well,, yes . . . er . . . he . . . um . . . told me – and I know he must be out of his depth a bit, as I was, but . . .'

Mimi smiled. 'Cleo, my dear girl, Dylan wasn't slightly out of his depth. And it's very sweet of you to fight his corner, but I can assure you that he doesn't need you as his champion.'

'No, I'm sure he doesn't, but, well, jobs are scarce these days, and delivering cars for Mortimer must be like a dream and I know his flat goes with the post and –'

Mimi laughed. 'Oh, dear. Cleo – yes, Dylan is Mortimer's delivery driver. But please don't lose any sleep worrying about him. He won't lose his job. Or his home. Dylan is my son.'

Chapter Twelve

A week later, on a unseasonably warm September afternoon, Cleo looked up from the cooker as a shadow loomed in the caravan's open doorway.

'Go away!'

'That's not very friendly,' Dylan said, stepping inside and brandishing his mobile phone. 'I've even switched this off especially for you.'

'Is that supposed to impress me? Because it doesn't. Please go away.'

'We need to talk.'

'No, we don't. Go away and leave me alone.'

'No.' Dylan, wearing jeans and a navy-blue sweatshirt, didn't smile. 'We had a date today, remember?'

Cleo stopped stirring the suppurating blackberries and waved a deep-purple dripping spoon threateningly in his direction. 'Yes, but that was arranged before –'

'Before what?' Dylan ignored the spoon's glutinous threat and dropped lazily onto one of the tiny kitchen chairs, stretching his long legs out in front of him. 'Remind me. I've been away all week and –'

'You know very well before what,' Cleo hissed. 'Before I knew that you were Mimi's son. Before I knew that you were a lord or an earl or a duke or whatever you are. Before I knew that you'd be at that supper party, and, worse, as a member of the family. Before I knew that you were just a spoilt brat waste of space.'

Dylan looked shocked. 'Blimey, Cleo, that's a bit harsh, even for you. And why would I have told you anything about my parentage at our previous meetings? It wasn't relevant, and anyway you kept a few fairly pertinent secrets yourself, didn't you?'

'Such as?'

'Such as, why you didn't tell me that you worked for my mother?'

'Because I didn't know she was your chaffing mother, did I?'

'No, but you knew I worked for Mortimer because I'd already told you. Why didn't you say then that you were my mother's – Mimi's – new PA? That we both worked at Lovelady Hall? I would have considered that the natural thing to do.'

Cleo said nothing. Damn him. He was right there, of course. She should have told him. So why hadn't she? Because she was playing some silly game, wanting to surprise him, that's why. Well, she'd managed that, hadn't she?

She sighed. 'OK, yes, I should have mentioned it. But I didn't want to. For, well, for all sorts of reasons – but, God,

I wish I had. How embarrassed did you think I felt at that sodding dinner party?'

'Why embarrassed? You were absolutely great. And you looked so sexy in that waitress outfit. I was in shock, though, when I saw you. Thought I was dreaming.'

'Yeah, right.' Cleo left the blackberries and clattered a dozen or so scalded bottles on to the draining board. 'But everything has changed now, hasn't it? We met by chance, we seemed to get on well, we've had a couple of fun times together, but now, well, now it's all over.'

'Why?'

'Because of who you are. What you are.'

'Really?' Dylan laughed. It didn't sound humorous. 'And what exactly am I?'

Cleo slowly counted the empty bottles. Several times. She was finding it difficult to concentrate. Right – keep focused. With the bottles she'd already amassed, washed and ready in the shed, there were more than enough for the Razzle Dazzle Damson. And for the Blackberry Blush if Mad Molly's recipes worked and the wine fermented more or less overnight. Which she hoped fervently that they would as there was now only a week until Harvest Home.

Harvest Home at Lovelady Hall. Dylan's home. Dylan's minor stately home.

Oh, God . . .

'I'm waiting,' Dylan said slowly, 'to find out why we can no longer be friends?'

'You're my employer's son. You've probably got a title. You mingle with ladies like Jessamine –'

'Don't remind me. I've still got earache. Have you ever tried sitting next to a Clanger all night?'

'Jessamine was your hot date.'

'One of my overworn stock phrases. Jess was forced on me for Saturday night because Blondy Burgess, who donates gazillions to my mother's charities, couldn't make the party and sent sweet Jessamine instead. And etiquette said that she needed a supper partner. And my mother thought –'

Cleo sniffed. 'And if Blondy had been available, would you have partnered her, under parental orders?'

'Hardly. Blondy Burgess is a man. He's Jessamine's father.'

'Oh.'

'Anyway, enough of Jessamine – she's happily in the past – please carry on with why we can no longer be friends simply because I'm Mimi's son.'

'Because it changes everything, can't you see?'

'No, but I'm all ears.'

Cleo sighed and tried not to look at him. She had to do this. Even if it broke her heart. And, she thought miserably, it probably would. Hah! Steady, staid, sensible, doing-the-right-thing-all-her-life Cleo Moon had been stupid enough to tumble head over heels for the one man she could never have.

Fantastic.

'Right. Well, as you know, at first I just assumed you were some sort of rather sweet and amusing Hooray Henry who'd fallen on his feet by finding a wonderful job driving super-cars around the country. A job that required very little intellect but a great deal of charm. Charm, which you admitted you used, to get as many women into your bed as possible. Fast cars and even faster women – fair enough, every boy's fantasy lifestyle come true.'

'Mmm.' Dylan nodded. 'OK, can't deny any of that. I still fail to see why you working for my mother should make one jot of difference though.'

'Because it does. Upstairs, downstairs ring any bells? We're poles apart. No shared life experiences, no shared nothing. Our backgrounds couldn't be more different.'

'God, where do you get your ideas from? Somewhere in the 1800s? I don't give a toss about your background.'

'Don't you? Well, let me fill you in anyway. My parents live in Hazy Hassocks. My mum is a school secretary and gives herself airs and graces because of it. My dad works in a factory – blue collar – although my mum pretends he's management and makes him take his sandwiches in a brief-case. I don't see much of them any more for reasons I won't bore you with now. Oh, and I was born in a council house on the Bath Road Estate. See?'

'Thanks for sharing, but I'm not in the least interested.' Dylan shrugged. 'It's who you are that I like. Not where you came from. As it is with all my friends. And you aren't ashamed of your roots, are you?'

'Of course I'm not!'

'Good. I loathe inverted snobs. Or snobs any way up actually. And none of that makes any difference to us being friends.'

'It does.'

'No, it doesn't. I think, whatever you might say to the contrary, that you *are* an inverted snob and a closet Bolshevik to boot. You're probably Red Ron Reynolds's second in command.'

Cleo flinched, thinking of Elvi and Zeb. 'No, I'm bloody not!'

'Sorry, but that's the way it looks to me. You're saying that because you're so-called working class and I'm so-called not, that we can't be friends, aren't you? That because of your preconceived outmoded notions of the class system, never the twain shall meet? That because of the accidents of our birth, we have absolutely nothing in common and therefore must live in our separate boxes?'

'No!' Cleo shook her head. 'Don't twist things.'

'Then, why?' Dylan sniffed. 'Oh, and I think your blackberries are burning.'

'Bugger!' Cleo snatched the huge saucepan's handle and hauled it from the cooker.

'Careful you don't spill anything.'

'Shut up!'

'Humour bypass alert.' Dylan snorted happily. 'And what are you brewing today?'

'Blackberry Blush. And don't change the subject.'

'Wouldn't dream of it? Oh, I haven't missed the Damson test-drive, have I?'

'No.' Cleo stirred the huge vat of blackberries, hoping they weren't too burned. No, they seemed OK. 'Oh, look – just try to see this from my point of view. All the time I was growing-up, my mother had this huge class chip on her shoulder. It was drummed into us that we were the lower orders. She desperately wanted to climb higher, but it didn't matter how much she yearned to be upper class, sadly breeding is in the genes. Before I became old enough to realise that she actually wasn't a very nice person – which is another story entirely – she was my mum and I loved her. And I *hated* the people who made her unhappy.'

'That's really sad, but –'

'You weren't there. It was all-consuming with her. It killed me as a kid to eventually realise that she could never have the one thing she wanted in life. She could use the right words, avoid the wrong ones, speak with strangulated vowels and read *Tatler*, but she'd never be a lady.'

'Can't imagine why she'd want to be.' Dylan frowned. 'Given some of the ladies I've known. Never mind, go on.'

'She was a snob and it ruined her life. And mine. She aped the upper classes and it was just sad. I felt sorry for her, of course, but I also hated the fact that there were people who simply took for granted the things that she'd die to have and never could.'

'People like me?'

Cleo nodded. 'Exactly. When we first met, naturally I knew you were well bred, and well educated. OK. That didn't faze me. Whatever problems my mother has, I'm not afraid of *class*.'

'Good. Carry on.'

Cleo wasn't actually sure that she could. Not without letting him know that the main reason she felt they could no longer be friends was now nothing to do with her mother's aspirations and everything to do with her own wanting to be more than that – and now knowing it really, really wouldn't work. Forget Elvi and Zeb – there was no way on earth that Dylan, with his background, and his reliance on the Pashley-Royle fortune, and his endless collection of *suitable* upper-class girlfriends, would ever consider a serious relationship with anyone like her.

Older, working class, a family skivvy – and infertile.

And as for Mimi and Mortimer – oh, just forget it!

Oh, yes, Dylan would happily bed her, probably in the age-old tradition of Cleo's favourite historical romance novels where the young master had his pick of the under-stairs staff, but there could never be a proper relationship.

And, she thought sadly, that was the one thing she wanted.

'OK,' she leaned against the draining board and looked at him, hoping that her true feelings wouldn't show. 'We can't be friends because I *despise* what you are.'

'Despise? Jesus Christ! That's a pretty bloody insulting word. And you've just said –'

'I don't mean your wealthy upper-class pedigree, that's not the issue – or your fault. The issue is what you've done with the gifts you've inherited. Which is precisely nothing. You're just a lazy little rich kid.'

Dylan frowned. 'Don't hold back. Say what you mean.'

Cleo ignored the jibe. 'OK, a very charming lazy little rich kid, but it's been so easy for you, hasn't it? You've taken everything for granted – education, money, all the trappings of a wealthy and privileged upbringing – and then took the easy way out. You didn't even need to look for a job. You just started working for Mummy – oh, well, in this case, Daddy. Driving cars most blokes would kill for. Bedding women. And . . . And, well, just wasting your time in hedonistic pleasure, and never having to worry about earning a proper living or worrying about money – simply because you could.'

There! She swallowed. Now Dylan would just storm out and she'd never see him again.

But he didn't.

He laughed. 'Rant over? OK. And touché – because you're right on most counts there. But can you blame me for taking the easy ride? Isn't that what most people would do in my circumstances? However, you did get one thing very wrong in that deadly character assassination.'

'I don't think so.'

'Yes, you did. Mort isn't my father, he's my step-father. My second step-father, actually. The first one decamped when I was at school. Which, in case you're interested in adding it to my list of sins, was Millfield. Followed, I'm gutted to admit because it adheres to your stereotype, by Oxford. Although you might be happy to know that I didn't complete my degree and was sent down at the end of my second year.'

'See?' Cleo shook her head. 'You had the privilege of being educated at one of the greatest universities in the world, and you threw that away too. Because you could. Because it didn't matter. Whereas kids like . . . like Elvi next door are startlingly intelligent and deserve to go to Oxford, but there's probably no way on earth her family can afford for her to go there and —'

'That's a real shame — and actually I think you'll find the major universities are increasing their state school intake these days — but the system is definitely not my fault,' Dylan argued. 'And why I left Oxford is nothing to do with this discussion. So, leaving educational opportunities to one side, where had we got to?'

'God knows,' Cleo sighed. 'Oh yes, the fact that Mortimer isn't you father.'

'Ah, yes . . . not much more to say, really. After step-daddy one had buggered off, my mother met up with Mort and fell in love with him. And he with her. And they still are. So, adorable as he is, Mort's not my father. My father was some snake-hipped rock star.'

'Really?' Cleo blinked in surprise, fascinated now despite her anger. 'So, Mimi's first marriage was to a famous musician was it? Crikey. So is that where the Maguire comes from?'

'Lord, no. Maguire is my mother's family name. The rock star remains nameless and faceless . . . so many gigs, so many hotel bedrooms apparently. No, I've never had the slightest interest in tracing him. My mother was seventeen when I was born. So, yes, you're right, I'm a bastard.'

'Oh, look, no — I didn't mean . . .'

Dylan laughed. 'In her youth, my mother was what the red-tops then called a "wild child". I think I must have inherited her anti-establishment genes, thank God. She shook off all the trappings of a comfortable and wealthy home life and a finishing school education and became a bit of a barefoot contessa on the rock scene. And I'm so bloody glad she did.'

Cleo felt the first stirrings of guilt. 'Oh, I just assumed –'

'Assumption is the mother of all fuck-ups,' Dylan said cheerfully. 'Now you've got all that class crap off your chest, and I've bared my overprivileged soul, why don't we carry on where we left off last Friday and get a move on with this wine? We really should make sure Mad Molly knew what she was talking about and that it's drinkable and not like neat Domestos, shouldn't we?'

'We should,' she agreed sheepishly, 'as we've only got a week until –'

'Harvest Home? That's when you're intending to uncork it, right?'

'Right,' Cleo admitted. 'Something else I suppose I should have told you.'

'Yes, you should. But now I know all about that too, from my mother, of course. She doesn't know about the wine, naturally, but she's been raving about the way you've got everything organised this week. She says it'll be the best Harvest Home ever – because you're a "simply super little trooper, darling".'

Cleo laughed at the spot-on impersonation. 'That's very flattering – I only hope I've managed to pull everything together to her satisfaction because I haven't seen her at all. Because she's been fund-raising round the country, I've had to handle all of it on my own. It's been a hell of a week. Oh, and did she ask you how we knew one another?'

Dylan nodded. 'I told her the truth. About me being dazed and confused and forgetting that Olive no longer lived here. She told me I was lucky you didn't run me off the encampment with a twelve-bore.' He sighed. 'My mother is still slightly out of touch with reality. But basically lovely.'

Cleo smiled at him. 'She is – and, Dylan, I'm really, really sorry for being such a precious prat. I shouldn't have – Well, can we forget all about, well, all of the other stuff?'

'Did you mean it?'

'Yes – well, some of it. Most of it. It's been with me a long time. Oh, I can't expect you to understand. But I probably shouldn't have let off steam quite so vehemently.'

Understatement, Cleo thought.

'No, you probably shouldn't. And a lesser man may well have been cut to the quick and turned on his heel twirling his moustaches, or whatever spurned suitors do in your class-conscious fevered imagination.'

'You're not a spurned suitor. And you don't have moustaches.'

'I could grow them if you liked.'

'I don't.' Cleo shook her head quickly. 'So, as a magnanimous and generous clean-shaven unspurned non-suitor, can you forget our little, um, difference of opinion?'

'Not really.' Dylan stared assembling bottles. 'Because it's taught us a lot about us, don't you think? But if we're going to stay friends it's probably better not to dwell on it. I always think it's nice to have things out in the open, even if they're all based on crap. And for your information only, in case you think I'm hiding anything else about my blue-blooded background, I have a younger step-brother who's really cool.'

Zeb.

Cleo knew, under the circumstances, she should say that she knew. But Zeb was Elvi's secret and would stay that way. Oh, Lordy, there were still so many machinations going on . . .

'He's called Zeb,' Dylan continued. 'And I also have a half-sister – from my mother's brief first marriage. She lives in Australia. Married. Two kids. And this will make you laugh – she's called Florence.'

Cleo paused in opening the cupboard by the cooker and hauling out the air-locked demijohns of Razzle Dazzle Damson. 'Why would I laugh? Florence is a nice name. Pretty. Old-fashioned – not at all funny.'

'Mmm.' Dylan nodded. 'But I wasn't called Dylan because my mother had a penchant for the music of Bob Dylan or even the poetry of Dylan Thomas.'

'And?'

'And, if I said that it wouldn't have surprised me if Zeb had been christened Brian, and it was touch-and-go whether or not he actually got named Dougal . . .?'

'So?' Cleo frowned.

'Zeb is short for Zebedee.'

'Zebedee?' Cleo paused for a moment, then shrieked with laughter. 'No way! You mean – you're Dylan because . . . because you're named after the spacey rabbit in *The Magic Roundabout*?'

'Precisely. My mother's ongoing obsession. And please be

assured I only share that information with very, very good friends.'

'Then I'm flattered, and your secret's safe with me,' Cleo giggled. 'Now, let's get on with getting this fermented wine decanted into bottles before it's too late.'

Chapter Thirteen

Raking through the winemaking equipment for funnels and corks, Cleo felt that they'd aired their differences and managed to resume their easy-going friendship. She hoped knowing that was all it was ever going to be would be enough for her.

While Dylan concentrated on decanting the rich, ruby-red wine into the odd assortment of bottles, Cleo wondered if he'd told Mimi where he was spending this afternoon.

Nah. That would be a step too far down the classless society path. Cleo chuckled to herself. One couldn't have it all, could one?

And this, Cleo realised, watching Dylan happily manhandling the demijohns, was a darn sight better than nothing.

So near and yet so far. Ah, well . . .

Eventually, the filled and corked wine bottles stood on the draining board, glowing like deep-crimson fire in the sunlight.

'Maybe Molly did know her winemaking onions. It looks

fantastically clear, and it smells just right,' Dylan said as they stood back and admired their handiwork. 'Vibrant mucky tones of rubber and creosote with a little under-ripple of dead mushrooms.'

Cleo punched him.

'Ouch. So, how many bottles have we got?'

'Thirteen. And a bit leftover.'

'For test-driving?'

'Yes –' Cleo nodded '– but it's still not going to be enough for Harvest Home, is it? Thirteen bottles won't go very far. That's why I wanted to make the Blackberry Blush today as well.'

Dylan frowned. 'Did you use the Lovers Cascade water for that too?'

'Yes, of course. If we believe Mad Molly, then it's the only chance we've got of making it drinkable in time. Why?'

'Because we collected it over a week ago. It'll be rancid by now. And we haven't got time to get any more today if you want to brew another batch.'

'I thought of that. I froze it.' Cleo smiled smugly. 'In every little plastic container I could find. Stacked them in the chest freezer in the shed. Melted them as needed. Next question?'

Dylan held up his hands. 'I'm impressed. No more questions. Well, just one – do you think we should make another flavour, as well as the damson and this blackberry? This'll be your first Harvest Home – but let me tell you, they don't hold back on their drinking. Oh, I know there'll be plenty of other booze at the party courtesy of Mort's cellar, but if the wine's a hit and then runs out it'll be carnage. What other sorts are there?'

'All Mad Molly's stuff is over there on the table. Have a look. I've got tons of fruit in the freezer, there's enough Lovers Cascade water for another gallon or so, which means we could make just over another dozen bottles of something – so take your pick.'

While Dylan leafed through the books' fragile pages, Cleo tipped the leftover Razzle Dazzle Damson into a spare bottle and looked for two glasses.

'You know,' Dylan murmured, 'there're all sorts of scribbled crossings outs and cautionary notes on all these recipes – just like there was on the Razzle Dazzle. Sadly, they've all been blurred by damp or nibbled by mice and are indecipherable, but Mad Molly really does seem to want to add something to warn anyone who makes this stuff about – No, damn, I can't make it out at all.'

'I wouldn't worry about it too much. Look, there's no way on earth I'd put anyone at risk. I've thought about those notes a lot, and my guess is that Molly's warnings are in case anyone else got hold of these recipe books in the good old days, and mixed in some noxious poisoned herbs or something.'

Dylan nodded. 'Like she must have done? Yeah, that makes sense. Whereas we in the twenty-first century, being horribly aware of the dire consequences of pissing off the health and safety brigade, have made Boringly Safe Wine?'

Cleo laughed. 'I hope not! I hope it's Wildly Exciting Wine. But after all, we do know we've made the wine with

163

proper ingredients, don't we? We haven't added anything in the least toxic and know exactly what's in it. It can't possibly hurt anyone, can it? So, have you found another recipe you like?'

'I have.'

'And?'

'Sloe Seduction.'

Oh, God, he was so gorgeous . . .

'OK.' She smiled brightly. 'Sounds like fun – and I've got loads of sloes. So, you follow Molly's instructions about what to mix into the blackberries – I think it's just sugar syrup, which is over there, and those grated lemons, oh, and the tannin, into the Lovers Cascade water and store the buckets in the warm cupboard, and I'll start defrosting the sloes.'

He grinned at her. 'I love it when you're all bossy. Reminds me of –'

'I don't want to know! Just get on with it.'

'Yes, miss. Of course, miss. Whatever you say, miss.'

She hurled the tea towel at him. 'Seriously, if we can get the Blackberry Blush done today and start the sloe one off as well, then we'll have – what? Around three dozen bottles of wine for Harvest Home. Will that be enough?'

'For me? Plenty, thanks. The others will have to make do with the Pashley-Royle contribution of barrels of real ales and champagne mountains of Cristal and Krug, poor sods. OK, lead me shackled to the coalface . . .'

It was almost dusk by the time they'd finished. The kitchen was awash with fabulous rich, fruity scents, and deep-purple stains from the blackberries and sloes adorned nearly every surface.

'I'm totally knackered.' Dylan slumped back on to the kitchen chair. 'But I reckon we'll have made enough wine to keep the villagers happy. Wonder what proof it is?'

'Lethal I should imagine.' Cleo pushed her hair away from her face. 'Which is all to the good. Thanks for helping. You've been a star. Especially after all those crass things I said earlier.'

'I know.' Dylan beamed. 'I'm lovely like that – even if I am an upper-class sponging playboy who has never done a decent day's work in his life. Right, now I think we deserve a little treat, don't you? Where's the leftover Razzle Dazzle Damson?'

'Here.'

'Grab the glasses then, and we'll go and test-drive it in style.'

Cleo looked wary. 'You haven't got a Lamborghini or something parked outside, have you? I don't think you should be driving after drinking this stuff – even if it is only one glass.'

'Wouldn't dream of it. No car today. I walked from Lovelady. And I have a much better idea for the ideal spot to toast our winemaking future enterprise. Come on.'

Following him, Cleo locked the caravan, looking round warily in case Elvi was anywhere in the vicinity. She really didn't want to be confronted by Elvi right now. Not while she was with Dylan. How could she explain that? It was all far too complicated.

Fortunately, Mimi's absence and the Harvest Home organisation had kept Cleo working late all week, and she'd arrived home each night exhausted and only fit for a bath and a lovely wallow in front of the television. Elvi, even if she had wanted to visit and discuss all manner of teenage angst and heartbreak, would have found Cleo sound asleep on the sofa with a rerun of *Friends* playing to no one but the fripperies.

So whatever Elvi had decide to do about Zeb and their forbidden love affair, still remained a mystery.

Cleo had somehow imagined that Dylan was going to head in the direction of Lovers Spinney once they'd left the caravan site, but he turned towards the village instead.

'Such a gorgeous evening,' he said cheerfully. 'Far too nice to stay stuck indoors, especially after all our hard work. Can't imagine why people want to keep hopping off abroad when it's like this. Nothing beats autumn in England when there's a hint of an Indian summer round the corner, does it?'

Cleo, who hadn't travelled very far outside England ever, simply nodded. It was typical of extremely wealthy people, she thought sadly, to assume that everyone could afford to pop off on foreign jaunts at the drop of a hat.

'It'll make Harvest Home much easier if it stays fine,' Cleo agreed, 'as it's traditionally supposed to be held in the open air, isn't it? You must have had some stinkers when it poured with rain or was freezing cold.'

'We have, and everyone grizzled a lot and huddled in the barn and got very drunk very quickly and went home early on those occasions.' He grinned at her. 'But somehow I've got a feeling that this one is going to be just perfect.'

Cleo exhaled. She somehow doubted it. Not with all that star-crossed lover stuff floating around, not to mention the role reversal of the Pashley-Royles waiting on the villagers, and the likes of Ron Reynolds getting tanked up on what was probably neat alcohol. And then there were the added Lovers Knot oddities of Rodders, Salome, Jerome, Mrs Hancock and the rest to throw into the mix.

Lordy, it didn't bear thinking about.

Lovers Knot was really pretty though, she thought dreamily, as they walked across the green side by side. So silent, so cut off from the rest of the world, and with the leaves of the spinney surrounding them in glorious autumnal colours and the gauzy setting sun slanting across the cottage roofs, it was truly idyllic.

'I thought this would be an ideal spot to test-drive the Razzle Dazzle Damson,' Dylan said, indicating the rustic bench opposite the huddle of pretty cottages. 'Quiet. Picture-perfect countrified. Every city dweller's dream of rural bliss. And as everyone else in Lovers Knot seems to be incarcerated indoors glued to their television sets, we should be completely undisturbed.'

Amused and impressed that he displayed perfect manners in waiting for her to be seated first, Cleo sat down beside him, close but not touching. She'd never touch him again.

Sod it.

'Mmm.' She breathed in the warm sweet-scented air. 'It's perfect. Just like a spring evening. So still. So quiet. And if this plonk of Mad Molly's turns us into drunken slobs after one sip, we won't have very far to crawl home.'

'Right.' Dylan flourished the bottle of damson wine. 'The moment of truth. Was Mad Molly truly insane, or did she really have some sort of deal going with the Lovers Cascade fairies?'

Cleo held the glasses as the Razzle Dazzle Damson glugged fruitily and crimson clear.

'Bugger,' Dylan sighed, holding his half-filled glass up to the sunlight. 'How boring was that? I at least thought there'd be small elfin creatures whizzing round in a smattering of stars, or distant shrills of supernatural laughter.'

'From overexcited snotlings, I suppose?' Cleo raised her glass to his. 'Nah. Nothing. Shame. Although it seems as though Mad Molly was right on one thing – this looks like a perfectly drinkable red. So the Lovers Cascade water must have speeded up the fermentation process, only obviously using the more boring and prosaic chemicals-in-the-rocks method.'

'Cheers anyway.' Dylan chinked his glass against hers. 'Despite our clearly insurmountable social differences, here's to our home-made wine being the talk of this year's Harvest Home.'

'I'll drink to that,' Cleo said happily. 'Cheers!'

But before they'd managed to raise the glasses to their lips, a husky voice interrupted them. 'Evening, young Cleo. And young master Dylan.'

Cleo turned her head and groaned.

Rodders in his dirty coat and even dirtier cloth cap, was

stomping across the green behind them, his vast collection of extendable poles slung over his disreputable shoulder.

'Just needs to check that there drain beside the bench,' Rodders said, crashing the poles to the ground. 'Mr Burnham up the cottages is 'aving trouble with his lav again. You carry on 'aving yer wine. I won't get in yer way.'

Cleo looked at Dylan and giggled.

'Whoa.' Dylan grimaced as Rodders wrenched the top off the drain with a lot of clanking. 'Is that him or the effluent?'

'Both I think,' Cleo muttered. 'So much for this being the idyllic spot for the wine tasting. Oooh, dear, that reeks.'

Rodders poked and prodded the murky depths with huge enthusiasm. And sang. Loudly. Off key.

'Yoo-hoo, you two!' Mrs Hancock, carrying a huge, overfed tabby cat in her arms, waved at them from the deep evening shadows outside the general stores. 'Lovely weather, isn't it?'

'Christ,' Dylan groaned, his hand over his nose. 'She's coming over.'

'Don't you like cats?' Cleo yelled above the singing and the rodding.

'Love cats. Adore cats. Just didn't want to share this moment with anyone except you.'

'Ah, sweet . . . Oh, God. That smell is truly foul. Er, hello, Mrs Hancock. Is this one of yours?'

'Just found him up there by the big houses. Poor pet, clearly starved. I'm going to take him home and feed him up. He'll soon fit in nicely with the rest of my little family.' Mrs Hancock settled fussily beside Dylan on the bench with the cat on her lap. 'Hello, Rodders. Mr Burnham's lav blocked again, is it?'

'Ah. Bad this time. Up to the brim.'

Dylan snorted.

'Careful,' Cleo chuckled. 'You'll spill the wine.'

'It somehow suddenly seems to have lost its appeal.' Dylan leaned across and tickled the fat cat under its tabby chin. 'Ah, bless. He's purring.'

I'm not surprised, Cleo thought wistfully.

'Oh, no way.' She blinked as Rodders got to grips with the blockage and the aroma grew even stronger. 'And, dear God . . .'

'Hiya, Cleo and Mr Maguire.'

'Hello, Jerome,' Dylan said warmly as Jerome galloped across the green towards them. 'That's a nice hat.'

'Thank you. This one's my best Davy Crockett,' Jerome said cheerfully, carefully tethering his imaginary horse to an imaginary hitching post before squeezing himself alongside Cleo. 'One day I'm going to get a Hopalong Cassidy hat, but that'll be a Stetson and it won't be furry, which is a shame.'

Cleo nodded with sympathetic understanding. Words, she felt, were unnecessary.

'Is that wine?' Jerome stared at their glasses. 'I'm not allowed to have wine. Mum says it makes me go silly.'

'Your mum's right,' Dylan said. 'Wine makes people go very silly indeed.'

Jerome nodded wisely, and watched Rodders and his delving intently for a moment, then leaned across Cleo and

Dylan. 'Excuse me, please. That's a lovely cat, Mrs Hancock. I think he belongs to Mr and Mrs Dryden in the big houses. I think his name's Fluffy. It'll say so on his collar.'

'His name's Michael and he belongs to me now,' Mrs Hancock hugged the stout tabby even tighter. 'And don't you go fiddling with his collar.'

Cleo and Dylan looked helplessly at one another.

'Got 'im!' Rodders shouted triumphantly, reeling violently as the rods lost their purchase and disappeared into the drain with a disgusting slurping sound. 'Ah! That's dislodged the bugger!'

'God almighty!' Dylan closed his eyes. 'That's rank.'

'And that's blasphemy, Mr Maguire, if you don't mind me saying so.' Jerome flicked the tail of his raccoon-skin cap jauntily over one shoulder. 'You shouldn't blaspheme.'

'No, I shouldn't. Sorry,' Dylan muttered.

Cleo looked at him. His shoulders were shaking.

'Welcome to the true rural idyll of Lovers Knot,' she giggled. 'And so much for the perfect bucolic tranquillity and seclusion of an autumn evening.'

'And the wine-tasting,' Dylan said. 'Somehow the ambience has gone.'

'Let's go somewhere else then,' Cleo said as Rodders started hauling all manner of unmentionable detritus from the drain. 'We could go back to the caravan. I could cook us something – and we could have the Razzle Dazzle Damson test-drive as an accompaniment.'

Dylan sighed. 'Sorry, Cleo. I'd really love to, but I can't. We'll have to make it another night. I've, um, got other plans for this evening. In fact –' he glanced at his watch '– I'm late as it is. I do apologise, but I'll have to love you and leave you.'

I just wish you could love me and *not* leave me, Cleo thought wistfully.

Dylan stood up and held out his hand. Cleo, feeling as though someone had just snuffed out the sun, ignored it as she got to her feet.

'Promise you won't drink the Razzle Dazzle Damson without me?' He smiled at her. 'And I'll see you soon. Really soon. At work if not before?'

She sketched a fleeting smile. 'Yes, yes, of course. And, um, thanks for your help this afternoon.'

'My pleasure. Again. It's been brilliant fun. Oh, sorry, but I've really go to dash.'

And with Rodders, Jerome and Mrs Hancock all waving him goodbye, Dylan strode off in the direction of Lovelady Hall.

Off to spend the night with some gorgeous society lady, Cleo thought miserably. Someone called Annabelle or Jemima or Polly. Someone who was used to eating samphire and holidaying in places like Juan-les-Pins. Someone who was eminently suitable for the gorgeously sexy but way-out-of-her-league son of Mimi Pashley-Royle.

Sadly, she raised the glass of wine to her lips and took a small sip. Oh, it tasted absolutely wonderful, like liquid sunshine. She swilled it round her mouth, delighting in the flavours that burst onto her tongue, longing to drink the whole glass. But no, she couldn't do it. Not without Dylan there to share it.

She'd have to behave as if it were a proper tasting session . . .

Cleo turned and spat the mouthful of wine into Rodder's open drain.

Jerome looked at her with deep sorrow. 'Was that nasty, Cleo?'

'Um, yes, sort of.'

'I do that with my mum's cocoa,' Jerome said confidentially. 'When it has grit in it. Cocoa shouldn't really have grit in it, should it?'

'No, it shouldn't. My wine was, um, a bit gritty too. Well, I suppose I ought to go home now.'

With them all making their village-polite farewells, Rodders replaced the drain cover, Mrs Hancock and fat-cat Michael hauled themselves to their feet, and Jerome unhitched his imaginary horse.

The floor show was over.

In the gathering twilight, Cleo turned and trudged back towards her caravan.

Jerome, his racoon-skin cap tails flying, galloped past her, pointing his imaginary six-shooter. 'Bang-bang! You're dead!'

I might not be, Cleo thought sadly, watching Jerome canter towards the caravan park, but I think my dreams definitely are.

Chapter Fourteen

'Ohmigod.' Elvi's hand shook as she drew the final smudgy lines of kohl round her eyes. 'It's today. It's really, truly today.'

Harvest Home. At last. At long, long last.

And Zeb was *here*. Well, not exactly in Lovers Knot Caravan Park of course, but home at Lovelady Hall. She knew he was. He'd texted her at just after midnight when he'd arrived. And he'd driven from Gorse Glade *in his own car*. How totally mint was that? *She* had a boyfriend with a *car*. And he'd come home in it – to see *her*. Well, OK, for his parents' party too, but mainly to see her.

And he'd had to get special dispensation for a weekend pass and miss Saturday morning studies to even be allowed out of Gorse Glade.

And he'd done it for her.

Zeb was *here*.

And tonight she'd be with him again.

Elvi, glowing from the shower and smothered in Angel, jigged excitedly in the tiny crowded space between the foot of her bed and the miniature fitted dressing table-wardrobe unit, tripping over discarded clothes.

All week she'd been wondering what to wear, trying on everything she possessed, wishing she had enough money to buy something new, but now it didn't matter.

Now she knew it just had to be her favourite super-trendy skinny jeans and black vest, with the tight black and grey pinstripe waistcoat over the top. And her flat silver ballet pumps because she didn't want to be taller than Zeb. And some silver bangles to make the Kate Moss-ish 'boyfriend' outfit look slightly more feminine.

Elvi grinned at herself in the tiny mirror. Her freshly washed hair looked OK and she hadn't developed any spots. And as Zeb had only ever seen her in her school uniform and without any make-up on, anything would be an improvement, wouldn't it?

Oh, it was still only ten o'clock. At least ten hours still to go. How on earth was she going to be able to wait until this evening?

Elvi knelt on her just-less-than-single bed and pulled up the blind.

Fabulous!

The sun sparkled from a cloudless azure blue September sky, the morning was already warm, and the leaves, tinged with gold, hung motionless. It was going to be perfect.

Next door, she could see that Cleo's curtains were open. Cleo was probably already up at Lovelady Hall, sorting out the seating and organising the streams of villagers as they arrived with the food and running around with clipboards and a mobile phone, no doubt being driven insane by Mimi every step of the way.

Lucky, lucky Cleo. She was, at this very minute, breathing the same air as Zeb . . .

Elvi smiled. Cleo was so lovely. So sensible about everything. It was shame she hadn't been in all week, Elvi thought, because it would have been great to tell her that she'd taken her advice and gone to the clinic in Winterbrook.

Sophie and Kate had been a bit of a pain, wanting to know why she wasn't catching the after-school bus home, but she'd eventually said she had a dental appointment – not that she thought they believed her as they knew her dentist was in Hazy Hassocks – and managed to escape.

The clinic people had been great, as Cleo had said they would be, and it hadn't been too embarrassing, and they hadn't preached or anything. And now she had a supply of contraceptive pills in her bedside drawer, hidden under her make-up bags well out of sight of the eagle eyes of her mum, or, even worse, the prying fingers of her younger brothers.

The lady at the clinic had said the pills wouldn't become effective straight away, so she and her partner must take extra precautions to start with, then there'd been some other gross stuff about infections and diseases – which of course couldn't possibly apply to her and Zeb, but she'd listened anyway and nodded.

So, that was all sorted. Not that Zeb knew, of course. They'd texted each other about everything, but not *that*. *That*, Elvi thought, would seem as though she was some sad slapper – and anyway, when *it* happened it would be wonderful and spontaneous. She'd hate Zeb to think she'd *planned* it.

What they hadn't actually planned was how they were going to behave tonight. Elvi shrugged. It didn't matter. Not any more. The only thing that mattered was that she and Zeb were going to be together.

And there was nothing her dad could do about it.

Her dad, she knew, would say he wasn't going to Harvest Home tonight, like he always did, because he wasn't going to play silly buggers and dance to the whims of the likes of the Pashley-Royles. But he'd go, like he always did, and glower for a while, then get a bit drunk and eventually enjoy himself, not that he'd ever admit it.

All that stuff she'd said to Cleo about her dad's views on the class system and her fears that she and Zeb wouldn't ever be together, had been true, of course, Elvi thought. But then, that night she'd been panicking that Zeb might not want to see her again. She'd got herself really putridly *down* about the whole thing. Since then Zeb's texts had reassured her a million times that she had absolutely nothing to worry about. Leave it to him, he'd said, he'd manage everything. And she totally believed him now.

So, if only, Elvi thought wistfully, her dad would talk to Zeb at Harvest Home tonight and realise that he was a normal person. A gorgeous, lovely, funny, normal person. That this class thing was ridiculous. That no one cared about it any more.

It wasn't going to happen . . . Or maybe it would . . .

177

Elvi shook her head. It really didn't matter. She knew, with all the ferocity of a teenager madly in love for the first time, that if it came down to choosing between her dad and Zeb – well, her dad would just have to lump it.

Her parents would be upset, of course, but she was sure her mum would be able to talk Dad round eventually. After all, they loved her, and this was her happiness they were dealing with here.

Anyway, Elvi thought as she picked up her iPod, she'd just play it by ear tonight. She'd wait for Zeb to make the first move, then she'd follow his cue. And if her dad did anything crass she knew she'd hate him for ever. And if he was *rude* to Zeb – well! Elvi puffed out her cheeks. That didn't even bear thinking about.

Oh, God – still nine hours, fifty-six minutes to go . . .

At Lovelady Hall, Cleo, in her work outfit of jeans and T-shirt, consulted her mental tick-list. She gazed at the hay bales surrounding the courtyard for seating; the long trestle tables already covered in starched white cloths; the spit erected in one corner for the pig roast already blazing away; the sound system set up for suitable cheerful dancing music; the dozens of fairy lights twisted round every conceivable structure; and at the ancient bunting hanging listlessly in the still, warm air.

All there. All in order.

Harvest Home was going to be just perfect.

Nearly midday. She'd been at Lovelady since first light, making sure that her arrangements had all gone flawlessly;

that everything was in place; that the electricians had been in and connected up all the wires properly; that everything worked exactly as it should.

Just before nine o'clock the totally stunning gardener, Rocky Lancaster, had arrived with his coterie of youthful apprentices and fixed hanging baskets of tumbling autumnal flowers and foliage around the courtyard.

Cleo had allowed herself a moment's sheer pleasure, watching so many gorgeous young men climbing ladders and bending and stretching and displaying firm flesh and even firmer muscles.

Although, she'd thought to herself afterwards, divine as Rocky Lancaster is, I wouldn't swap him for Dylan . . .

Then she'd had to give herself a severe mental telling-off for even thinking such a stupid thing about someone who clearly had no time for her at all, and had busied herself immediately in counting paper napkins, suddenly overwhelmed with longing.

Not that she'd had time to dwell on her foolishness for long. A never-ending stream of villagers had started arriving with their contributions for the party, and she'd been swamped by the vast quantities of food – all of which now reposed under cling-film wraps in Mimi's towering American-style refrigerators.

Ticking off the items on her clipboard as they were delivered, Cleo had been delighted that her organisational skills really seemed to have worked. There had been no duplications, everyone had brought exactly what they'd said they'd bring, and it all looked wonderful.

And her own contribution to the party, just over three dozen bottles of wine, was nestling in the icy-cold, hushed and darkened confines of the Pashley-Royle cellar. Manoeuvring so many bottles down into the cellar had threatened to defeat her, but just as she'd been going to call for help, she'd discovered an ancient dumb-waiter device – clearly designed for hauling flagons of mead up to the Lovelady Hall dining rooms in the good old days – and with much creaking and eye-watering clouds of dust, Mad Molly's assorted brews disappeared from view.

So, the wine – still properly untested – but looking gloriously, drinkably *real*, was safely here. As was Mary Benwell's goat's cheese and Geoff Glass's apple pies and the Phlopps' sponge cakes and practically every other home-made party delicacy anyone could wish for. And some, she thought, that you really wouldn't want to eat . . .

Rodders had brought misshapen pork pies, and Wilf and Maudie, with Jerome galloping alongside, had produced a sort of gelatinous pea and ham soup which they assured her was 'right tasty' eaten cold. Salome had supplied cheese and onion tarts – which Cleo had thought was very apt – and Mrs Hopkins had made a trifle liberally scattered with hundreds and thousands and an awful lot of cat fur.

But on the whole, Cleo nodded round the courtyard again, she really thought it was all going to be perfect.

Except for Dylan.

Infuriatingly, Dylan had again been away from Lovelady all week. She knew from Mimi that he'd had to go 'up north' on Monday to deliver a Ferrari for a Premiership footballer. But would that really have taken him all this time? Surely not. Cleo had convinced herself by Thursday that Dylan had fallen into the French-manicured clutches of an abandoned WAG and wouldn't be seen again until he appeared on the pages of some glossy celeb magazine.

'I hope he remembers to come back in time for Harvest Home,' Mimi had said distractedly. 'It won't be the same without him.'

Too damn right it won't, Cleo had thought despondently.

And how did he get back home from his trips away, anyway? Did he hitch-hike on the entrance to the motorway slip roads, clutching trade number plates? Cleo had seen this phenomena many times and never quite understood what was going on. Or did he simply catch a train back to Reading railway station and wait for the local bus to Lovers Knot from there? Cleo somehow couldn't see Dylan on a bus, mingling with the likes of Belly and Flip. Maybe a taxi for the return trip was supplied by Mortimer as part of the job? Or maybe, and far more likely, whichever bit of feminine pleasure he mixed with his prolonged business, always drove him safely back to Berkshire as a thank you?

It was all a bit baffling and maybe something she'd ask him when she saw him again. *If* she saw him again. If he hadn't decamped properly this time with someone called Georgiana or Aphrodite who was fresh back from topping up her tan in Tobago or having her toenails waxed in Monaco.

Anyway, Cleo thought now as she counted boxes of paper plates and plastic cutlery and polystyrene beakers, Dylan had made it quite clear at the abortive wine-tasting that he wasn't interested in her as anything more than a friend, hadn't he? He couldn't have spelled it out any clearer. She blushed at the memory. She'd invited him back to the caravan and he'd immediately turned her down. For a much more pressing engagement.

Oh, Lordy . . .

Well, she wouldn't make the same mistake twice. Friends, yes; anything else, no bloody way. Even if it did break her heart.

'Cleo!' Mimi, dressed in white linen trousers and a vivid yellow jumper, waved from the archway. 'Good morning, Cleo, dear – or should I say afternoon? Sorry to have left you with all this, Mortimer and I have been having a little lie-in in preparation for the festivities, then we had a leisurely breakfast in the morning room.'

OK for some, Cleo thought, beaming back in her best employee-of-the-year fashion.

'My word, dear! It's all looking absolutely wonderful!' Mimi gazed round the transformed courtyard. 'Thank you so much. We've never had it looking so, well, organised and glamorous. Oh, this is definitely going to be the best Harvest Home ever. You've worked wonders. Is the food all here?'

'Yes. Everything is in the fridges.'

'So,' Mimi continued, smiling happily, 'there's nothing missing at all. Super. The weather is forecast to stay fine and unseasonably mild, and I've even got my boy back in time for the celebrations.'

Cleo's heart skipped a silly beat. 'Oh, er, good. Um, that's lovely. Dylan finally made it home last night then?'

'Dylan? Oh no, dear. I haven't had a peep from Dylan. His mobile telephone's off and no one seems to have seen him for days. You haven't heard from him, I suppose?'

Cleo shook her head. 'No. But, I mean, he's hardly likely to contact me, is he? And he doesn't even have my mobile number.'

She realised he'd never even asked her for it. Really, Cleo thought, she should have read all the 'I'm not interested' signs, shouldn't she? They'd certainly been written clearly enough.

'Never mind.' Mimi gave a little shrug. 'No, actually I was talking about Zeb. My younger son. He's home from school for the weekend. Gorse Glade, you know. You haven't met him yet, have you?'

'Zeb?' Cleo said faintly. 'Er, no . . . no, I haven't . . .'

Chaff it. So Dylan was still absent, and somehow she'd almost forgotten about Zeb. Oh, Lord. She still had the Zeb–Elvi thing to worry about, didn't she?

'I'll get him to pop out and say hello as soon as he appears. I think he's still in bed. You know what teenagers are like.'

Cleo nodded. She clearly remembered her brothers being revoltingly lazy.

'Zeb's a poppet – if a little odd sometimes. Hormones I think. It's his age. Clever boy though. Sciences. All gobbledegook to me, I'm afraid. But Dylan . . . Ah, Dylan's a law unto himself.' Mimi sighed indulgently. 'I'm sure he'll be here if he wants to be. He's such a naughty boy – as no doubt you already know, having become such good friends.'

I've got a pretty good idea, yes, Cleo thought, still smiling the necessary bright smile.

'He's certainly amusing and good company,' Cleo said non-committally. 'But I don't really know him that well, of course.'

'No one does. He's an enigma. But a little word of warning – don't encourage him too much, dear. Oh, I know I shouldn't say this, as his mother, but really, he will take advantage of you being a pretty girl, Cleo. He's got his father's wicked inclinations.'

Cleo tried to remain impassive as Mimi's face momentarily flickered back to the glory days of her misspent youth.

'Um, no, I wouldn't dream of encouraging him.'

'Good, good – Ooh, yes!' Mimi struck a light-bulb-moment pose. 'I knew there was something else. Your own contribution to the eats? Have you –?'

Cleo, seeing no reason at all for any further secrecy and delighted to get away from discussing Dylan's inherited penchant for mass seduction, nodded. 'Drinks, actually. Home-made wine. I brought it up with me earlier and put it in the cellar. I hope that's OK?'

'Perfect. Perfect,' Mimi gushed. 'Wine! Oooh lovely! I adore home-made wine. So simple yet so rustic. What a woman of many talents you are, Cleo, dear.'

Phew, Cleo thought. That went better than she'd expected.

'Of course,' Mimi continued, 'it will also mean that the villagers won't need to drink so much of our fizz. Mortimer will be absolutely delighted. Could save us pounds. Make sure they're served your plonk first, dear, won't you? And plenty of it. Oh, did I say that I'm putting you on as our wine waitress tonight?'

Right, Cleo thought. Clearly a health and safety choice. It would be far less socially irritating to the Pashley-Royles for Cleo to tip Razzle Dazzle Damson over Rodders than it had been for her to hurl samphire at Jessamine.

'No, you didn't. But that's fine. And appropriate under the circumstances.'

'Absolutely.' Mimi beamed round the courtyard again. 'Right, now I must just go and have another little nap before starting to titivate myself for tonight. So tiring, being a hostess, don't you find? Anyway, Cleo, why don't you do the same? Pop back to your encampment and have a siesta? You've worked so hard in seeing to everything and it's going to be frantically busy tonight, and if it all goes well, you may still be here in the morning.'

Only in my fevered dreams, Cleo thought, trying not to look too wistful.

'That sounds like a good idea. And I'm quite tired, actually. Thanks, yes, I probably will.'

'No, thank you, my dear. You're a treasure. An absolute treasure.' And still smiling, Mimi drifted away back under the clock arch.

Yeah, right, Cleo thought, and how much of treasure would you really think I was, if you knew the sort of thoughts I was harbouring about your beloved son and heir, eh?

And me, scum from the trailer park . . .

She giggled to herself as she walked round the corner of the Hall to her car – and collided with a tall, skinny boy.

'I'm so sorry!' He smiled up from his mobile phone, flicking a long black fringe from his eyes. 'I do apologise. I was texting and not looking where I was going.'

'My fault.' Cleo beamed. 'I was miles away. I'm Cleo – your mother's new PA.'

'Zeb Pashley-Royle.' He held out his hand. 'It's very nice to meet you. I've heard so much about you. Mother thinks you're a gift from the gods. You've been a star in organising all this Harvest Home stuff this year. Mother usually forgets the most vital things.'

Shaking his hand, Cleo realised why Elvi was so smitten. Zeb, with his low-slung skinny jeans – so low-slung that his hip bones showed – his scruffy cashmere sweater, his silky spiky hair, his good manners and his absolute charm, was every teenage girl's dream.

She wondered if she should say that she knew Elvi, then decided it was better not to. Just in case that particular embryo love affair had already bitten the dust.

'I'll see you again tonight?' Zeb enquired politely, his long fingers hovering over the buttons on his mobile, clearly desperate to continue his text conversation.

Cleo, really hoping that it was Elvi he was texting, nodded. 'You will. Sometime before eight o'clock.'

'I'll look forward to it.' Zeb smiled again. 'And it's been a pleasure to meet you.'

Well, Cleo thought as they parted company, a private education certainly taught you perfect manners. A

seventeen-year-old boy who didn't snarl and spit? Blimey –
that was a first . . .

'Just gone seven o'clock,' Amy Reynolds called round the
caravan. 'Boys! Get yourselves smartened up!' She looked at
her husband and Elvi across the living room. 'And what
about you two? Well, Elvi's been ready for hours, obviously – so what about you, love?'

'Not going,' Ron Reynolds muttered from his seat in
front of the television. 'Can't be arsed.'

Elvi, who had been bouncing off the furniture all day,
glared at her father. 'Dad! You always say that! You know
you're going.'

'Do I?' Ron's eyes softened. 'Well, we'll see. Maybe this
year it'll be different.'

It'll certainly be that, Elvi thought, hugging her phone to
her chest. She and Zeb had spent the last ten hours counting
down the minutes. They'd made, checked and rechecked
their arrangements to meet at least a hundred times. Even
her mum had commented on the number of texts Elvi was
receiving.

Less than an hour to go! She'd see him in less than an
hour! If she lived that long . . .

'Ah, Cleo's just left.' Amy peered through the living-room
window. 'She looks really lovely. Tight jeans and a fab
turquoise top, proper going-out make-up, and her hair all
over the place and gleaming like a shampoo ad. She'll turn a
few heads tonight up at Lovelady looking like that.'

'Cleo always looks lovely,' Elvi said.

Amy puffed out her cheeks. 'She looked really scruffy when she came home just after lunch, so she must have spent ages getting ready for tonight. Her curtains have been pulled all afternoon, if you get my drift.'

'Don't be so damn nosy,' Ron laughed. 'That poor girl works her socks off up at Lovelady Hall. She was off before it was properly light this morning. I passed her when I was going to get my paper. She's probably been grabbing some much-needed shut-eye before the bloody Pashley-Royles squeeze the last drop of lifeblood out of her tonight'

'I just wondered if she might have been entertaining.' Amy moved away from the window. 'You know . . .'

'There's no need to be grossly cryptic.' Elvi grinned. 'I'm not a child you know. Go on, Mum, spit it out – although I happen to know that Cleo is very happy being single.'

'Do you, Miss Brainbox? Well, let me put you straight then. I happen to know that Cleo has been seeing someone on a fairly regular basis. I don't miss much from here, you know. Not much gets past me.'

'Women!' Ron huffed, hauling himself from his chair and heading out of the living room.

'Where are you going?' Amy called.

'For a shower – not that it means I'm going to be joining you tonight. You'll not catch me acting all grateful to them easy-living buggers like the rest of the hoi polloi. I'm just feeling all hot and sweaty. Need to freshen up a bit.'

'There!' Amy beamed across at Elvi. 'He *is* going. I knew he would be. God knows why we have to go through this palaver every time . . . He's dying to get his hands on my pickled eggs – and I told him no way – not until they're opened up at Lovelady tonight . . . What was I saying? Ah, yes, about Cleo's secret lover.'

'She doesn't have a lover, secret or any other kind.'

'Oh, no? Then why has Dylan Maguire been making several visits in the last weeks?'

Dylan Maguire!

Elvi swallowed. No way. Cleo would have said, wouldn't she? Especially when she'd told her all about Zeb?

'You've got that wrong, Mum. Dylan was always popping in next door when Olive lived there, but not now.'

'Yes, now.' Amy nodded. 'Last Saturday, and the week before that, and sometime in the week before that, too. And he turns up either without his car, or he leaves it parked up at the entrance to the site, so my guess is they don't want anyone to know he's there. What's that if it's not a candle-thingy affair?'

'Clandestine.'

'That's the word.'

Elvi exhaled slowly. Cleo was her friend. Her confidante. Why the hell, if she was seeing Dylan Maguire, hadn't Cleo mentioned it?

Oh! And she'd trusted Cleo with *everything*, hadn't she? And Dylan Maguire was practically Zeb's brother! Oh, it just went to show you couldn't trust putrid *anyone*.

Dylan Maguire was a bit old – but pretty hot, of course. Not as hot as Zeb, natch, but he certainly managed to pull. And he had a fearsome reputation. He was so not what Cleo needed.

189

Elvi checked her mobile again. Forty-four minutes and counting!

Now who should she believe? Cleo, who she'd trusted with her most desperate secrets? Or her mum, who was known in Lovers Knot as an inveterate gossip?

No one, Elvi decided. Putrid no one.

It would have to be her and Zeb against the world. And tonight, at Harvest Home, they'd show everyone that true love really did conquer all, wouldn't they? And as for Cleo – Elvi sighed. She'd never trust Cleo again as long as she lived.

Chapter Fifteen

'Good God!' Cleo stared at the courtyard in total delight.

In the twilight, with the fairy lights twinkling and the flames from the pig roast leaping, and the music plinketty-plonking from the speakers, it was even more wonderful than she'd ever imagined it could be.

Lovelady Hall's Harvest Home. Perfect bucolic bliss.

Exactly as it had been for hundreds of years.

Well, almost. Clearly as they were now in the twenty-first century, there had been some updates. The invention of electricity must have improved things considerably. Health and safety would have had a field day in the times of candles and flares. Cleo reckoned the celebrating Lovers Knot ancestors had probably set fire to an awful lot of hay bales pre-Faraday.

But otherwise, surely nothing much had altered? The entire hamlet had turned out, well, was still turning out, as people streamed under the clock arch. Cleo, watching the noisy arrivals, had had no idea there were so many people living in Lovers Knot.

Everyone from the large imposing hidden red-bricked villas, the small council estate and the tiny shuttered cottages, the surrounding farms, the one-and-only shop, and of course from the caravan site, had made the annual pilgrimage.

'We'll give them something to drink as soon as they've found a hay bale and are properly seated,' Mimi said to her as, with Zola and Zlinki, Mortimer and Zeb – still congenitally attached to his iPhone – they ferried huge platters of food from the fridges to the centre stretch of trestle tables. 'Oh, and the soft drinks for the kiddies are over there . . . They'll all be OK to start with, getting settled, chatting to one another and discussing the decorations and the state of the country and the weather. All the usual stuff. Then they'll want to start drinking.'

'So early?' Cleo puffed, buckling under the weight of a salver of sausage rolls. 'They'll be completely trollied by ten.'

'I fervently hope so.' Mortimer hefting, double-handed, trays of cheese and pickles and hunks of home-baked bread, beamed at her. 'Then they won't need our champers. Which means all the more for us. Could you just clear space down there, please, Cleo. Thank you, my dear.'

Cleo had wanted to laugh at Mimi and Mortimer, but managed not to. They'd clearly selected their outfits from the Country Casuals department of their favourite Rich People's store, and looked like Torvill and Dean Go Sunday Walking in identical too-blue denims, cream shirts and matching gilets.

Mimi surveyed the landscape of food and nodded happily. 'As soon as you've done your first round with the drinks –

oh, and don't give them a choice, Cleo, just pour them a beaker of whatever you've uncorked; we really can't spend all night catering to *whims* – we'll make our sorties with the food. We'll just keep topping them up throughout the evening until it's all gone or they've had sufficient – whichever comes first. And Zeb is going to make sure they've all got a plate and knives and forks and a napkin. Aren't you, darling?'

'Darling' seemed to have disappeared.

'Goodness me!' Mimi shrugged expansively. 'Now both my sons have gone missing. And on the very night they should be here. Whatever am I going to do with them?'

Assuming this was a hypothetical question, Cleo tactfully said nothing. Bugger, though. It meant Dylan still wasn't back. Oh, well . . .

'I'll go and collect the first bottles of wine then,' she said. 'I'll use that space on the end of the table as a bar.'

Pushing through the tightly packed throng of very noisy up-for-a-party villagers, Cleo headed for the wine cellar.

In her dreams she'd imagined that Dylan would be here to help her with this. That they'd be laughing together as they uncorked the first bottles of Razzle Dazzle Damson. That they'd toast one another beneath the sparkling fairy lights and at long last discover whether Mad Molly's fast-fermentation fix really worked.

She sighed. Stupid things, dreams.

In the cellar's dim coolness, having loaded all thirteen bottles of the damson wine, Cleo hauled at the grubby ropes of the dumb waiter. With a lot of clanking and groaning, it disappeared upwards. First batch despatched. So far so good. Now all she had to do was run back up the stone steps to the kitchen, transfer the bottles to one of Mimi's hostess trollies and wheel the lot into the courtyard.

Having pulled the bottles of Blackberry Blush and the Sloe Seduction forwards so that she'd be able to reach it more easily on the return journey, Cleo switched off the cellar lights, climbed back into the kitchen, loaded the wine onto the trolley and prepared to find out – at last – if her home-made wine was even slightly palatable.

The villagers, now all seated on the hay bales, cheered as she appeared. Several of them drummed their feet in anticipation.

Grabbing the first bottle in one hand and a corkscrew in the other, Cleo held her breath.

'Wow – don't you look gorgeous?' Dylan, looking slightly dishevelled in his rumpled tuxedo and undone bow tie, but still totally mind-blowingly sexy, appeared from the deep shadows behind the scorching, crackling blaze of the pig roast. 'And please let me do that.'

'Thank you.' Cleo knew she was blushing and hoped Dylan would think it was reflection of the spit's flames and not her silly girly reaction to both his compliment and his much longed for arrival.

He reached for the wine bottle. 'I see you're starting with the damson. It must be OK then? Good choice. Sorry I had to miss the taste test. And even sorrier I'm so late. I, er, got delayed.'

Flicking a glance behind him to see if he was indeed

194

accompanied by a slender Galliano-garbed WAG and happily seeing no one but Mortimer and a selection of villagers, Cleo breathed a sigh of relief. It didn't matter that Dylan had no doubt just tumbled from the four-poster bed of Georgiana or Aphrodite, she told herself. The only thing that mattered was that he was *here*.

And she decided not to tell him that the Razzle Dazzle Damson was still untouched by human hand or gullet. It was too late now anyway . . .

'Still cutting it a bit fine, weren't you?' she hissed. 'Your mother's gone all po-faced. She thought you weren't going to turn up at all.'

'As if. Let's get this first batch poured out, then we can talk. Here goes – I wouldn't have missed this for anything – ah –'

The first cork flew out – disappointingly without any enchantment whatsoever. No fluttering fairies, no prancing unicorns, not even a sniff of a snotling.

Cleo picked up another corkscrew and a further bottle, still simply ridiculously delighted that Dylan was there. 'You won't have any time for talking, you're on serving savouries. Only don't give anyone the pork pies.'

'Why? Do you have a secret penchant for them? Do you want me to keep you some back?'

'No way. Rodders made them. They don't look, um, normal.'

'That figures. What about the smell?'

'As you'd expect.'

Dylan laughed, uncorking bottles at the speed of light.

'Oh, I do love this place. There's nowhere like it on earth. Right – is that the lot open?'

Cleo nodded. 'And you can't help me. I'm supposed to be *the* wine waiter. Solo.'

'And I always say everything's better with two.' Dylan grinned at her. 'We'll just give them a splash each to start with and see how far it goes. You start at the clock arch end, I'll take the pig roast side, and we'll meet in the middle. Which is a pretty good analogy for us really, don't you think?'

Cleo gave him what she hoped was a haughty stare, grabbed two bottles of wine and set off on her rounds.

The villagers, eager now to get their hands on as much food and drink as possible at the expense of someone else, held out their beakers like obedient children. Cleo knew most of them and, as far as she could see, the only family missing was the Reynolds. She hoped that Ron hadn't caused a fuss about coming to Harvest Home. Elvi would be heartbroken if she'd had to miss it because Ron had turned into the Mussolini of Lovers Knot. Again.

Pouring the Razzle Dazzle Damson into the first beakers, Cleo watched proudly as the crystal-clear red wine glugged perfectly. Just like the real thing.

Magic!

Returning time and again to grab more bottles, she and Dylan managed to give everyone at least half a beaker of damson wine.

Mortimer, bouncing up and down with the microphone, switched off the music and clapped his hands authoritatively. 'Right, ladies and gentlemen of Lovers Knot! Before you drink yourselves into a stupor, can I just say that Mimi and I – and our family – are delighted to welcome you all to Lovelady Hall for yet another successful Harvest Home. We will be attending to your every need – so eat, drink and let's all be merry!'

Mimi took the microphone from her husband. 'And I'd just like to add, because praise where praise is due, a very public thank you to Cleo Moon. Without her, this year's Harvest Home would have been a far more meagre affair. She's worked tirelessly to make sure tonight goes with a swing.' Mimi beamed across at Cleo. 'So, thank you, my dear.'

Cleo, scarlet with embarrassment, smiled back. Oh, Lordy . . .

Everyone clapped and cheered – Dylan more loudly than anyone – and raised their beakers.

Briefly, through the drifting aromatic smoke from the pig roast, Cleo finally spotted the Reynolds – Ron, Amy and their two boys – sitting on the hay bales with Mrs Hancock and Salome. Phew – that was OK then . . . She squinted again. Oh, but there was no sign of Elvi . . .

'Three – two – one . . .' Dylan handed a beaker of Razzle Dazzle Damson to her. 'Here's to us . . . Oh, listen – how very apt.'

Someone had put UB40's 'Red Red Wine' on the sound system. Waving their beakers, the Lovers Knot crowd roared along with the chorus.

'Cheers.' Cleo smiled, and took the very first sip of her very own Razzle Dazzle Damson wine.

It was absolutely delicious. Divine. Delectable. Full-bodied: fruity, rich, total nectar. She could taste the warm summer sun turning to sugar in the autumn damsons, and the wonderful pure bite of the wild fruit on her tongue, and the sparkling clarity of the pure Lovers Cascade water.

Absolutely scrumptious . . .

Cleo swallowed the mouthful, relishing the flavour.

Oooh, but it was . . . strong! So very strong . . .

Afterwards she wasn't sure exactly what had happened. Or how. Or when. Everything just telescoped together: the music, the noise of the crowd, the colours of the lights. Everything blurred together and became a swirling, noisy, vividly hued mass.

'What the hell?' Dylan's voice echoed from miles away. 'Cleo? This stuff is total nectar, but what's going on? I've only had a drop and . . . Is it me – or . . .?'

'It's not you,' she said faintly, watching in stunned amazement as, all around them, everyone drained their beakers and leaped to their feet. 'Dylan, don't drink any more!'

'But it's fantastic –'

'I know, but just don't drink any more. Not yet . . .'

Aware that something very odd was happening but not knowing what, Cleo, putting her beaker of Razzle Dazzle Damson down on the trestle table, was simply overwhelmed by the insane urge to rush home and make a cake.

A cake like she'd never made before. The biggest cake in the world. A massive towering, gooey chocolate cake oozing with cream and dripping with exotic liqueurs and squishy with raspberries and decorated with dark cocoa shards and drizzled with . . .

'Bloody hell,' Dylan groaned. 'I really want to drag you into bed. Now. Here. This minute.'

Cleo laughed, and laughed, and laughed. She clapped her hand over her mouth. It didn't help. The laughing just carried on through her fingers.

Oh, Lord – if he'd said that to her at any other time . . . But not now. Not when she needed to go home and cook.

She giggled. 'And I just want to make a cake. I'm literally aching to make a cake. And I think everyone's gone mad.'

They watched in disbelief as Mortimer started haggling loudly with no one over the price of an unseen car, extolling its virtues and admiring its invisible paintwork, while Mimi tore off her gilet and threw herself into a wildly energetic and vaguely sexual solo dance.

All around them the Lovers Knot villagers were on their feet, acting out their own strange fantasies with no sign of embarrassment whatsoever.

It was like a method acting class aided by hallucinatory drugs.

Amy Reynolds was finger-wagging and gossiping loudly to mid-air like an extra in *Oklahoma*; Ron was gesturing wildly and orating like an old-style trade union agitator; Rodders was clearing imaginary drains with gusto; Salome was propositioning all and sundry while swinging her handbag round her head; Mrs Hancock was stroking everyone and offering saucers of milk; Raymond and George in their hand-knitted Fair Isle tank tops were Morris dancing; and

Jerome – on his imaginary horse – had taken a flying leap and cleared the pig roast's flames with a rebel yell.

People were dancing, singing, telling jokes, running round kissing virtual strangers, flirting, arguing, shouting, laughing . . . And all with total wild abandon.

'They've gone crazy!' Dylan shouted, ducking as an elderly lady from the council houses forced her way between them while juggling several paper plates, his words still slightly slurred. 'They've all gone bloody crazy!'

The mayhem grew.

Belly and Flip, arms linked, were doing the Dance of the Little Swans atop three hay bales, pointing their matching stout laced-up toes prettily.

Cleo, still fighting the compulsion to rush home to the caravan and start baking, blinked in astonishment.

'It's the wine,' she said faintly. 'It's got to be the wine.'

'But when you tested it?' Dylan frowned, rocking on his feet. 'Did it have this effect on you?'

She shook her head and wished she hadn't. Everything whizzed round in a rainbow blaze. She'd had one sip. Just one sip . . . Whereas everyone else had quaffed theirs in one go . . .

Belly and Flip fell off the hay bales.

'I, um, just swilled it round my mouth and spat it out after you left. No one's actually drunk any until tonight. Er, you don't happen to have flour and eggs and sugar and three pounds of chocolate on you, do you?'

Dylan groaned. 'And that's the most erotic thing I've ever heard in my life.'

'I don't want you to smother me with them,' Cleo hissed, nimbly avoiding a couple from the red-bricked villas who were tangoing erotically across the courtyard. 'I want to use them in my gateaux.'

She laughed again.

So did Dylan.

And everyone else joined in. The noise rose in a crescendo of merriment. A tidal roar of guffaws swamped the courtyard of Lovelady Hall.

'Did you hear that?' Elvi murmured. 'That noise? Like a rumbling explosion? Sounded like it came from Lovelady – or maybe it was thunder?'

'Didn't hear a thing,' Zeb said, kissing her again. 'I only have olfactory organs for you.'

Elvi giggled.

Zeb laced his fingers slowly with hers. 'Anyway, we'll be fine here even if it does rain.'

'Mmm,' Elvi sighed, shivering with delight as he pushed her down again. 'It'll be so romantic, snug and cosy, under these trees, listening to the raindrops pattering on the leaves.'

They curled against one another in the darkness, ecstatically happy just being together.

Elvi stroked Zeb's slender face. This was what love was all about, she thought, dreamily. Being together. Just sharing romantic never-to-be-forgotten special moments. Just knowing there was only one person in the whole world who could make you feel like this.

'Will your parents wonder where you are?' Zeb asked between kisses. 'It must have been ages ago that you said you just needed to go to the loo.'

Time had ceased to exist. Elvi had no idea if they'd been in Lovers Spinney for minutes or hours or days. And she didn't care.

'Doubt it.' Elvi smiled into Zeb's bony cashmere-covered shoulder. 'Not once they've had a putrid drink and Mum starts gossiping and Dad finds people to argue with. What about yours?'

'My mother will possibly wonder why they're a waiter short but she's pretty cool. I'll just tell her the truth.'

'No way!' Elvi rolled over on their rustling cushiony bed of fallen leaves. 'She'll go ballistic.'

'Why should she? She adores me and she was young once – she'll understand. And she's always taught me to follow my heart.'

'Yeah, right. But not with the horrid ex-cleaner's brat.'

Zeb laughed. 'You have such funny notions about my parents. Now yours – they're something else.'

'I think Mum would be fine, well, about, um, us, er, seeing one another and being in love and . . .'

Elvi stopped. It was OK talking about love. She and Zeb loved each other. They both *loved* and were *in love*. They both knew it. They'd said so a million times.

She couldn't mention sex though. Not yet.

'And your father?'

'Would want you trundled to the guillotine with the rest of the bourgeoisie.'

202

'Oh, good.' Zeb smiled cheerfully. 'Can't wait to meet him. Would you like another drink?'

'Please.' Elvi sat up slightly, not wanting to move an inch away from Zeb's beautiful slender body. 'Does your mother know you've pinched a bottle of her best champagne?'

Zeb shook his head, passing her the bottle, and laughed as she swigged from it and the bubbles trickled from her lips. 'They've got loads of bottles of fizz. They won't miss one. Anyway, Mother was more interested in making sure the villagers all got bladdered on the new PA's home-made wine first.'

He kissed the bubbles from her chin. Her body immediately sparkled more than any champagne and she giggled.

Then she stopped.

'Cleo?' Elvi said faintly as she passed the bottle back to him. 'Cleo made the wine for Harvest Home?'

'Apparently.' Zeb swallowed another frothy mouthful. 'Do you know her? She's very pretty – nowhere near as pretty as you, of course – for someone as old as that, and my mother says she's simply wonderful at her job.'

The champagne and being with Zeb – at long, long last – had gone straight to Elvi's head. And she was still very cross with Cleo.

'She's having an affair with Dylan.'

'Who is?'

'Cleo.'

'No way!' Zeb forgot about being achingly cool. 'Dylan? My brother Dylan?'

'The very same.'

'But Dylan, well, I know he's a serial shagger, but he's never . . . not on his own doorstep. That was something he taught me from an early age.'

'Did he? You seem to have forgotten that little home truth, then? I mean – not that we're, um . . .'

Elvi stopped. She couldn't possibly say shagging. Kate said it about her and Mason all the time. It was, she thought, such a hatefully harshly gross and unromantic word for something as gloriously wonderful as making love with the only person in the world who'd ever matter.

Not that she knew – yet – of course, but she would.

Zeb smiled gently at her. 'No, I know. I didn't mean us. I'm delighted that you're on my doorstep. It was more a hypo-thetical observation. But Dylan . . . oh, he's ace but he's a bad boy sometimes. He says his interpretation of the family motto is "Never the Same Bed Twice". And I've never known him see anyone locally before. Cleo is certainly gorgeous, and def-initely his type of woman, but an affair? Are you sure?'

Elvi repeated what her mum had told her.

'Phew. Sounds likely then.' Zeb exhaled. 'Fancy that. Maybe Dylan's fallen in love at last.'

'I hope so,' Elvi said. She might be cross with Cleo for not telling her about Dylan, but she still cared about her. 'Cleo's had a real rough deal in the past. The last thing she needs is to messed around by a love rat.'

'Maybe it's *exactly* what she needs,' Zeb chuckled. 'No, sorry . . . But can't you see the irony here? Both sons of Lovelady Hall in love with girls from the Lovers Knot cara-van park?'

Elvi giggled. Mimi and Mortimer would have a total fit.

'I don't know if Dylan's back tonight or not,' Zeb said, passing the champagne bottle back to Elvi. 'But I'll definitely have to ask him about Cleo.'

Elvi stopped in mid-swig. 'Please don't. I . . . I don't want there to be any trouble, if they are, well, together, and they're happy. They haven't said anything so they must want to keep it a secret.'

Zeb pulled her towards him again. 'Like you do? About us? When I want to tell the whole world. I've told everyone at school. I've even told Dylan, but I made him swear not to say anything because of the village gossip. I'd hate it if your father heard it from someone else. But haven't you told anyone?'

Elvi smiled in the darkness. 'Only Cleo. I told Cleo.'

'Ah . . . And she didn't tell you about Dylan? And that annoys you?'

Elvi blinked. She loved him so much. He was so wonderfully perceptive. She nodded.

'She must have had her reasons then. You obviously trust her.'

'I do. Did.'

'Then carry on trusting her. She's kept your secret so we'll keep hers. That's only fair. Oh, bugger – we've finished the champagne. We'll have to think of something else to do now . . .'

Chapter Sixteen

Cleo clutched the edge of the trestle table as the urge to make the world's most incredible cake receded. The crazy world of Lovelady Hall seemed to be resuming normality again.

Slowly, the colours separated, the lights stopped dazzling her eyes, the music became tuneful once more, and the courtyard stopped spinning.

The villagers all looked slightly bemused. Staring round them, they seemed rather confused to find themselves standing up and sheepishly returned to their hay bales.

Even Zola and Zlinki, who had, Cleo seemed to remember, been recently involved in barristerly barracking one another from opposite sides of an invisible courtroom, suddenly skipped happily towards the food table together and picked up salvers of home-made delicacies.

'What the hell happened there?' Dylan blinked at her, still clutching his almost-full beaker. 'Did I miss something?'

'Not sure . . .' Cleo frowned. 'I vaguely remember – No,

it's gone. Hang on – it's coming back. Ah, right – no, surely not? How weird – I wanted to go home and make a cake. God knows why.'

'And I'm pretty sure I wanted to –' Dylan grinned. 'No, possibly not the best thing to share with you. But wasn't everyone . . . being . . . well, mad?'

Cleo nodded slowly. She knew they had been. Although, looking at them all now, sitting on the hay bales again, tapping their feet to the music, grabbing handfuls of food from the passing trays and looking perfectly normal, it was impossible to believe.

So, was it possible that the Razzle Dazzle Damson had had a rapid mind-altering effect? That for a short space of time it removed all inhibitions and – but then what?

'I say!' Mimi called imperiously, swanning past them with two serving platters of assorted pickles. 'Has anyone seen my gilet? I seem to have mislaid it.' Her eyes softened. 'Dylan! Darling! When did you get back?'

'Earlier. A few minutes ago, I think, or maybe it was longer. I seem to have lost all track of time, but you already knew I was here. I spoke to you when I arrived.'

Mimi frowned. 'Did you? How very odd . . . I don't seem to remember. I do remember – no, it's gone. Definitely having a senior moment.'

Dylan laughed. 'I somehow doubt that. But I did say hi when I got here.'

'I'm sure you did, and of course I'm delighted that you're here, but if you've only just arrived you missed a real treat, darling. Cleo uncorked her damson wine. It was delicious.

In fact we must have some more. Do go and get some more bottles PDQ, Cleo.'

Cleo and Dylan exchanged glances.

'Er, yes, OK.' Cleo nodded. 'And, um, Mimi, when you'd drunk the wine, did you feel, well, a bit odd?'

'Do you know,' Mimi chuckled, 'I think it rather went straight to my head. I think it made me slightly squiffy. I vaguely remember wanting to dance wildly like I had in my youth. In fact, now I think about it, I rather think I actually did it. I did! I let my fantasies run away with me, didn't I? Oh, goodness, please tell me I wasn't too, um, free-spirited? Was I dancing too, too madly?'

'Er, no, not really. You were just, well, going with the flow,' Cleo said diplomatically. 'You were very good.'

Mimi preened. 'Was I? Thank goodness I managed to remain fully dressed then. When I used to go to rock festivals as a youngster, I'd take all my clothes off and just let my spirits run free. Ah, I was the star of the circuit in those days . . . Isle of Wight, Reading, Glastonbury. People used to say they'd never seen anything as uninhibited as my dancing. Happy days, sweethearts, happy days.'

Watching her drift away towards the hay bales again, Cleo grabbed Dylan's arm. 'That's it!'

'What's what?'

'The Razzle Dazzle Damson. It *is* magic!'

'Magic?' Dylan frowned. 'And you were the one who pooh-poohed the snotlings.'

'Forget the snotlings. This is real magic. Mad Molly's real magic. No, I know you're going to think I'm as mad as she was, but just think this through for a minute. We used the Lovers Cascade water which – either by science or practical magic – enabled the wine to ferment and become drinkable in a remarkably short space of time, right?'

'Right, but –'

'Dylan!' Mortimer beckoned from the other side of the table. 'Stop chatting up the prettiest girl in the place – after your mother, of course – and come and grab this plate of apple pies! You're supposed to be waiting on our guests.'

'Yeah, OK, just one minute.' Dylan turned to Cleo again. 'Go on with your hypothesis.'

'I don't think it's that exactly, but, oh well, remember those scribbled-out and blurred warnings we couldn't read on the back of Molly's recipes? What if they were saying that yes, the Lovers Cascade water would make the wine brew quickly, but anyone making it must be aware that it would also have other effects? Magical effects?'

'Like making my mother want to do the Dance of the Seven Veils?'

Cleo giggled. 'Yes, sort of. What if Mad Molly's Razzle Dazzle Damson recipe did exactly that? Turned anyone who drank it into a, well, into a Razzle Dazzler? Enabled them to shake off their inhibitions and perform – or at least try to – the very thing closest to their heart at that moment? Let them show off with no fear of criticism? Gave them the opportunity to live out, publicly, their most secret desires?'

'Or the one thing they're best at?'

Cleo nodded. 'Exactly.'

Dylan laughed.

'Don't laugh,' Cleo said quickly. 'It all makes sense. Why are you laughing?'

'Because, after just one sip, I'm pretty sure I was on the verge of, um, behaving towards you in an inappropriate manner – given the time and the place – not to mention your ingrained aversion to the upper classes. But –' he looked at her '– with all due modesty, I've been told I'm, um, very good at it, and you're amazing at making cakes, and my mother was clearly the Isadora Duncan of the rock-chick set.'

They stared at one another.

'And we just *wanted* to – er – well, do what we're best at because we only had a drop. But the others drank it all . . . And then,' Cleo said slowly, 'once the wine has been drunk, and had a chance to work its way round the system, and the Razzle Dazzle part has happened, then the effect fades, and so does a lot of the memory of what's happened. It becomes a bit blurred and dreamlike. So, people went slightly crazy, happily living out their fantasies for a little while, but like all the best morning afters, they can recall some, but not all, of what they did.'

Dylan laughed. 'Fantastic! Didn't I tell you that Lovers Cascade was enchanted? Clever old Mad Molly. So, what's next on the wine list?'

'Oh, no. I don't think we should, just in case –'

'Of course we should,' Dylan insisted. 'Where's the harm? The effects are short-lived, everyone has a blast, then it's over with no lingering embarrassment. Everyone's just had so much fun. It'll really make this the best Harvest Home ever.'

'Dylan!' Mortimer roared. 'I'm supposed to be carving the meats, and I've got apple pies *and* vegetarian pâté here, both good to go!'

'He's been watching too many American television cookery programmes.' Dylan grinned. 'OK, Mort! I'm on my way.' He looked at Cleo. 'But not until we've collected the next round of wine bottles. What's this one? Blackberry Blush?'

'Yes, but —'

'It'll be fine. What can Blackberry Blush do that's so awful? Cause embarrassing flatulence? Bring on a mass rash of blue joke-telling?'

'Oh, God, let's hope not.'

Dylan shrugged. 'If the process is the same with Blackberry Blush as it was with Razzle Dazzle Damson, whatever happens it'll only be temporary, won't it? And we'll all laugh at the time because we find it funny, and afterwards maybe feel a little uncomfortable that we've shed so many inhibitions in public — because there's no one more uptight than the Brits — then, just as quickly as the wine kicked in it'll kick out again, and any embarrassment will gradually fade away.'

'Yes, OK — but should we even be experimenting like this? We shouldn't be test-driving this on other people. I don't think it's right to —'

'Cleo, how do you feel right now? After tasting the wine? Drunk? Ill? Angry? No, if you feel anything like I do — like the rest of the villagers clearly do — then it's probably the best feeling in the world. Look at them, Cleo — they may not remember *exactly* what they've just done, but they know they've had a really great time doing it, and the after-effects are clearly amazing. I've never seen such a chilled-out, happy bunch.'

Cleo gazed round the courtyard. In the darkness, illuminated only by the fairy lights and the flames from the pig roast, everyone was relaxed and smiling, eating and chattering and laughing.

And, yes, didn't she feel exactly the same? As though she'd had the best fun night ever, followed by a sound and dreamless ten-hour sleep? Peaceful, on cloud nine, ready for anything?

And she already knew that she'd added nothing harmful to the wines, didn't she? So, if the Lovers Cascade rocks – or Mad Molly's magic – had added a little extra pizzazz to the home-made wine, it wasn't actually going to hurt anyone, was it?

'OK.' She grinned at Dylan. 'Race you down the cellar steps!'

Elvi stirred in Zeb's arms. How wonderful, she thought, it would be to live together. To be together all the time. To go to sleep together and wake up together, and spend every minute together just being in love.

They'd talked about everything for what must have been hours. Stuff they couldn't cover in their texts. All their hopes and dreams. About their respective schools and homes and friends and everything. They'd laughed and argued and laughed a lot more. She looked at his thin face, half-obscured by the long black fringe, and her heart actually hurt with loving him so much.

Zeb was sooo beautiful. And so lovely. Now she knew that he wanted them to have a proper relationship – but not here. Not tonight. Not like this. Not until she was ready. Not until she felt it was right for her.

Elvi, knowing that Kate said boys all wanted you to do it all the time, marvelled at his self-control. And even more at his gentle respect for her.

'What are you thinking about?' Zeb opened his eyes.

'You.'

'Boring.' He grinned. 'God, Elvi, you're the most beautiful girl in the world. And you're clever and funny – and I really do love you.'

'I love you too.'

'And now –' He wriggled into a sitting position '– I want to go and speak to your father.'

'Nooo!' Elvi squeaked. 'You can't. He'll kill you.'

'Of course he won't. Let Cleo and Dylan have a cloak and dagger affair if that's what they want, but it isn't for me. Us. You do love me, don't you? And you want to carry on seeing me?'

'Yes. Yes. For ever. But . . .'

Zeb uncurled his long body and got to his feet, hauling her after him, then circled her waist with his arms. 'Then we're going to be open and honest about it from the start. With my parents as well as yours. They'll be OK. Trust me.'

Elvi shook her head. 'Honestly, you don't know my dad.'

'I know his reputation.' Zeb kissed the tip of her nose. 'So this will be my Lovers Knot rite of passage moment, won't it? Braving Red Ron Reynolds?'

'You're mad to even think of it,' Elvi sighed. 'And he's bound to be grossly obnoxious. He's not like that, really he isn't. He's a sweetie. But he's got this huge working man versus the landed gentry thing going on. Always has had, always will do.'

'So you've said a million times. And I'm still not scared. I think he deserves to know that I love you, respect you, will care for you – and this isn't just a silly boy–girl thing.'

'He'll probably laugh at first and say we're too young to know anything about love, and that we don't even know each other properly, and it's all pretty words, then he'll start getting putridly angry about your privileged lifestyle and all that crap stuff.'

'Words,' Zeb said confidently. 'All words. Words can't hurt us, can they?'

'Maybe not,' Elvi said doubtfully. 'But anyway, whatever he says – please believe me – I will never, never stop loving you or seeing you. But your parents – they'll be even worse, won't they? They'll definitely say you're too young and that you're throwing away your education and your whole future.'

'Nah.' Zeb shook his head. 'They'll love you. And it's not as if we're doing anything stupid, is it? We both want to get really good A levels and go to uni; I want to be a physicist and you want to teach. Why can't we do all that when we're together?'

'They'll say I'm a distraction.'

'Which –' Zeb kissed her '– is absolutely true. You are

214

driving me out of my mind. So, if you think you can spend the rest of your life with a mindless, babbling fool –?'

Elvi wrinkled her nose. 'Tough one. I'll have to think about it.'

'No time like the present then. Think about it while we run.' Zeb grabbed her hand and started to lead her through Lovers Spinney towards Lovelady Hall. 'Anyway, we ought to show our faces at the yawn-making Harvest Home, oughtn't we? Not, of course, that we'll have missed anything exciting.'

Dylan and Cleo lined the bottles of Blackberry Blush on the bar end of the trestle table and uncorked them quickly, watched intently by the villagers who had just been served huge hot roast pork sandwiches by Mortimer.

Cleo inhaled the wine's rich, deep fruity autumnal fragrance. Oooh, gorgeous.

'It looks perfect.' Dylan held the bottle up to the fairy lights. 'Clear as crystal. So,' he said, smiling at her, 'I wonder what little surprise Mad Molly has in store for us this time?'

'I'm having second thoughts.'

'It'll be wonderful.' Dylan glugged some into the nearest beaker. 'Look at it! Dark purple, full-bodied, glowing, just asking to be drunk. And you never know, this one might not be quite as, um, magical as the Razzle Dazzle Damson.'

'So you do believe that it is? Magic, I mean?'

'Cleo,' Dylan said softly, 'I believed it was magic long before you did. Everyone in Lovers Knot believes in magic. Just remember never to mention that you've made this from Mad Molly's recipes, that's all. Right? Ready to go?'

'Aren't we going to test it ourselves first?'

Dylan shook his head. 'We'll have ours afterwards – when we've seen what effect it has.'

'That's a bit cruel.'

'Just sensible.' Dylan gathered up four bottles of Blackberry Blush. 'I don't know about you, but if it is funny flatulence then I'm prepared to give it a miss. I do have some sense of dignity and decorum, although you probably won't believe it. Right, we'll use the same routes as last time, and then it'll be light the blue touchpaper and stand well back.'

'But what if –?'

'What can possibly go wrong? The wine is made from totally safe ingredients. No, my money's still on the flatulence. Like the baked beans scene in *Blazing Saddles*. Mad Molly would probably have found mass burping and farting amusing – especially if she served her wine in polite company. Ready? Let's go.'

Cleo, her earlier enthusiasm waning rapidly, started pouring the Blackberry Blush into the proffered beakers. The villagers, she noticed, were still mellower post-Razzle Dazzle. They all smiled happily at her through their slices of pork and chunks of home-made bread.

'Lovely wine, Cleo. Dead strong,' Amy Reynolds said, holding her beaker out and laughing. 'It made us all go a bit daft, didn't it? It usually takes three or four bottles of Diamond White to get me to that stage. I was having a right old rare-up, wasn't I? Mind, I like a good argument. Oh, and you haven't seen our Elvi, have you? She said she needed the loo when we first got here but that was ages ago and I haven't seen her since. I checked the lavs but there was no sign of her.'

'I'm glad you liked the wine. Have some of this one.' Cleo, pretty sure that Elvi was with the delectable Zeb, smiled. 'I'm sure Elvi's OK. She's probably met up with a friend or something. After all there's nowhere she can get lost round here is there?'

'That's what I keep saying.' Ron Reynolds nodded cheerfully. 'And Amy's right, this here wine's a bit of all right, Cleo. I gave one of my best speeches just now I reckon. I always used to address the brothers a bit tanked up. Great days. Great days.'

'I'm pleased it's, um, made you happy.'

'Right happy. The bloody Pashley-Royles have certainly pushed the boat out with this lot. Must have cost them a fortune. Give us a drop more, love. I'd hate to think that I wasn't getting my fair share.'

As soon as all the beakers had been filled, Cleo, reassured that no one had suffered any ill effects, flew back to the trestle table.

'I've poured us two small glasses,' Dylan said. 'But I still think we should wait.'

The music on the sound system changed abruptly to The Move's 'Blackberry Way'. Cleo frowned. How on earth did that happen? There was no one near the equipment. Was it simply coincidence?

Or something else?

'Sod it,' Dylan groaned. 'Look. How disappointing is that? They're all drinking – and nothing's happened. No mass wind-breaking, no burping, and definitely no blue jokes.'

Cleo heaved a huge sigh of relief. She really thought she'd have to run for cover if the Blackberry Blush turned the whole of Lovers Knot into a universal Chubby Brown.

'Looks like this one is boringly non-magical, then.' Dylan raised his beaker. 'Just a fabulous wine in its own right.'

'Maybe – but I still think we should only have a little sip – just in case . . .'

'OK. Cheers, then.'

'Cheers!'

They each took a mouthful of the Blackberry Blush.

Oooh, Cleo thought, it was really lovely. Possibly even nicer than the damson. Honey sweet. Rich and delicious. She smiled, remembering collecting the blackberries with Doll, and the Lovers Cascade water with Dylan. And then, simply mixing the two together, with the aid of Mad Molly's ancient recipe, had produced this . . . this fabulous nectar.

It *was* magic.

She beamed at Dylan. 'I love you.'

Oooh no! She didn't really say that, did she? Had she spoken aloud? She clapped her free hand to her mouth. What had happened then? Where had that come from?

Oh my God!

'I love you, too.' Dylan smiled. 'I'm completely besotted with you. I think you're the sexiest woman I have ever met in my life. I wanted to drag you into bed the first time we met. You're beautiful and funny and I want to spend the rest of my life with you.'

Cleo laughed.

'Jesus.' Dylan blinked at her. 'Did I just say that?'

'You did!' Cleo said delightedly. 'And I wanted you to take me to bed, too. Still do. And I don't care about your class or your amoral behaviour and all the other women or anything. I think you're the most drop-dead gorgeous man on the planet, and I think about you all the time. I am obsessed by you, Dylan Maguire.'

They giggled together like children.

'However,' Cleo continued, no longer in control of her words and not caring, 'there is one thing I really don't like about you.'

'Spit it out.' Dylan laughed even more. 'Tell the truth.'

'It's the way you waste your life. Such a shame. You've got so much to give and yet you spend your life in one long round of self-gratification. You just use your privileges on pure pleasure. I don't like that at all. And I never will.'

'Christ!' Mortimer puffed, pushing past them. 'I bloody hate Harvest Home! I can't stand all this damn daft traditional nancy countrified stuff. I don't want to wear fox-hunting outfits and be a haw-haw. I want to go down the Weasel and Bucket and play darts with the boys. I only do this for Mimi. I love Mimi.'

Cleo and Dylan stared at his retreating figure in surprise.

'Damn,' Dylan sighed. 'Before Mort muscled in I'm sure I was going to say something else, but – Oh, hell. The Phlopps are heading this way, and – bloody hell! Belly's just hit Flip – or maybe it's the other way round, I can never tell them apart.'

'They wouldn't fight,' Cleo said in disbelief. 'No way!'

219

'True. I've just seen them with my own eyes,' Dylan chuckled. 'Ask them yourself if you don't believe me.'

Cleo, now sure the whole world had gone mad, shook her head. Belly and Flip were inseparable, and had never, as far as she knew, exchanged a cross word.

'Do you know,' Belly said chattily as she pranced by, looking smug and clutching her empty beaker, 'I sometimes used to think about killing Flip. She pinched my one and only boyfriend when we were younger. I still hate her for that. I'm glad I slapped her. She deserved it.'

Flip, following close behind with a plate of the Phlopps' home-made cakes piled high, beamed at Cleo. 'She's right. I went all out to get him, even though I didn't want him. We've always shared everything, you see. I wanted to know what it was like to 'ave a boyfriend too. I'd never 'ad one of me own. It weren't up to much, to be honest – and nor was 'e.'

'Oh, right.' Cleo, not knowing if there was anything she could possibly say to either of these confessions, peered at the heap of cakes. 'Oh, did you make those? I wanted to make cakes but Mimi said you and Belly always did it. They look superb.'

'They are,' Flip gurgled. 'But they ain't ours. They're Dame Helen Mirren's.'

'Sorry?' Cleo blinked in astonishment. 'I had no idea you and Belly were on close culinary terms with Dame Helen.'

'Bless you! Course we're not. No, what I meant was if they was good enough for Dame Helen's character to pass off as 'er own in that *Calendar* fillum, then they was good enough for us. We idolise Dame Helen.'

220

'Yes, but —?'

'In the fillum,' Flip said seriously, 'Dame Helen passes off some shop-bought cakes as home-made and wins a prize for 'em. Me and Belly has been doing the same at Harvest Home for years.'

Cleo laughed. 'You mean your delicate and perfectly baked air-light fancies are really from Marks and Spencer?'

Flip nodded. 'Yep. But don't you go telling no one, young Cleo. I don't know what made me tell you now, truth be told. Me an' Belly swore each other to secrecy.'

Dylan roared with laughter.

As Flip trotted away in the wake of her sister, Cleo turned slowly and looked at the rest of the villagers. They were still chatting while munching their way through their doorsteps of pork, but their conversations were no longer light-hearted. While she couldn't hear exactly what was being said, it was clear that more than a few home truths were being aired.

Truths . . .

Telling the truth. Shooting straight from the hip. Enough to make anyone blush . . .

'Shit!' She looked at Dylan. 'It *does* work. It *is* magic. The blush bit comes in because everyone is being totally honest about their innermost feelings.'

Dylan paused for a moment. 'Christ, yes. Listen to them.'

Amy and Ron Reynolds were going at it hammer and tongs about his political views. Wilf and Maudie were talking loudly over each other as they harshly criticised one another's families. The joint-mustachioed Raymond and

George were having a frank and open discussion about their intense dislike of facial hair.

And the Phlopps had fallen out over a decades-old disagreement.

And Cleo had told Dylan the truth.

Oooh, dear . . .

'Blackberry Blush must be Mad Molly's equivalent of sodium pentothal.' Dylan laughed. 'Unbelievable! What a star she was – concocting some sort of rustic truth drug. And what a party piece that must have been in the good old days.'

'It isn't doing too badly now either,' Cleo said anxiously, watching as the discussions became ever more heated. 'And, um – about what I said . . .'

'Yes?'

Cleo frowned. Much as she wanted to say it had been complete nonsense, her lips simply wouldn't form the words. She tried to clamp her teeth together. That didn't work either. 'It was the absolute truth.'

Bugger!

'All of it?'

'All of it.'

Dylan whooped cheerfully. 'So was mine! I've never used the "l"-word before. Well, and meant it, I mean. I've always had to say, "I love you," because it's good manners when you're sharing someone's bed and body, but it's never been the truth before. How weird.'

'Scary, you mean,' Cleo muttered, praying that the Blackberry Blush wouldn't work in the same way as the Razzle Dazzle Damson and that this time the memories would be wiped swiftly away. It was wonderfully amazing that Dylan had said he loved her, of course, even though he would perhaps not remember and it meant nothing, could come to nothing.

'Not scary at all. I think it's brilliant that thanks to the Blackberry Blush we've all lost our inhibitions and become more communicative. Honesty is always the best policy, isn't it?'

'Well,' Cleo considered, 'sometimes it's better not to say exactly what – Oh, chaff and double chaff! Lambs to the slaughter . . .'

Elvi and Zeb, hand in hand, had just drifted dreamily into the courtyard.

Chapter Seventeen

Elvi frowned round in the semi-darkness. 'What on earth's going on here? I thought it was supposed to be a jolly party for the hoi polloi – my dad's words, natch – but this looks more like putrid *Question Time*.'

'They all seem very serious,' Zeb agreed, looking equally confused. 'I'd expected everyone to be out of their skulls by now, with a brawl or two going on, and maybe a bit of an argument here and there, but this is strange.'

Elvi peered at the villagers, all of whom seemed to be deeply involved in airing their views. Very loudly. Very forcefully. And all at the same time.

How peculiar.

Oh, help – and her dad was arguing more than most. On his own. She gave an ironic snort. It was often said in Lovers Knot that Red Ron Reynolds could start a fight in an empty phone box, and there was the living proof.

Zeb squeezed her hand. 'Come on, let's get the family

intros out of the way, then we'll grab something to eat. I'm starving.'

'Me too.' Elvi giggled as they pushed their way through little knots of highly indignant villagers. 'I know love is supposed to suppress the appetite, but I can't wait to get my hands on a plate piled high with a bit of everything on offer. Are you sure we couldn't just sneak off and eat without having to speak to my parents?'

'Absolutely,' Zeb said firmly. 'Duty before pleasure as the Gorse Glade maxim goes.'

'Does it really?'

'Nah – oh, your mother is waving at us. She hasn't changed a bit.'

'And you can cut that out.' Elvi squeezed his fingers tightly. 'No flirting with my mum. That's strictly against the rules.'

'Elvi, love!' Amy Reynolds, who appeared to have been having a bit of a ding-dong with her nearest neighbour, broke off and beckoned eagerly from her hay bale. 'Elvi! Oh, I'm so glad to see you. Where have you been? I was worried sick. I thought you'd been abducted. I was going out of my mind.'

'I'm sorry, we should have realised you'd be worried.' Zeb held out his hand. 'It's very nice to meet you, Mrs Reynolds.'

'And you, dear,' Amy fluttered. 'What lovely manners. And are you a friend of Elvi's?'

'Hair's funny. Too bloody long at the front and then all them spikes,' Ron stopped his solo spat and growled. 'Looks like a bloody hedgehog.'

'Dad!' Elvi was mortified.

'Tell the truth, that's my motto. Where have you been? And what have you two been up to, eh?'

'Nothing.' Elvi blushed. 'Well, just talking and that. What on earth's happening here? Why is everyone shouting at everyone else? And how much have you had to drink?'

'Can't answer the first two, but the third's just two glasses of wine.' Ron nodded happily. 'Great wine. Mind you, paying thousands for a bottle of wine is pocket money to the likes of the Pashley-Royles isn't it?'

Elvi tightened her fingers on Zeb's hand. 'Mum, Dad, this is Zeb. And yes, he is my friend.'

'Little Zeb!' Amy screamed excitedly. 'Of course! I thought I recognised you. Well I never! Haven't you grown?'

'I should hope so, Mrs Reynolds.' Zeb smiled. 'I was probably three when you last saw me.'

'But I didn't know you knew each other.' Amy looked puzzled. 'Elvi, you've never mentioned little Zeb Pashley-Royle to me, have you?'

Hardly little, Elvi giggled to herself. 'Er, no, but we only met again recently.'

'Pashley-Royle?' Ron suddenly puffed out his cheeks. 'One of *the* Pashley-Royles? One of these here Lovelady Hall Pashley-Royles?'

Elvi whimpered. Oooh noooo . . .

'Mimi and Mortimer's son, yes.' Zeb held out his hand once again. 'I've been looking forward to meeting you, Mr Reynolds.'

'Dad!' Elvi hissed. 'Shake Zeb's hand!'

Ron Reynolds frowned as he lumbered to his feet. 'I was going to. I was brought up properly, you know.'

Elvi held her breath as they shook hands very briefly.

'So.' Ron sat down again and looked up at Zeb. 'You're Elvi's friend, are you? And you know all about her background, do you? And you think that she's a *suitable* friend, do you?'

'Absolutely,' Zeb said bravely. 'I think Elvi is beautiful and intelligent and I've never met anyone like her. Mr Reynolds, you and Mrs Reynolds are clearly wonderful parents.'

Elvi smirked. One–nil to Zeb.

'Ah, well, yes, we've done our best,' Ron said quickly. 'But don't you think you can soft-soap me, my lad. I was young once, you know. I know all about what lads want at your age. And I've lived here all my life. I know what goes on between rich boys and the village girls.'

'Really?' Zeb continued to smile. 'I do love hearing the stories of the, um, olden days. Er, not, of course, that you're that old. I mean, you must be about the same age as my mother, and she's, um, quite young, really . . .'

Ouch, thought Elvi. Big hole. Stop digging.

'Ah, well, we're all old to you kids. But more importantly, we're from the caravans and you're from the big house,' Ron continued. 'Doesn't that say anything to you?'

'Only that good parenting will produce great children anywhere.'

Two–nil to Zeb. Elvi grinned.

Amy smiled happily. 'Well, I think it's lovely. You make a lovely little couple.'

227

Elvi wanted to hug her. 'Thanks, Mum.'

'Couple?' Ron snorted. 'They ain't a couple! They're just kids. So, young Zeb, you think that Elvi is going to be your girlfriend, do you?'

Zeb shook his head. 'No.'

What? Elvi held her breath.

'She's already my girlfriend. But she's also far more than that,' Zeb continued. 'I love her, Mr Reynolds.'

There was a brief silence.

'Love?' Ron roared. 'Don't be so bloody daft! You mean lust, lad! Lust! And I don't care who your bloody parents are, you ain't lusting after my daughter.'

Elvi sighed. And it had all been going so well.

'Dad, don't. We love each other. But it won't interfere with school or anything.'

'Too right it won't!' Ron spluttered. 'Because it isn't going to happen.'

'Aw!' Amy was gooey-eyed. 'I think it's lovely.'

'I'm not lusting, Mr Reynolds.' Zeb stood his ground, but Elvi could feel him shaking. 'I respect Elvi too much for that. But I do love her. And she loves me. And with due respect, there isn't anything you can do to alter that.'

Yay! Elvi cheered mentally. Three–nil to Zeb.

Ron scowled. 'Listen, I've spent my life fighting for the rights of the working man. I've been their voice when the likes of the Pashley-Royles tried to gag them. All over the country there are still little people who are being crushed underfoot by the ruling classes – and I will never sit back and let that happen.'

228

'I can absolutely understand your socialist views,' Zeb said, sounding a bit unsure. 'And I can only applaud them. I think a man should have principles and stick to them. But honestly, I don't think you can talk about the ruling classes any more. Since the demise of Old Labour and the trades unions, the them versus us, er, thingy has gone, hasn't it? And financial power has shifted, hasn't it? All blurred together. The fat cats aren't, um, the upper classes any more. We're all slaves. None of us are free, if you ask me. Today we're all in the same boat. Fighting for survival. And to survive we have to pull together. You know, divided we fall . . .?'

Wow, Elvi thought. Four–nil to Zeb! The Gorse Glade education scores bonus points.

Amy clapped her hands.

'Poppycock!' Ron blustered. 'That's fine for the likes of you to say – you've had it all on a plate, lad. I've had to sweat for every penny. You can't even begin to understand with your cushy life and your fancy education – paid for by the likes of me.'

'And my father,' Zeb interrupted. 'My father was a working man – still is.'

'Pah!' Ron snorted. 'And for all your fine words, you're still not seeing Elvi. When Elvi is old enough to have a boyfriend it'll be someone from her own class. Someone who understands the struggle.'

Elvi interrupted, 'Bloody hell, Dad, you sound like something from *Animal Farm*. You're way out of date. And I don't want to argue with you. But I do love Zeb and . . .'

'You're too bloody young!'

'Hardly,' Amy said, still beaming. 'I wasn't that much older than Elvi is now when we got together, wasn't I? And you'd got me pregnant just before my nineteenth birthday.'

The silence was deafening.

'Pregnant? With me?' Elvi muttered.

'Yes, yes,' Ron said brusquely. 'But that was different.'

'You always said I was a honeymoon baby!'

Amy chuckled. 'We just had our honeymoon a bit before the wedding, love. The way it's always been.'

Elvi turned away. This was all too putridly gross. Way, way too much information.

'At least we got married straight away, soon as we knew,' Ron said, looking a bit shamefaced. 'And we was always going to wed, wasn't we? We just had to bring the date forward a bit.'

Zeb shuffled his feet. 'Um, maybe we'd better leave it there. It's been nice meeting you, and –'

'Zeb! Darling!' Mimi Pashley-Royle drifted towards them with plates of cakes. 'Where have you been? You've missed the start of a fab party, darling. I danced! And we need you to take round that funny trifle thing that Mrs Hancock made. I've peeled the fur off the top. Choppy-chop, darling, oh, and who's this gorgeous girl?'

'Elvi,' Zeb said. 'Elvi, my mother – who of course you know.'

Elvi, still feeling pretty sick at knowing that her parents had ever been young and had sex, shook hands.

'Elvi?' Mimi tried to furrow her surgically enhanced brow. 'Elvi Reynolds? Really? My! What a lovely young

230

lady you've grown up to be. Oh, darling, are you two an item?'

'Yes,' Elvi and Zeb said together.

'No,' Ron snapped.

Mimi flicked her eyes to the hay bales. 'Ron! Ronnie – of course! Now I'm not remotely surprised that you have such a beautiful daughter. What a divinely sexy boy you were. Do you remember – oh, the fun we had when we were all growing up in the village together? Oh, the things we used to get up to! You were sooo naughty!'

Now everyone stared at Mimi.

Amy leaned forwards. 'Ron? What's she talking about? You didn't go out with Lady Pashley-Royle, did you?'

'We didn't go out much,' Mimi giggled delightedly. 'Oh, but he was a devil. He used to help out in the stables in the days when father had horses. Wonderful hands . . . So totally irresistible. We had such an amazing summer together that year before they packed me off to school in Switzerland. Of course, I ran away from there and – But that's another story . . . But I've never forgotten my early introduction to the art of love, and it was all down to Ronnie. So amazing to be deflowered by someone who knew what they were doing.'

'You weren't so bad yourself.' Ron blushed.

Amy glared. 'But me and Ron were together from when I was seventeen.'

'Ah, yes, but he's quite a bit older than you, dear, isn't he? My age. Not that there's anything wrong in that, of course. But Ronnie had already sown his wild oats by the time he

231

met you. Several times. Your Ron had built up quite a reputation. Love 'em and leave 'em – that was his motto – until he met you, naturally.' Mimi continued to smile delightedly. 'Of course, experience tells and Ron's a wonderful lover, don't you agree?'

'Well, yes, but –'

'Enough!' Elvi yelled. 'What the hell's going on here? Even if this gross stuff is true – which I don't believe – it must have been years and years ago, so why are you all talking about it now?'

'I've actually got no idea,' Mimi said happily. 'But it's best to be honest, don't you agree? I was absolutely heartbroken when I found out that my sexy Ronnie – who swore he'd stay single for ever if he couldn't marry me – had married fat Amy.'

'I was never fat! Well, yes, OK, I was a little plump when we married. But that was because –'

'You were pregnant!' Mimi finished triumphantly.

'And you –' Ron grinned wolfishly at Mimi '– were already on husband number two by that time – and had three children. Young Dylan was – what – fifteen or so by then? And you'd got little Florence, and Zeb was a baby. So, you didn't actually pine for me, did you?'

Elvi and Zeb stared at their collective parents in complete horror.

'How could you?' Elvi hissed at her father. 'You . . . you putrid hypocrite! All these years you've been spouting your lefty cants at all and sundry, and saying that the likes of the Pashley-Royles should be boiled in oil, and you'd had a . . .

a fling with Mimi. The wealthiest girl in the area, no doubt. And the only one with a title.'

'It wasn't a fling, dear.' Mimi gave a little shiver of happiness. 'It was a full-on affair. My very first. And you always remember your first, don't you?'

'Very Lady Chatterley,' Zeb said. 'Mother, how could you?'

'Lord, don't be so po-faced, darling! We were young and absolutely bursting with hormones. Ron was super . . . super . . . And so enchantingly and excitingly politically left wing, even then.'

'But hardly politically correct.' Elvi sniffed.

'Oh, sweetheart –' Mimi beamed '– don't be so intense. I was a closet pinko myself back then, you know. And already kicking against the pricks of my sheltered upbringing. You have no idea what fun Ronnie and I had, planning the downfall of the aristocracy in the seclusion of Lovers Spinney with the sun hot on our naked sated bodies.'

Zeb groaned.

'Darling! Get a grip. You youngsters didn't invent sex, you know. Anyway, so much to do. It's been lovely talking to you, I do so enjoy a trip down memory lane. And you –' she smiled at Elvi '– must come to supper really soon. How wonderful – my Zeb and sexy Ron Reynolds's little girl. How truly wonderful.'

Mimi, still smiling, drifted away.

Elvi shook her head. It was all too much. 'Don't say another word.' She looked at her dad. 'Please. I can't cope with any further gross revelations.'

Ron pushed his plate to one side. 'It doesn't alter –'

'Yes it does,' Elvi said fiercely. 'It alters everything. You were giving Zeb a lecture on rich boys seducing poor girls, and you . . . you did it the other way round. You were Mimi's bit of putrid rough!'

'It wasn't like that. We were kids,' Ron said. 'Just kids. All kids together. It was well over thirty years ago. And she was a game girl. A real goer.'

'Excuse me, Mr Reynolds,' Zeb said quietly, 'but that's my mother you're referring to.'

'Exactly.' Ron nodded. 'Your mum and me had a bit of a thing going on. It was fun and no one got hurt, but it didn't last because we were too different and far too young. Exactly the same reasons why you and our Elvi won't last. Only I had nothing to lose, and our Elvi's got everything. Her education, her prospects, her future . . . No, I'm sorry, but I can't allow it.'

'You can and you will,' Elvi snapped. 'And if I get pregnant like Mum did – then that's tough. It'll be all you deserve for being such a two-faced liar. You and your leftie cants. All for the working man! Workers of the world unite! Rise up and flatten the aristocracy! That's all I've ever heard from you. All my life. And you've just proved it's all crap, Dad, and you bloody know it.'

And still clutching Zeb's hand, Elvi turned furiously away from the hay bales before anyone could see her cry.

Zeb brushed his fringe from his eyes. 'I think I really ought to be handing round some food. And it might be better if we never mention any of this again. I don't want Elvi to be upset. Shall we forget it, Mr Reynolds?'

'Suits me.' Ron nodded.

'But what I still don't understand,' Amy's voice rang plaintively, 'is why we've brought all this stuff out in the open now. OK, so everyone has skeletons, but why are they all tumbling out of the closet tonight? What on earth is happening here?'

Chapter Eighteen

It was exactly as if someone had flicked a switch across the courtyard scene, Cleo thought. One minute the Harvest Home crowd had been baring their souls with no holds barred, and the next they were back to eating and chatting merrily, all antagonism forgotten.

Blackberry Bush, Mad Molly's rustic truth drug had worked its magic spell, and just as quickly, normality – or what passed for normality in Lovers Knot – had returned.

So what had happened after her own sip of Blackberry Blush? What secrets had she spilled? She frowned. Nope – she couldn't remember very much at all. Vaguely, there was something she'd said that she possibly shouldn't have, but, no, it had gone.

She shrugged. It probably wasn't that important.

But how odd, she thought, even if she couldn't remember what had happened after the Blackberry Blush, that now – after just two small mouthfuls of extremely strong wine – she should be seeing things with such amazing clarity. Her brain felt clear, her energy levels sky-high.

'Er.' Dylan stared at her. 'What were we talking about?'

'I've got absolutely no idea. I vaguely remember that your mother asked you to help with the food – and Mort said something else – and oh, yes, I saw Elvi and Zeb arrive . . .'

'And I can guess what they'd been doing, especially as I taught him all he knows,' Dylan said cheerfully. 'So I'm not surprised he's hooked up with the prettiest girl in Lovers Knot. Present company excepted, of course.'

'Oh, of course. But I wonder where they've got to now?' Cleo mused. 'I'd love to see Elvi tonight – I haven't talked to her for ages. Hopefully Red Ron hasn't let rip and got them both in tears. I'll just go and get the final batch of wine, then see if I can find her.'

Dylan raised his eyebrows. 'You're going for another brew then, are you?'

'Yep. It's the last one – and their beakers are empty. And the Blackberry Blush's truth-telling doesn't seem to have done them any harm, does it?'

Dylan shook his head. 'Quite the opposite. Like with the Razzle Dazzle Damson, they all look exceptionally happy. Although, unlike the Razzle Dazzle, I can't remember a single thing I said or did. But I feel really good – which, of course, is something you're never going to experience for yourself, are you?'

'Feeling good?'

'Feeling me.'

'Nope,' Cleo laughed. 'In your dreams, Mr Maguire. But,

hang on, that rings a bell – you know, I've got a feeling that . . . No, it's weird. You know, I'm sure there's something that happened after we'd tasted the Blackberry Blush I should remember, but this time it's like waking up after a vivid dream. You think you'll have total recall but it all just gently slips away. Never mind, it'll probably come back one day.'

'Dylan!' Mortimer called across the courtyard. 'I need you!'

'Glad someone does,' Dylan muttered. 'I'm clearly not needed by the Lovers Knot ice maiden over here. Unless you want me to help with the wine? And a cosy interlude with a devastatingly sexy man in a dark cellar?'

'No, thanks. I can manage perfectly well without the added, er, attraction. You go and hand round plates of what-ever's next on offer and flirt with the village ladies instead.'

Dylan brightened. 'Sounds good to me. Oh, and what's the final brew? Did you make the crab apple or the elder-berry?'

'Neither. I brought your special selection: Sloe Seduction.'

'Bloody hell!' Dylan laughed delightedly. 'Can't wait to see what that one does. Don't start without me.'

'Wouldn't dream of it . . .'

Having got to grips with the dumb waiter, it didn't take Cleo very long at all to haul the final bottles of wine up to the courtyard. She'd just finished arranging them on the trestle table, and was watching Zeb and Dylan working the hay bales double-handed, serving the villagers, laughing and chatting.

What fabulous-looking boys they were, she thought wistfully. Well, Dylan wasn't a boy of course, but he was younger than her, wasn't he? And he looked so damn sexy in his evening suit. And Zeb, with his low-slung tight jeans, and his beautiful hair, was exceptionally attractive.

Oh, dear, Zeb – and Elvi . . . She wondered what had happened when Elvi and Zeb had come face to face with the Reynolds. She really hoped that Red Ron Reynolds wouldn't spoil things for Elvi.

'I want to talk to you.'

Cleo looked up. 'Elvi! Goodness me, you look like a supermodel. But how lovely, I was just thinking of you. Er, are you OK? You look as if you've been crying –'

'I'm fine, thanks.' Elvi's face was dark-shadowed in the September night. 'But I told you everything. Everything. So, why didn't you tell me?'

'Sorry? Not with you. Tell you what?'

'One –' Elvi indicated the array of wine bottles '– that you were making wine for Harvest Home. I'd have loved to have helped you. And two, that you're having a putrid affair with Dylan.'

Cleo laughed. 'Sorry, I'm not laughing at you. Just at the idea. Me and Dylan? No way, Elvi! You've got that sooo wrong.'

'Mum says he's been to your caravan. You never said. I told you all about Zeb, and you still didn't tell me about you and Dylan.'

'No, because there was nothing to tell. There's no "me and Dylan", Elvi, love. Honestly. Look, be a star and help me with uncorking this lot and I'll explain it all . . .'

Quickly, Cleo told Elvi about the wine-making, and about Dylan. Well, most of it. '. . . so,' she finished, 'the two things were linked so I couldn't really talk about the wine without telling you about Dylan, and as there's absolutely nothing to tell about Dylan, I thought it was a non-topic.'

Elvi wrestled with the corkscrew. 'OK, sorry, then Mum clearly put two and two together and made ninety-seven. As usual. But, you are friends with him? And did you tell him about me and Zeb?'

'Yes, we're friends and no, of course I didn't tell him anything that you'd told me in confidence. God, Elvi, what sort of friend do you think I am? Zeb himself told Dylan about you two, not me. In fact, I still haven't said that I knew anything about it. OK?'

'OK. Elvi smiled faintly. 'As my life seems to be falling apart at the moment it's nice to know I've got at least one friend I can rely on in Lovers Knot.'

'What? Have you and Zeb split up?'

'No, course not. Me and Zeb are together for ever. But – well, earlier, when we came back from . . . from . . . um . . . talking . . . and I introduced him to my mum and dad, oh, Cleo – it was so putridly weird and awful. It was like they'd gone mad.'

Open-mouthed, Cleo listened to Elvi's story of the no-holds-barred skin-crawling litany of family home truths.

Oh, lordy. Home truths. Blush-causing truths . . .

Quickly, Cleo knew there was no way she was ever going to let anyone know that the Blackberry Bush had been responsible for the soul-baring. Not even Elvi. She'd have to feign innocence . . .

'Oh, you poor thing.' She hugged Elvi, feeling horribly guilty. 'That's awful. How embarrassed must you have been? But – um – I wonder why on earth your dad started telling the truth about everything? And – er – your mum? They'd kept all that a secret for, well, for ever, I suppose. Not to mention Mimi? Fancy Mimi and Ron – um – no, perhaps that's best left alone. And what an old fraud your dad is!'

'I know. I was mortified,' Elvi sighed. 'Trust them to decide to tell us all sorts of putrid stuff tonight of all nights. I blame the drink. My mum and dad are rubbish drinkers. A couple of glasses of wine and they think they're on Jeremy Kyle. I never want to get old!'

Cleo pulled an agonised face. 'It must have been really awful . . .'

'Yeah.' Elvi shrugged. 'But now I *know* everything – and so does Zeb – and it's horrid and sick-making to think about, but it does mean that neither my dad nor the Pashley-Royles have a leg to stand on. They were way worse than us.'

'It certainly sounds like it.' Cleo winced, trying not to think about it in too much detail. 'And yes, OK, look on the bright side – you might know stuff about your parents that you wish you'd never heard, but as you say, you and Zeb now have the upper hand. So, forget the nasties – you and Zeb?'

'Are mint,' Elvi said with renewed enthusiasm. 'Truly. And I took your advice and went to the clinic – not –' she looked seriously at Cleo '– that we've slept together yet. But when we do . . .'

Cleo swallowed the lump in her throat. 'Elvi, I'm so proud of you. You're so sensible and lovely. Your mum and dad must see that. And Zeb clearly adores you. You're very lucky.'

Elvi exhaled. 'S'pose so. And I'm glad you're not having an affair with Dylan. I mean, he's dead cute, but he's got such a bad reputation. He's a serial cheater. My nan would have called him a lounge-lizarding gigolo. And after Dave the Rave nicking off with Wobbly Wanda, you so don't need anyone like Dylan Maguire in your life, do you?'

'Um, no, I don't suppose I do. Anyway, it's not going to happen, so don't worry about it.'

'Nah. OK.' Elvi smiled. 'Now we've got all that sorted out, I'm going to go and find Zeb again. We've got to make the most of every minute together. He'll be back at putrid Gorse Glade tomorrow. Thanks, Cleo. See ya.'

Watching Elvi undulate through the crowd and then seeing Zeb turn, and his eyes light up as he pulled her into his arms, Cleo sighed.

So sweet. First love . . . Exquisite.

And, Cleo thought with a pang, actually she'd really quite like a lounge-lizarding gigolo in her life. Ah, well . . .

She hefted the Sloe Seduction bottles on to a tray and, as Dylan – the lounge-lizarding gigolo in question – was still handing round plates of food on the far side of the courtyard, made a solo wine-waitering trip.

The sloe wine, Cleo thought as she poured it into the

proffered beakers, was even darker than the Blackberry Blush. Midnight dark. Inky. With a delicious uncorked scent of wild west winds and sparkling cold fresh air and a hint of the tangled briars and dense foliage of Lovers Spinney.

And what if it was called Sloe Seduction? What harm could it do? Most of the villagers were pretty merry by now anyway. Even if it lived up to its name, a few harmless kisses and a little meaningless flirtation couldn't hurt anyone, could it?

Mad Molly, being of a more chaste era, probably would never have made anything *iffy* – would she?

'Don't –' Dylan shuddered, joining her once more at the trestle table '– ever suggest I chat up the villagers again.'

'Why? Did Mrs Hancock make advances? Did Maudie show you her hidden tattoo? That's a joke, by the way. Oh, no, the Phlopps didn't suggest that you come back to their caravan and watch their collection of Val Doonican videos, did they?'

'Believe me, they'd have been preferable. No, Salome took my friendly chat-up lines seriously and offered me a cut-price deal. With extras.'

'Lucky you,' Cleo giggled. 'Why are you surprised? You keep telling me how irresistible you are to any woman with a pulse. Poor Salome. You've probably broken her heart.'

Dylan still looked sick. 'And that's not even the worst thing. Zeb has just been telling me that –'

'I already know.' Cleo pulled a face. 'Elvi told me the same story. It all came out thanks to the Blackberry Blush. Your mother and Red Ron? Can you believe it?'

243

'Actually, yes.' Dylan poured them two beakers of Sloe Seduction. 'But I never, ever, want to think about it again. I wish that would stay forgotten like whatever else we all talked about.'

'But it might make things a lot easier for Zeb and Elvi. Ron can hardly object to them seeing one another now they know the truth, can he?'

'Apparently he's currently loudly denying that he said anything of the sort. As is my mother. Neither of them seem to remember a thing about that conversation. But they both look as guilty as sin, so I know who I believe. So, I need a huge slug of Sloe Seduction – and let's hope it erases all those unpleasant images that I know will haunt my tortured dreams for the rest of my life.'

'OK, then. Let's see what happens this time.' Cleo handed him the wine. 'Cheers!'

They raised their beakers.

The music immediately changed from a middle-of-the-road easy-listening track to the Pointer Sisters' wildly sexy 'Slow Hand'.

Cleo stared again at the sound system. Again there was no one near it. How bizarre. Maybe someone had a remote control . . .

'Wow,' Dylan said, swallowing the first mouthful. 'This one's truly fantastic. Really dry and crisp, but with a proper depth to it. I think we should have a proper drink this time. Why should we miss out? I reckon Mad Molly was spot on with Sloe Seduction.'

Cleo swallowed a mouthful, too. 'Mmmm, it tastes like

heaven. Sooo – do we just stand back and see who seduces who?'

'Shouldn't that be whom?'

'Dunno, do I? I'm a thick hick from the sticks, ain't I?'

'You're very beautiful.'

'So are you.'

Cleo stopped. Ooops. Was that the wine talking? She didn't think so. She'd said it perfectly rationally. Bugger.

Dylan laughed. 'It's OK. We can swap compliments. Friends do that. So, what's happening?'

'Nothing,' Cleo said in some frustration. 'Everyone seems perfectly normal. How disappointing. I'd honestly thought this one was going to be a mild liquid aphrodisiac that would at least have people squeezing knees and kissing cheeks.'

'It looks as though Zeb and Elvi have bathed in it,' Dylan laughed, motioning with his beaker across the courtyard. 'Mind you, they probably don't need any sort of artificial help.'

Cleo watched them, clinging together in the deepening shadows, bodies entwined, Zeb's spiky black hair mingling with Elvi's chestnut bob. 'They're completely oblivious to anyone or anything. Bless – it's so lovely, isn't it?'

'I guess so. Zeb seems truly serious about her. Clearly all my detailed instructions on how to love 'em and leave 'em fell on deaf ears.'

'And he obviously hasn't inherited your mother's libido, or her desire to share it with all and sundry.'

'No, but I have.'

'Yes, I know.'

They laughed together. Then stopped.

Something very odd was happening in the courtyard.

It was growing rapidly dark, a deep, warm, black velvet darkness. The fairy lights dimmed. The flames from the spit leaped higher, casting a lone path of shimmering golden brilliance across the cobbles.

From nowhere, a zephyr of exotic fragrances wafted across their faces, leaving the scents of sandalwood, musk, ylang-ylang and jasmine hovering tantalisingly in its wake.

The music suddenly became louder. Bad Company's 'Feel Like Making Love' oozed sexily into the unnaturally warm night air.

'Bloody hell. Mad Molly's magic works again,' Dylan said softly. 'This time the wine is creating an aura. Everything's sensual. It's affecting the atmosphere rather than the drinkers. Jesus, Cleo, what exactly have we unleashed here?'

'I've no idea.'

Stupefied, Cleo watched as people stood up from the hay bales and moved together and started dancing. Slow, erotically charged dancing.

Sloe Seduction . . . yes, absolutely.

The music changed to 'Je T'aime' and as Serge Gainsbourg and Jane Birkin breathed and moaned, even more villagers took to the floor, close together, eyes shut in bliss, bodies touching.

The most unlikely people were swaying, tightly clasped in one another's arms, almost making love to the music. Some of them had arrived at Harvest Home as couples, others were virtual strangers. It didn't seem to matter.

Sloe Seduction's magic had transformed them all.

People like Maudie and Wilf, who both had arthritis and limped heavily, had been turned into slow-dance experts. Amy was dancing with Jerome. And Raymond and George were happily entwined, their bodies moving as one.

Mortimer was with Zola, and Rodders was moving smoochily with Zlinki.

Practically everyone was dancing now.

Except Zeb and Elvi, Cleo noticed dreamily. They were still wrapped up in their own little paradise.

The music changed again. Phyllis Nelson urged then to 'Move Closer' this time. Everyone did.

'Incredible,' Dylan breathed. 'I can't believe this. And, yes, I do want to dance with you – desperately want to feel you in my arms – but I'm fighting the urge.'

'Well don't,' Cleo whispered, her body already floating away on the music. 'Do what you do best and give into temptation.'

She slid against him, her hands resting on the shoulders of his tuxedo, just in time to see Red Ron Reynolds and Mimi practically recreating their youthful love affair under the clock arch.

'Summer (The First Time)' was playing now.

Perfect, Cleo thought dazedly, as she and Dylan danced together, and for the first time she felt his arms around her and his body touching hers.

Absolutely perfect.

Dylan, as she knew he would be, was a brilliant dancer. She sighed blissfully and wriggled even closer. The warm darkness and the glorious scents and the eroticism of the music had removed the last trace of her inhibitions.

'Happy?' Dylan murmured into her hair.

'Blissfully.'

He smiled down at her. 'Me too. This really is magic.'

And he kissed her.

Chapter Nineteen

'*And*? Then what? You can't stop there!' Doll wailed as she dished up several plates of lasagne in her steamy kitchen. 'You can't just leave it at that. What happened next?'

'Nothing.' Cleo sprinkled French dressing on the mixed salad. 'Well, nothing that I can remember. In fact I can't remember much at all. And no, I wasn't drunk. Although maybe I was just a little tired and confused.'

'So you keep saying. Me, I'm keeping an open mind on that one. But your home-made wine was drinkable?' Doll rescued deliciously fragrant garlic bread from the oven. 'I mean, it didn't make anyone ill? It'll be OK for my mum's party?'

'Oh, definitely. Everyone really loved it. Mimi says she's never had so many compliments. Everyone in Lovers Knot says it was the best Harvest Home ever – although . . .'

Cleo stopped. If she wanted to be the sole supplier of home-made wine to Mitzi Blessing's party and beyond, it might be prudent not to tell Doll too much about the strange effects it had had at the previous week's shindig.

'Although what?' Doll grabbed two small plates. 'I'll just go and give these to the kids – you take Brett's – oh, if you could manage the salad and the bread. I'll come back for the rest in a moment. No, go on. What I really want to know is what happened after you *think* Dylan Maguire kissed you.'

Cleo, following Doll into her comfortably cluttered living room, smiled to herself. So did she. She already knew some, but not all.

And everyone at Harvest Home seemed to have reacted in the same way. Everyone remembered *something* about what had happened after the Razzle Dazzle Damson. No one remembered *anything* they'd said or done after the Blackberry Blush. And they all had the strangest, vaguest, dreamlike recollections of the steamy, sensuous atmosphere caused by the Sloe Seduction.

It was sooo annoying not being able to remember anything clearly.

'Not much happened, as I said.' Cleo handed lasagne, salad and bread to Brett, Doll's husband, who was snuggled in the fireside chair happily engrossed in a repeat of *In the Night Garden* with the two toddlers. 'Everyone just carried on partying and having a really good time – and Dylan was, well, just Dylan.'

'And another thing I don't understand,' Doll said once she and Cleo were ensconced on the sofa with their dinners and the baby was happily being spoon-fed a watered down mush of lasagne, 'is why you never mentioned Dylan Maguire to me before. I'm your best friend. You're supposed to tell me everything. And even I know Dylan Maguire – by reputation only, of course – and he's D. D. G.!'

'What's D. D. G.?' Brett queried from beneath his heap of toddlers.

'Drop Dead Gorgeous,' Doll laughed across at her husband. 'Don't you know anything? And – just from a very happily married woman's personal observational point of view, of course – Dylan Maguire is definitely D. D. G.'

Cleo nodded. 'He is. Which is precisely why I didn't tell you about him before. You'd have jumped to all the wrong conclusions and have been off into Winterbrook choosing your wedding outfit – Oh, this is fab, Doll. I never know how you manage to cook so well when you've got the kids to look after and work part-time at the dental surgery.'

'Great organisational skills and the best husband, mum, and sister support system in the world,' Doll said briskly, 'and don't change the subject. I think you're holding way too much back. You said you *think* he might have kissed you. I'm damn sure if Dylan Maguire kissed me, I'd remember it.'

Brett grinned complacently from the fireside chair.

'Well, yes,' Cleo sighed, spearing a forkful of salad, 'so would I. But I don't. And if he did . . . er . . . we did, then it was definitely a mistake. Honestly, I think we were just so carried away with the success of the whole wine thing and the fact that I'd managed to organise Harvest Home at my first attempt without any major disasters, that the events of the evening all became a bit blurred.'

After the sensual ambience of Sloe Seduction had worn off, and Lovelady Hall's courtyard had resumed normality, she and Dylan had still been locked in one another's arms.

They'd blinked sheepishly at each other, laughed a bit, and

unpeeled themselves. As had every other mismatched couple in the courtyard. That much she remembered. But no more.

And this was the aftermath of – what? What exactly had they done?

Cleo remembered everything prior to the dancing, and everything after it, but not the enticing middle. All she was left with was some hazy memory that maybe, just maybe, she and Dylan had kissed. Properly. Mind-blowingly properly.

But she didn't *know*.

And she hadn't asked. And even if she had asked, Dylan wouldn't have remembered. And she so wanted him to remember kissing her . . .

She knew that after the Sloe Seduction, the Harvest Home hooley had roared on to its conclusion, with everyone saying they felt as high as kites, and relaxed and wide awake and really, really happy and wasn't it odd that they couldn't really remember much about what they'd just been doing.

But there had been some longer lasting after-effects. Cleo knew it. The three wines had created very different reactions, but each one had left its subliminal mark.

As the last stragglers had drifted under the clock arch in the early hours of the morning, they were still talking happily about vague recollections of behaving badly, of dancing stupidly, of singing, of arguing – and flirting with completely the wrong people.

Mimi Pashley-Royle had been extremely coy around Ron Reynolds as they all helped clear up the after-party detritus. The Phlopps had eyed one another speculatively and muttered about the past being best left there, and Raymond and George had appeared next day in the general stores, clean shaven.

People who had never even passed a glance at each other before, now smiled bashfully as they walked their dogs on the village green.

New friendships had been forged through shared but barely remembered memories of Harvest Home. Everyone was dimly aware that things were different, and that something at Lovelady Hall had happened to change them, although exactly what seemed to float nebulously in and out of their consciousness.

Cleo knew that nothing in Lovers Knot would ever be quite the same again.

And, if this was wrong in any way, then it was all her fault.

'. . . Cleo, wake up!' Doll nudged her. 'I was saying – so, tell me all about you and Dylan. Are you seeing him now? As in *seeing* him?'

'No.' Cleo shook her head as Doll's oldest child staggered unsteadily across the room, clambered onto her lap, narrowly missing the lasagne and put sticky arms lovingly round her neck. 'Oh, sweetheart, mind you don't get garlic bread on your – ah, too late . . . No, and I never will be. We're just friends. He's gorgeous, of course. The most beautiful boy in the world. But way, way out of my league. He's Mimi Pashley-Royle's son, for heaven's sake. Practically nobility. And he's just far too posh for a council house chick like me.'

'Oooh, lovely,' Doll drooled, 'do you remember how we used to chase after the dead posh boys in our youth? Not –'

she shot a glance at her still-grinning husband '– in any sort of serious way, of course. But we used to think they were so cool, didn't we? With their uniforms, their accents, their charm and their oozing confidence.'

Cleo laughed. 'Poor things – they must have suddenly known what hunted foxes felt like. We were quite merciless in our stalking, weren't we? But we wouldn't have known what on earth to do with one if we'd captured one, would we?'

'Which, it sounds to me, as if you now have.'

'No, I haven't, believe me. We're friends, but Dylan Maguire has more women in his harem than any man could even dream of. Rich, glamorous, eminently suitable women. And honestly, I do think he's just a charming waster. I can't be doing with someone who has no concept of what it's like to be a real person, and have to worry about bills and down-to-earth stuff like that.'

Doll picked up the baby and kissed it thoroughly. It gurgled regurgitated lasagne down its chubby chin. 'Get your claws into Dylan and you won't have to worry about them either.'

'No way! It's not going to happen. And anyway, after Dave I really don't want another man in my life.'

'Yes you do.' Doll bounced the chuckling baby up and down. 'After Dave, that's exactly what you want. Need. Must have. Anyway, you'll be bringing Dylan along to Mum's party, won't you?'

Cleo shook her head. 'I honestly hadn't thought about it. We're not, um, a couple. We've never had a date or anything, but, yes, OK, I'll ask him. He enjoys a party. Although no doubt he'll be heavily involved with Georgiana or Aphrodite that night and turn me down.'

'Georgiana and who?'

Cleo flapped her hands round the sticky toddler. 'It doesn't matter. But even if Dylan doesn't come with me, I'll definitely be there. As will my wines. How many bottles do you want?'

'Me personally?' Brett asked lazily from his armchair. 'About twenty. As Mitzi's having a No Bloody Kids rule at her party and my mum and dad are babysitting, I intend to make the most of it.'

'How many glasses do you get from a bottle?' Doll asked. 'Four? Five?'

'Something like that. And assuming Mitzi will have invited the entire population of Hazy Hassocks, Fiddlesticks, Bagley-cum-Russet and all points south, that's going to be an awful lot of bottles.'

'Which we'll pay you for,' Doll said. 'So, work out quantities and a price and let me know. And if the wine goes down as well as it seems to have done at Harvest Home, then Mum's really interested in the two of you joining forces.'

Cleo smiled happily. 'That's brilliant, Doll. Thanks so much. Me and the infamous local witch Mitzi Blessing in corporate cahoots!'

'My mum is *not* a witch!'

'Oh, yes she is,' Brett hooted.

'Right, so while you're planning on how to mix your winemaking activities with your dalliance with the D. D. G.

Dylan *and* being his mother's ace PA, there's one more thing to think about. Ah, but before that – who wants pud?'

'Me-me-me-me-meeeee!' the children shouted in high-pitched unison.

'Yes, please,' Cleo said, thinking that another thousand calories or so wouldn't make much difference. 'But what else do I have to think about? It's not the theory of relativity or a sneaky equation or quantum physics, is it?'

'Nope.' Doll stood up and dumped the baby on Cleo's lap where it snuffled happily round the already in-situ toddler. 'It's much more taxing than that. Your costume for the party.'

'Costume?'

'Outfit. Whatever. It's a 60s Sixtieth Birthday Party, remember? Everyone in appropriate fancy dress? Me and Brett are taking the easy way out and going as hippies.' Doll giggled. 'Of course, with our Lulu being the real thing, she'll no doubt come in her normal rag-bag clothes, but there's plenty of scope. It's just that fancy dress is compulsory, so give it some thought over the next couple of weeks. OK, kids, stop whining – pud's coming right up!'

Chapter Twenty

'A fancy dress party?' Dylan frowned at Cleo two days later as they pored over Mad Molly's battered collection of recipes in the caravan. 'What? Like a masked ball?'

'Absolutely chuff all like a masked ball.' Cleo grinned at him. 'And you know it. Anyway, Doll, er, wondered if you'd like to, um, come with me? It's in a fortnight's time. I told her you'd be too busy, but –'

'I'd love to come.' Dylan beamed. 'I can't think of anything I'd like more than spending hours and hours with you dressed in hot pants.'

'Is that me dressed in hot pants? Or you? And hot pants were 1970s, anyway.'

'Bugger. Ah, well, it'll have to be a miniskirt then. Don't know what you'll be wearing.'

Cleo laughed. And felt ridiculously delighted that she'd be going to Mitzi Blessing's party with Dylan. That would set the Hazy Hassocks tongues a-wagging. Not that they needed much . . .

'So you'll come? Brilliant. Although a party in Hazy Hassocks village hall may come as something of a culture shock.'

'I have been to village hall parties before.'

'Oh, I wasn't talking about it from a social standing point of view,' Cleo laughed. 'Just a survival one. Anyway, we'll have to leave the vexing question of suitable party costumes until later, because we've got a much more pressing problem. Which wines should we make to blow Mitzi's socks off?'

'I assume you're speaking metaphorically there.' Dylan flicked through the mass of faded, crackling pages. 'But I'd say definitely not the three we made for Harvest Home. We have some idea of the effect they'll have. And as you've already said you'd really like to go into business with Mitzi Blessing's Herbal Country Cooking Company, I suggest we try something maybe a little less inflammatory.'

'That'd rule out the Crab Apple Captivation and Elderberry Ecstasy then?' Cleo frowned. 'Because they sound as though they might lean towards love potions. I've got some other fruit though – I picked pears and some really nice apples from those scrubby trees growing wild at the edge of the spinney, and – oh, yes – I've got loads of plums.'

'OK . . . yes, they sound good. Pears, apples and plums should turn into three fruity robust country wines, which we'll have to make in vast quantities if what you've said about Hazy Hassocks parties is true. Which means collecting tons more water from Lovers Cascade. How empty is your freezer?'

'The one in here? Filled to bursting with fruit. The chest freezer in the shed? Empty. Which also means, if we're going to make enough wine, we'll have to make at least three trips to Lovers Cascade.' Cleo shivered, listening to the howling wind and lashing rain outside. The Indian summer had been a brief-lived affair. 'Still, at least getting wet in the waterfall won't matter this time. We'll be drowned long before we get there.'

Dylan shook his head. 'There's absolutely no point in both of us getting soaked, is there? So you start preparing the fruit, and I'll go and dig out all the containers and collect the water.'

'Are you sure?'

Dylan nodded. 'I've got a Hummer outside. One of Mort's finest deals. I've got to deliver it to a thrash metal guitarist in Bexley Heath later tonight. It's built like a tank and the size of a bus, so I might as well make use of it. One trip to Lovers Spinney – all the water we'll need in one hit – and I get to wear your dressing gown again.'

They looked at one another and laughed.

'I've been collecting loads of other suitable water containers, too. They're all in the shed. So, if you're happy to get wet, that's brilliant. Oh, and can I ask you something?'

'Anything.' Dylan's eyes crinkled at the corners. 'Especially if it's about getting wet.'

'It's about how you get back from Mortimer's delivery trips. Do you hitch or what?'

'Hitch? *Moi*? One of the privileged and overpaid upper classes? Perish the thought! No, Mort always makes sure I have a return train ticket. Second class you'll be delighted to hear. And then I grab a cab for the last bit. Satisfied?'

Cleo blushed and looked away. Only Dylan could load one word with that much overt sexuality. 'Mmm – thanks. It'd been puzzling me – and I hate being puzzled. OK, um, now I'm going to defrost and chop like mad, and have a look at the recipes, and ponder the vexing question of what to wear to Mitzi's party. Oh, and when you get back, there's a cherry and chocolate cake in the tin . . .'

Dylan took well over an hour to collect the water. He dripped into the kitchen, absolutely saturated, rain trickling from his flattened hair, and with his jeans covered in slimy mud.

Cleo shrieked with laughter. 'Is that Lovers Cascade water or snotlings spit? Oh, no – I'm sorry, but you look really, um, I mean, you poor thing . . . Thanks so much for doing that for me.'

'Us, and the future of our winemaking venture.' Dylan shook himself vigorously and peeled off his leather jacket, then spotted the small mountain range of fruit. 'Oh, well done, you. You've worked far harder than me. Have you chopped everything?'

Cleo nodded. 'Pears there, apples on the draining board and the plums are here . . . But, oh, I'm sorry, honestly. You're soaked right through. And you've still got to work. I shouldn't have let you go out tonight. You'll be so cross with me if you die of pneumonia.'

'I went to a public school, remember?' Dylan kicked off his boots, sloshed across the kitchen in his socks, and emptied water into the sink. 'We were positively encouraged to get wet. For character building amongst other things. Can I put my boots by the cooker to dry out?'

'Of course. Is it still raining?'

'Hammering. And blowing a gale. You're much better off in here – it's really snug.'

'Snug', Cleo thought. What a lovely word. Along with 'cosy'. It was all she'd ever wanted her home to be. And something that the Winterbrook semi had never quite achieved.

Dylan pushed his sopping hair from his eyes. 'Actually, it really wasn't too bad. Once you're wet, you're wet – although the Hummer might need quite a bit of valeting when it and I get to Bexley Heath later. And I only fell over twice, but there was no one around to see me so my super-cool image is still intact, even if my dignity isn't. So, if I could just grab a shower?'

'Grab away. You know where everything is – including my dressing gown. And while you're in there, I'll drag the containers into the shed and decant as much water as possible into the freezer.'

'All done,' Dylan's voice echoed from the tiny bathroom above the first swish of the shower.

'Really?' Cleo smiled happily. 'What a star you are. I'm beginning to think you're not such a useless waste of space after all.'

'Gee, thanks.'

'If you throw all your clothes out into the corridor, I'll put them on a fast wash and then straight into the dryer. And as soon as you're out of the shower, we'll have coffee and cake? OK?'

'Far more than OK,' Dylan said happily, as he closed the bathroom door. 'Oh, and I've been giving some thought to our 1960s characters for the fancy dress party, too.'

Cleo smiled even more. He *did* want to go. 'Really? I haven't come up with anything remotely 60-ish apart from hippies or mods and rockers or maybe something to do with the Beatles. Is your idea better than that?'

The shower roared.

Dylan raised his voice. 'I thought we could go as Sonny and Cher. Preferably before he died and she became reconstituted.'

Cleo erupted with laughter. 'Brilliant! And the costumes won't be too difficult to put together. Clever. I'm dead impressed. Which one are you going to be?'

'Cher – as if you needed to ask.'

Still smiling broadly as she gathered up Dylan's soggy clothing and switched on the washing machine, Cleo returned to Mad Molly's recipes.

Sonny and Cher – a proper couple . . . well, at least until the divorce.

Stop thinking along those lines. Concentrate on the wine-making. Look at the book and read the recipes. Right – so what had Molly called these?

Pear Prank, Plum Pucker and Apple Affinity.

Mmm, OK . . . So if, just if, they *were* magical, they might well involve a bit of harmless fun, a little partyish kissing, and some unsuitable but mercifully brief pairings.

They'd be fine. Nothing much there that wouldn't happen at a normal Hazy Hassocks party anyway.

Cleo scanned the recipes – yes, she already had everything she needed, even extra raisins for the Apple Affinity. As long as Mimi didn't find her too much PA-ing overtime in the next couple of weeks she'd be able to have all three flavours made and ready to go well before Mitzi's party.

Fifteen minutes later, Dylan pattered out, bare-footed and wrapped in the fluffy dressing gown, from the bathroom. He smelled clean and warm and tantalisingly of Toko-Yuzu.

'You found my Molton Brown, then?'

'Is that OK? I used the shower mousse and the body lotion.' He smiled. 'It's really, really nice. I like it a lot. That actually worries me a bit. Can I hack at the cake now, please? I'm starving.'

'Take the whole tin through.' Cleo nodded. 'And I'll make coffee and then shove your clothes into the dryer. They should be dry well in time for you to head off into the uncharted wilds of Bexley Heath.'

In a haze of oriental bath essences and clutching the cake tin, Dylan headed happily into the living room.

Joining him, minutes later, with two mugs of coffee and plates and knives, Cleo helped herself to several chunks of cake from the tin, then curled her feet under her in the fireside chair.

'You know,' Dylan said lazily from the sofa, 'I used to think that this was the nicest place on earth when Olive lived here. But now, with the rain beating on the roof and the wind rattling the windows and the fire glowing, it's even better.'

'Really?' Cleo scooped up chocolate cake crumbs. 'No doubt because of the scintillating company?'

'What?' Dylan frowned. 'No way. It's all because of the cake. I think I could elope with your cake and set up home and live happily ever after.'

'And talking of fairy-tale endings,' Cleo said, knowing that she had to ask, 'have you heard from Zeb since –?'

'He's phoned me a couple of times. He and Elvi are still red hot. But, you know, the odd thing is, because they were so besotted with one another at Harvest Home, they – apart from the underage kids – were the only people who didn't drink any of the wine. So they're the only ones who witnessed the shenanigans – and the only ones who can remember what happened.'

Cleo stared at her plate. Had she really eaten three slices of cake? She'd be the fattest Cher on record. 'I know.'

'How come?'

'From Elvi. She popped in last night. I, er, wasn't going to mention it because we knew most of it and guessed the rest – and most of it is just too embarrassing to even think about.'

Please, please, Cleo prayed silently, don't let Zeb have been so observant as Elvi had obviously been.

Elvi had said an awful lot about what she'd seen at Harvest Home. She'd also said that she thought Cleo must have added something hallucinatory to the wine for it to have the effect it'd had. There had been a lot of wild speculation from Elvi about where Cleo had got her hands on mind-altering substances.

As it was straying pretty close to the truth, Cleo had vehemently denied it.

Dylan chuckled. 'I'm still not sure exactly what we did – or said. Hopefully it wasn't too awful. Although I've got a feeling we might have said – No, it's gone again, isn't that odd? I still get these little flashes of memory, but they disappear just as fast.'

'Me too. But, um, Elvi said, even though they missed Razzle Dazzle Damson, not that that mattered because we sort of remember that one, apparently Blackberry Blush *did* make everyone searingly honest – so whatever your mother and Ron Reynolds got up to in their youth was the absolute truth. And Elvi intends to use it to her advantage.'

Dylan helped himself to more cake. 'Zeb does too. I think that inadvertently we've produced the answer to their starcrossed lovers' dilemma. So, that's a plus point for the wine, isn't it?'

'Mmm. Um, did Zeb say anything to you about the effects of the Sloe Seduction?'

'I think he was on planet Lurve and heavily into his own seduction by then. No, he didn't notice much, although he did say the courtyard went sort of funny, and it was weird to see so many old people being disgustingly close together and doing *slow* dancing.' Dylan laughed. 'He was so shocked by it, it was funny to hear him. He sounded like some apoplectic old colonel dissing the youth of today.'

'Elvi said much the same – only with a lot more "putrids" thrown in,' Cleo giggled in relief. 'They're very moralistic, these children, aren't they?'

'Putridly.'

Cleo stared at the empty plate again. Phew. So Zeb hadn't mentioned to Dylan anything about their own particular Sloe Seduction dancing antics. Elvi had. With extravagant detail and a huge amount of amused relish.

'Oh, yes.' Dylan leaned forwards and placed the lid carefully on the cake tin. 'Zeb did happen to mention that they watched us dancing. Together.'

'Really?' Cleo scrambled to her feet. 'I'll just go and see if your clothes are dry.'

'He said –' Dylan stared at her, the faintest hint of a smile on his lips '– and I quote: "no idea what was in that stuff or how much you had to drink, but you and Cleo were really getting down and dirty".'

'Did he?' Cleo tried to laugh. It sounded like the shriek of a strangled budgie. 'I mean, did he? Bless him. What a quaint old-fashioned phrase. Such innocence. I mean, I know we danced together. I do remember that much. I don't remember exactly *how* we danced, but we can hardly have been at *Boléro* standard, can we?'

'And then,' Dylan continued, not even trying to hide his amusement, 'he said, "You two were well into it – well, for olds anyway, which was frankly pretty gross – snogging each other's faces off . . ."'

Chapter Twenty-one

The coach to Gorse Glade, lashed by a ferocious autumn storm, travelled exceedingly slowly along the winding Berkshire lanes in the darkness.

Come on! Elvi urged. For God's sake, get a move on!

'Practically a full house for Social Integration,' Sophie, sitting beside her, said. 'I know it counts towards our grades for the Citizenship certificate, but as it's not compulsory I'm surprised so many of us turned up tonight.'

'I'm not.' Kate leaned across the swaying aisle. 'How often do we get to see inside a posh boys' school? Not, of course, that I'm in the slightest bit interested in the posh boys. My Mason says . . .'

'Whatever your Mason says,' Sophie sniggered, 'always ends in "innit" and is mostly balls.'

'Children,' Elvi giggled, 'play nicely.'

She leaned her head back in her seat. Sophie was right. Most of the lower sixth had turned out on this cold, wet and windy October night simply because Gorse Glade was so totally outside their own sphere of experience.

Of course, that wasn't her reason for being here.

She sighed with impatience, her fingers itching to stray to her school bag and remove her mobile phone. But she couldn't. Mobiles were banned by Winterbrook Grammar School. If you were caught with one it was confiscated until the end of term. There was no way on earth Elvi was going to risk her only line of communication with Zeb being cut off.

Of course a lot of the other girls just bought another phone, but she couldn't afford to do that. No, she'd just have to sit here, crawling towards Gorse Glade, praying that Zeb would be waiting.

In his last text before she'd boarded the coach, he'd said he'd be there, waiting for her. Dying to see her. Counting the seconds. They had no idea how they were going to play it from there. But they'd think of something.

Elvi, completely obsessed by him and loving him to distraction, was terrified that during the journey something awful would happen to stop them being together. What if the coach broke down? What if they never got there at all? What if –?

If only she could text him . . .

God! How did people ever *cope* before there were mobiles and email? Her mum had said that when she was Elvi's age they didn't even have a phone at *home*. And if she wanted to get a message to anyone, or talk to a boyfriend, or make arrangements with her friends, she had to use the putrid phone box outside the Lovers Knot general stores.

How archaic was that?

And, even more shocking, her nan had told her that as well as the phone box, she used to write *love letters* to her boyfriends and they used to write back. Letters! Letters that had to be stamped and posted and delivered and arrive and answered and posted back again.

That would have taken *months*!

Ohmigod, Elvi thought. How grossly awful it must have been to be in love in the olden days.

The coach trundled on. Mind-numbingly slowly. Sophie went to sleep. Kate – clearly prepared to risk everything for her man – was texting Mason and swigging from a bottle of Lucozade and WKD.

Elvi groaned to herself. The coach must be going backwards. They'd never, ever get there . . .

But they did.

'Come along, girls!' Miss Chamberlain shouted bossily. 'No dawdling! Out of the coach and into the entrance hall. It's still raining hard and I don't want any of you catching colds. Come along – quickly!'

They poured off the coach into the storm.

Elvi's heart was thumping so hard she was sure everyone could hear it.

This was it. Oblivious of the screaming wind and rain, she stopped and stared at Gorse Glade for a second.

How beautiful. How lucky Zeb was.

The sixteenth-century abbey, bathed in the glow of muted floodlights, looked amazingly gothic, especially in the darkness and the lashing rain. Sprawling and mellow, with well-worn steps and a multitude of latticed windows, it was like something from a dream.

'Cool, or what?' Sophie breathed, forgetting to be unimpressed. 'No wonder they get so many Oxbridge entrants. This sort of place would make you want to study even harder, wouldn't it?'

Elvi nodded, too excited to speak.

Kate, hastily pushing her mobile phone out of sight, gazed at the splendour, open-mouthed. 'Wow! It's like, totally awesome.'

'Girls!' Miss Chamberlain's shriek was spiralled away by the gale. 'Come along! Run!'

The other Winterbrook staff members, Elvi noticed vaguely, had already bustled inside to be greeted by the Gorse Glade masters, all of whom were wearing their gowns. She walked slowly, her hair whipped across her face, the rain stinging her eyes, because Zeb may well have walked on this very spot. His feet had trodden the path she was now treading. They were sharing the same earth.

'Elvi! Stop daydreaming. Come along. Hurry up.'

Elvi, knowing that she was now only milliseconds away from being with Zeb, hurried.

The inside of Gorse Glade exactly matched the exterior. Old, cared for, totally beautiful.

Elvi's mouth was dry as she followed the other girls into the panelled and gilded assembly hall. There were portraits on the wall, and real velvet curtains, and chandeliers twinkled subtly, casting pools of gentle light on the gleaming wooden floors. Everywhere smelled of lavender.

There was no excruciating electro pop here. Soft classical music swept through the hall, and a pimply youth handed them each a real faceted crystal glass of something amber and sparkling.

'Not alcohol, is it?' Miss Chamberlain snapped. 'These girls are all under eighteen. I don't want them touching alcohol.'

Kate sniggered.

'Non-alcoholic,' the pimply youth assured her in wonderfully deep, well-modulated tones. 'We don't allow alcohol on the premises in Gorse Glade.'

Elvi smiled to herself.

'Reports will be written on your behaviour, as you know,' Miss Chamberlain said, rubbing her hands vigorously together. 'We have two hours, girls, and I don't want you to waste a minute of it.'

Believe me, Elvi thought deliriously, I don't intend to.

'Right, off you go and mingle. No hanging around on the periphery. And exchange views. Talk, girls, and listen to what is said. Talk, listen and learn the art of conversation. This is an important part of your education. And remember, I – and the other staff members – will be watching you.'

I sincerely hope not, Elvi thought, her eyes already raking the crowd of Gorse Glade boys for Zeb.

'I say!' Henry Bancroft, still pink and white and fluffy-looking, bore down on her. 'Don't I remember you?'

'Er . . .?' Elvi frowned at him. 'Yes, of course you do. It's me – Elvi.'

'I know jolly well it's you,' Henry hissed. 'I'm acting here.

Just in case anyone overhears. I was Ophelia in last term's *Hamlet*, you know.'

Christ, Elvi thought.

'Er, right.' She smiled at him and raised her voice. 'Yes, I think I remember you from our Soc Int at Winterbrook. Um, Harry, isn't it?'

'Henry,' he stage-whispered. 'Just follow me across the hall. Talk normally. Lovely weather, isn't it?'

'It's like a monsoon out there.'

'Ah, yes, um, did you have a nice holiday?'

'You're not a hairdresser,' Elvi giggled. 'And where's Zeb?'

'Not here.'

Elvi's heart stopped beating. She felt sick. Her fingers tightened on the stem of her glass.

She knew it.

Something had happened to keep them apart. She'd never see him again. He'd changed his mind. The awful parental revelations at Harvest Home had suddenly made him realise they had no future together.

'He's, er, been taken ill,' Henry brayed loudly, looking across at the be-gowned Gorse Glade masters. 'Poor boy. Felt terribly nauseous after tea. We had mushrooms.'

Oh God, Elvi thought. Zeb had caught salmonella or beriberi or something equally as awful and was going to die.

She'd have to die too. She couldn't possibly live without him.

It was just like Romeo and Juliet. 'Tainted Love'.

She'd have to eat poisoned mushrooms too. She didn't like mushrooms. She didn't supposed that mattered.

'Keep talking,' Henry whispered. 'Keep smiling and keep behind that crowd of boys over there.' He raised his voice. 'Yes, poor Zeb, it was very sudden. Very sudden indeed. '

Totally distraught and unable to smile, Elvi was only vaguely aware of Shellie and Bex, the lower sixth's social climbers, practically gagging to scramble on to the first rung of the Gorse Glade dating ladder by squealing excitedly at everything the group of boys were saying. And of Kate in a deep and presumably intelligible conversation with the pimply wine-bearer. She couldn't see Sophie. She didn't care.

'But . . . but . . . is he . . .?'

'What? Oh, yes, absolutely! Didn't stand a chance! Went down like a . . . like a . . . stone!'

Oh, God, Elvi thought. 'Is he unconscious?'

'What? Oh, yes. Completely. In fact, it's much worse than that.'

Elvi knew she was going to pass out. She clutched Henry's arm.

'Ouch! Through here.' Henry held a door open for her. 'Don't look back. I don't think anyone's seen us. This part is out of bounds, but under the circumstances . . . er . . .'

Had Zeb already died? Was Henry taking her to see his body? Gorse Glade, she presumed, would have a private chapel. That must be it. Zeb was dead! Henry was taking her to make her final farewells!

Elvi whimpered. She still vividly remembered going with her mum and dad to the Motions funeral directors in Hazy Hassocks when her beloved Gramps had died, and staring in horror into the coffin, with the candles at each end and the sickly sweet smell of air-freshener and awful music playing. And recoiling in horror at his unfamiliar waxy face, smiling in a sort of sinister way, and with far too much lipstick and blusher.

Zeb was dead . . .

'There,' Henry said as, after traipsing along a maze of spotlessly clean and panelled corridors, they reached the top of a flight of highly polished stairs. He indicated a stout oak door. 'In you go.'

'Aren't you coming in with me?' Elvi whispered.

'Er, no. Not my scene,' Henry brayed nervously. 'I'll come and get you in just under two hours.'

'Two hours?' Elvi swallowed. 'I can't stay in there for just under two hours. On my own.'

Henry looked at her strangely and pushed the door open.

Holding her breath, knowing that this was the most awful moment of her entire life, Elvi stepped inside.

The door boomed shut behind her.

The small oak-panelled room was warm, and dimly lit by a single small gold-shaded lamp, and there was reggae music playing softly in the background. No flowers, no candles, no coffin.

'Hi.' Zeb, very alive, totally beautiful and completely naked, grinned from his bed. 'I thought you'd never get here.'

Elvi burst into tears.

'Oh crap,' Zeb groaned, leaping out of bed with no apparent embarrassment. 'I knew you wouldn't want to. I said to

Henry this was pushing things too far too fast. Don't cry, Elvi, please don't cry. We don't have to do anything you don't want to.'

Elvi sniffed back her tears and stared at him in wonderment.

He encircled her with his thin arms and pulled her against him. 'There was no way on earth I could have stood just making small talk in the hall with all the others when all I wanted to do was – But that's me being selfish. I'm so very sorry.'

'I thought you were dead,' Elvi hiccupped with delight, feeing his body against hers. 'But you're not.'

'Er, no . . . I'm very much alive, as you can, um, tell. What the hell did Henry say to you?'

'He said you'd eaten poisoned mushrooms.'

'That's Henry for you – always over-egging the pudding. And I'm sorry but this seems a bit weird – talking like this.'

'I don't want to talk.' Elvi stroked his slender face, her fingers hovering on his lips. 'I really don't want to talk.'

Some million years later, Elvi moved her head on the pillows. Such lovely pillows. And so many of them. Goose down, she reckoned. Like the duvet. And fresh white linen. And she was in heaven – and she hadn't eaten poisoned mushrooms to get there.

'OK?' Zeb moved his arm slightly underneath her neck, pulling her even closer to him. 'Still awake?'

'Just about. Floating. And very OK.' Elvi kissed his naked shoulder. 'Er, are you?'

'Oh God, yes.' Zeb smoothed her tangled hair from her eyes. 'More vodka?'

'Please. Oh, this is just the most wonderful time of my life.'

'Mine too,' Zeb said, sloshing vodka haphazardly into their glasses. 'I've never, ever been happier. Never. Ever. I love you.'

'I love you too.'

Chinking glasses, they gulped the vodka, then smiled at one another, totally delighted at their cleverness.

They didn't need to talk, Elvi thought dreamily. Not at that moment. Their bodies had said everything there was to say.

So this was it. She knew what it was like to be a woman. Twice over. And it had been wonderful. Not tacky like Kate had made it sound, or scary, or awkward or anything. Just amazing.

She was sixteen and in love with the most wonderful boy in the world. And he loved her. And because of her dad and Mimi Pashley-Royle getting drunk on fabulous, fabulous Cleo's home-made wine there was nothing in the world to keep them apart.

She sighed happily, feeling Zeb's skin touching her skin, so close to him that she could feel his heart beating, listening to the wind and the rain outside.

'I never want to leave here. I want to stay snuggled up with you. I want to look at you all the time and touch you all the time and listen to your voice all the time. I want to live in this room for ever.'

'Me, too.' Zeb kissed her. The vodka splashed on to the duvet. 'But this is just the start of our happy ever after, isn't it? This is how we'll always be. Oh, not in this room, obviously, but soon – as soon as we go to university – we can get a flat together, and study together and live together, and it'll be like this all the time.'

Elvi smiled at the blissful dream . . . then stopped and shook her head. 'No it won't. It can't be.'

'Why not?'

'Because you're already in your A-level year. I've still got almost two years to go. You'll go to Oxford a year before me, then I'll go to Durham –' She caught her breath. 'And we'll be miles apart and then there'll be years and years of studying, and we'll never see each other, and we'll be ancient and grossly decrepit by the time we get our degrees and –'

'Sssh.' Zeb kissed her again. 'I've thought of all that. I've got a plan. A very secret plan. A plan that only we will know about.'

Elvi blinked at him. 'OK, go on, but I don't see what . . .'

'I'm going to fail.'

'*What?*'

'I'm going to fail my As,' Zeb said happily. 'Spectacularly badly. Then I'll have a resit year, which will mean we'll be taking our A levels at the same time. And of course, the second time I'll pass all three with flying colours, as will you at your first attempt. And I'm not going to go to Oxford, I'm going to apply to Durham. I've looked at the prospectus online and they do a brilliant physics course there. So, we'll both be up at Durham. At the same time.'

Elvi was open-mouthed. 'You'd really do that for me?'

'I'd do anything for you, Elvi. Anything in the world. But I'm doing it for me too.' Zeb grinned at her. 'How the hell do you think I'd survive apart from you? These last few weeks have been torture. So, we've just got to get through the next couple of years – and I shall come home to Lovers Knot as often as I can – then we can be together for ever.'

'In Durham.' Elvi squeaked with ecstasy at the brilliance of the plan. 'In a little flat, and seeing each other all the time. Sharing everything. Living together . . . Ohmigod.'

'Like it?'

'I love it!'

Zeb moved even closer and she kissed him. And he kissed her back. And then they spilt the rest of the vodka and giggled a lot. Then somehow they were rolling over and over on the bed, laughing, and slid, blissfully entwined and entangled in the duvet, to the floor.

'Oh, I say!' Henry's voice bellowed into the room. 'Oh-I-say!'

Elvi sat up on the floor, grabbed part of the duvet to her nakedness, and grinned at him.

'Bugger off, Henry.' Zeb emerged from under the other end of the duvet. 'This isn't the floor show.'

'Actually,' Elvi giggled, 'I think it probably is.'

'You've got five minutes,' Henry hissed. 'The staff are just making their farewell speeches and congratulating one another that nothing went wrong.'

'Bugger.' Elvi, still clutching the duvet, scrambled around for her clothes. 'Henry, close your eyes. Where's my bra?'

'Here.' Zeb handed it to her. 'Oh, and these are yours. And this. And this.'

She leaned over and kissed him.

'I love you, love you, love you,' Zeb said, kissing her as she frantically pulled on her school uniform. 'And I always will.'

'Get a move on!' Henry urged, his eyes tightly shut. 'Please get a move on! We could all get unfrocked for this.'

'I've already been unfrocked,' Elvi giggled.

Dressed, raking her fingers through her hair and eventually locating her school bag, Elvi then clung to Zeb for one final time.

He kissed her lingeringly. 'Oh, shit, I so don't want you to go. But I'll be home in a couple of weeks. We've got a free study weekend looming. And you can come here any time you like. We'll work out a plan.'

'Mmm,' she murmured into his skin, not wanting to ever let him go. 'I like your plans.'

'Elvi!' Henry was red-faced. 'They haven't missed you yet, but please come on!'

Kissing Zeb goodbye, Elvi tore herself away and, with one last lingering look, followed Henry from the room.

'And that's everyone,' Miss Chamberlain said with some relief as she counted heads on to the coach. 'Right, driver, home, James, and don't spare the horses.'

Elvi sat in the darkness, completely unable to stop smiling, and trying not to look at Kate and Sophie.

279

'So?' Sophie said as soon as the coach had pulled away from Gorse Glade and the noise of the engine would prevent the teachers overhearing. 'Give. All of it. Where were you? Who is he? Why the hell didn't we know about him, and it, and all of it, before?'

'Yeah.' Kate leaned across the aisle. 'We're your best friends. We want every little last tiny detail.'

'Nothing to tell.' Elvi beamed.

'There's loads to tell,' Sophie said huffily. 'You could start with why most of your uniform is on inside out.'

Ooops. Elvi giggled.

'Look,' Kate said. 'No one else noticed you were missing, but we did. We were going to say something, like, in case you'd gone to the loo and got locked in or lost in all those corridors, then that fat Henry –'

'He isn't actually fat,' Sophie interrupted. 'He's more stocky. Like a rugby player. I like a big boy myself.'

Elvi stared at her.

'Yeah,' Kate sighed. 'She pulled. Gross, if you ask me.'

Sophie sighed. 'Actually, it's all rather lovely. And Henry's dad is a bishop. Don't you think that's so bloody sexy? You know, like in "Son of a Preacher Man"?'

'No.' Kate shook her head. 'Like I said, it's gross. Anyway, fat Henry haw-hawed a lot and said we couldn't report you missing because you weren't and that we mustn't worry because you were OK and you'd be back in time to catch the coach – and now we want all the sordid details.'

'There aren't any sordid details,' Elvi said dreamily. 'Only beautiful ones. And I'm keeping them all to myself.'

'No, you're not.' Sophie grinned. 'Henry clearly knew all about it, so we want a name at least.'

'Zeb Pashley-Royle.' Elvi caressed each syllable lovingly with her tongue. 'I've just spent the last two hours in bed with Zeb Pashley-Royle.'

Kate and Sophie stared at her in shock and awe.

'My secret lover,' said Elvi, suddenly laughing out loud. 'Not such a secret any more. But always and for ever my lover.'

Sophie wrinkled her nose. 'Now you sound just like one of my gran's Doris Day records.'

'Doris who?' Kate frowned. 'Anyway, you mean that you and this Zeb, have —?'

'Made love? Mmm, we have.' Elvi shivered blissfully at the memory. 'Three times.'

'*Three times*?' Kate said in amazement. 'In less than two *hours*? Me and my Mason never —'

'Bugger you and your Mason,' Sophie said faintly, gazing at Elvi in jealous admiration. 'In less than two hours . . . That must be a record.'

'No, that was Doris Day,' Elvi shrieked with laughter. 'Oh, I do so adore social integration, but I adore Zeb Pashley-Royle even more . . .'

Chapter Twenty-two

October had followed the pattern of late September, and was exceptionally cold and windy. But at least it wasn't raining. Standing outside a dark and dismal Hazy Hassocks village hall, dressed as Cher, Cleo shivered.

'You're bang on time.' Doll emerged from the hall's side door. 'That's great. Me, Brett, Lulu and Shay are here just to set out Mum's food and your wine and let the JB Roadshow get their stage stuff organised. Zillah's with them – you remember Mum's friend Zillah?'

Cleo nodded. Zillah Flanagan had lived in Fiddlesticks; she'd rather sensationally married one of the JB Roadshow a few years back.

'And Amber, Lewis and Jem are with her, of course. And Gwyneth and Big Ida – and everyone else is coming from Fiddlesticks and Bagley-cum-Russet. And Clemmie and Guy Devlin from Winterbrook. This is their first evening out without Emerald Star – they've left her at home with YaYa and Suggs.'

Cleo nodded again. It probably didn't seem at all odd to anyone local that the Devlin's cherished first baby was being cared for by Suggs the ferret and YaYa Bordello the outrageous drag queen. Cleo knew that YaYa, being Clemmie and Guy's best friend, had very recently taken on the dual role of both godmother and godfather to baby Emerald Star.

'Then there's Joss, Freddo, Sukie, Derry, Phoebe and Rocky – oh, yes, Rocky works on the Lovelady gardens sometimes, doesn't he, so you'll know him – and . . .'

Cleo continued to nod as Doll excitedly listed the guests. Everyone she knew was going to be at the party. Well, almost everyone.

'. . . and – Cleo? Are you still with me? I said, is the wine all in the car?'

Cleo, feeling slightly guilty at her lack of concentration, nodded again.

'Fantastic. Oh, before I forget, here's your money. In cash – I thought you might prefer it that way.' Doll handed Cleo a bulky envelope. 'Best get the business transaction out of the way before we're all too sozzled to remember.'

'Thanks so much, but you haven't tried the wine yet,' Cleo protested, pushing the envelope into the hippy and hopefully Cher-like shoulder bag. 'It might be awful.'

'Of course it won't be awful. I've heard some amazing reports about your Harvest Home brews. We've had loads of Lovers Knot people in the dental surgery this past week or so, and they were all raving about it. If it's half as good as they say it is, then we'll have underpaid you.'

'Let's wait and see, shall we? You might be wanting a refund.'

'No way.' Doll stopped. 'Are you feeling OK? You don't sound very partyish.'

'I'm fine, um, just a bit tired. Er, Mimi's been really cracking the whip this week. I've been doing loads of overtime at Lovelady.'

'But you still enjoy it?'

'I love it,' Cleo said honestly. 'It's a great job. Every day's different, but that doesn't mean that I still wouldn't love the opportunity to be part-time partner in your mum's catering business too.'

'And she's really up for it. It'll be like the start of Fortnum and Mason all over again. Or do I mean Marks and Spencer? Goodness!' Doll shivered. 'That wind's freezing. We'd better stop nattering and get the wine inside, otherwise the guests'll be here and baying for blood.'

'Have you got a barmaid, or do you want me to?'

'No way. I told you, you're here as a guest. You've just got to enjoy yourself. We're all organised. We've set out a table at one end for the bar, which Fern and Timmy Pluckrose from the Weasel and Bucket in Fiddlesticks are going to run for us. And the food is on a table at the other end on a help-yourself basis. That way there won't be the usual scrum.'

'And have you got other drinks, too? For those who don't like wine?'

'All tastes and inclinations catered for.' Doll laughed. 'Fern and Timmy are supplying beer for the diehards and spirits for those who can't face a party without a g and t – so with your wine there should be plenty of booze to go round. Now, I'll just pop back in and get the blokes to do the heavy lifting.'

Cleo stood alone again in the icy-cold blustery darkness and hoped the wine would be OK. Would be what Mitzi wanted. She was sure it would be. She couldn't worry about it – it was too late to alter it – and, after all, it was one of her smaller problems right now.

Each of the wines had looked perfect when she'd decanted them into the bottles. As before, the Lovers Cascade water had ensured a rapid fermentation process, and the wine had been crystal clear and smelled wonderful. She had a good selection of Pear Prank, Apple Affinity and Plum Pucker carefully stacked in the car. More than enough for Mitzi's party.

Someone suddenly flicked on the outside security lights, making Cleo blink.

Brett and his brother-in-law Shay emerged from the hall. Brett was dressed, as Doll had been, in a selection of multi-coloured flowing robes over jeans, with a garland of flowers in his hair. Shay, she noticed with some surprise, was in a retro football strip.

'He's come as the 1966 World Cup winning team,' Brett explained as they hauled the bottles from the car. 'Lu's here as her normal hippy self, but she said Shay had such lovely legs it was a shame not to show them off.'

Shay aped a catwalk pose and pouted.

Cleo almost smiled.

'Right –' Doll emerged again as Brett and Shay hefted the bottles inside '– that's that well under way. Oh, and now I can see you properly under the light, you look absolutely amazing. How long did that take you?'

'Ages,' Cleo said through chattering teeth. 'I've never used hair straighteners before. Elvi had to do it for me in the end. And my eye make-up took even longer. I think I look like a panda, and these false eyelashes are bound to fall off . . .'

And she'd probably split the skin-tight floral bell-bottoms that she spent hours making from scraps of fabric scrounged from everyone in Lovers Knot. And the charity shop faux-fur trimmed waistcoat would make her sneeze, and the white T-shirt was obscenely tight, and all the bells, beads and flowers round her neck would strangle her before the night was out.

Hopefully.

'And your other half? The sweet Sonny? The D. D. G. Dylan Maguire – who I can't wait to meet?'

'Isn't coming.'

'*What?*'

'Don't ask. Please. Tonight I'm a solo Cher,' Cleo sighed. 'I'll just have to pass my self off as another hippy. And can we go inside now, Doll? I'm freezing.'

Inside the hall, despite her gloom, Cleo smiled. Banners and balloons were festooned everywhere, the JB Roadshow were busily setting up their soul-band equipment on the stage, Fern and Timmy were busily stacking her home-made wines to their best advantage, and there was more food heaped on the table than anyone could possibly want in a lifetime.

It was going to be a great party. Such a shame Dylan couldn't be bothered to be there to share it.

Cleo sighed.

Dylan had taken a Maserati Gran Turisimo to Jersey at the beginning of the week. He hadn't come back. And his mobile was switched off.

And this time she couldn't excuse him by saying he didn't know her number. He did. And even if he'd lost it, he'd have been able to contact her at Lovelady Hall, wouldn't he?

If he'd wanted to.

She sighed again.

Dylan had promised he'd be back in time. Promised. He'd laughed about the irony of taking the Maserati to an island with roads like footpaths and a 40 mph maximum speed limit. He'd been as thrilled as she was with the new wines they'd made. He'd been even more delighted with the Sonny outfit she'd concocted for him. He'd tried it on and posed in front of the caravan's one and only long mirror and said he couldn't wait for the party.

And now he wasn't going to be there.

'Cleo!' Mitzi Blessing, followed by her gorgeous live-in lover Joel, both dressed as Sergeant Pepper Beatles, bounced up to her and kissed her. 'It's great to see you again. And don't you look lovely? Exactly like Cher in her early days. Um, sorry, love, I was just going to be typically tactless and say it was shame you haven't got a Sonny in tow tonight, but I know after the divorce and everything . . .'

'I'm more than happy being a solo Cher,' Cleo lied.

'Good.' Mitzi looked relieved. 'And I'm sure you'll meet someone just right for you before too long. Like I did with Joel. After my divorce from Lance −' Mitzi cast a glance across the room to where her ex-husband and Jennifer, Mrs Blessing Mark Two, were hovering by the bar, dressed as John and Yoko: the hippy years '— I didn't even think about finding anyone else. I was old and frumpy and —'

'Luckily, old and frumpy turned me on,' Joel laughed. 'And still does.'

Mitzi, clearly knowing she looked anything but old and frumpy, giggled girlishly.

Cleo smiled at them both. Just because she was feeling as miserable as sin really didn't mean she should spoil everyone else's fun.

'I don't know — maybe I'm better being single.'

'For a while, maybe, 'Mitzi agreed. 'But you're such a beautiful girl, it would be such a pity for you not to be happy again with another man. Someone will come along, when you least expect it, and — whoosh — it'll be all rainbows and fireworks. You'll see.'

But I've already seen, Cleo thought sadly. And yes, he came along when I least expected it, and I've had all that rainbow and fireworks stuff. And having had it, and because it was with Dylan and he's the only man I'll ever want and can't have and because he clearly doesn't want me, it'll never come again.

Mitzi was still smiling happily. 'Oh, and before I forget, or get too tiddly, your wines look fantastic. Such wonderful colours, and so clear. Home-made wines are very tricky to get right, so I'm really impressed. So, you'll be up for a bit of a merger, will you?'

'Oh, er, well, yes,' Cleo mumbled. 'I mean, yes, of

course, I'd love to, but only if you think the wines are good enough.'

'We've been hearing about nothing else at the surgery,' Joel laughed. 'Every filling I've done this week seems to be for someone who thinks your wines are the best thing they've ever tasted. And apparently they have a really odd effect – "mind-blowing", I think was the most commonly used description – but then with no after-effects at all, except a sense of being wide awake, extremely happy and raring to go.'

'Which all sounds pretty magical to me,' Mitzi laughed. 'And exactly what I'm looking for to go with my herbal food. So, shall we get together sometime next week and have a chat to sort out the details?'

'Yes, please. Thanks so much – I'd love to.' Cleo nodded enthusiastically.

She'd do it. But she'd do it alone. Like being a solo Cher, she'd be a solo vintner. Dylan clearly couldn't be bothered. Again.

Mitzi beamed. 'Wonderful. I'll give you a ring. Oh, I suppose I ought to go and circulate. There are so many people arriving – and Lav and Lob came with us and if I'm not careful they'll have eaten all the food before anyone else gets a look in.'

Cleo gazed across at the food table, and laughed at Lavender and Lobelia Banding, Mitzi's geriatric next-door neighbours, who were hovering round the still cling-filmed goodies like impatient vultures.

But why on earth were they wearing long johns on their

skinny bodies and Wellingtons on their feet? And what the heck was that on their heads?

'Are they supposed to be, um –?'

'They're spacemen. Moonwalkers. Neil Armstrong and Buzz Aldrin. Or so they told me. The first man on the moon landing thing in 1969, you know? The, um, all-in-ones are their interpretation of spacesuits.' Mitzi kept a straight face. 'The helmets are Perspex goldfish bowls, with a hole cut in the front so they can shovel food in.'

'And the cycle helmets balanced on top? With flowers stuck on?'

'Will probably fall off and kill someone,' Joel sighed. 'The flowers are their second attempt at decorating the helmets in a 60s fashion. They're made of plaster of Paris and stuck on with Elastoplasts. Their first choice was with Martians made from lino. They wilted fairly spectacularly.'

Mitzi smiled at her elderly neighbours lovingly. 'Bless them. Lav and Lob always wear their cycle helmets. Day and night. In case of accidents. A fancy dress party wasn't going to stop them. Not that they've ever been on a bike in their lives.'

Cleo nodded. After Rodders and Jerome and the rest of the Lovers Knot villagers, the Banding sisters seemed positively normal.

As Mitzi and Joel moved off to greet their guests, still more people poured into the hall and headed straight for the bar. Recognising many of them, Cleo waved and smiled. It was weird though, being alone in such a huge crowd. Oh, sod and damn Dylan Maguire.

There were lots of hippies, and several unsuitable miniskirts, and a fair few mods and rockers who growled at each other with mock-menace. And from the start of the decade there was a rash of rock 'n' rollers – the men with their teddy-boy suits and their partners in full skirts and petticoats and ankle socks.

Everyone had dressed up for the occasion.

The hall was packed. As the stage burst into a blazing flurry of floodlights, the JB Roadshow, in their satin shirts and velvet trousers, roared into their opening number – 'Sock It To 'Em JB'. Everyone yelled with delight and rushed to the middle of the floor and started dancing.

And kissing.

Kissing anyone within reach. No one seemed to object. There was an awful lot of laughter. And even more kissing. Partners swapped partners mid-dance and carried on kissing their new ones.

Was that the effects of the Plum Pucker, Cleo wondered. Mmm, probably. She smiled to herself. At least tonight she'd be able to observe the effect her wines had, wouldn't she? As she was driving she wouldn't be drinking, so it would be a great opportunity to see exactly what happened.

Unlike the Harvest Home wines, tonight's brews didn't appear to alter the atmosphere. They only affected the drinkers. There seemed to be no magic force at work suddenly changing the JB Roadshow's music as it had at Lovelady. Which meant that the wines weren't all the same. And the magic – or chemicals – all reacted differently.

Fascinating.

The Plum Pucker was clearly extremely effective. The kissing had reached new heights – or depths – depending on your point of view.

Dylan, Cleo thought irritably from the edge of the floor, would certainly go along with the Plum Pucker ethos. Kiss the one you're with. Any old one. Any old where.

Sod him.

She wondered where he was. Well, no, she didn't. She knew very well where he was. She knew he was still in Jersey, obviously, and probably with some glamorous female mega-rich ex-pat tax-evader; she wasn't entirely sure about the laws on tax exiles, but was pretty sure that anyone who lived in Jersey must be a millionaire at least twice over.

Money, money, money.

Whatever Dylan might say to the contrary, he'd been born into money and he couldn't live without it. There was no point in hoping otherwise.

The JB Roadshow belted into a Sam and Dave number. More people were on the dance floor. Now, as well as the kissing, there were people pinching one another, or pulling odd faces, or making others jump by creeping up behind them and shouting loudly in their ears.

Pear Prank kicking in, Cleo thought.

A bit juvenile, more playground stuff, but probably OK for this sort of party. So far, so good.

And again, unlike Harvest Home, the wines were all being drunk together, so the effects were multiplied. Cleo wasn't sure if the Apple Affinity had made a difference to the several entwined couples still visible, but Pear Prank and Plum

Pucker were certainly running in tandem. It was a scary sight.

The kissing was still going on. And the pranks were becoming ever more . . . prankish. Everyone was screaming with laughter.

Finding herself caught up between two wrinkly Mick Jaggers – one in velvet loon pants, a singlet and a lot of scarves, the other from the Hyde Park concert era in a white pleated frock and bangles, and both of whom had to be drawing their pensions – Cleo was swept onto the dance floor.

Realising it was pointless to protest to either of them that she really didn't want to dance, she simply stood and swayed as they clapped and pouted and postured around her.

'Having a good time? Good! Knew you would!' Doll yelled as she passed, clasped in the arms of shaven-headed 60s mod compete with parka. 'And the wine is divine! Mum's thrilled to bits with it!'

Cleo did the noisy-party thing of smiling and flapping her hands in acknowledgement.

As the Mick Jaggers continued to strut their stuff around her, she was aware that things were subtly changing on the dance floor.

Several couples who had joined forces during the Plum Pucker, now seemed to have sneaked away to the darker corners, leaving their original partners abandoned in the middle of the floor. Apple Affinity at work? Yes, it looked like it.

God, these wines were all made for Dylan. Now it was

definitely a case of love the one you're with all round Hazy Hassocks village hall.

Cleo was slightly cheered to notice that after a few more sips of Apple Affinity, the abandoned partners started pairing up with one another, chatting happily and dancing. That was nice, she thought. She wouldn't want anyone else to feel as lonely as she did.

The Hyde Park Mick Jagger suddenly blew an enormous raspberry at Cleo.

Pear Prank still going strong, Cleo thought, backing away. Possibly one to avoid in future . . .

The JB Roadshow were soul-singing their way through Otis Redding's greatest hits. There was an awful lot of Hazy Hassocks groping going on in the middle of 'Dock of the Bay'.

'I-got-you-babe!' A very put-on hoarse voice echoed from behind Cleo, just as a pair of hands grabbed her round the waist.

Oh, the Pear Prank was becoming really boring now. Still, at least someone had recognised that she was supposed to be Cher and not just another hippy . . .

Cleo swirled round, ready to bop the loon-panted Mick Jagger on the nose if he didn't let go.

'Hi.' Dylan beamed at her. 'Sorry I'm late. And you look sensationally sexy. The real Cher has some very serious competition.'

He was dressed in his Sonny outfit: flared jeans, a pink and purple flowered shirt, a furry waistcoat and umpteen floating scarves, bells and beads.

He still looked totally delectable, damn him.

Completely thrown off kilter, Cleo wriggled free and simply stared at him in silence for a second. But only for a second.

'You'll have to have "I'm sorry I'm late" engraved on your tombstone,' she said crossly. 'Along with "I got held up." It'd give a ring of truth to the old adage of "he was even late for his own funeral", wouldn't it? Anyway, who was she this time? A Jersey socialite? A rich ex-Brit with a beach-front villa? A glamorous local with a mega-nouveau riche daddy?'

The Mick Jaggers pranced a little closer so as not to miss a word.

'Fog.'

Cleo frowned. 'Yeah, right. It's been blowing a sodding gale here all week.'

'The whole island was fog-bound,' Dylan repeated. 'Jersey isn't just down the road a bit. Don't be so insular. And you're beginning to sound like a nagging wife.'

'And you've had plenty of those. Oh, not your own, of course, but –'

'For God's sake!'

'You could have phoned me.'

'Yes, I could. And I should. But I thought I'd be home far sooner. And when I knew I wouldn't be, I, um . . . Anyway, I'm here now. I wouldn't have missed this. I've been looking forward to it. How are the wines going?'

The Mick Jaggers suddenly skipped round together, holding hands and singing 'Satisfaction'.

'See for yourself.'

295

'Cleo –'

'Ah, brilliant! At last!' Doll, having shed her skinhead, bounced across to them and hiccupped to an unsteady halt. 'Sonny and Cher reunited! Hello, I'm Doll.'

'Dylan Maguire.' Dylan smiled and held out his hand.

Doll clasped it with both of hers. 'Oh, w-o-w! How fabulous are you? You're even more deliciously sexy than Cleo said you were.'

Cleo groaned.

'She's been really miserable,' Doll continued happily, trying to uncross her eyes. 'She thought you weren't coming. She'll perk up loads now you're here. See you both later.'

Doll shimmied away and the Mick Jaggers started singing 'Honky Tonk Women' in descant. It clashed horribly with the JB Roadshow's 'Mr Pitiful'.

'You really thought I wasn't coming?' Dylan yelled at her above the brass section roaring from the stage. 'You thought I'd miss this?'

Cleo nodded. 'Why wouldn't you? It's clearly bottom of your list of important things to do.'

Dylan looked extremely irritable. 'We can't have this discussion here – can we find somewhere quieter?'

'It's not a discussion and I'm perfectly happy here.'

Dylan glared at the Mick Jaggers who seem to have forgotten the rest of their Stones repertoire and had resorted to the 'Hokey Cokey'.

'This is bloody insanity!' He caught hold of Cleo's hand. 'Come on – please, Cleo. I need to talk to you. Seriously talk to you. We can't go on like this.'

'Like what exactly? And we don't need to go anywhere else to talk. I've been dumped in village halls before. It won't be a first for me. Let me tell you, at Nina Cardew's thirteenth birthday party, Robbie Knight broke my heart right here in this very hall and –'

'Cleo, please, please stop being so obtuse. We need to talk.'

She shrugged and followed him off the dance floor. She'd heard those awful 'we need to talk' words before. From Dave. When he told her about Wobbly Wanda and wanting a divorce. She'd coped then and she'd cope now.

Might as well just get it over.

'Where are we going?'

'Outside.'

'Oh, now this really is just like being a teenager again. Sneaking outside from the youth club discos with the captain of the school football team for a fag and a snog.'

'Fascinating,' Dylan snapped.

Outside the wind was still howling and the air, after the tropical heat of the village hall, felt bitterly cold. Cleo shivered, her hair, beads and flowers whipping wildly round her face.

'Over here, quick, it's bloody freezing,' Dylan beckoned, pointing a set of car keys into the darkness and getting an answering signal of amber flashes. 'I've got the car.'

A Ferrari? An Aston Martin? Cleo wondered. It would be quite a coup to be dumped in a luxury car. Not, of course, that she could really be dumped, could she? You had to be going out together to be officially dumped.

This'd be a first then. Dumped *before* the relationship had even started.

'Oh.'

She stared at the unremarkable silver saloon in surprise.

'My car,' Dylan said, opening the passenger door for her. 'Not one of Mort's.'

He hurried round to the other side, slid in behind the wheel and started the engine. The car purred into life and the heater kicked in. Cleo shivered again. Still, look on the bright side, at least she wasn't going to be dumped out in the cold like one of Mrs Hancock's rescued kittens.

'We can't go anywhere. I didn't say my polite goodbyes and thank yous. Are you kidnapping me?'

Dylan laughed. 'I'm sure they'll understand, and no. I'm going to do something I should have done ages ago.'

Cleo felt a little treacherous flicker of excitement. 'Really?'

He drove the car carefully out of the dark and crowded car park, slowed, indicated, and headed away from Hazy Hassocks.

At least, Cleo thought, she knew exactly what effect tonight's wine had had. She wasn't leaving manic mayhem behind her – just fun and jolly japes and a bit of harmless flirting. Hopefully, they were exactly the sort of thing Mitzi wanted to complement her herbal cookery.

'Where are we going?'

'I'm going to show you what a waste of space I really am.' Dylan looked across at her in the darkness. 'I'm going to do something I should have done when we first met. I'm going to introduce you to my real life.'

Chapter Twenty-three

Cleo wasn't sure that she recognised the town. She knew they'd left the snaking lanes of Berkshire behind, and then travelled along the A34 and on to the M4, and after that, with the dizzy glare of the stream of headlights in the darkness and the constant swish of Saturday night traffic, she'd completely lost her bearings.

Dylan, clearly not wanting to talk while driving, had turned on the CD player. The car, beautifully warm, had echoed to the strains of various compilations, varying from the Pet Shop Boys through Def Leppard and on to Nickelback.

Cleo had leaned her head back in her seat. So, where were they going? And what did he consider to be his real life? Not Lovelady Hall, that much was obvious. So, had Dylan got a minor stately wife and children stashed away somewhere? Living in a moated castle with peacocks and fountains? Was this his way of putting an end to her silly dreams once and for all?

Or was he going to take her to some slinky members-only nightclub or luxurious casino, all dark and sensuous, where the only qualification for joining was a Coutts bank account, several million stashed away in Switzerland and a full house of platinum cards in your wallet? Not as a treat, but just to show her that he really was out of her league.

Or, maybe it was to really see how the other half lived? To show her the mansions and manor houses of his other women? The natural habitat of Georgiana and Aphrodite. Just to prove to her that someone from a tiny caravan, in the madness of Lovers Knot, was never going to be suitable for the son of Mimi Pashley-Royle.

Determined not to ask any questions, Cleo simply stared ahead of her.

'You're very quiet,' Dylan said, eventually switching off the CD player as he steered the car through a sodium-lit clone-town-centre maze. 'Are you all right?'

'Fine, thanks. I didn't think you wanted to talk.'

'I do, but not yet. Later. There's something I have to show you first. Anyway, we're nearly there now.'

Cleo looked at the urban landscape in some astonishment. It was such a long time since she'd been properly out on the town that she'd forgotten about the nightclub spillage and the swathes of youngsters falling over, fighting, vomiting and passing out in the road, still clutching their alcopops.

This really was another world, she thought, and surely just as alien to Dylan as it was to her?

Blue flashing lights and wailing sirens screamed past them, and ahead a gaggle of hi-vizzed policemen were struggling with a gang of youths outside a brightly lit nightclub door-way. Several girls in miniskirts flashed their chests at them as they passed. More were fighting with apparent hatred. It was all so aggressive and brutal. Where was the laughter and the fun? Why did no one seem to be having a good time?

God, she was too old for all of this.

Thankful that she'd left her teenage years way behind in the relatively calm climes of Winterbrook, Cleo was glad the car doors were securely locked.

Dylan drove along a dark and dimly lit alleyway, slowed down, indicated and then stopped the car.

Cleo stared at the towering, scruffy buildings surrounding them, their wired-up windows and grimy walls covered in the remnants of tattered fly-posting and badly executed graf-fiti. Surely this couldn't be the end of their journey? This mean and dirty alleyway, with litter piled in the gutters and black rubbish bags ripped open by scavengers – animal or human, Cleo wasn't sure – spilling their rotting contents across the road?

This had to be the haunt of muggers and druggies and every other member of the underclasses so reviled by the newspapers and social-conscience television programmes. Cleo shuddered.

'Come on, then.' Dylan smiled at her. 'Don't look so scared. It's OK. Oh, and you'd better have this . . .'

He reached over to the back seat. Hopefully, Cleo thought, it's a baseball bat or a pepper spray. Or preferably both.

It was his leather jacket.

'Put it on. I know it's a shame to cover up all that voluptuous gorgeousness, but it's pretty cold out there.'

Cleo slid into the soft warmth, and sighed. It *was* Dylan. It smelled of him.

'But what about you?'

'I'm OK. I'm used to it – anyway, this furry waistcoat is surprisingly warm. And please don't look so frightened. I promise not to let anything happen to you.'

'We're going out *there*?'

'Yes . . . look, Cleo, this is very important to me. I could – and should – have told you a long time ago, but I didn't. The only person who ever knew about it was Olive, and as you kept saying you didn't want to be Olive's replacement – No, sorry, that's a weak excuse. Just trust me. I'll explain everything later. Oh, and if you could just grab those carrier bags and pass them over – thanks.'

Despite the warm hug of the leather jacket, Cleo shivered again as she clambered from the car. The wind seemed far more vicious in the narrow alleyway, keening and whining, slamming icy fingers against her face and tangling her hair.

And she was scared. Very scared.

Dylan held out his hand. She clung to it, all thoughts of being haughty and stand-offish forgotten in this frighteningly foreign world.

What the chaffing hell was going on here?

The dark alley seemed deserted. In the distance she could hear the constant wail of the emergency services' sirens and the occasional harsh and guttural shout carried on the wind from the drunken nightclub boys.

'Hi, Stevie,' Dylan said suddenly. 'I hoped you'd be here.'

Oh, God – Cleo blinked. Now Dylan had gone completely doolally. He was talking to himself. And now what was he doing? Rooting about in one of the bulging carrier bags? And getting out – what? Was that a pashmina? Oh, Lordy, she was stuck in a deserted alleyway, chaff knew where, with a cross-dressing madman.

'Thanks, Dylan.' A voice echoed from the darkness. 'Didn't expect to see you tonight. Cold, innit?'

'Very. Anyway, that should help a bit.'

'Thanks, mate. That's snaz. And you all dressed up for a party or summat?'

Dylan flicked at his Sonny selection of beads and flowers. 'Fancy dress. Pretty neat, don't you think?'

'Dead heavy.'

Cleo squinted at the heap of newspapers piled in the doorway. And swallowed.

A thin, pale-faced boy was huddled in the middle of the rubbish, with a couple of sheets of cardboard round him as a makeshift windbreak. He was enthusiastically wrapping himself in the thermal blanket Dylan had just given him.

'Hey.' He stopped and grinned. 'She's dead chung. She your girl?'

'You'll have to ask her that,' Dylan laughed. 'And she'll tell you no bloody way. But yes, I'll agree with you that she's pretty chung.'

Stevie laughed and then coughed. A lot.

'And here's a packet of cigarettes – not that I think you should have them until that bronchitis has cleared up but I know you want them – and there's some chocolate there, too.'

'Cheers. You're dead cool. See ya.'

Dylan moved on and, giving the huddled Stevie a last look of total sympathy, Cleo followed him, her head reeling. What on earth was 'chung'? Before she could ask about it, and also if Stevie was some ex-public schoolboy chum of his, fallen on hard times, Dylan had stopped by another bundle of rags.

An elderly man and an equally ancient woman, all toothless and with wild, straggled hair, surfaced from their ragged covers and beamed gummily with obvious pleasure at seeing him.

'Evening, lad. Evening, miss. Not your usual night, is it, Dylan? Got any booze?'

Dylan delved into the bag again and produced a six-pack of lager and a large packet of biscuits.

'Try to make this last, Tommy. And ginger melts, Nancy. Your favourites.'

'Thanks, Dylan. You're a gent.'

They moved on again, quickly emerging from the alley into what looked like an abandoned car breaker's yard. There was only one flickering light here, and in the shadows Cleo was sure she could see things scuttling amongst the wind-blown urban tumbleweed. Broken sheets of rusty corrugated iron slapped and slammed, flapping and grating together in the bitter wind like massive broken limbs.

Surely no one could be trying to sleep here? Not in this cold and mess and disgusting debris?

'Dylan!' A couple of men loomed from the shadows. 'Come and have a warm.'

Dylan took Cleo's hand again. 'Mind where you step – there's a lot of rubble and broken glass. Are you still OK?'

Cleo nodded. She couldn't speak. This was way out of her comfort zone, but more than that, she was desperately sorry for these people, horribly ashamed and even more bemused.

She knew all about homelessness, of course. She'd often bought sandwiches and takeout coffees for the rough-sleepers in Winterbrook during her lunchtime shopping sessions. She always gave money to Shelter and the Salvation Army at Christmas. And she'd never passed the *Big Issue* seller outside the library in Hazy Hassocks without buying a copy.

She knew all about it, but she'd never seen it close up before.

It was truly awful.

But what was Dylan doing here? And how did all these desperate people know him? Was he systematically dumping the Pashley-Royle fortune in this anonymous town? Like *The Secret Millionaire* on television?

And even if he was, then why? When she knew how much he revelled in the material things his privileges brought him? It was all really, really weird . . .

And made even more so because so very recently she'd been in the cosy, noisy, happy atmosphere of Mitzi's 60s Sixtieth party, surrounded by people she'd known all her life – or most of it. And now – Cleo shuddered again – she was in this strange, scary place with a man she clearly didn't know at all.

They stumbled across the uneven ground, and ducked inside a sort of roofless shed. Cleo gazed around at the makeshift beds and the piles of bags and boxes fashioned into little cells, with tarpaulins draped over them in order to keep out the worst of the weather. Several grubby sleeping bags were heaped in a corner, along with empty bottles and cans and the remnants of fast-food containers.

Several men and a few younger boys, all muffled in dirty coats and pulled-down woolly hats, were warming their hands round a blazing fire alight in an oil drum.

'Cosy,' Dylan said. 'You need that fire tonight. Jim, I've got your throat pastilles, and some more cough mixture. But get to the doctor as soon as possible. And, Al, here's some pasties – cheese and onion – I know you won't eat meat. And I've got some cigarettes and beers in this bag – try to share them round the others. Where's Mick?'

'Horspital,' one of the men said sadly. 'Went orf on Thursday. Amberlance took 'im. Mind, it's probably the best place for 'im. He weren't getting no better.'

They all smiled at Cleo. She smiled shakily back. They seemed friendly enough, but she was still frightened.

'She's a pretty girl, Dylan. She looks dead like Cher. What's 'er name? Is she new?'

'Cleo. And no.'

'Um . . . hello,' Cleo said uncertainly.

They all said hello back.

'We can't stop,' Dylan said. 'Give Mick my best when he comes out of hospital. And take care.'

'Ar. Will do. You too. Night, Cleo.'

'Er, goodnight.'

They made their way, slowly and carefully, back out of the breaker's yard and on to another dark and dingy street.

'Dylan, please tell me: what's going on? Oh, I mean – I'm not stupid, I know what you're doing. But I don't understand –'

He grinned at her in the darkness. 'I'll explain everything later. I promise. And I haven't gone mad. But, you're really OK with this? You don't want to go and wait in the car?'

'No. Of course not,' Cleo said quickly. 'But –'

'Not much longer, then I'll tell you everything. I'd intended to tell you tonight anyway but – Ah, hang on.'

Dylan suddenly dived off at an angle across the road, still holding Cleo's hand. She thought, fleetingly, how odd they must look – Sonny and Cher – ducking and diving in and out of seedy streets, traipsing round squalid broken-down abandoned buildings, in their floral flares and bells and beads and flowers.

She laughed to herself. It was just another deliriously mad episode in her equally deliriously mad friendship with Dylan, wasn't it?

'Kath?' Dylan was bending over a bundle of rags in a boarded-up shop doorway. 'Kath? This isn't your usual haunt. Did you get moved on?'

'Hello, Dylan. Yeah. Because of the bloody kids really. They wouldn't leave me alone. The cops is fine. They keeps an eye on me, but the bloody kids ain't got no respect any more. Hey, who's this? You been cheatin' on me?'

Cleo peered at the woman who was possibly the same age

as Mimi Pashley-Royle, but who couldn't have been more different. Broken teeth, deeply lined face, thin hair and wearing what was possibly her entire wardrobe of grubby cardigans and quilted anoraks.

'I'm Cleo.' She smiled before Dylan could say anything. 'Pleased to meet you. Er, is there anything you need?'

Kath gave a cackling laugh. 'Bless 'er. Lovely manners! Just like you, Dylan. No, Cleo, duck, I'm OK for most stuff, ta. Just needs the bloody kids to leave me alone. Ain't got a spare Rottweiler or two, 'ave you?'

Cleo looked helplessly at Dylan. Why was Kath here? Surely she could be helped in some way? Surely there must be some sort of housing available? Surely she didn't have to live on the streets? And probably die on them, too. Weren't there hostels? B & Bs? Anything?

'I've got you a clean blanket.' Dylan delved into the carrier bags again. 'And some fruit juices – I know you like a bit of orange juice. And go and get those eyes checked out. Promise me? You know the doctor at the drop-in centre sessions will sort you out with everything you need for free, don't you?'

'Ah, I do.' Kath nodded. 'Thanks, Dylan. You're a proper godsend, you are. Bye – and bye, Cleopatra. You look after him, my duck. He's one in a million, he is, for all his la-di-dah ways.'

La-di-dah? *La-di-dah*! Cleo had a sudden ker-ching! moment. Of course! Like mother like son!

Cleo sighed as the realisation struck home. Duh! How thick was she? Dylan was working for Mimi. Mimi was

308

always off doing something for her charities, wasn't she? Copious good works amongst the less fortunate. Cleo had never been sure what Mimi's pet fund-raising issues had been, but she knew now.

Dylan was simply carrying on in the family tradition. Well, it was still really good of him – and amazing that he knew all these people so well and helped them and that they liked him, of course – but again, it was something that had fallen into his lap. Like delivering the cars was working for Mort, this charity stuff was working for Mimi.

'One more stop then we're done for the evening,' Dylan said cheerfully as they hurried along a maze of back roads, passing reeling drunks and crowds of noisy jostling youths. 'And then we can talk properly. Not too cold are you?'

She shook her head. 'How could I be cold? I don't even know what it's like to be really cold – not after seeing all these people sleeping on the streets. Sleeping on the streets every night. How awful must that be? I think what you're doing is brilliant. Mimi must be very – Oh, where's this?'

'Last port of call for tonight. Again, not scheduled, but they'll probably be very glad to see us.'

Dylan rattled quickly through a series of coded button-pressing on the panel set in the brickwork, then quickly pushed open a glass door in a tall, thin terraced building. The door swished closed behind them. It was like an old-fashioned clinic, Cleo thought. All shiny yellow walls stuccoed with notices, flyers and posters, and harsh overhead lighting, and a reception desk. And it was blissfully warm.

It smelled of school dinners and in the background she

could hear voices. Not the abrasive voices of the streets out-side, but voices raised in conversation and laughter.

She breathed a sigh of relief. Normality. Well, almost.

'Dylan! Angel! This is a nice surprise.' A plump motherly looking woman appeared behind the desk, then screamed in delight. 'Get you! Don't tell me – hippies?'

'Sonny and Cher.'

'So I see.' The woman ran beady bright eyes over Cleo. 'Very nice. Very nice indeed. So, was it for a bet?'

'A fancy dress party, Annie. A fancy dress party that I cut short because – well, long story. Anyway, I thought I'd just drop in while I was passing and see how things are going.'

'OK. We're full, of course. But an extra pair of hands . . .' Here Annie stopped and once again gave Cleo a quick once-over with the beady eyes. 'Or two, always comes in handy.'

Cleo caught the inference. 'I'm more than willing to help out at, er, whatever it is. I'm not afraid of hard work. And I'm Cleo. It's nice to meet you.'

'And you, dear, 'Annie said. 'And nice to know you're not simply decorative. Go on through, then Dylan – you know the way.'

Cleo followed Dylan through two more security doors and into a brightly lit room. It looked like the games room in a church youth club, with scattered comfortable chairs, a billiard table, a television set showing a dancing programme in lurid colours, various board games dotted around, and an overflowing bookcase in the corner – and it was full of men.

'Is this a homeless shelter?' Cleo asked, embarrassed as a barrage of catcalls and wolf whistles greeted her entrance.

310

'Sort of. But not an official one. It's a halfway house,' Dylan said, grinning at the whistles and raising his hand in greeting as various rough, gruff voices called out to him. 'The blokes can have a bath, a bed for the night and a hot meal. It's run by volunteers and works on a first-come first-served basis and is always full – particularly on cold nights like this.'

'And what about drinks and stuff?'

'It's strictly no alcohol. They have to leave their cans and bottles at the door. And they're searched too. No knives or weapons of any kind. And no drugs either. If anyone is caught fighting or stealing then they're banned. Never allowed back in. Most of them simply won't risk that.'

'Pretty rigid rules then. And it's just for men? No women?'

'No. There are far more men than women on the streets, and it would be insane to offer them shared accommodation in a place like this, because – well, just because. There's a women's hostel in this town, too – which is rare – but there simply isn't enough space for everyone.'

Cleo, still blushing at the continued whistling, shook her head sadly. She'd had absolutely no idea that there was homelessness on this scale, not in this country, not in the twenty-first century.

Then, still being whistled at, she hurried through the room in Dylan's wake and walked straight into the source of the school-dinner smell.

In a brightly lit canteen, three youngish girls and a man with dreadlocks were frantically dishing up massive plates of food to a long line of men.

'Hi, Dylan!' They all waved ladles cheerfully. 'Bloody hell! What have you come as?'

'Sonny and Cher,' Dylan said, sounding slightly weary. 'Long story. This is Cleo – and can we help?'

Still bemused, but delighted to see where Mimi Pashley-Royle's fund-raising had gone, Cleo joined the others behind the counter and was soon sloshing out plates of either stew or curry and huge scalding mugs of tea to a succession of cold and hungry, and very grateful, takers.

She wondered vaguely if she'd wake up in a minute. Or if this was another side effect of Mad Molly's wine: was she really still in Hazy Hassocks village hall, at Mitzi's party, suffering some grand magically induced delusion?

No, she couldn't be. It had to be real. She hadn't touched a drop of wine all night, had she? All night . . . And which night was that exactly? The last couple of hours had turned her world completely askew. She had no idea what time it was or even where they were. But somehow, it didn't matter.

She was doing something useful, she'd seen things she'd never seen before, and it would change her attitudes for ever.

And she had Dylan to thank for that. Rich, spoilt, upper-class – and absolutely gorgeous – Dylan Maguire, who had come into her life with a tumult of rainbows and fountains – and magical waterfalls.

She giggled.

'OK?' Dylan looked at her. 'You're a star, Cleo, really you are. You must have been scared witless out there and this . . . Well, this is all familiar territory to me, but to you it must seem –'

'Strange? Yes, it does. More mash or rice? There you go. It's like a bit of a bad dream, really. But an eye-opener too. I'll never take anything I've got for granted again.'

Dylan grinned. 'You're brilliant. And as soon as this lot have gone, then we'll go too.'

'So soon?' the man with the dreadlocks chuckled. 'Not stopping to help with the washing-up?'

'Not tonight, Lou, no. I'll be back next week for my usual shift, but tonight I've got far more important things to do.'

'So I see,' Lou laughed throatily.

Cleo blushed.

'So, are you comfortable with all this?' she asked once the last plate of food had been dished up. 'Do you feel at home?'

Dylan shook his head. 'No. But I know I can escape back to my home and live the life I want to live at any time I choose. These people have no choice. They're stuck with what they've got. So, if I can help to make their crappy lives a bit more pleasant on occasions, then I will.'

Cleo smiled happily. 'There. I knew you weren't all bad. So, are we done here? Is there anywhere else we have to go?'

'Oh, yes,' Dylan said, leading her out from behind the counter. 'There's certainly somewhere else we need to be. But for that we'll have to get back in the car.'

Cleo heaved a guilty sigh of relief. She really understood now why Mimi funded these ventures but sent Dylan to do the dirty work on her behalf.

'So? Where next?' she said as soon as they'd left the hostel. 'And if it's some hospital or anything I don't mind –'

'It's nothing like that.' Dylan smiled down at her as they

retraced their steps back to the car. 'But it is something that I hope will come as a pleasant surprise. Something that might just convince you that you've got me all wrong.'

'You've already done that. Tonight. You're amazing. I apologise for everything I said about –'

Dylan put an icy finger on her lips. 'Don't. Please don't. Not now. Save it for later. Later you might not even want to say it.'

'OK, but – So, where are we going?'

'Home.' Dylan grinned at her. 'Home to Lovers Knot.'

Chapter Twenty-four

The journey back to Lovers Knot from Clone Town – Cleo still had no idea where they'd actually been and presumed, that for the purposes of the visit, it really didn't matter – was far more cordial than the outward one had been.

With the sad images of everyone she'd just met still swirling through her head, and seeing Dylan through new eyes, Cleo huddled in the delicious warmth blasting from the car's heater and appreciated every single tiny little gram, calorie, therm or watt – science never having been her strong point.

She turned her head and looked at Dylan's profile in the darkness. Yep, he was still totally gorgeous. Still the Most Beautiful Boy in the World. Only now, she thought, smiling in the reflected lights of the motorway traffic, she knew he was not only gorgeous, but compassionate and generous as well. It was a heady combination.

And, she reflected, as the eclectic in-car entertainment moved from the Beach Boys to Black Sabbath – and you didn't get much more eclectic than that – she'd pay far more attention to typing up Mimi's charity correspondence in future. Now that it meant *something*. Now that it was *real*.

And there must be something she could do as well: raise money, raise awareness, just help . . . After tonight, she knew she had to do something. And she would.

But what other surprises could Dylan possibly have in store for her back in Lovers Knot? There was nothing, she reckoned, nothing on earth that could come as more of a shock – albeit a very pleasant one – than having discovered that Dylan wasn't simply a womanising, playboy egoist.

'Can I ask you something?'

'Anything.' Dylan nodded, moving the car smoothly into the outside lane of the M4 as they picked up speed. 'Unless it's please can we stop and find a loo, like my mother always seems to want do when we're as far from a service station as is physically possible.'

'That's a woman thing,' Cleo said cheerfully. 'We all do that. No, no that's fine – I had my comfort break, as my mother would tweely say, at the hostel, thanks very much for asking.'

'I wasn't.' Dylan grinned at her.

She grinned back. 'No, actually I was going to ask if this surprise you mentioned earlier involves going back to my caravan? Because, if it does, I'd love to get out of this ridiculous Cher outfit and become Cleo the Normal again. There are only so many hours a girl can be comfortable in a pair of flowery flares, made from bits of other people's curtains, two sizes too small.'

Dylan nodded. 'I was thinking much along the same lines. Oh, not about you taking off your flowery flares – although now you come to mention it . . .'

'Concentrate on the driving,' she giggled. 'Do *not* think about my bell-bottoms. Or even my bell bottom.'

'OK, I'm trying . . . No, it's not working. But, yes, I'm pretty desperate to dump Sonny's fluffy waistcoat and the flowers and beads, not to mention these weird flappy jeans.'

'Which means you'll be wearing my dressing gown again?'

'Sorry to disappoint you –' Dylan changed lanes to avoid a small car dawdling in front of him '– but I have a change of clothes in the boot.'

'Your loss. And, actually –' Cleo pulled herself up in the seat '– that's something else I'd like to ask you about. Tonight –'

'I said I'd tell you all about tonight when we got home.'

That 'home' word again. Cleo sighed happily. 'No, not that bit of tonight, but going there from the party was impromptu, wasn't it? That, um, visit wasn't scheduled?'

'No, it wasn't, but –'

'And yet, you had blankets and stuff already to hand in the car. How come?'

Dylan sighed as they reclaimed the right-hand lane and gained speed again. 'Because sadly, most of the rough sleepers need the same things. I always have a stash of fully equipped bags in the car, so wherever I go, I've always got plenty of blankets, beer, cigarettes, biscuits, chocolate and non-prescription medicines for coughs and sore throats and aches and pains.'

Cleo nodded. It made sense.

'Oooh, the A34 already – we should be home before dawn.'

It was, Cleo was surprised to notice on the digital dashboard clock, still not quite midnight. Mitzi's party would still be roaring away in Hazy Hassocks. Only four hours since they'd left. Would anyone have missed her? Nah. Doll, if she was sober enough, would have noticed both Sonny and Cher were missing and jumped to all manner of wrong conclusions. Cleo sighed. She'd have the devil of a job convincing Doll that she and Dylan were not an item now . . .

So many things had happened since she'd left the village hall, time seemed to have lost all meaning. She hoped everyone had had a great time. Oh, and the wines! She'd almost forgotten about the wines! How could she?

Please, please, let Mitzi have absolutely loved the Plum Pucker, Pear Prank and Apple Affinity.

Cleo smiled to herself in the darkness as the countryside flashing past outside the car took on ever-more recognisable shapes, and much-loved landmarks loomed. Of course Mitzi would love the wines. They'd added just that extra little bit of oomph to an already OTT Hazy Hassocks party.

Yes, life was definitely on the up. She'd go into business with Mitzi, and carry on working for Mimi Pashley-Royle, and possibly help Dylan out with the homeless charity stuff too – if he wanted her.

Huh! Dangerous territory.

'Zeb's home at Lovelady this weekend,' Dylan said

suddenly in a gap in Ozzy Osbourne's ongoing musical declaration that he was 'Paranoid'. 'He and Elvi seem ecstatically happy.'

'They are.' Cleo nodded, deciding not to share Elvi's confidences about the course the Social Integration had taken at Gorse Glade. If Zeb had already shared that with Dylan that was OK. She certainly didn't want to be the one to divulge their secrets. 'It's lovely, isn't it?'

Elvi had made Cleo roar with laughter when she'd told her about Zeb's clever plan to get her into his room, and the fact that, thanks to the over-egging Henry, Elvi had thought he was dead; and had made her sigh with romantic nostalgia when Elvi had described the delight of finding Zeb very much alive.

The intervening interlude had been tastefully glossed over, but Cleo got the drift. Elvi and Zeb were now lovers in every sense of the word – and intended to stay so.

It had been, Cleo thought, rather touching that Elvi and Zeb still both thanked the Blackberry Blush for loosening their respective parents' tongues, thus effectively putting paid to any further opposition to their teenage love affair. Not that either Elvi or Zeb knew anything about the magical properties of the wine, of course, just that it must have been very strong and 'got the putrid olds totally bladdered'.

'And now,' Elvi had said, her eyes shining, 'all we need is for you and Dylan to get it together.'

'You said Dylan was *so not* what I needed, if I remember,' Cleo had said with mock severity. 'You can't change your mind now.'

'Can and have.' Elvi had twirled round in the caravan. 'You're brilliant, Dylan's dead sexy, I'm in love, Zeb's in love, and we want the whole damn world to be in love as well.'

'Even if it's with the wrong person?'

Elvi had stopped twirling. 'Dylan's not the wrong person. Anyone with half an eye can see you're perfect for each other. Zeb and I agree, all he needs is the love of a good woman to put an end to his cheating ways.'

'And I'm going to be that good woman, am I?' Cleo had said. 'No, love, you and Zeb are one thing – me and Dylan are quite another. We're happy just being friends.'

'You've gone quiet again,' Dylan broke into her thoughts. 'Are you asleep?'

'If I had been you'd have just woken me up, and no, actually I wasn't. I might be a whole five years older than you but I haven't yet reached the stage where I need a nap every ten minutes. I was just thinking about Zeb and Elvi and happy stuff.'

'Good,' Dylan said as they turned off the A34 and headed for the familiar Berkshire villages. 'Because it's important that you don't let the homelessness eat away at you. You have to stay positive and not let it get you down otherwise you'll never be able to help any of them. I used to get really depressed and angry that whatever I did was never enough – now I realise that anything that makes even the smallest difference is a good thing.'

He was lovely, Cleo thought as the road signs announced that Hazy Hassocks and Bagley-cum-Russet and Fiddlesticks were now merely miles away. He was lovely and her friend –

and she'd have to hope that throwing herself into so many new ventures would be enough to stop her longing that it could be more.

'That's better,' Dylan said half an hour later, emerging from the caravan's bathroom in his own tight denim jeans and a black sweater. 'Remind me the next time we have an invite to a fancy dress party not to come up with any more bright plans about our costumes. I've no idea how hippies managed to have a normal life with all those bells and beads and things flapping around.'

Cleo, no longer a Cher-alike, now in black jeans and a soft scarlet sweater, nodded. 'And tripping over their flares every step of the way, not to mention having their circulation cut off. I'm so glad we didn't live in the putrid olden days, as Elvi would say. Right? Coffee? Marble cake?'

Dylan shook his head. 'No, thanks. I'm not stopping.'

'OK . . .'

Cleo tried valiantly to hide her disappointment.

She'd half expected to find a massive bouquet of roses on her doorstep, or a huge box of chocolates, or something. Anything. Dylan had said there'd be a surprise, but there had been nothing, and now he wasn't even stopping.

He must have forgotten. Cleo tried really hard not to mind. She'd got used to disappointments, hadn't she? She could – and would – cope with this one.

'And neither are you.' Dylan beamed. 'Grab your coat. You've pulled.'

Cleo giggled. 'Where on earth are we going now? It's

horribly late, or horribly early depending which end of the day you're looking at – surely, we're not –'

'Just put your jacket on and trust me. I promised you a surprise, didn't I?'

'Oooh, yes.' Cleo's heart soared. 'Don't tell me – we're going to all-night Big Sava to wander round the aisles with all those people who dash out at two o'clock in the morning to buy frozen peas in their pyjamas.'

'What an exciting life you must lead.' Dylan frowned. 'Sorry to disappoint you, but we're not going anywhere near Big Sava. Right, have you got boots on? Good. Come along then . . .'

Chapter Twenty-five

Five minutes later, Cleo stood with Dylan on the edge of Lovers Spinney and felt the first stirrings of doubt.

What the chaffing hell could be going on here? Was Dylan intending to make an overnight collection of Lovers Cascade water for their next batch of wine? Well, that would, Cleo admitted, certainly be a surprise, but not quite what she was expecting.

It was extremely dark and very cold. And the spinney made all sorts of odd rustling and moaning noises.

'Trust me?' Dylan squeezed her hand.

'Yes.'

'Right, then wait here for just a little while. I won't be long.'

'OK.'

Cleo held her breath as Dylan flicked on a torch and made his way into the inky blackness of the spinney's tangled branches.

Now she was alone. Completely alone. In the pitch dark. Her heart started dancing a little samba under her ribs.

'Get a grip,' she told herself. 'You've just seen people who have to survive in the darkness, all alone, always, night after night. This is Lovers Knot, not some scary urban landscape. Even if someone does come along it'll only be Rodders or Jerome or Salome out on their nightly prowl.'

The 'little while' seemed to last for several agonisingly long hours, but eventually she saw the return flicker of Dylan's torch and heard him making his way back towards her.

'OK, we're all set. Give me your hand.'

She did, and shivered as his fingers closed round hers. It had nothing to do with the cold.

Carefully, by torchlight, they made their way through the spinney, branches catching their hair, tree roots snatching at their feet, slithering and sliding. Totally mystified, Cleo clung to Dylan's hand and hoped she wouldn't fall over, disappearing from view, screaming wildly.

Just as they reached the top of the steepest incline, the moon appeared from behind the dark, towering clouds, sliding across the bruised sky, spilling silver through the quivering canopy of leaves, tipping the branches with white light.

'Perfect timing.' Dylan gazed upwards. 'And it's a full moon.'

'And I'm an empty Moon,' Cleo giggled. 'I knew I should have had a chunk of marble cake. I haven't eaten since – Oh my God . . .'

She stopped and stared down into the fairy glade.

She couldn't speak. Tears blurred her eyes.

With Lovers Cascade thundering its dancing, iridescent, non-stop torrent as a backdrop, the glade was alight with candles.

Dozens and dozens of tiny flickering candles. Everywhere, at every level, pinpricks of light swayed and eddied, making the fairy glade a place of shimmering magic.

And there, in the middle of the short, springy grass was a tiny wrought-iron table and two chairs, with a fat pillar candle on either side, guttering and casting leaping shadows.

'Come on.' Dylan smiled gently at her. 'Hold my hand again.'

He led her downwards and across the grass to the table. Again, it was oddly warm and still.

Magical.

'Madam.' He pulled out a chair for her.

Stunned, she sat down, gazing around her at the enchanted beauty of it all. This was absolutely amazing. Far, far more astonishing than anything she could ever have imagined.

So incredibly beautiful . . .

And Dylan had created it.

Just for her.

'OK?' Dylan sat down opposite her, then reaching under the table, produced a bottle and two crystal glasses. 'As we haven't been able to have a drink all evening, I thought that –'

'Dylan,' Cleo interrupted him. 'Thank you. Thank you so much. This is – is incredible. Absolutely stunningly incredible. I can't believe it. It must have taken you ages.'

'Mmm, a bit. That was why I was so late at Mitzi's party. Setting it up took longer than I'd imagined it would, and then I had to think of some way of getting you here and lighting the candles without you knowing, and –'

'And you managed it. It's the most lovely, beautiful, original wonderful surprise I've ever had – and now I think I'm going to cry.'

'Oh, God, please don't. As long as you like it. You see –' he leaned across the table and took her hands '– I had to prove to you how much I care for you. It had to be something relevant, somewhere that meant something to us both – not just taking you out to dinner or talking things over in the caravan. It had to be special, because you are. I don't think you have any idea how special you are.'

'But, I'm . . . and you're . . .'

Dylan laughed. 'Very succinct. And I said we had to talk. Because we do. So, can I talk first?'

Cleo nodded. Even if he said they had no future together she thought it wouldn't matter quite so much now. Not here. Not in fairyland.

'Have you noticed anything different about me?'

'You've had a haircut?' Cleo was still too stunned to even think straight.

'I've had my mobile phone switched off for weeks. When we've been together.'

Cleo nodded. 'Now you come to mention it, but why?'

'Because, once I'd met you I didn't want to talk to anyone else. Because once I'd met you there *was* no one else.'

Cleo smiled at him, loving his beautiful face in the

dancing, gentle light. 'Selective memory there. You've been away all the time, when you've been delivering cars for Mort. And it's taken you far, far longer than it should have done. And I know all about Nesta and Alicia and Georgiana and Aphrodite –'

'Who the hell are Georgiana and Aphrodite?'

Cleo shrugged. 'They don't matter – what I mean is, I know why you deliver supercars for Mort. Because they – and you – are babe magnets. It's a perfect opportunity for you to spend time with umpteen women and –'

'That's *used* to spend time with umpteen women. Past tense. There have been no other women since we met. Apart from Jessamine – and she was only a supper partner, as you well know. I haven't wanted any other women since the day you hit me with the rubbish bag.'

'Oh, but –'

'And the other reason I drive Mort's cars around the country isn't because it satisfies my overblown macho ego – it's because it means I'm in different towns at different times, which means it gives me the perfect opportunity to do my outreach stuff all over the country.'

Cleo stared at him, feeling hellishly guilty. 'You mean, all those times you were late back from your delivery trips, you weren't –?'

'Romping with Georgiana and Aphrodite? No, I was helping out at shelters, going round the streets with the rough sleepers, doing whatever was needed wherever I was needed.'

'And you didn't tell me?'

'Not at first. Because I didn't know you well enough to share it with you. I've kept it a secret from everyone for so long that it didn't actually occur to me to tell you. And then later, I couldn't tell you because I thought you'd just think I was bragging, or trying to prove that I wasn't simply a spoilt brat. But now, apart from Olive, you're the *only* person I've told.'

'Well, and your mother, of course. As they're Mimi's charities –'

'How carefully do you read my mother's correspondence when you're typing her letters?'

Cleo frowned. 'Well enough. I'm a competent typist, my spelling's OK –'

'But do you know which charities you're writing to and about?'

'No. They all have acronyms, but, I know now, after tonight . . .'

Dylan leaned back in his chair for a moment, then he smiled. 'My mother's charities are all very worthy ones. The ones that give her the maximum kudos. My mother is a kind and generous woman, but homelessness wouldn't give her any brownie points among the great and the good. My mother knows nothing about what I do.'

Cleo swallowed. 'You mean that since Olive I'm seriously the only person who knows?'

'Well, apart from all the other outreach workers, yes. But then, they don't know about my Lovers Knot life. So, yes, you, Cleo Moon, are the only person who knows about both. You're that important to me. I had to tell you – not just because I know you think I'm an idle waste of space who squanders his time and money in some constant privileged ego trip of fast cars and fast women – which of course, used to be half the attraction – but because I needed you to know the truth. I want to know if you can share it with me?'

Cleo closed her eyes. Suddenly it was all far, far too much to take in.

She opened her eyes and stared at him. 'Dylan, I owe you the biggest apology in the world . . . I'm so very sorry for jumping to every wrong conclusion, but –'

'It was even the reason I was sent down from Oxford. Not because I spent too much time being a rich brat, but because I was never at lectures or tutorials. Never handed in any essays. Never did any work. That's where it all started.'

'And you never told your mother? You let her think that you'd been, er, sent down for, well, some misdemeanour?'

Dylan laughed. 'Yeah. And she obviously accepted that, knowing that I was very much her son. After all, she ran away from her finishing school – she certainly couldn't censure me for doing much the same.'

'And, when you were up at Oxford, you just decided that you wanted to help homeless people?'

'Yeah, well, I started off just chucking money at the poor blokes on the streets as I passed, then I stopped and talked to them and got to know them, and about their backgrounds. After that I got involved with soup runs, and then the night shelter, and it all seemed so much more important than my degree. It was real, Cleo. And I'd never had a real life. It had all been so cushioned and perfect. And the street people I

met had had lives once too, but they'd lost them – and I felt
so bloody helpless.'

Cleo sighed and squeezed his hands even tighter. 'You're
the most amazing man I've ever met. So, whatever money
you make from Mort's deliveries goes to help people like the
ones we met tonight?'

Dylan nodded. 'And whatever else I can claw from my
inheritance. My disgusting wealth isn't going to be wasted. I
just had to let you know all this, but I couldn't do it until I
knew I could trust you, and that you'd understand.'

He leaned across the table and kissed her very gently. 'I
love you.'

'I love you, too.'

He sat back and smiled at her. 'So? Shall we drink a toast
to our future? To your winemaking ventures with Mitzi
Blessing? To our secret life on the mean streets? Oh, and to
you becoming Mrs Dylan Maguire?'

'*What*?' Cleo blinked at him. 'I mean – do you mean . . .?'

'That I want to marry you? Yes.'

Cleo wanted to run across the fairy glade and turn cartwheels. She felt as though she could just take her feet off
the ground and float happily and touch the moon that
was bathing them with silver. Dylan wanted to marry her!
Her!

'But . . . but –' she looked at him in wonderment '– but
we haven't even had a proper date yet, have we? We haven't
been out together . . . haven't, um, well, had a relationship,
or well, anything . . .'

So?' Dylan shrugged. 'We can start that now. Who cares if

it's all the wrong way round? Everything about our friendship has been unconventional and topsy-turvy. So, why change now? Cleo, I love you. I want to spend the rest of my life with you. That's all that matters to me.'

Ohmigod . . . Cleo beamed at him with total love and happiness.

'So, will you? Marry me? Live with me? Be happy with me for ever and ever?'

Suddenly, Cleo's wondrous happiness died as swiftly as someone snuffing out a candle.

'I can't.'

Dylan looked stricken. 'What? Oh, God, Cleo, have I got this all wrong? I thought —'

'You're the most wonderful man I've ever met. This is the most incredible setting for a marriage proposal any woman could ever dream of. I think you're totally incredible. But I can't marry you.'

Dylan shook his head, his shoulders slumped, he stared down at the table.

'Dylan,' Cleo whispered, 'I love you. I'll love you for the rest of my life. And there's nothing I want more than to marry you, but I —' She swallowed. 'I can't have children.'

'Is that all?' Dylan laughed with relief.

'*All?*' Cleo shook her head. 'It's *everything*. You must want children. Every man wants children. You'd be a fantastic father. It's not fair that —'

'And if there's one thing I know it's that life's not fair. What about you? Do you want to be a mother?'

'Yes, of course I do. I've always wanted to be a mother.

The IVF failed so many times, and it's killed me for years that –'

'So, OK, you can't give birth to children, which must be shattering for you, but that doesn't mean we can't have them. We'll foster. We'll adopt. We'll fill our home with children. We'll be like Mrs Hancock is with her cats – we'll have all those poor kids that other people don't want. We'll give them a real home – a fabulously happy home with love and laughter – and we'll be their parents. Their real parents. You and me. Cleo, are you crying?'

'Yes,' Cleo sobbed. 'Yes . . . Yes . . .'

'Is that a yes to the crying or the children or the proposal or all of them?'

She nodded again, and Dylan leaned over and gently wiped the tears away.

'Now I'm the happiest man on the planet – and I'm welling up too – so let's toast our engagement and impending parent-dom, and all the other amazing things that lie ahead.' Dylan's hands shook as the cork popped out of the bottle, and bubbles frothed on to the table. 'Here's to us. Cleo, I love you.'

'And I love you – so very much. Oh, and this isn't one of Mad Molly's wines, is it?'

Dylan shook his head, smiling at her. 'No, this is Krug – bought with my very own pocket money. We'll save Mad Molly's wines for injecting a touch of enchantment into our relationship when it looks like it might be needed. Although something tells me,' he said softly pulling her towards him across the table, 'that we'll never need anyone else's magic for that.'

And then he kissed her. Slowly and tantalisingly. And dizzy with love, somewhere in the moonlit fairyland euphoria, Cleo knew that this time she'd remember the kiss for as long as she lived.

Read on for a sneak-peek of

Happy Birthday

by

CHRISTINA JONES

available now from Piatkus

Chapter One

Outside Hazy Hassocks' drowsy midsummer church, Mrs Finstock, the vicar's wife, was energetically executing a solo version of 'YMCA' to a small but seemingly appreciative audience.

Resplendent in a lilac tulle two-piece, she leaped up and down in the middle of the road, her arms waving wildly, her generous bosoms dancing beneath the glimmering fabric. Her lilac hat, a mass of feathers from some exotic and possibly protected bird, danced too, albeit to a slightly different beat.

'Is Mrs Finstock *dancing*? In the *street*? In *this* heat?' Phoebe Bowler, the perfect size ten, ash-blonde-bobbed, designer-frocked bride-to-be, sitting beside her father in the back of the rose-scented white limousine, giggled delightedly. She leaned forwards and stared at the spectacle through the blur of her veil. 'Yes – she is! Oh, bless her. She's always so funny, isn't she?'

'Funny wouldn't be my word for it,' Bob Bowler muttered, looking rather anxiously from his daughter to the now star-jumping Mrs Finstock. 'I'm far too nervous to find anything amusing – especially the vicar's wife having one of her turns.'

'Vicar's wife is she? Blimey . . .' the limo's chauffeur joined in as he slowed down and, despite the efficacy of the car's expensive air-con, took the opportunity to mop the sweat from his forehead. 'Looks to me like she's found the communion wine and had a hefty swig or three. Ah – she seems to have stopped prancing – yep, she's waving at us now. Hope she don't want us to join in. Too darn hot for any of that old nonsense. Maybe she just wants to tell us something. Shall I stop, duck?'

Phoebe smiled happily. 'May as well, seeing as we're outside the church and it's nearly midday, the wedding's at noon and I'm half of the main attraction.'

As the limousine purred to an opulent halt, the vicar's wife stopped dancing up and down and bustled busily towards the driver's window. Her face glistened under its generous coating of Crème Puff. There were little beads of moisture in the bristles above her upper lip.

'Thank goodness I caught your attention.'

Difficult not to, Phoebe thought, beaming the prenuptial smile that had been impossible to suppress since she'd woken in her parents' semi that morning. 'Actually, we thought you were dancing.'

'What? No, no . . .' The vicar's wife squinted into the depths of the flower-and-ribbon-bedecked car. 'Oh, Phoebe, dear, don't you look lovely. Now, I don't want to worry you – but we've got a bit of a delay. We're not quite ready for you.' She pulled a face at the driver. 'Would you mind awfully driving round the block again?'

'Fine by me,' the driver said with a nod. 'Allus happens at every wedding. Five minutes or so OK?'

'Lovely.' Mrs Finstock bared her teeth in an agitated smile. 'Five minutes should be perfect.'

'What sort of delay?' Phoebe's prenuptial beam slipped slightly. 'Not something wrong with our planning, surely? I've timed the whole day to perfection. It's taken me months to get this show on the road. Oh, I know – don't tell me – Clemmie hasn't arrived yet. She's so useless about time. I knew I should have forced to her to be at our house with the rest of the bridesmaids instead of coming straight from Winterbrook. Trust Clemmie! I'll have to have serious words with her later.'

The vicar's wife nodded vigorously. 'That's the ticket. Good girl. Nothing to worry about. Now, off you pop.'

The driver replaced his cap, wiped his face and the limo moved slowly away.

Phoebe got a quick glimpse of her nearest and dearest in their wedding finery, a sea of rainbow colours, outside the church, sheltering from the searing midday sun in the mellowed portals before the car rounded the bend into the High Street.

As she'd suspected, there was no sign of Clemmie in the throng.

'I'll drive back out towards Bagley, shall I?' the driver asked over his shoulder. 'No point getting caught up in the Saturday shopping traffic in Hassocks, is there? Who's this Clemmie, then?'

'My chief bridesmaid.' Phoebe settled back into her seat. 'Or matron-of-honour I suppose I should say seeing as she's already beaten me to the altar. Lifelong best friend.

Scientifically brilliant and amazingly clever, but a complete pill-brain when it comes to common sense or being organised. She'll owe me big time for this.'

'Ah, but you go easy on her, duck. Everyone'll expect the bride to be late anyway, won't they? Goes with the territory.' The limo driver headed away from Hazy Hassocks' main street and out into the narrow lanes surrounding the large Berkshire market village. 'Five minutes or so won't make any difference, will it?'

With a sigh, Phoebe shook her head. Well, it wouldn't. Not really. But, any delay to her minutely crafted day was slightly irritating. She was never late for anything. Not ever. Possible disruptions, interruptions and disasters were all carefully factored into each of Phoebe's plans. Trust dizzy, disorganised Clemmie to be the one to mess things up.

That was the trouble with having someone like Clemmie as a best friend. Especially an extremely loved-up, newly married and even more newly pregnant Clemmie.

Secretly, Phoebe was a teensy bit miffed that Clemmie had met, worked with, fallen in love with and whirlwindly married the divine Guy Devlin within six months, and was now merely seconds later expecting their first baby, while she and Ben – having been together since school – had taken the more sedate, orderly, well-planned route to everlasting love.

After a fifteen-year relationship, they'd become engaged, planned the dream wedding down to the finest detail, and had decided to start a family in another year or two when they'd left their rented Hazy Hassocks flat and sensibly saved enough to scramble onto the first rung of the mortgage ladder.

Clemmie, with no regard for planning or organisation, had simply characteristically plunged in. It was all rather annoying to someone like Phoebe who rarely even decided on what to wear without consulting her astral charts and considering all the possible options at least three times.

'Nervous?' Bob Bowler broke into her thoughts and squeezed his daughter's hand.

'About Clemmie being late? No, of course not. Well, not really.' Phoebe looked serenely at her father through the ice-white froth of her veil. 'Par for the course with Clemmie. She's probably having morning sickness or something – as long as she manages not to have it on her frock it'll be fine. She'll turn up eventually. Why on earth would I be nervous?'

'Because it's your wedding day and I'm petrified.' Bob Bowler chuckled rather shakily. 'I've never been father of the bride before.'

'Well, I've never been the bride before either and I'm absolutely calm.' Phoebe smiled at him and reached across the rear seat of the pink-rose-strewn limousine and patted his grey-trousered leg. 'There's nothing to worry about, Dad. Today will run as smoothly as any military campaign. Stick with me, kid, and you'll be OK.'

Bob shook his head, running a sweating finger round the tight collar of his morning suit. 'You're scary, Phoebes. Cool as a cucumber. I thought brides were supposed to be a mass of nerves.'

Phoebe gazed out on the scorching blue-sky June morning as the limo swept through the glossy Berkshire lanes close to her parents' semi in the tiny village of Bagley-cum-Russet and circled once more towards the church in nearby Hazy

Hassocks. Even the weather had come up trumps. As she'd known it would.

She smiled blissfully. 'I'm not worried – not even about Clemmie – because everything is going to be perfect. What could possibly go wrong?'

'Don't even expect me to answer that.' Bob moved his top hat from his lap to the acres of silver leather seat beside him. 'I'm not going to tempt fate.'

'Fate,' Phoebe said firmly, 'can't be tempted. Fate is on my side. And I've planned today with minute attention to detail and a time-line never before seen in the history of weddings – not to mention it being astrally charted, of course.'

Bob snorted. 'You and your astrology! Do you really think a deck of tarot cards and some sort of star-sign mumbojumbo can forecast –?'

'Absolutely,' Phoebe said happily. 'I used my charts to plan the exact day, time and place for this wedding. All the portents pointed to this day being the perfect one for our marriage. And after all, Ben and I know each other inside out. You wait and see – he'll be as calm as I am. We're just looking forward to it being the best wedding anyone can ever remember.'

Settling back in the limousine's smoothly purring luxury, Phoebe rearranged her slim-fitting silk frock and checked her mental tick-list. Yes, it was fine. Apart from Clemmie being late, everything was simply perfect. This, her and Ben's wedding day, was truly going to be the happiest day of her life.

Seven and a half minutes later, the limousine pulled up outside the church again. This time there was no sign of the vicar's wife and the guests had all disappeared.

'There,' Phoebe said cheerfully, 'see? No problems. Clemmie's obviously arrived intact and they're all inside waiting. Blimey, I bet Ben's chewing his fingernails, though. I promised him I wouldn't be late.'

The limo driver struggled out and held the door open. A tidal wave of heat swooshed into the car.

'Proper scorcher you've got,' the driver said, as Phoebe, in her slender strapless column of silk, wriggled the pooled hem round her high-heeled white sandals and clutched her small bouquet of pale-pink rosebuds. 'Still, you know what they say, duck? Happy the bride the sun shines on . . . Now – where's the photographer? You'll need some snaps of you and your dad together before you gets going.'

Bob Bowler frowned towards the church as it shimmered beneath the June sun. 'Yes, where is the photographer, Phoebes? I know you've got the camcorder bloke waiting in the porch to film us coming up the path, but I thought –'

Phoebe sighed in exasperation. 'Why can no one be relied on? Yes, the photographer should be here – maybe he was late as well. As long as he arrives for the after-the-event pics I'll be OK. Oh, well, at least we'll have it on film.'

Bob smiled moist-eyed at his slender, blonde daughter in the exquisite ice-white silk dress, short veil and diamante tiara. 'You look gorgeous, Phoebe, truly. I'm so proud of you. Let me just straighten your veil a bit. Now, you take my arm and we'll be off. Are you feeling OK?'

'Fine, Dad, honest. Not a tummy-dancing butterfly, trembly hand or nerve in sight.'

Phoebe gave a wide beam to the crowd of Hazy Hassocks Saturday shoppers all clustered round the church gates. The Saturday shoppers beamed back. Several clapped.

'Phoebes . . .' Clemmie, tall and beautiful in a filmy dress of dusky pink, her mass of unruly dark-red hair caught up with white rosebuds, suddenly appeared from the porch and hurried down the church path. 'Oh, you look so lovely . . . I'm so sorry . . .'

'It's OK. You're here now. And you look stunning yourself. Have you stopped being sick? Have you got the little flower girls under control? And has Mum stopped sniffling? And has my nan left that awful hat at home and –'

'What? Yes, but, Phoebes –'

'Don't worry, Clem – honestly. I'm used to you being late for everything. I should have factored it in on my list: ten minutes extra in case Clemmie doesn't turn up.'

'It wasn't me . . . isn't me . . . Phoebe, listen –'

'Oh, Clem, stop fretting about it. I'm cool – now let's get on with this.'

Clemmie gave Bob Bowler a beseeching look, then held out her hand. 'Phoebes, come over here . . . please . . . There's something I've got to tell you.'

'Not now!' Phoebe laughed. 'Whatever it is can wait until after the wedding.'

'No it can't.' Clemmie swallowed. 'Phoebes, sweetheart . . . Oh, Lordy, there's no easy way to say this. There's not going to be a wedding. Ben isn't here. He isn't going to be here. He's called it off . . .'